THE
DEFAULT
WORLD

Advance Praise for *The Default World*

"Naomi Kanakia's tour de force novel of a trans adventuress among the tech elite is a beautiful cis nightmare in the mold of *Manhunt* and *Tell Me I'm Worthless*, ripping off bandage after bandage around body politics and the belief that money and dreams can reshape how we treat each other. The questions her unforgettable antiheroine Jhanvi asks—and the conversations on friendship and what it asks of us that this sparkling, often brutal book will start—are worth your attention."
—**JEANNE THORNTON**, author of *Summer Fun: A Novel*

"*The Default World* is the wild, often hilarious and troubling story of Jhanvi, an angry, witty trans woman who tells it like it is. She's entitled, demanding, outrageous, funny, careening, an extremely entertaining and sometimes horrible person who I can't help loving and rooting for."
—**MATTHEW KLAM**, author of *Sam the Cat and Other Stories*

"*The Default World* takes a scalpel to constructed myths of joy, allyship, and solidarity within and surrounding queer communities, exposing with unwavering scrutiny the messy networks of insecurity and vulnerability that hum and throb through trans lives and experiences. A heady mixture of satire, exposé, and hard truth-telling."
—**BISHAKH SOM**, author of *Apsara Engine*

"Bananas, grody, uninhibited, histrionic, mortifying, funny, and awful. As a satire of contemporary tech-bro burner hippiedom, it's a riot. As a dissection of what it costs to make it as a trans woman in a dude's world, it's harrowing."
—**CAT FITZPATRICK**, author of *The Call-Out: A Novel in Rhyme*

"*The Default World* is the best sort of novel, one where you fall in love with every one of the tragic, flawed characters, all of them in the midst of great change. And one which ends, as all novels probably should, with an apocalyptic, disastrous sex party! I loved reading this book not only for its story and characters but because it felt deeply honest to me. I was immersed in its world, and recommend it to everyone."
—**MATTHEW ZAPRUDER**, author of *Story of a Poem: A Memoir*

"This fierce, fearless, and unflinching novel interrogates who we are and what we want. How do we know who we are among an onslaught of identities? And if we don't know who we are, how can we know what we want? Naomi Kanakia's unexpectedly tender conclusion is that the truth is in kindness, in closeness, in feeling."
—**TAYMOUR SOOMRO**, author of *Other Names for Love: A Novel*

THE DEFAULT WORLD

NAOMI KANAKIA

THE FEMINIST PRESS
AT THE CITY UNIVERSITY OF NEW YORK
NEW YORK CITY

Published in 2024 by the Feminist Press
at the City University of New York
The Graduate Center
365 Fifth Avenue, Suite 5406
New York, NY 10016

feministpress.org

First Feminist Press edition 2024

NEW YORK | Council on
STATE OF | the Arts
OPPORTUNITY.

This book was made possible thanks to a grant from the New York State
Council on the Arts with the support of Governor Kathy Hochul and the
New York State Legislature.

▲ ▼▼
ART WORKS.

This book is supported in part by an award from the National Endowment
for the Arts.

First printing May 2024

Cover design by John Elizabeth Stintzi
Text design by Drew Stevens

Library of Congress Cataloging-in-Publication Data

Names: Kanakia, Naomi, author.
Title: The default world / Naomi Kanakia.
Description: First Feminist Press edition. | New York City : The Feminist
    Press at the City University of New York, 2024.
Identifiers: LCCN 2024000516 (print) | LCCN 2024000517 (ebook) | ISBN
    9781558613164 (trade paperback) | ISBN 9781558613171 (ebook)
Subjects: LCGFT: Transgender fiction. | Novels.
Classification: LCC PS3611.A493 D44 2024 (print) | LCC PS3611.A493
    (ebook) | DDC 813/.6--dc23/eng/20240111
LC record available at https://lccn.loc.gov/2024000516
LC ebook record available at https://lccn.loc.gov/2024000517

PRINTED IN THE UNITED STATES OF AMERICA

For the one who deserved this more than I did

1

"Excuse me, but are you trans?"

Jhanvi looked up from her soda water. The guy asking the question was one of the servers: tall, scrawny, with acne and a loose ponytail.

"I'm sorry," he said. "Is that rude? You look amazing. You're, like, a goddess."

"Uhh, yeah," she said. "I'm trans."

"I am too!" His voice had gotten higher, and Jhanvi closed one eye. Was he a trans man who was partway there, or a trans woman who'd barely begun? "I'm Tony," he said. Or was it Toni? Really, the unusual thing here was that he'd even asked—Jhanvi assumed most people saw her broad shoulders and heavy brow and clocked her instantly.

"Do you live around here?" He was holding a tray of glasses in one hand, but he touched her shoulder with the other. "I would've noticed you before." A woman in leather pants stood behind Toni, shifting her weight, trying to sidle past the oblivious server.

The woman finally twisted around Toni, her hand already sprouting a phone as she walked past them, and Jhanvi let out her breath, turned her attention to Toni.

"Uhh, I'm visiting," Jhanvi said, shrugging a bit.

"I knew you couldn't live here," Toni said. "Sometimes I feel like the only trans woman in San Francisco."

She! Jhanvi's smile got brighter and more authentic. Other trans women were friendly to her if she met them at a trans meet-up or brunch or dance party, but if she saw them in public? No fucking way; they usually cut her dead, out of a fear, perhaps, of being clocked. She saw them sometimes, noticing them from a slight patchiness to their hair or the top-heaviness of their shoulders. When she made eye contact, they'd look stolidly onward, pretending they hadn't seen her, and the utter hatred and despair would boil up inside her, and she'd think *fuck you*, and swear to herself that if she was ever beautiful and cis passing, she'd be different. She'd see people, acknowledge their humanity.

"Hey!" Jhanvi said. "It's so nice to meet you! Yeah, I should be around a lot, I think my friend comes here? I've been to this bar with him, anyway."

"A friend?" Toni's voice rose, pulled so high into her nose that Jhanvi could hear the nostril hairs quivering. Toni would learn to relax her vocal cords someday, let her lips and tongue do more of the work of feminizing her voice. "Who is it? How do you know him?"

Jhanvi's ears suddenly got hot. She'd never stopped feeling like the geek in the locker room, panting out some obviously fake story about all the sexing he'd done.

"He's ... I guess ..." Jhanvi shook her head. "No, Henry is a sex friend. I shouldn't be embarrassed. He's really, really good looking. It's pretty absurd." This assessment of Henry's looks was a recycled line, something she repeated like a mantra when thinking about and discussing her visit.

"Oh wow, can I see?" Toni's hair brushed against Jhanvi's shoulder as she propped herself on the edge of a stool to peer at Jhanvi's phone.

"He *is* beautiful," Toni said. "Where's he from?"

Henry's best feature was his skin, swarthy but with perfect golden undertones that made his picture shimmer slightly on the phone screen. He had dark eyes and prematurely graying hair and beautiful white teeth.

"Look at that jaw," Toni said. "It's like something you'd see on TV."

"He's so beautiful," Jhanvi said. She'd been saying the words in the weeks leading up to her visit—*he's so beautiful*—because she knew that was the consensus. It wasn't her personal opinion of him, but that didn't matter—she wasn't sure anymore what she actually liked in a man. Everyone's appearance was buried in too many layers of social meaning. What mattered was not how he looked, but that other people loved to look at him. Henry needed to be beautiful, somehow, for the calculus behind the visit to work.

"Well, girl, where is he?" Toni's hand still rested on Jhanvi's back.

"I have no clue," Jhanvi said. "He's supposed to meet me here. He's one of these fire-eaters, right? Not that punctual, those people. He lives on this street, but the code he gave for his door didn't work, and he's not responding to my texts. But it'll come together."

She gave a broad smile. Hopefully not too manic, because she really was at peace with her stranded state.

But Toni's forehead creased. "Oh no," Toni said. "Is there someone you can call? Another roommate?"

"I'll be fine."

"Well," Toni said. "I live with my dad, but I can ask him if . . ."

"Don't worry about it. If my friend doesn't work out, I have other people to call."

"You are so chill," Toni said. "I'd be freaking out."

"Oh . . . yeah," Jhanvi said. "I mean, what's the worst that can happen? You sleep rough for a night. Or drink coffee, smoke some meth, stay up." Pausing for a second, assessing Toni's eyes, Jhanvi sensed the need to adjust her story. "But I'm not really here to see him. I'm just crashing at his place." Toni relaxed, took a breath, and Jhanvi winked.

This was amazing! She was totally pulling this off. Being a woman was really good. If only people knew. It was so good—at least, if you'd been born a man. Of course, that made no sense—being trans was awful, a short train to death and despair—but not for her!

Nope. In certain, very limited circumstances, it was an improvement. Like, she'd once sat all night in this exact same bar—literally this exact one—getting drunk by herself, trying to work up the courage to talk to girls during her "learn to pick up women" stage. After saying hello to three girls, she just gave up, because she could see how unwelcome she was: some red-faced Indian nerd, trying too hard, in expensive jeans and a shirt that did little to hide his paunch and flabby arms. Well, look at her now, talking to a stranger like it was nothing.

"Okay," Toni said. "I gotta go, but order a drink, I'll tell the bartender to comp it. Let me know if your friend gets here, I want to see him!"

Jhanvi squeezed closer to the bar, basking in that belonging, that sense of "I know someone." She ordered a hamburger, figuring Toni could comp that too. It was Sunday afternoon and the bar was relaxed. She saw four people shooting pool, two guys messing with a jukebox, groups of friends squeezed into booths, gushing over flights of beer.

Everything here was different from Sacramento: it was in the texture and taste of the place, in every detail. If you knew both cities, you couldn't mistake one for the other. People in SF were so thin, so tall, so beloved of the gods. At this same kind of bar in Sactown, there'd always be that weedy, desperate grumble, that feeling of being down. Even at a hipster bar, the guys would be bandy-legged, in T-shirts, with bushy eyebrows and baseball caps, and the girls would be in shiny T-shirts and unfashionably low jeans. Not that they would be poor, or even low class, but the whole aura would just be resentful and wounded—not like here. Sacramento always had an aura of second best, of loserdom. That was also what people said about this place: San Francisco wanted to be New York—and it was true. But that made Sacramento even more pathetic—it envied something that was already ersatz and fake.

She watched a gaggle of perfect girls at a nearby table, somewhere between twenty-five years old and a very well-preserved thirty-two, speaking indecipherable syllables in high, liquid voices as the brittle bristles of their eyelashes cut the air and tunic hems swished around their stretchy leggings. Her eyes followed one girl's legs down into a pair of high-heeled shoes, glossy black, attached by a strap around her ankle.

The sight made Jhanvi shiver, and when the girl's eyes briefly turned to her, Jhanvi dropped her eyes, though she knew it was weak and creepy to break eye contact so fast, as if she'd done something wrong. She should've smiled and looked away slowly instead.

"Okay!" Toni said. "I took my break to come tell you. I just saw you stand up, and wow, you're stunning."

Jhanvi colored. She was about six feet four inches, an Amazon, and big in all her dimensions—she chose her clothes more by what fit than by any sense of style. But today she'd come in a bright orange dress with buttons down the front, a bit more of a tunic than a dress on her. She had a momentary vision of herself, a giantess propped on this stool, her chunky heel locked into the foot bar, and her hair teased to frame her face and then pulled back. She knew her makeup was on point, with long lashes and smoky black around her eyes and a bright red, almost orange lip that matched her dress.

Women sometimes complimented her looks, but Jhanvi always wrote them off. She was just tall. She knew her broad shoulders, square build, and brow bone read as inescapably masculine. Not to mention that her clothes rarely fit—they bulged at the belly and were baggy on her hips. Tights and leggings rolled down, not finding any purchase on her soft, round midsection, and dresses that were knee-length on cis women were too short for her, while ankle-length gowns stopped dowdily at the top of her calf.

"Thanks," Jhanvi said. "How's your stuff? Are you on hormones?"

"No," Toni said. "I'm sort of backwards, I'm identifying as a girl to see if I can do it, and then I'll start hormones."

"Totally. That's the right thing to do," Jhanvi said. "This is the hardest part, and by the way, if you ever feel like, oh, you know, you're not a real trans—that people like me are better than you, further along—that's silly. Don't believe that, because you're at the hardest part, trying to tell people, get them to believe, you know..." She realized her intended wording—*something other than what they see*—might be insulting.

"Hey, thanks!" Toni said. "That means so much. You are so cool."

They smiled tentatively at each other, and for a moment Jhanvi felt the slide into her old self—into the fear and the confusion, the sense that something was slipping away and could not be recovered. She'd sat across from so many women in so many bars, or at so many house parties, trying and failing to find the right words.

Jhanvi sometimes had trouble—everyone did, she knew—assigning the proper gender to people who were early in transition, but in this case, watching Toni's thin frame and her graceful movements, the long, fitted shirt—a man's shirt, but still—hugging her hips, Jhanvi thought, *okay, this works*. Jhanvi could probably gender Toni correctly without slipping up.

"So, uhh, what're your plans? Why are you visiting?" Toni said.

"Oh!" Jhanvi said, raising one finger. Now was the moment to test out her cover story. "Yes, that's it. I'm gonna get married."

"What!" Toni said. "Are you kidding? To who? To Henry?"

Jhanvi inwardly murmured *to whom*. "Sorry, that's a new line I'm trying out, as a way of explaining my plan. I read in a book you should try out each conversational gambit over and over, using slight variations, to see which one works best." Jhanvi tried to ignore Toni's confused expression and continued.

"No, I, uhh, so you know all these tech-bro types have great trans benefits at their jobs—like, lots of money for surgery and hair removal and whatever you need, and Henry is always telling me to learn to code and get a job here. And I'm like, *Or I could just find a techie and marry them for their benefits.* And he always laughs, because it's just a line. But a little while ago, Henry was texting and complaining to me about his girlfriend, Audrey, and how they were poly and she didn't want to marry him, and all this stupid, pointless drama they were having over this party they all run, and he mentioned one of his friends had paid a hundred thousand dollars to rent out an event space—"

"For one night!?"

"No, for the year. But still, it's empty most of the time, nobody lives there. It's for this event they throw for Alterna-Fest. It's called The Guilty Party, it's a bit famous. His girlfriend, or his ex? She kinda runs it, and she's always online, talking about poly and kinky stuff, being an influencer, or whatever."

"Fire-eaters," Toni said. "They're so selfish. We get them in here all the time."

"Totally! So I got mad, and I was like, you guys have this much money to throw around, and I'm fucking earning twenty dollars an hour and happy about it, and fuck you. Forget the poly thing, she just doesn't want to marry you, Henry!"

"Truth bomb."

"Totally, and he got quiet and was like, *You're right, I know.* So we had a long talk, and I was like, *You are so valuable. I would marry you in a second.* And he was like, *Well, why don't you?*"

"Shit! He asked you?"

That wasn't precisely how it'd gone. But it sounded good this way.

"Yeah," Jhanvi said. "He doesn't care. He's game. It's a way of rejecting his ex's rejection."

Toni's face flushed, her eyebrows going up and her cheeks widening in a real smile. She threw her arms around Jhanvi. "Congratulations! That's amazing! Let me know if you need a witness! I'll do it, I'll take time off. Oh my god, is that too strong?

I'm sorry, you must have lots of friends. Do your parents know? What do they think?"

Jhanvi had no idea how her parents would react if this wedding became real—if they'd be happy or disgusted or confused. Jhanvi, married, was so far away from their conception of her as an alcoholic, drunk in a field, beaten to death. Maybe they'd be happy for her.

"This is amazing! I'm so glad we met!"

Interesting. If Jhanvi could've selected one superpower, it would've been telepathy. She'd have liked to pick apart Toni's excited reaction, figure out if she was excited because this resembled a romantic comedy and she assumed Jhanvi and Henry would fall in love, or if she was excited because Jhanvi would finally get the procedures she needed.

"You can witness for me, sure," Jhanvi said. "Oh hey, what's your number?"

Toni had some new app where you beamed numbers by tapping phones together. Jhanvi had never used it, so Toni reeled off her number the old-fashioned way, and when Jhanvi called it, Toni stared at the buzzing phone, blank eyed.

"So you can save my number as a contact."

"Oh!" Toni said. "Yeah!" She tapped on her phone. "So, if you get married, are you gonna stay here?"

"Probably," Jhanvi said. "I don't know. My life back home is good, but it's just like—this isn't how someone is supposed to be spending her life. You're not supposed to just sit around waiting for your real life to start. So I was like, what if I could get the same thing, but much quicker?"

Jhanvi smiled again. It was terrible even to think this, but it was so easy to talk with someone whose good opinion you didn't need to earn. Someone less important than her. She saw a silken web of connections spanning this room. Toni was a townie—and this world of yuppie San Franciscans was impossibly distant to her. By being both unemployed and visibly trans, Jhanvi's class status was effaced, and she had the ability to cut across the gap, bridging all the worlds—a position that, at least in theory, carried an awful power that allowed her to be forgiven for saying absurd things and being a useless sort of human being.

"Do I sound crazy?" Jhanvi said. "Because you have this look..."

"No!" Toni said. "This is a great plan. I am *so* impressed. You're like a character from a TV show. I love you *so* much."

"I mean, it's actually not a great plan," Jhanvi said. "In Sactown, I work at this co-op, Green Magic. It's really famous and shit, kind of like Rainbow Grocery here. And they pay really well if you become a member, which I'm about to. And Henry still needs to look up his job's trans benefits, see if they're actually that good. And it leaves me really entangled with him, really exposed. But, you know, after two years, I've only saved like two thousand bucks for a face chopping surgery, you know... hack at this brow bone, which is the minimum I'd need to pass... and doing it would cost five times that much and I'd have to fly to Spain or Thailand or Mexico... Kind of scary, you know, and what if something goes wrong with the operation? But if this marriage goes through, I'll be set—and my friend wouldn't be giving up anything! He just signs a form, and boom, I get the very best surgeon."

Toni's eyes flicked up to Jhanvi's brow, and Jhanvi said, "The chin, too. And the nose. Then some breasts, perhaps, and maybe liposuction, move some fat around, oh, and see if there's hair enough on my scalp to get some better coverage up front. Bottom surgery, I guess, if everything else is in place, and that's the last thing holding me back."

A lot of trans women were into being trans, or claimed to be. But if Jhanvi could've passed, she'd have left it behind, done like a 1970s trans person and moved to a new town, cut off everyone from her old life, and started anew. But that seemed too impossible even to dream about.

There was a pause in the conversation. Jhanvi sipped her

drink, then said, "The whole thing would be, like, a hundred and fifty thousand dollars. But Facebook or Google or whatever, they'd pay the bill."

Jhanvi saw something then in Toni's face, a tiny sort of inward sigh, and Jhanvi put out a hand, said, "Hey . . . you're like, what . . . twenty-two?"

"Uhh . . . yeah," Toni said. "Exactly."

"And you're thin," Jhanvi said. "What, twenty-eight-inch waist?"

"Yeah!"

"Five ten?"

"This is great."

"I know, I should work at a carnival. Look, your facial hair is sparse." She touched Toni's face, ran her thumb over the bristles on her chin. "It won't cost you nearly as much as it's cost me. Start doing lasering, invest in that. I got most of mine done a few years ago. You've got good hair on top. You've got that boyish frame, that's a nice basic start—no fat to take away, just fat to add, and that thin chest will look good even with small breasts. Oh, and most importantly . . ." Jhanvi pushed Toni's face from one side to another. "Your brow is good, doesn't protrude. Your chin might want some shaving down—might not, too—but at the very worst, you'll be a cute girl with a strong chin, like Kristen Stewart," Jhanvi said, naming a starlet beloved by the dykeish set.

Toni withdrew a bit. "You know, thanks. I've been online, there are forums, where you post your face, ask people to evaluate it, but . . ."

"People can be too mean, and they can be too nice," Jhanvi said. "And both are wrong. The thing is, if you're one of us, you've seen a lot of plain, scrawny guys transform. Sorry, I'm like such an asshole, talking about how much it costs. No, no, it's not your job to worry about that right now. And hey, absolute worst-case scenario, you don't pass. Like, that's the thing, I'll probably never pass, never look normal, and it's fine. I'm happy."

"No, you do!"

"I don't," Jhanvi said. "You clocked me right away. That's the definition of not passing."

"But I wasn't sure."

"Okay, okay," Jhanvi said. "The point is, you play the hand that you were dealt. A lot of girls look at me and they think, *I'd die before I'd look like her. Her life must be hard.* And ..." Jhanvi shrugged. "It's really not. You make it work. So, like, for myself ... I don't want to sit around at home waiting for the knife to turn me into a person. I want to start living right away, and if that stuff comes together later, then that's a bonus."

"Wow," Toni said. "You're awesome. This is so great. Hey ... I have to go back to work. Are you sticking around?"

"I want to, if I can find somewhere to live. The co-op back in Sacramento is waiting to hear from—oh, you mean am I gonna stay here, right now?"

"It'd be great if you moved here, but I did mean right now, yeah." Jhanvi nodded, and Toni waved as she went back to work.

Jhanvi pulled out her phone and saw a few texts from her boss, Monica, asking if she needed a loan to pay the buy-in. The co-op had a buy-in fee for membership, but Jhanvi knew she could get it—even if her parents wouldn't believe she needed it, some cousin or family friend would wire the money, swearing that if she was scamming them, this would be the last time they'd speak to her. Jhanvi wrote back, *No I can get the money. I just need to ask someone. Can you hold the spot?*

Monica: Why aren't you in today? It really doesn't look good to be absent before the vote.

Jhanvi: I'll be in next week.

Monica: That doesn't work. You need to show up, so people don't think you're taking this for granted! Can you make it by the end of the week?

Jhanvi: Ok.

When she'd been drinking, Jhanvi had lived a few days at a time. Now the co-op meeting curtained her future: after it, she could imagine nothing, saw no vision of a Jhanvi she recognized, and the implied nonexistence was actually far preferable to her normal vision of the many lonely years to come.

Another text came. Henry said he was out of town with his housemates—they were planning and vision boarding for The Guilty Party.

He explained that his roommate Katie had stayed home, but she was checking on some things at the dungeon, so she might not be around, and maybe Jhanvi could ring the bell, and Henry was really sorry, but he was gonna be out of touch for a few hours since they were about to enter the medicine tent.

Jhanvi texted back, *Why didn't the code work? Can you recheck it for me?*

She stared at her phone, willing him to respond, but it remained blank. It would be easy to go insane with resentment. All she wanted was a couch to crash on, and her college friends literally rented out a whole empty warehouse for their sex parties—although they hated when she called them that. But Jhanvi reminded herself she wasn't owed better treatment— she was a parasite, a leech, a terrible person—and someday she would destroy them all. She shook her head slightly; she got these stray destructive thoughts sometimes. Violence and anger weren't something she'd totally left behind when she'd stopped being a man.

Jhanvi stayed at the bar, nursing her drink, hating herself for the hangdog look she knew was on her face. Toni came by, put a hand on her shoulder, said, "Everything okay?" and Jhanvi reassured her that everything was.

"Umm, here." Jhanvi handed over her phone.

Toni rested her hand on Jhanvi's arm again, with her long, thin fingers, and Jhanvi sighed, thinking about how Toni would someday hate her fingers and her hands, think *why couldn't they be more demure?* It crept on you slowly, these sorts of feelings. As your dysphoria boiled away, it also became more concentrated, along with the desire to cut and carve away and dispose of your remaining masculinity.

"Stay here as long as you want!"

"Thanks."

Jhanvi's eyes caressed the wooden paneling behind the bar and lingered on the glittering rows of bottled liquid. What if— what if—what if she relapsed right now? She'd go on quite a bender, and then, after a month or a year, she'd end up in a hospital, and that would be a new bottom, and in some AA meeting, she'd say, *Well, I was in San Francisco, and I was looking for any answer other than "get a job, work hard, save some money, and put your life together"* and everyone would laugh at the dumbness of her plans, and some unctuous twenty-years-sober queer would come up to her after and say, "How you holding up?" and she'd go to barbecues in his backyard, and eventually live in his spare room and listen to his problems getting along with his kids, and some night she would go online and block her San Francisco friends one by one so she wouldn't be triggered by photos of their beach bonfires and sewer raves.

A man at the bar jabbed her with his elbow. She caught his eye, and he looked studiously away. She let her gaze pass over all the men in the room, sweeping laser-like, watching the row of eyes flutter toward the ceiling to avoid meeting her gaze. She was a monster—she was the nineties sitcom trope come to life: the sad, ugly trans woman. But no. Let 'em think what they want. Let 'em die in a pit. She'd live better than them all.

Maybe she'd just smash open Henry's window with a rock and crawl in. His roommates were all prison and police abolitionists—what were they gonna do, call the cops?

Jhanvi gathered her bag. Toni said, "Oh, you heading out?"

"Yeah, I'll wait at their door."

"Cool. Where do they live?"

"Just up the street? Like, right nearby?"

"Huh, literally on this street? Why not just wait here?"

"They have a stoop."

"Okay, but . . ."

Toni fluttered over, and they pored over the map on Jhanvi's phone. "Oh no, oh no," Toni said. "You don't want this. Just leave them a note, how 'bout that? There's, like, well, I don't wanna scare you, but okay, well, in Sacramento do you have, like—okay, have you noticed SF has these, uhh . . . it's got these camps? I mean it sounds crazy to say, but literal tents, people on the streets—the police can't do a thing, though I call them like every day, and—"

"Thanks, but we have tons of those in Sacramento. It's fine."

Toni was standing close, and Jhanvi felt the urge to squeeze the other woman around the waist and wondered if she could get away with it. She had always wanted to engage in these impulsive feminine touches and caresses but had never known how.

"I can deal with the unhoused," Jhanvi said. "Or whatever people say these days: folx temporarily experiencing a lack of housing."

"This isn't temporary, they're like major crack addicts. And that guy at the corner—there's a spot in the door of an abandoned storefront—he's really offensive. He called me a faggot the other day. I literally hate him. You really shouldn't go out there."

"Toni," Jhanvi said. "I'm not that kind of trans."

Now the other girl looked confused, and Jhanvi was reminded that she was so young—oh god, it was working! Jhanvi was already seeing and treating her like the beautiful young woman she would become, the girl Jhanvi would envy and fear. Jhanvi took the chance to rub her hand on the girl's upper arm, imagining the geometric tattoo that would someday encircle it.

"People don't bother me," Jhanvi said. "I'm not that kind of trans. I'm, like, well, it's not that I'm ugly . . ."

"You're not—"

"I am, but some ugly transes also get harassed—it's that I know I'm unworthy of being noticed—that I don't walk around pretending to think some man might care. I don't threaten them."

Now Toni frowned. "Look, SF can be really—"

"I'll be fine, I swear."

Jhanvi gathered all her stuff, and Toni drifted along behind her to the door, muttered, "You have my number . . ."

Jhanvi was lost in her own thoughts and hardly noticed the bright light surround her as she left the bar, the burst of street noise. She tottered on her chunky heels—they were so uncomfortable. Half her bag was shoes, she really shouldn't be wearing these—they were too small by far, at least by a size or two. But she took a step, and her bag's wheels clicked behind her. Walking down the street, she examined every face for some evidence that they saw her as worthy of comment—other trans women swore people looked at them all the time, but maybe Jhanvi was simply too self-absorbed—she felt that she moved invisibly through the world.

Sure enough, a pup tent sat in the doorway of an old closed-down bank. A head poked out, shaggy hair and shaggy beard, reddened skin, indeterminate race, but probably white. Jhanvi's eyes skipped away when they met the man's.

When she reached Henry's stoop, she smoothed her tunic so it lay close to her legs and sat down, resting her back on the iron gate.

2

Nobody ever forgot meeting Jhanvi—she was too huge and too odd—so even though they'd only met once or twice before and Katie didn't remember her name, she knew the other girl recognized her face.

"Sure, sure," Katie said. "I'll let you in."

Katie wore leggings, a crop top, and a sports bra: the Sunday uniform of the sporty San Franciscan. Jhanvi noticed her gluteal muscles shifting under the spandex as they ascended the carpeted stair. At the top, Katie said, "Just one sec."

Jhanvi drifted through the house. It was very San Franciscan—the top floor and attic of a Victorian. The hardwood floor was deeply scarred—the last tenants, ten years ago, had cooked meth. That was the explanation Henry usually gave, although Jhanvi wasn't sure why that would cause long black gouges in the floors. The apartment was bisected by a long hallway, with bedrooms on either side and a kitchen and dining room sprouting off the back.

Individuality was prized in the Fun Haus, but not everyone had the interior design skills they needed to really express themselves, so the result came off as trying a bit too hard. The rooms contained an assortment of bean bag chairs, minimalist Swedish furniture, heavy thrift-store tables, and couches with stains layered like geological strata. The bedrooms varied mostly in color palette: the front den, Audrey's room, was decorated in reds and oranges, while some rooms had warmer lighting and leaned into the hardwood look. Katie's stood out for its extreme minimalism: she slept on a bamboo mat and kept all of her possessions in her closet, with nothing in view but a standing desk and her laptop.

There was another bedroom upstairs, but Jhanvi had never gone there.

Like most buildings in this part of San Francisco, it had once been a grand multigenerational manor house with plenty of space for servants and poor relatives to scurry about. The house had been split in half vertically, and each half sold off separately, then each owner had duplexed their own half. So this apartment was about a quarter of the original house, and everything had an oddly narrow feeling. Even the walls seemed ad hoc. For instance, the front den had a big chandelier and a boarded fireplace—it had clearly been a sitting room or something. The now dining room had been where the servants took their lunch. The upstairs had been, perhaps, where the maids slept. The whole thing made Jhanvi want to reread a Zola novel.

The four roommates each paid under a thousand bucks a month, since the apartment was rent-controlled—like most of them needed it, with their six-figure tech jobs! Market rate for these rooms would be something like eighteen hundred each. The downstairs apartment had recently rerented for twelve thousand a month. The landlord was on Henry and his friends like a hawk, always trying to force them out, and he refused to do repairs, so the roommates did their own plumbing and replaced broken fixtures themselves.

Jhanvi scouted the front den, looking for the router—she had a pay-as-you-go data plan, so she needed to get off cell data. You could normally get the log-in data from a sticker attached to the router. She traced the wires behind a chair, then knelt on all fours, trying to reach the box behind it.

"What're you doing?"

"Oh." Jhanvi sat up, smiled. Katie stood in the doorway, holding a giant mason jar full of what looked like cloudy urine but was probably kombucha. "Wi-Fi password."

"You won't find it down there."

"I was looking on the—sorry."

Jhanvi struggled to her feet. Katie was tall, maybe 5'9", but Jhanvi was a good half foot taller. She slouched a little. "Sorry. I thought it'd still be in my phone, but it wasn't."

"We set up a guest network," Katie said. "We were worried too many people had our old password."

As a kid, Jhanvi had been socially awkward, couldn't read social cues. Most times, she felt like she still couldn't, but on occasion, her consciousness surged, and from the slight angle of a foot, the twitch of an eyelid, she realized, *This person finds me weird. I am somehow scaring them.* She could be scary, Jhanvi knew: once on a dark street, a woman had turned, glanced at her, then turned back a few times as Jhanvi closed the gap between them, until, with the flapping of her sandals, the woman had sprinted across the street and away from the looming stranger.

"Hey, sorry," Jhanvi said, reaching out a hand apologetically. "I feel as if I'm annoying you."

Katie lost a fraction of her injured reserve. "No." She shook her head, wrapping her arms around herself. "Sorry, I haven't showered." Jhanvi saw a flash of her armpit—shaved, perhaps, or maybe her hair was so blond it didn't matter. Katie was a chilly Viking princess, transported to a San Francisco apartment to encounter a dark-skinned tranny nobody.

"I'll keep out of your way," Jhanvi said.

"The network is FunHaus, with the 'ay you' spelling of house. And the password is . . ." She lowered her voice. "We try not to say it too loud, it's *fuckthepolice.*"

"Okay," Jhanvi said. "Why?"

"Well . . ." Katie's eyebrows furrowed. "The carceral state is a tool of white supremacy, and we think—"

"No, I meant why do you whisper it? So people who live on the street don't hear? And steal your Wi-Fi?"

Jhanvi felt the terrible urge to grin. These people were so absurd. When she'd tried to explain what they were like to her trans friends in Sacramento, they had been like, *Oh, so they're terrible yuppies.* And yes, that was true, but they were so much more. They said and did everything they ought to say in order to be good, but somehow they still weren't. In spite of how hard they tried to be good allies, there were prickles that betrayed their essential lack of comprehension that *they* were the real problem with this country. Jhanvi sometimes used that to justify her own plans: *Why should I work so hard when they make all this money without any effort? I could literally survive for three years on one of their end-of-year bonuses.*

Her trans friends were like, *Oh yeah, but they'd never give that money up, they're greedy, money-obsessed white people.* Except Jhanvi knew better—they didn't spend the money! Look at this house! It was a dump. They weren't spending their preposterous salaries. They saved all their money for years, then blew it on twelve-thousand-dollar carbon nano-fiber bikes or years-long sabbaticals to work on organic farms. And somehow, Jhanvi knew she could get ahold of it—and not by stealing—but simply by providing them with entertainment. She'd seen it done by others who had hung around, like this tall lanky guy with white-guy dreads—Nasal Xylophone. He'd hung around Fun Haus for half a year, claiming to be a spiritual medium or something.

Jhanvi couldn't use that dodge, but something else would come up, she knew. Some gamble, some scheme or scam to make her way and get what she needed to transition fast. Maybe this marriage plan would even work. Henry hadn't totally dismissed the idea. There was nothing inherently unworkable about it.

"Yes, we want to keep our password private," Katie said. "Oh, that reminds me—we have a few house rules. Here, I actually meant to laminate them, but let me, can I—actually, I'll email them—but we need to have a meeting. But there are rules, they are—"

"Don't put meat on the veg counters, don't call the police, etcetera—"

"Or be racist or homophobic, or bring anyone here who is ..."

"Got it," Jhanvi said, trying hard not to roll her eyes. It was like Katie imagined a guest saying, *Oh no, I'm a racist, and this house is anti-racist—guess I'll go stay somewhere else!*

Jhanvi heard shouting that sounded like it was coming from downstairs, and Katie got a terribly severe look. "There's a man, Chris, who sleeps next door. He sometimes rings the doorbell to ask to use our bathroom. Do not, and I repeat, *do not* call the cops on him. You don't have to let him in, but don't call the cops. They hassle Chris literally every day, and I'm pretty sure it's a guest associated with this community. Fire-eaters have a real equity problem, as I'm sure you know."

"Oh," Jhanvi said. "Uhh, no, it isn't anyone in this house calling the cops."

"You'd be surprised," Katie said. "This house is actually going through a huge transition. It's caused a lot of chaos."

Chaos? Jhanvi noted that to bring up later with Henry. Maybe she was talking about his and Audrey's slow-moving de-couple-ment.

"No, I meant, I, uhh, I know who calls the cops on him. I met the—them."

"What?" Katie's eyes narrowed. "Who?"

"Just ... someone who works here, on the street."

"Who?" Katie insisted. "I've talked to the owners of the stores. And our neighbors downstairs. Who is this person? What the fuck is their problem? This is so infuriating. How do you know this person?"

"From around," Jhanvi said. "Just around."

"Can I talk to them?"

"Uhh, let me check ... I ... I'll ask."

"Oh. And are you only visiting? Or is there a job ... or ... ?"

Jhanvi felt a sense of terrible resistance, almost a physical force, clamping down on her heart and throat. She wanted to be bold and different—to give off that main character energy—but she also deeply felt that telling Katie about the marriage plan would be a mistake. And yet, she'd been on the sidelines of life for so long, had not said so many things she wished she had, and she'd told herself, *Coming here is only worthwhile if I'm gonna be different,* so she pushed forward with her plan.

"I'm, uhh, gonna find someone to marry me," Jhanvi said. "For their trans benefits. Like . . . a green card marriage sort of thing." Free electrolysis marriage? It wasn't as catchy. This idea needed better branding.

"Oh." Katie pursed her lips. "That's interesting."

"Is it?" Jhanvi said. "Or is it insane?"

"N—no, no," Katie said. "I don't know. I've heard some companies have good benefits."

"I too have heard that."

They were still standing in the open doorway of the den. Jhanvi hated the shyness of her own glance, how it was almost difficult to look at the other girl, with her narrow face, wide mouth, and pale hair, so delicate and fine—like the golden thread spun for the miller's daughter each night by Rumpelstiltskin.

"So . . . can I just sit here until Henry gets back?"

"Well . . . this is actually part of Audrey's room. I mean, when she and Hen were together they used to leave it open, as a sort of den, but now—"

Jhanvi frowned. "Oh, did they actually break up?" Jhanvi knew Henry liked her because she was easy and fit into the confines of his open relationship. But if he was single, he'd find another girlfriend instantly, and they'd probably be monogamous.

"No, no, no, they just wanted their space," Katie said.

"That sounds like breaking up."

"They're life partners. But their relationship is evolving."

"Err... all right," Jhanvi said.

"Maybe you should go in the living room? I'll be around if you need anything."

Jhanvi didn't ask for the code to the front door—she was afraid Katie would refuse.

The living room had a terrible bare quality, as if scouring winds had blown away all ornamentation and swept dust into all its corners. The wood was worn and the rug was a mottled green. Jhanvi sat on the couch, which was cold and leathery, with grains or crumbs worked into all the crevices. She plugged in her ereader (it'd run out of charge on the bus). After it blinked back into operation, she opened her current book—a sci-fi novel about a future war with space communism—but kept shivering. Finally, she went to the den, found a fleece blanket, and brought it back, feeling like a criminal.

She was in one of her fallow periods, reading-wise. During the last three years, she had tried to educate herself in the greats of Western civilization, but since deciding to come out here, she couldn't concentrate—even sci-fi pew-pew spaceship laser novels were too much. Instead, she worked herself into a web of daydreams, holding her future self tightly—the woman at the end of this road, the person who'd be gifted with a winning personality, who'd *be* someone.

Or maybe she'd be a monster, a Grendel's son (daughter?) walking through the streets of San Francisco with a heavy tread, her hands hanging down, fingers splayed out, jaw frontthrust, her long coat swishing around a broad frame with breasts bolted onto the chest. She'd have control over her voice, dropping it deep and raising it high, and over her eyes, scorching everyone with her gaze. Be the bad trans, be the bad trans—she would show them—all the indeterminate someones. She would be tall and dark and dangerous, eye-catching in her awful ugliness.

And of course, she dreamed too of slimming down—that another few years on the hormones would carve the excess muscle from her shoulders, redistribute her paunch, reshape the skin of her eyes and nose, and with careful cutting, she'd alter the rest. She'd walk around passing beautifully, super-model tall, with a hint of shimmer around her cheekbones, smiling and experiencing life, reaching that stage that some girls spoke about, where you went days without thinking about being trans.

The thoughts spun through her mind. Her life would finally matter. People would like her, she'd have a personality, an essence.

It was so frustrating how an inner self kept failing to gel: she was interesting, thoughtful, with much to say, and smart observational material to use in the "conversation space" (as fire-eaters called the warm-up to their partying). In the four years since she'd left this city, since she quit drinking and started on hormones, she'd cast away her old self: Nikhil, the angry nerd-boy, and she'd even learned to read social cues some-times. And yet . . . and yet . . . despite all that experience and the wealth of insight it gave her, a new personality hadn't quite coalesced. Something big was still missing from her life. A real personality needed a driving urge, something outside itself, and she honestly cared about nothing so much as transition-ing, passing, and being beautiful, in that order. If the Devil had appeared with an offer: you can look like Katie for one year, at the cost of an immediate death afterwards—like the cursed bargain made by the queens who'd kept fucking in bathhouses in 1982, '83, '84, until they sickened and grew KS—she'd have taken it without hesitation.

For a lot of people, the essential self was entangled with work, but Jhanvi was waaay off the career track. When she'd lived in SF right after college, she'd drudged for a nonprofit, because the job was respectable, but hadn't actually cared about its mission.

In Sacramento, she'd liked the working-class quality of grocery store life. At first, she had enjoyed the cool people, the authenticity, the sense of being separate from her social class. She'd befriended other trans women, going out with them to bars and cafes, gossiping, watching them take drugs and whirl away their lives. She had thought, *Okay, so I will be one of these people. A queer radical type. We'll live separate, in our own superior community.* But when they'd invited her to join the co-op—giving her profit sharing and a job for life, essentially—she had gone out for dinner with her landlord-slash-boss, Monica, who'd gotten her the job, and a bunch of her coworkers, and they'd toasted her, talking about how lucky she was, and how far ahead of the curve. But she'd known: *This isn't my place. These aren't my kind of folks.* And yes, it would've been easy to justify her rejection: to say she was gentrifying this worker-owned co-op, that they were only giving her a spot because they liked to think the place wasn't too good for a Stanford grad. And she didn't precisely think she was better than them. Because she wasn't—she was not a good person, and she was of very little use to anyone. But they just weren't her people. To them, she was interchangeable with any other hard-luck case that might've shown up at their door. It wasn't something she could put into words, other than to say, *This isn't where I belong.*

And yet ... and yet ... when she'd come to San Francisco the first time, she'd failed miserably. So maybe she didn't belong anywhere.

After a few days of moping about the co-op job, Jhanvi had thought: *I can whine to myself all day long about how it's impossible for a trans woman to find her place in society and how everybody in SF rejected me and how I'm stuck in this dead-end job with these people who don't understand how special I really am. Or I can do what I really want, which is to go back to San Francisco.*

And with that, she was irresistibly reminded of a conversation she'd recently had with Henry. The marriage idea. Rotating it in her mind, she'd been drawn to its simplicity. In an instant, through the force of her own personality, without bowing and scraping, signing up for shifts, saving money, hurting her back, and without having to live in Sacramento, Henry's money could turn her into a real girl.

About three years before, right after she left San Francisco, she'd been texting Henry, and he'd suddenly said: *What are you wearing?* The change had been so abrupt and sudden, almost comical, it had seemed like a line. They'd hooked up once before in college, but he'd never mentioned it again, and she'd assumed it was a drunken mistake. But she'd made up an outfit—a short skirt with garters, etcetera—and he'd asked about her thick cock, so she'd mentioned it poking out from the skirt. And then, over text, she'd sodomized him and called him a bad boy. The next day, she texted, *That was intense*, and he wrote, *Yea, that was nice.* Nothing more. But it had happened again, infrequently.

She knew male biology and psychology, how before a man came, he became pliable and left-brained, so she'd started taking advantage of the run-up, while he stroked himself, forcing him to say he loved her and stuff like that. Almost invariably, a couple weeks would go by afterward where they didn't talk. And god forbid she initiated the session—he would go cold and sometimes they wouldn't speak for a month.

She'd mentioned this to her trans friend Charli in Sacramento, and Charli laughed, saying, "Oh yeah, we've all got one of those," like it was a hobby, but to Jhanvi, this wasn't a small relationship. She wasn't the kind of trans girl who had a bunch of hookups and tricks. She had this, and nothing but this, and its very regularity—including the fact that Henry needed to hold her at arm's length afterwards—was reassuring. *It is possible to treat me as an object of desire after all.*

During their last sexy text, a week ago, he'd said she could come and live in the house in SF and work from home, and he could stop in at lunch, and they'd fuck, maybe in Audrey's bed, and she wouldn't know. And Jhanvi had said, *What's in it for me?* And then she had mentioned the marriage plan, and he hadn't shied away. She had told him she'd come to visit, to explore, and in the days afterward he hadn't been standoffish, he'd seemed effusive, telling her: *It's gonna be so great to see you in person. Audrey is being a pill. Just need a break.*

She'd written back: *Imagine how she'll feel after we get married.*

That would be insane, he wrote. *It would be a relief actually.*

The odd thing was that she knew Henry wanted to get married, to be monogamous, but Audrey insisted on this poly thing, and yet wanted to be his "life partner" too. He'd happily have sworn fidelity to her, but swearing lifelong cuckoldry was too much. Or at least that's how Jhanvi saw it. And maybe, maybe . . . maybe Jhanvi could do something for him. Make him feel small, which he obviously needed—look at how Audrey dominated him—and large, manly, and needed, at the same time. Maybe he'd decide Jhanvi could be his one and only? Or at least a valuable addition to the stable. So she'd bought a ticket.

On her bus ride to the city, as her eyes flitted over outlet malls and rolling hills, an idea had occurred to her: *I've done it. I've left society behind.*

And now, in this empty apartment, as the cold crept around the blanket, Jhanvi thought of the perfect term to describe herself: *I'm an adventurer.* It brought to mind con artists, dwarven rogues stealing from dragon hoards. *I'm an adventurer.* To others, it'd sound juvenile, absurd, but it's what she was.

• • •

"An adventurer?" Henry asked.

They were on his bed. He was long-limbed, his dark wavy hair flecked with premature gray, and one of those classic physiques with all the muscles outlined. He was nerdy as well—they'd met in their college gaming society. Jhanvi's attraction to men was complex—she was more attracted to what they represented than to their bodies, but she remembered Toni admiring his picture. He was objectively very good looking. Her fingertip twitched, and she imagined reaching out a long arm toward him, like Adam on the Sistine Chapel ceiling, about to receive the spark of life. Her nails were freshly done, a bright orange that she regretted—with her tan skin, it made her look jaundiced. She loved orange, but she mostly loved how it looked on tanned white women, how it made them radiate heat and light.

"Like, a Dungeons & Dragons thing?" He pushed back a lock of hair.

"You know what?" Jhanvi said. "Sort of exactly that. Except cooler." She mentioned a cult movie where the hero—a hitman played by an actor who was a former Black Panther—kept musing on how he wanted to be a wandering adventurer, someone who did good.

"Well yeah, but that was Samuel L. Jackson. And, you know—a movie."

"Totally," Jhanvi said. "Actually, maybe I should do good—that would really organize my life."

"Is this a bit?" Henry asked. "I was telling Audrey some of your classic college bits. Like your alter ego, Hassan? Remember him?" That was the name she gave people at parties so they wouldn't know who to hate after she vomited or blacked out. But he'd grown, developing into an entire character of his own. Eventually she met a real Hassan, a Saudi prince, and convinced him to make Nikhil (her birth name) his alter ego. But she'd thought the roguish part of her had disappeared when she stopped drinking.

"It wouldn't be entirely inaccurate to call it a bit."

"It's a good one. Like, this is San Francisco. I think a lot of fire-eaters think of themselves as adventurers, so they'd probably love that kind of talk."

"Would they?" Jhanvi asked. "Or would they make fun of it?

I think to be quirky and weird, you need money or beauty or charm. Or something. I don't know."

"Jhanvi," he said. "Stop being so negative. There is some really exciting stuff happening here." He was pacing around, and then he sat on the beanbag chair in a corner of his room and picked at the strings of a ukulele with his long fingers. "There's a girl in the house, Roshie. She's got some great ideas. We're, like, right on the verge of taking it to the next level—all buying property together—doing it up, like a real community."

"Sure you are."

"I'm serious. I've gotten really into this whole idea of, like, the community coming together and being self-sufficient—doing stuff that in the olden days the whole village would've done."

Fuck you. The thought came instinctively to Jhanvi's mind, and she just as instinctively said to herself, *No, that's not fair.*

Sometimes Henry brought out a side of Jhanvi that she didn't like, and she knew exactly why. During their senior year in college, when they were drunk, he'd blown her. Her entire time in college, she'd seen other people get drunk and hook up, and she'd wondered, *Why is that not happening for me? What is wrong with me?* But for once, it'd actually worked! They'd ended up together at the end of the night, grunting and sweaty and fumbling unpleasurably with each other. And the next day she'd texted him shyly, *Hey I should return the favor, or, like, maybe we should do other stuff,* and he'd been like *Sorry, I totally had a good time, but I think maybe that was a one-off, since we're friends and stuff.* He wasn't rude, but it'd destroyed her. Until then she'd been a straight guy, wondering why she was so different from everyone, why she could never feel at home. She'd hoped this sexual incident, the first in her life, could be an unlocking. Like, maybe, finally, she could experience what everyone else spent so much time going on about. But he'd tossed the key back into her face. Not his fault, of course. You don't owe someone your body. Jhanvi blinked rapidly, trying to stop herself from crying. She hadn't thought about that night in years.

She leaned forward, trying to stay focused. "That sounds super exciting! So, what would you do?"

"Maybe buy the building where we have the dungeon. Roshie's negotiating with the landlord. Roshie's incredible. She's amazing. She's like . . . okay, this is going to sound weird, but I never understood being an adult until I met her. Like, everything you always thought you needed permission to do? She just does. Like . . . she went out and organized the tenants in the building into a little union! She is nuts. I actually can't wait until you meet her."

"What does Katie think about all this?"

"Oh," Henry said. "She might not join. She's worried about displacement and stuff. Sad. She might stay here."

"And Audrey would be okay with that?"

He waved a hand. "We're figuring it out. I told her there'd be a studio in there, with better lighting for her videos. Sort of like a YouTube house, or whatever, but for fire-eaters."

Jhanvi narrowed her eyes. "You know . . . it's totally okay to break up with Audrey. You don't have to go along with whatever she wants."

"Nah, nah, we're working it out," Henry said. "So, what're you in town for? You mentioned some big plan. Ready for your triumphant return from the provinces?"

Once again, Jhanvi had come to that crossroads: the place where she had to reveal herself. She could hear traffic noise from Divisadero Street below, with cars honking at each other and people shouting. Maybe Toni had ended her shift at the bar. She thought, *Toni is more human than any of these fucks.* Jhanvi flushed with sudden rage, and, just as automatically, hated herself for it.

"Well, uhh, you remember that marriage plan, right?" she said. "Like, about finding some techie? And scamming their company out of their trans benefits?"

"Right on!" he said. "Now that's a good bit." He reached out a hand, and they high-fived like high school bros. He grabbed his desk chair and sat in it backwards, like he was the bad kid in an after-school special, and leaned toward her. "Remind me what you were thinking."

"Tech companies," she said, "have insane trans benefits. Besides healthcare—the best—they offer tens of thousands of dollars a year for 'cosmetic' procedures insurance won't cover, but stuff you really need, to like, be gender-affirmed. You know, nose jobs and hair removal or whatever."

"You're looking great, by the way."

"Sure, sure," Jhanvi said. "But what do you think? Is that insane?"

"No," Henry shook his head. "No, this is a good idea. But what's better is if you, like, made it an app. Made it a movement."

Jhanvi's eyes went wide, not because the idea was smart—it wasn't—but because somehow Henry's words cut to the core of what San Francisco had become. Nothing here was ever allowed to be purely personal—it always had to be larger than life, to disrupt all of society.

"Mmmhmm," Jhanvi said. "An app, to, you know, match people who have good health insurance with people who need it."

"It could be for all kinds of chronic conditions!" Henry said. "Not just being trans. Like, stuff that's expensive. Anything."

"Yeah," Jhanvi said. "But . . . they would have to get married."

"Or do domestic partnership."

There were legal issues with the latter, Jhanvi had researched it, but Henry was on a roll, laying out points as his fingertips tapped against his taut thigh, expanding the idea. His eyes were dancing, and Jhanvi was filled with a sudden contempt for him. Which was insane! She actually liked this guy—he was such an old friend, a good guy—and he was willingly entering into her madness. But at the same time, she knew, without a fragment of doubt, that under no circumstances whatsoever would Henry go through with this marriage plan.

"Insurance companies would try to take it down."

"Okay, but how?" Henry said. "How could they prove you're not 'really' married?"

"Prove it's transactional."

"But there's no exchange of money! In fact, they could move in together for the duration—even sleep together—like, it could be a genuine dating vehicle. And we could have prewritten prenups to protect people's assets. There could even be an aspect like an old-world *ton*—if the person dies, you get their stuff—not to be morbid."

"Then that *would* be transactional."

"Hahaha, yeah, okay," Henry said. "Hey, you should put this on the idea board. Like, to introduce yourself. We find that guests work well when they enter the life of the house. Or anyway, so sayeth Katie—she taught a seminar recently on how to cause less friction with our guests."

"Don't call the cops."

"Well, that goes without saying, but yeah," Henry said. "Just how to be good community citizens, both to San Francisco and to the friends of our friends—like, I'm working on an app to export our extended social graph—because if you think about it, all your friends are, well, not my friends, but my community too."

"Totally," Jhanvi said, wondering whether Toni, or some of her dad's Indian college friends, would be welcome in this house.

"Anyway, the idea board is out in the hall. You should really take your shot."

"You think?"

"Totally, yeah. And sorry, I'll email everyone, introduce you around."

"K."

They sat for a few more seconds, then Henry clapped his knees, got up. Jhanvi stood as well and watched as he dragged his desk chair in front of his computer and sat. She watched the muscles in his neck, and let her eyes trail up to his wavy hair. She had a brief glimpse of Henry fucking her ass. They hadn't hooked up in person since that time in college, but their sexts were pretty involved. And they'd been intimate once before, so it wasn't impossible!

Jhanvi sat on his bed again, sighed, started reading her book. He smiled crookedly at her, put on his headphones. He had come home pretty tired, insisting he was about to sleep, but they'd talked for a few hours anyway, having fun, eating a late dinner at a burrito place. She was too shy to ask him to pay, even though that's what an adventurer would do.

When Henry said he needed to concentrate, Jhanvi laid out Henry's sleeping bag and mat, which still reeked of bonfire smoke, and shyly slipped off her leggings and tunic. For a moment she was in her underwear on his floor, with her elbows pushing on her small, perky breasts. She huddled up— the house was always cold, especially at night.

Henry was still at his desk, and his eyes didn't fall on her. The old anger flared up. *Look at me.* This was pathetic. Not even an adventure: just another embarrassing moment she could never reveal to anyone. She crawled into the sleeping bag.

She rewatched a dumb sitcom on her phone, turning up the volume on her headphones when she heard his housemates talking in the hall. At some point he left without inviting her, and he didn't come back. Although they lived in separate rooms now, he'd said he still spent most nights with Audrey, when she didn't have someone else over.

Jhanvi spent a couple hours crafting a very fine, very eloquent email on her phone. *Henry, we've known each other for years, and I was wondering, since you thought the idea was so good, whether you'd be willing to . . .* The moment she hit *send*, she plugged in her phone and closed her eyes to sleep.

3

A couple mornings later, Jhanvi came out of Henry's room and saw Audrey standing in the hall wearing nothing but boxer shorts, toweling her wet hair and looking at the board where Henry had written down Jhanvi's idea.

Jhanvi's eyes drifted from the girl's bare breasts to the interlocking tattoos on her arms and back and shoulders—they were vaguely mechanical, something like the gears of a clock.

"Oh hey," Jhanvi said.

"Hey," Audrey said.

Jhanvi walked into the front den, where she usually spent her time. The sky outside the window was a terrible gray from SF's famous fog, and even inside the apartment, a chill permeated her body. She rooted through her bag looking for a second pair of socks and didn't turn when Audrey dropped down on the couch.

She was short, maybe 5'3" or so, and her brown hair was perpetually in a ponytail. She looked like a gymnast, slight at first glance, almost elfin, but her arms and thighs and back were knotted muscle.

"Oh hey," the girl said. "Don't leave. The room's for everybody, at least during the day. I only really need people out when I'm shooting a one-on-one."

"Uhh, okay," Jhanvi said. Her tired brain stuttered. "Katie said . . ."

"Everything's up in the air, I know. I'm so glad you're here to keep Henry company. It'll be so restorative, don't you think? I'm so impressed you got him to agree to this marriage idea. Henry can sometimes be sort of *too* introspective, you know?"

Jhanvi's forehead and ears were suddenly damp. She'd pressed Henry for an answer the day after she'd emailed him, and he'd mumbled something vaguely affirmative. She'd expected it to fall apart, but the next day he emailed her a web link about getting a marriage license and asked her to sort it out. He was working hard on a big release for the next few days, but on Friday she and Henry were planning to head to the courthouse.

"I'm just so impressed with him. And it makes me happy that he's really, like, moving on," Audrey said. "Hey . . . you've spent more time with him these past days than anyone. How is he? How's he holding up?"

Apparently, they hadn't broken up. They'd "uncoupled." But since they still lived together, albeit not in the same room, and screwed nightly, Jhanvi didn't really understand the distinction. Except she knew from what other people had said that this was considered a big emotional tragedy—a broken love. It was like one time when some girl cried to Jhanvi over how she'd never ever find love, and Jhanvi realized the girl had just broken up with some perfectly good guy because he "just wasn't going anywhere in life." Emotionally the girl might *feel* hopeless and bereft, and Jhanvi might sympathize in some way, but the reality bore no relation to the abyssal plains of Jhanvi's loneliness.

Jhanvi shrugged. "He's okay. Misses you, obviously . . ." The conversation sat awkwardly, and she felt a pang in her stomach. She had a sudden flash of contempt for this girl. "Let him feel his feelings. It's okay to feel bad about a breakup."

"Did he call it a breakup?"

"I mean the uncoupling."

"But I don't know if that word is right either. We're trying something really new. I don't have the answers. I thought, with you and the marriage plan—it seemed like maybe Henry would get on board with it."

Jhanvi brushed a strand of hair out of her face. Audrey squatted like a gargoyle on the arm of the couch. "It's not really new," Jhanvi muttered.

"What?"

"It's not new," Jhanvi said. "You're breaking up. It's just slow and messy and complicated because you're mostly but not totally compatible,"—because Audrey wanted to keep fucking other people—"but that's a really normal problem."

"Did he say that?" Audrey rubbed at the corner of her eye with a fingertip. "Look, you love Henry, I can tell. Everyone loves him so much. I am so lucky to have him in my life—and I would never, ever want to lose that. I really envision us living together forever. Like, raising kids together, maybe even our own kids. But definitely being part of each other's lives."

"Sure." Jhanvi shrugged.

"It's just, this is the point in people's lives when they're supposed to abandon their friends and fall into their little two-by-two Noah's ark pairs, and I think Henry and I both just totally reject that."

Jhanvi had heard so many people talk like this in her life. *Nuclear families suck. We can't keep building these towns and cities full of detached homes, occupied by two lonely, friendless married people. We need real community! We should be there for each other. We should do something bold and new and creative.*

The idea was inherently attractive, because it dispensed with the need to find love. But it just didn't work. Like, what if her "found family" had a stroke? Would Audrey spoon-feed them? Or if they lost their job, got depressed, couldn't or wouldn't work? Would Audrey cover their rent? No fucking way. Once you realized how shallow friendship really was, you realized it was stupid to give up a decent guy.

"Most people would prefer their twenties to never end, I guess," Jhanvi said.

"Yeah, but the default world just assumes you're gonna abandon everyone besides your partner. It's so sick! That just really upsets me sometimes. I get so many messages from people who've been so burned by our societal expectations about romance. Cheating. Messy divorces. People who just couldn't be each other's everything and are really upset about it. It's so weird to me, but I get it. They just haven't heard of anything different."

"They've never heard of just sleeping with whoever you want?"

"You're funny." Audrey smiled, but didn't laugh. "I mean they've never heard it *can* work and *can* be good and satisfying and sustainable and long lasting and nurturing and have room for friendship and children and careers and everything people need."

Did it work for Henry?

Jhanvi kept her face neutral. "It's good they have you to tell them."

"Hey, give me a minute." Audrey slipped through the sliding door and into the back of the room. "Don't mind me," she said, her voice muffled. "Just getting dressed."

She poked her head back through the doorway. "Hey, you're into makeup and stuff, right? Or is that rude?"

"Umm, yeah," Jhanvi said.

"Cool," Audrey said. "Have you seen my corner?"

She slid the door open and emerged in jeans and a relish-colored tank top that showed off her tattooed biceps. Behind her was a king-sized bed and long racks of clothes along one wall. The doors folded inward, banging into a dresser. Jhanvi followed Audrey to the corner with a vanity, complete with lights and a mirror. Audrey sat down on a swiveling stool and Jhanvi crouched by her side. Audrey pulled open a drawer, revealing dozens of jars of foundation. Another drawer had a hundred lipsticks. A third had eye and lip pencils. Everything was stuck with printed labels and stacked in trays from the Container Store.

"I'm a little type A," she said. "So I organized everything by parts of the face. Here's the primers, the foundations." She went on opening and closing drawers, revealing every single thing a person could need. Jhanvi's eyes got wider and wider. Her own experiments with cosmetics had consisted primarily of trying to find drugstore-brand foundations that actually matched her skin tone.

"We're a similar shade," Audrey said, holding up one arm. "I'm pretty tanned. We should hang out sometime. Most people around here aren't that interested in makeup."

"Uhh, yeah," Jhanvi said. "This is insane."

"It's my hobby. I got into it like two years ago—I was appearing on TV, and they did me up, and I was like . . . wow. Made me really regret all the videos I did without it. I've kinda been deleting some of my old content because of that."

Jhanvi looked at her. "But you don't usually wear anything, I think?"

"Oh, it's not for every day," she said. "But yeah. Most of my friends are fire-eaters and they're too anti-capitalist to be really into makeup."

"Totally," Jhanvi said. "And all the sex sweat would melt it off anyway."

Audrey looked at her. "What do you mean?"

"Your group, Trial By Fire," Jhanvi said. "How're the plans for the orgy going? You run it during AlternaFest, right? Henry has told me a ton about the dungeon."

Actually, he'd told her the dungeon was a source of massive house drama: Audrey had been on the verge of losing her lease—the landlord wanted her out because he suspected her of having fires there as part of The Guilty Party. But some other girl in the house had stepped in and paid the jacked-up rent, and now there were tussles between her and Audrey over who really controlled the "event space" (slash sex dungeon).

"It's not an orgy," Audrey said. "It's all kinds of things."

"Okay. Okay . . ." Jhanvi said. "It's not an insult."

"That's fine, it's just, people get confused about us," Audrey said. "Are you coming back to town for AlternaFest? We're normally really full up with guests here, but now that Henry has his own room, maybe he could put you up."

AlternaFest was a citywide festival hosted every spring, meant to promote alternative lifestyles of all sorts. In some ways, it was the straight answer to San Francisco's famous bondage festival, the Folsom Street Fair, and every year it got bigger and bigger. The year before, it had over two hundred thousand guests, which had created concern about whether it'd gotten too mainstream.

"I dunno," Jhanvi said. "I think I'm probably here permanently. So I'll be around."

"Oh," Audrey said. "Huh. I thought you were here for just a week."

"Three weeks." Jhanvi had called in sick for the last few days, after Henry had agreed to the marriage plan. They needed the time to get the license and get her registered on his insurance. Once she at least had the marriage license, she'd feel safe telling Green Magic to fuck off. Monica would be disappointed—the meeting to usher her into the co-op was on Monday. But she'd probably understand.

"But I have a house-sitting gig lined up after that," Jhanvi said. That was overstating the case. She'd been emailing other friends for a week, and the closest she'd gotten to a nibble was her cousin Meena, who was thinking of spending two weeks in Japan for a business trip and had said maybe Jhanvi could stay and feed her cat. But the trip wasn't certain yet.

"Weird. Does Katie know? I think Henry told her you were leaving this Sunday."

"No . . . I have an email from him."

"Oh, well, we should talk. Katie is really serious about us being anti-police. We've had a lot of meetings about it. That's been really hard on her."

"What's been hard? The existence of police?"

"Yeah. And the incarceration state. Racism. Injustice, people not getting it. Being selfish, making San Francisco unlivable. We're all really trying to be the solution and not the problem."

What a crazy bitch. Jhanvi *was* notionally a member of the downtrodden and the oppressed, and she didn't get as upset about that stuff. All she needed was a sandwich and a room of her own and a few hundred milligrams of estradiol and spiro.

"Well, okay," Jhanvi said. "I mean . . . the most important thing to me is this, uhh, this marriage plan. Like, you know, this green-card marriage type thing I'm doing. 'Free vagina marriage?' We'll have to workshop the name."

"Mmmhmm," Audrey said. "Henry said you were working it up as a business idea. Are you gonna pitch investors? Or bootstrap?"

"N—no, I mean doing it. For me, personally. I don't care about turning it into a thing for other people. Also, I guess it's kind of . . . illegal? To do? I mean it's not morally wrong, obviously, but still."

"Sorry—just my Google mind—always trying to figure out how to scale an idea."

Later, when Audrey was gone, Jhanvi couldn't resist going through her stuff. One whole section of the wall was bondage stuff: collars and handcuffs, whips and whatnot. On the clothing racks, Jhanvi saw short skirts and slinky fabric and outfits that looked as if they belonged under red lights: things she'd only seen on TV—dresses with cutouts and tabs and laces that went all up and down, so you couldn't possibly wear underwear or it'd show. Beneath her clothes there were rows of shoes, almost all with insanely high heels.

Jhanvi was afraid to sit on Audrey's bed, which was covered in a very fluffy down comforter. She closed the doors as she left, then went online, pulling up Audrey's profile and friending her on Instagram. She scrolled through photo after photo of Audrey dressed to the nines, with her hair done and her face shaded and contoured, wearing tiny dresses and high heels. In one picture, a friend of theirs, Achilles, was holding on to her.

She texted Henry right away, *Wait are Audrey and Achilles hooking up?????*

He wrote back, *Think they've hooked up. I'm not sure.*

And you're okay with that????? Wasn't he your friend first?????

It's okay, so're me and Katie.

Wait wut? You've been SLEEPING with her? Who else is sleeping with who? ARE YOU ALL SLEEPING WITH EACH OTHER? WHAT ABOUT KATIE AND AUDREY??????

Yeah they have something going on too, he texted. *But, I mean, most TBFers are poly, you know that.*

Most people drive cars, but they're still opposed to driving their car off a cliff, Jhanvi replied.

Are you creeped out or something?

What? No. I don't care. Just surprised. But in a good way. Part of me thought you were, like, pining after Audrey and weren't even doing the poly thing.

Lol.

Would you fuck Achilles? Or be fucked by him? she asked. *Aren't you a bit bi?*

Not now, I'm at work.

It's just a question.

Later, he said and stopped responding.

Jhanvi closed the door to the den and turned on the space heater in the corner, then she spat into her hand and pulled her cock out from under her dress, trying to feel aroused by the idea of being with Henry. With her cock flopping around, she lay on the couch, tweaking her nipple and rubbing herself.

She normally couldn't get off without porn, but she tried very hard to imagine herself as Audrey, wearing that lace-up dress thing, her mouth painted utterly red, her eyelashes long, bent over a table, with Henry taking her in the ass. Jhanvi's skin opened up and she felt the friction of all her clothes. The warm air from the heater drifted up around her, and she moaned. This was actually happening, quite surprisingly.

And yet, masturbation somehow didn't capture its crux. She didn't even want to come. If a spell had existed for sucking out Audrey's soul and taking her body, Jhanvi would've used it in a second.

The door opened and Jhanvi's face went red. Her dress was still shoved up around her waist! She fumbled to get dressed and a voice said, "Sorry, sorry, sorry!"

"Sorry!" Jhanvi yelled. "I'm so sorry!"

But she didn't hear any response.

After pulling herself together and making sure she didn't have semen stains on her dress, Jhanvi poked open the door. "Hello?" she shouted.

Again, there was nothing.

She went into the kitchen, and heard creaking above her. It must be one of the roommates—Roshie—the weird girl who'd paid the ridiculous rent for Audrey's dungeon.

Jhanvi looked down the hallway and spotted a figure in dark jeans and a white T-shirt bending over in front of the den. The girl must've come down from upstairs. "Hey!" Jhanvi said.

"Sorry!" The girl ran upstairs. "Sorry!"

Jhanvi went back to the room and spotted a note on the ground. It said, "Space heaters are expensive. They can double the house's energy bill. Please call me for other heating alternatives." There was a phone number too.

Jhanvi looked at the stairs. She'd hardly gotten a look at the girl—had only the vaguest glimpse of black hair. Dialing the number, Jhanvi said, "Hey."

"I'm sorry, but you should turn off the space heater."

Jhanvi laughed. "You're too much fun. You're Roshie, right?"

"It can cost literally hundreds a month."

"It's off, it's off," Jhanvi said. "Sorry."

"And your marriage plan is dumb!"

Jhanvi laughed again. She sat down abruptly, leaning against the wall in the hallway, looking up the stairs, as if waiting for a cat to emerge.

"Why?" Jhanvi said.

The disembodied voice floated out of the phone speakers. "Well, how long does it take to transition?"

"I don't know. A long time, years."

"Are people not gonna switch their jobs?"

"Maybe."

"And stocks—California is a community property state— you could take them to court to get their bonuses and stock options."

"Prenups."

"Usually don't hold up, especially when the assets come unexpectedly—not to mention, it's insurance fraud."

"Well, you're the only one who's brought any of this up," Jhanvi said. "Henry thought it was brilliant."

There was a long sigh—so long and so filled with tones that Jhanvi could hear it, not just through the phone, but from upstairs. The breath of that sigh drifted through the whiteboards and tacked-up notes, up and over the bikes hanging from the walls, and somehow made the apartment feel less cold.

The effect on Jhanvi went unobserved, even by herself—but she loosened her shoulders and her neck, and a shiver went through her body—a shiver not of fear, but of some sensation she had suppressed since entering this home.

"They're fire-eaters," Roshie said. "They're beautiful and fun and amazing, and I love them, but they're so impractical. Henry got hopped up on the idea of building a glory hole for one of our TBF events, and he made designs, and he was gonna put it in the alley behind the event space we rent, and I begged him not to, I was like, *I'm friendly with the person who lives above the space, Adriana, and she's super cool, and I* promised *her we wouldn't be a nuisance*, because her husband is sick and if he doesn't sleep well he could literally, like, die, and I promised her we wouldn't cause trouble, and in my mind, 'trouble' includes attracting weirdos to some shack to get blow jobs and not to mention hookers will end up using it to turn tricks and people will shoot up in it or go to the toilet, and if someone dies maybe they'll sue us, and he still went ahead and did it, and you know what happened?"

"It burned down?"

"Wait, you know this story?"

"Just seemed like what would happen."

"It burned down. So those guys are great if you want good vibes or a massage or to rig up a really cool light show— although even then, they can be a bit disorganized—but don't ever ask them about anything serious or important. And . . . wait . . . are you going to get all pissy and upset if I'm honest with you?"

"It depends."

"Huh? On what?"

"I can't hear you."

"On what!"

"I can't hear you," Jhanvi said, lowering her voice to make it seem like the connection was about to drop.

"On what!"

The shout now resounded through the hall. Jhanvi heard a door open upstairs and quiet footsteps flow down. The girl crept on bare toes and peeked around the doorframe, shouting, "Can you hear me now?"

Jhanvi smiled and put down the phone. "Yes."

"Oh." The girl took a couple steps into the hall. She was short and rectangular, with square shoulders and just the slightest hint of breasts and a butt. She had a ring in her lip and her glasses were chunky and black, but otherwise she was lacking in flair. She had severe straight bangs and long dark hair, and wore jeans and a gray hoodie zipped up to her neck. Her skin was brown, though not terribly so, perhaps a few shades darker than Jhanvi's. It was the shape of her nose and the cast of her mouth and brow that marked her as non-white.

"Oh. You're right here," she said. "Why were we talking on the phone?"

"You left a number," Jhanvi said.

The girl sat on the carpeted stairs and gestured with her hands. "So we've been having a big flame war for the past few days about this plan of yours. Everyone is like 'woohoo, yay Henry, go,' but meanwhile I'm doing research, and I have to be the bad guy and say 'no, no, no.' I was the one who discovered—what an idiot—that his trans benefits have to get paid back if he leaves before two years. Can you believe that? Just took actually *reading* his benefits docs."

"So what? Is he thinking about leaving?"

"But look at . . ." Roshie got up and went to the whiteboard, wiping an eraser through Henry's explication of Jhanvi's idea. "Okay, let's say as a result of this marriage, a person stays an extra six months at their job . . . and average length of job is two years . . . and each switch gives you a twenty percent pay bump . . ."

When Jhanvi looked at the numbers, she frowned. "Wait, is that really what Henry makes?"

"I mean, he's a senior engineer."

"He's twenty-eight."

Roshie's forehead creased, and she squinted at Jhanvi. "So? He's pretty good."

"Two hundred fifty thousand good?"

She shrugged. "I make double that."

"You're kidding."

Roshie kept writing, kept explaining, and Jhanvi said, "Okay, you can stop."

"No, look at the numbers, the amount it'd cost is like in the range of ..."

"Twenty-five thousand, yeah," Jhanvi said. "But actually, you've gotta project forward, because it shifts back all their other jobs, so those increases come later, too. So they always lag behind. Then also there's the chance of a crash or something that keeps them trapped at their job and ... huh, I wonder how we'd price all that in ... and also the risk of getting caught ... that's the major cost ... like if you get fired for fraud, your future is shot, that has a monetary cost. I had a friend who lost their job after having a psychotic break, and at their next one they made half as much."

"Oh, that's a good addition to the model," Roshie said. "Let's say the chance of being caught is ten percent."

"No," Jhanvi said. "More like two percent."

Roshie wrote for a bit. The fog was burning away outside, but the sunlight at either end of the corridor only increased the hall's gloominess. "Were you a math major?" Roshie asked, putting down the marker.

Jhanvi shrugged. "Econ."

"But ... you're not dumb," Roshie said. "The people around here, they can write code, but they don't use their brains—it's insane. I've been telling them, *Look, if you want to help, just give her the money*, but they say, *No, this way Facebook is paying*, and I'm like, *No, you're the one paying, you're just too dumb to realize it*."

"It's not a mystery," Jhanvi said. "The thing is, on some level, they *know* that all their talk about community is bullshit, but it's an illusion that makes them feel good. Like, have you ever heard that line 'They'd help me bury a body'? Do you have a friend like that?"

"Sure," Roshie said. "Tons."

"But do you really? Someone who'd potentially go to jail for you? No, of course not. The whole ride-or-die concept is a fantasy."

"I dunno, maybe in the default world," Roshie shrugged.

"Roshie!" Jhanvi said. "You're smarter than that. Come on. You're the only person who really believes this rhetoric. Don't let them sucker you. Just look at it honestly. You think they're dumb because they don't realize the obvious: they could just give me money. But they're not dumb. You know that. They don't do it because they don't want to. Because friendship doesn't work that way. It's all just words, Roshie. Everyone knows that besides you."

She could sense Roshie wasn't quite comprehending. The look in her eyes was a little too heavy, a little too studied.

"But . . . you're the one asking them to marry you . . ."

"I'm trapping them." Jhanvi hadn't realized it until she spoke the words. "That's how you deal with hypocrites. If I asked for money, they would give like a hundred bucks to my GoFundMe and be relieved and I'd have to pretend to be thankful, even though we would both know that's not enough. But if you hide the cost, pretend it's not there, then you dare them to say what you both know, which is that it's too high. And *maybe*, just maybe, they're too cowardly to come out with it."

"No," Roshie said. "You're wrong."

"About what?" Jhanvi said.

"You're wrong about all of it. Henry isn't like that, for one. We talked a lot over text about your marriage plan. He's excited about it."

"Sure he is," Jhanvi said.

"He is!"

"Look," Jhanvi said. "Ugh, I hate that thing where two people start arguing, and, like, after a while you can't figure out what they're disagreeing about anymore. It's so abstract. And you've got a built-in way to dismiss me. I don't deserve help. Just use that. I'm a leech. I'm not good for anything. Of course, you could also apply that standard to the guy who sleeps next door on the stoop, but it's not like you're giving him money either."

"If you hate everyone here so much, why are you even visiting?"

"I don't hate them," Jhanvi said. "It's just a game. And it's a really fun game, like when you get drunk and grab your friend and say *I loooooove you*, and pretend like your friendship will last forever. It feels good. Makes you feel safer in the world. And it's spiritually bankrupt, but it's okay, because we all *know* it's bankrupt. The only thing that worries me is this idea that maybe *you* don't know the truth. And that someday you'll ask these people for actual help, and the help won't be there."

"I don't put up with bullshit," Roshie said. "If I think a friend won't be there for me, I cut them off. Forever. You get one chance with me."

"That's what I was like, until, you know, I was living here in SF a few years ago, and I came out as trans, and nobody gave a shit. I mean, they were supportive, but they didn't give a shit. I lost my job, and they were like, *Oh, that's tough*. Nobody helped. When I left town, I hardly heard from anyone for years."

Roshie surveyed Jhanvi. "Yeah, that . . . I dunno. Sorry. Sucks. I think you're right that stuff usually works out that way in the default world."

"No, no, I'm not gonna let you get away with that. The default world is actually *better* at helping people than these guys. Like, the default world knows you can have excitement or security, but you can't have both. People who help you out when you're in trouble? That's your real-world community. For me, that means my family, it means Indian people, it means trans people. But community comes with rules. Like, my parents helped me, but they were like, *We don't want to get ostracized by our relatives, so let's keep your transition quiet*. Other trans people helped me, but they were like, *Here, abandon all ambition and work this shitty job because it's the best you can hope for*. If you take someone's help, you give up your freedom. That's the rule.

"But friendship is different," Jhanvi continued. "That's all about having fun. And having a bunch of responsibilities isn't fun. So yeah, you might help your friend move apartments or something, but if a friend is poor or sad or ugly or unfortunate or sick or disabled or just plain boring, then you drift away from them. And yeah, that sucks, but that's exactly why friendship is so brilliant and exciting and fun. Communities help each other out, but they're also full of annoying, tedious people. Here, it's dangerous. You have to provide value, or you're out. And that's why everyone here is so beautiful and interesting. A friend is just a person you hang out with whose company you enjoy. The minute the enjoyment stops, the friendship breaks, and that's *fine*."

"Mmmhmm." Roshie scowled a little, playing with the zipper on her hooded sweatshirt, running it all the way to her neck and back down.

"Sorry," Jhanvi said. "That was heavy. Normally I don't say stuff like that."

"It's fine," Roshie said. "You're wrong, but it's fine. And you know why?"

"Why? Because you paid a bunch of money for Audrey's event space?"

"Yeah. I think it's stupid, but I did it. Because she and Henry are my friends. And they said they needed it."

A devastating retort immediately came to mind: *You did it because you're trying to buy the friendship of a bunch of beautiful people.* But that was too much, too personal. And besides—Jhanvi took a deep breath—there was something about this tiny girl, standing there with hunched shoulders and a pugnacious expression—Jhanvi didn't like her, precisely, but she also didn't want to hurt her. "Well, you're probably different from them," Jhanvi said.

After a pause, Jhanvi continued, "So, umm, are you on your lunch break? Do you want to go eat something?"

Roshie looked at her again, and her expression was, if anything, more suspicious. "I don't eat out."

"Oh—okay. So . . . what do you do for fun?"

"Mostly work on the event space. We're getting ready for The Guilty Party."

Jhanvi's stomach grumbled, and she said, "I've got to eat. Come on. Let's go somewhere."

And Roshie, staring intensely at the ground, said, "Okay, sorry. See you later." Jhanvi wanted to grab her by the hand, to tug her away, over to the kitchen, or out the front door, but something about her body language was utterly forbidding. Jhanvi had an odd thought: *I wonder if she's ever been in love.*

4

The members of the Fun Haus had demanding jobs that kept them from hanging out together too much during the week. Dinners, though technically communal, were often just two or one of them. She'd never seen everyone from the whole house together in one place.

Jhanvi kept telling herself to go outside and explore the city, but what was there to see that she hadn't seen when she'd lived here? The same old yuppie bars and eateries where she couldn't afford anything. The same old naked men, massaging their swollen balls on the benches in the Castro. The same old Dolores Park, full of shivery huddling young people, drinking beer and playing frisbee and getting snuffled by overly friendly dogs.

She'd spent the last three days sitting inside, watching TV, looking at her phone, drawing up grandiose plans in a notebook. She'd known a few people in her life who she would've tentatively called *adventurers*. But they all had something she didn't. Like Synestra, another SF-based trans girl with no obvious means of support, was incredibly gorgeous. Maybe Jhanvi's best role model would be Nasal Xylophone, who'd mooched off these guys for three months before being kicked out. He'd been tall and dirty, with dreadlocks and a spacey affect. But even he had possessed some strange sexual power: Katie had actually slept with him.

Circling back around, she couldn't avoid the conclusion that being an adventurer required one of two things: money or sex appeal.

And yet, Jhanvi had succeeded in the longest con, manipulating Henry into marrying her. She had twisted their sex play into reality, psychologically dominating him, forcing him to submit to her demand. It was strange—that kind of manipulation didn't feel within her power—but it was a totally plausible interpretation of what'd occurred!

And whatever, he had agreed. A meeting had crept into his calendar, so they'd go to the courthouse on Monday instead. She forced herself not to harp on it, not to probe him or remind him of the plan. She needed to project confidence.

Now she only needed to plan for everything else. The co-op job was dead, probably. She had a bunch of unread texts and emails from Monica that she couldn't bear to read. The co-op meeting was on Monday, and Jhanvi would have to miss it. Henry would reschedule if she wanted, but if she let him go— no, it needed to happen now.

All Jhanvi needed was to marry, schedule her surgeries, then sit tight, have fun, support herself. She knew already the folly of trying to get a room in SF through open listings. Whatever people wanted here, it wasn't her. Even as a trans woman, she emitted some particle of desperation or uncool. In SF everyone assumed if you needed a room, and were cool, some friend of yours would hook you up with a rent-controlled spot.

Jhanvi had her chance, though: Henry's room. It was empty five nights out of seven! Surely he felt guilty leaving a room empty like that. She and he could share! His rent was only five hundred dollars. She could pay half or two-thirds of that, easily, just out of her saved surgery fund, for a while. And then, that dreariest of options—a job.

Jhanvi didn't believe satisfying work was possible. Even her techie friends seemed to complain constantly about their jobs. And all her work experiences had been meaningless, anxiety provoking, and demeaning. Sometimes she dreamed of being a dominatrix, fucking guys like Henry, but realistically, she was a slag. Jhanvi abhorred her thick-set body, with its broad shoulders and barrel shape. Sometimes she tried to be feminine, swaying when she walked, giggling, brushing a man's arm and flirting, but the mental doubling of herself made her sick—she had a transphobe inside her who saw Jhanvi exactly as they did.

But if you had to work and be unhappy, at least you should be rich, like her friends were. She hated their whining about their jobs, about the petty annoyances and meaninglessness—she would've loved to be their manager, to torment them, to laugh at their entitlement. She wanted somehow to hurt the members of this house.

Katie and Audrey fascinated her. The two seemed polar opposites: Katie was tall, light-haired, collected, and very politically active, while Audrey was shorter, auburn-haired, bubblier, and had worked for all the biggest and evilest tech companies in Silicon Valley as some sort of designer or project manager or something—Jhanvi still wasn't sure what the difference was between all those titles. But they spent hours together, often in Katie's extremely sparse room, from which Jhanvi not infrequently heard low voices and giggling.

Moreover, Katie, despite clearly being more thoughtful and competent, was a full-on sidekick. Jhanvi had seen her doing Audrey's eyelashes, editing her videos, and filming her—even moderating the comments on her channel. It was absurd. This woman had her own job! But she was completely subsumed in someone else.

And yet, that was the dream, wasn't it? To find someone you believed in so strongly that you'd give up your own individuality just to further their goals or dreams.

Today Jhanvi was in the kitchen, cleaning up after dinner—they'd said everyone who stayed a week needed to do at least one job shift—when the two of them came out of Katie's room. Katie wore a long furry coat and a silver jumpsuit with cutouts on the stomach and the hips that made her slender silhouette seem even more dagger-like than normal. Audrey, earthier, was in tiny shorts, a leather vest, and the highest heels, her face completely painted with intricate designs of gold and silver and white, so that she shone in the hallway light.

"Hey," Jhanvi said.

But Audrey spilled out, laughing, holding on to Katie's waist, and lifted a phone, taking a picture of the two of them from a high angle. Jhanvi's heart took another turn. *I own your man,* she thought. It wasn't true, but it gave her strength.

"Hey guys," Jhanvi ventured again. "Where you off to?"

On the few occasions she'd seen people around, the house was always suffused with sexuality. Audrey and Katie always had guys over and were always making out with them or being felt up in the hallways. Even when nobody else was near, they handled each other, with long hugs and arms on shoulders and light touches on bare skin. The other night, a group make-out had started in the den with Audrey and Katie and Henry and some other fire-eaters. Jhanvi had hung around the edges, trying to figure out how to insinuate herself, before slinking off to Henry's room.

They were talking to Henry now, who came out of his room in a leather vest and draw-string pants.

"Oh hey," he said. "What's going on?"

"You guys are pretty dressed up for a Wednesday," Jhanvi said.

They looked at each other, and Jhanvi felt the shift, some silent communication among them, and a heavy stare from Katie.

"How're you liking the city?" Katie said.

"Fine," Jhanvi said. "Lonely. I can feel it sucking out my soul, turning me into this needy, friendless banshee. I don't really like it."

"Oh," Audrey said. "Wow. Yeah. It can be lonely. Did you figure out how long you're staying?"

"Indefinitely," Jhanvi said.

"What?" Henry said. "You didn't tell me that."

"I did, sort of, but don't worry, I'll figure it out. I've got other friends I can crash with."

At that last statement, the roommates clearly relaxed. People were so interesting—if you were an outsider, they almost treated you like a nonperson. They didn't feel the need to hide how they felt. It was a bit like being a telepath. Everything was written in their body language.

"What's the event?" Jhanvi said.

"Something at this event space we're part of," Henry said.

"The dungeon?"

"What?" Audrey said. "What did you call it?"

"A dungeon," Jhanvi said. "The place you rent, in the Mission. Or, no, the place Roshie rents."

"Where did you hear that?" Audrey said.

Now Jhanvi was confused. "I'm sorry . . ." She took a few steps back. "I really have no idea what I said wrong."

"Dungeon is just a highly technical term for a place designed for a certain set of activities," Katie said. "We prefer to call it an event space. And, yes, Roshie contributed money toward affording a rent increase, but Audrey is the sole lessee."

Over the last day or two, Jhanvi had learned that Roshie was a bit of an outcaste. She did a lot of work on the event space, and she'd saved it by paying a year's rent in advance. But people were wary around her. To Jhanvi, the distance seemed to be at least partially racism and classism. Something about Roshie just came off very middle class. It was in her expectations and assumptions—the things she didn't understand about her roommates. Roshie was the child of store owners, Katie the child of doctors. The difference mattered somehow. Jhanvi, for her part, split the difference—she was the daughter of an engineer.

Of course Roshie knew how to ostracize other people, too. Jhanvi had knocked on Roshie's door a half dozen times, asking if she wanted to chat, and each time Roshie had said, *Not right now*, with no further elaboration.

"Can I come?" Jhanvi said.

They were silent for a long time, and Jhanvi burst out laughing. Being an adventurer was the most terrific sort of fun.

"It's really—" Henry said.

"Don't worry about it, hubs," Jhanvi said. "It's okay."

"We'll have some days that are open to guests, but first we—"

"Don't worry. When I'm naked, I'm basically a guy anyway, and I know you have different rules for that."

Most sexy spaces didn't allow unattached guys, to keep the gender ratio right.

"Oh, it's not that," Henry said. "Do you know Synestra?"

Jhanvi almost choked on her laugh. Of course she knew Synestra—the girl was a semifamous trans—absolutely gorgeous, with golden skin, a slender body, long legs, and high cheekbones.

"Does she have a dick?" Jhanvi said.

"We don't talk about that," Katie said.

"I just mean she and I are an entirely different kettle of fish."

"You're just not a member, Jhanvi," Katie said. "It's nothing personal." Her tone was sharp.

Jhanvi smiled. The only thing she truly disliked about these people was their relentless dissimulation. She had a fantasy of interrogating Henry—of strapping his arms and legs to a chair and tickling him until he broke down and told her the truth.

Admit that having my ugly body in your sex club will be uncomfortable for all involved. Admit you don't want to marry me. Admit you want me to leave before my three weeks are up, and you're just counting on Katie to do your dirty work! Admit it!

She had this crazy thought that even under duress, he wouldn't tell the truth—that he didn't know the truth—that he relied on Katie to intuit his desires and spare him from the terrible self-knowledge that he just wanted his poor trans friend to go away.

Jhanvi went into the den, and, researching further, realized getting the marriage license didn't itself constitute a marriage—they needed a ceremony for that. For a few hundred dollars they could have one on a balcony on the rotunda of the courthouse. Jhanvi booked it for the first opening, on Monday afternoon, and informed Henry in a group email, asking if anyone else wanted to come. No one responded. Then she made a fatal mistake, sending an apology, asking if maybe she'd overstepped her bounds as a guest. Katie wrote back instantly, *Let's talk this week.* Henry sent a simple *Don't worry about it.* The wedding email got no response.

She went to his bed, got naked, climbed under the covers—a man with long, thin hair and two blobs of subcutaneous fat on his chest. She didn't wipe off her makeup, just laid her head on Henry's pillow and lay there, her heart hammering, getting angrier and angrier. He had agreed to this plan! He'd agreed. He was supposed to be her friend!

She had a sense of spiraling. She had known, the moment the apology email went out, that she'd lost ground, hadn't played out the game to the end. But long hours still waited between her and Monday.

• • •

Jhanvi woke up suddenly when a person climbed into bed. She yelped, and Henry jumped back. "I'm sorry! I'm sorry! I was just going to sleep."

"Oh," she said. "Umm, sorry. Let me get out."

Jhanvi slid out from under the sheets, acutely aware of how sweaty and greasy and naked she was. In the dark and confusion, she looked for some night clothes. Henry was still in his beads and glitter, shirtless, sitting on the edge of the bed, looking at her inquisitively.

"Hey," he said. "Are you drinking again?"

Jhanvi was still groggy. "Huh? No!"

"You just seem mad," he said. "Hey ... hey, I've seen you naked before." He placed a hand on Jhanvi's back, and she shivered. "Come here a sec."

She was on his bed, and his arm was around her. Her shoulders bowed inward. Henry started to massage her shoulders, and she let him, even though the pressure was too hard, and his fingers were little battering rams, bashing at tired muscles which only wanted to be left in peace.

"Can we talk about earlier?" he said. "About the event space? Because Audrey got really mad at me for not having better boundaries with you."

"It's fine," Jhanvi said.

"The thing is, I wanted to talk about your feelings. About what this marriage means. And how you feel about me, and SF, and this whole scene."

The flare of anger and recognition was welcome, and she felt more awake. Words still wouldn't quite form, but she had contempt for him, for his friends. She no longer felt supplicatory. His room was tidy, with pens arranged in neat rows on his desk, and all the cords bundled up. His clothes were in plastic boxes, and she had a flash of insight—Audrey must've gotten them for him from the Container Store. She'd stage-managed his whole move-out/move-in process. Jhanvi had seen the way Katie or Audrey tidied up when they were in here, had seen the push and pull of it, how they exerted their control over him and resented him. The only man in a house of women.

"Why'd you come out here?" Henry said. "I don't mind, but it was so sudden. And what's the hurry with the marriage thing? We joked about it last week, and the next thing I knew you'd bought a bus ticket ... It was kind of quick ..."

Because you never want me to visit. You always put it off. Henry was so malleable. But once the pressure was off, he snapped back into his old shape.

"I just ..." Her voice was husky. She cleared her throat. "I just ..."

"Did I say something?" he said. "What made you come here? Because I've gotta be honest, I do feel a little pressured. Katie wants me to hire a lawyer. Do a prenup. You'd need a lawyer too. It can't get rushed. And a month or two, what's the hurry?"

"No hurry, just my life," Jhanvi said bitterly. Henry's fingers stopped pressing into the muscles of her shoulders, and he drew back. She felt the cars rushing past outside and the cold wind flowing over her as the fog slipped into the room.

"It was Roshie," she said. She felt minute shifts in his weight through the bed, felt him move forward, and she focused on those shifts, feeling so terrified, so out of her league, remembering all the conversations, all her life, when she'd begged other people for things—begged either overtly or implicitly. Once, she'd begged a man to take her on a date. A single date outside their apartments. And he hadn't even done the normal thing (agree to it, then ghost her). Instead, he'd gotten mad, told her she was manipulative.

"What about her?" Henry said. "I didn't even know you two knew each other."

"She lives upstairs, Henry!" Jhanvi said. "She's literally your roommate!"

"Okay . . ." he said. "Yeah, sorry. Just being stupid."

"Audrey took a hundred thousand dollars from her. And she paid, just to make Audrey happy. And you were like, *Rah rah, the community, rah rah, we manifest support for each other.*"

"Okay . . . I get you."

"But aren't I your community?" Jhanvi said. "Don't I get support? Everyone is acting like this is such a big deal. It's not. You can give me something precious for free. Do you see how insane you sound? How selfish?"

"I get it," Henry said. "Okay, I've got it. Let's do it."

"For free. And you're acting like I'm pushing you? Why do you have these benefits and not me?"

"I . . ."

And now Jhanvi choked off a high, maniacal laugh. Because anybody who wasn't in this stupid house would've said the obvious: *When you were drinking, I was working. I have skills, and companies are willing to pay for them.* But he couldn't or wouldn't say that.

"Unless you think you're just better than me?" Jhanvi said. "Deserve more? This is life or death for me. And it'll cost you nothing. But you got a corporate job out of college, and I was dumb and wanted to help the world, so I got a different one, and—"

"All right," Henry said. "Okay."

"This is life or death," Jhanvi said. "Look at me. Look at me. Just look at me. What crazy alternate world do you live in? What's the hurry? You ask me what's the hurry? What the fuck. Just *look* at me!"

"Okay," Henry said. "Okay . . . okay. Well . . . can you keep calm? Don't send out emails to the list. Don't ask to come to the dungeon. You're a guest here."

"Fine," Jhanvi said. "Whatever makes you happy."

She got dressed, and Henry left, probably to debrief with Audrey. Jhanvi huddled in her sleeping bag, replaying the conversation, going through all its paths like in a video game. Henry was one of her oldest friends, but it was astonishing how little she cared about his distress. He was a stone-cold yuppie gentrifier. Fuck him. She'd take what she could get.

But still, if anyone could crack her open and see the coldness and the rage inside, she knew they'd abhor it.

• • •

The next day, Thursday, she awoke to no word from anyone. The house email list was dead, and everyone had left for work. She texted Charli and filled her in, and her friend was incredulous. *You did what?*

They're all discussing me behind my back, aren't they?

Stay SAFE, girl. I'm worried they'll call the sheriffs on you. You've got rights! Squatter's rights!

Jhanvi wrote a text to Toni. They'd exchanged hellos a few times since they'd met, when Toni was smoking outside the bar, and she'd updated the girl on Henry's reluctant yes.

Booked a courthouse appt Monday to get the license, Jhanvi texted. *Ceremony's later that day.*

I don't work Mon. I'll be there! What should I wear? A dress or what

A suit? Don't be stupid. A dress, Jhanvi said. She didn't mention being iced out by the house. Toni still admired her, and she wanted to hold on to that for a few days more. Jhanvi was her Charli, at least until Toni went on hormones and Charlied herself.

Over the course of the day, Jhanvi spent a lot of time talking to herself. She had a long-standing argument to settle: if someone could see her real self, with all her violent, envious impulses, all her contempt and longing, balanced against her generosity, her sense of humor, and her indomitable will to make something of her life, would they think her life was worthwhile? Or would they think she was a waste of skin? Essentially, Jhanvi wanted to know if she was worthy of love.

Despite worming her way into this house with an unexpected rapidity, she just—she wasn't sure. The roommates didn't love her, they merely tolerated her. Her thoughts were inchoate. She wanted more. Those words went through her mind again and again. *Want more. Want more. This life is not . . .* but she couldn't complete that sentence.

The days were gray and cold, the streets outside looked bare. She had explored San Francisco a bit, noticing changes from when she'd lived there, and sat in coffee shops full of well-dressed, chattering girls with long, straight hair. She still wasn't sure—Who was she? What did she want?

Her boss called. She rejected the call, but the phone rang again. And again.

"I'm calling to ask if you're gone much longer," said Monica's flat, nasal voice.

"Hey, I don't actually know. I'll be home on Tuesday, maybe."

"I'm writing an email right now withdrawing your nomination. Should I say personal problems or what? Did you relapse? That's the problem, isn't it?"

"Sure," Jhanvi said. "I relapsed. I'm on a bender. Monica, I'm sorry. I just can't commit to the co-op right now."

Saying the words felt good. The world didn't explode, nobody burst through the door saying *you are ruining your life*. A sparrow falls, and perhaps God notices, but nobody else does, apparently.

"Can you find a meeting? I'll send you money for a bus ticket. I know the Castro Country Club has meetings . . ."

Monica was a middle-aged woman from the local trans community, a manager at Green Magic since long before she'd transitioned. She was the kind of woman who went to the public hearings when some new construction was being proposed and harangued the developers about how they were gonna avoid displacement. Jhanvi had met her in an AA meeting, and when her parents had kicked her out, Monica had given her a room and guided her into a job. She basically owed her life to the woman.

"Don't worry," Jhanvi said. "I'm just drinking once in a while, to celebrate. Look, I'm with friends." The lie slipped out by accident. It seemed unbearably trite to insist, *No really, I am sober for real! I'm just messing up my life with total forethought, not on impulse at all!*

"Jhanvi," Monica said. "Where are you right now?"

The conversation was such a mire. Jhanvi sank, exhausted, to the couch. She hoped messages wouldn't be passed behind her back, little strings pulling at her parents' phones over in India.

"Just with my boyfriend," Jhanvi said. "He lives in SF. I'm sorry, we know each other from college."

"Oh," Monica said. "Oh! Why didn't you tell me? Who is he?"

A short interrogation followed, and, like Toni before her, Monica got more and more excited. By the end, Jhanvi could tell she was beaming, her gravelly voice getting avuncular, reminiscing on the crazy moves she'd pulled as a kid. "I don't blame you for not wanting to be stuck here. It's not a place for kids. But Jhanvi, you're being safe, right? You're not getting trapped into a bad situation?"

"I top him, Mon," Jhanvi said. That wasn't a nickname she ever used with Monica, but it seemed appropriate. "What's he gonna do, beat me during the day, and let me beat him at night?"

"You laugh, but it could happen."

"We're good."

Monica said, "Okay then. I know you were embarrassed or maybe had to line up some ducks, but I'm glad to have an answer. The members were getting a little angry. You know Green Magic, always drama. Tommy angry as fuck, saying no white guy has a chance anymore."

"I've got it," Jhanvi said. "Give up my spot. That's fine."

"And your room?"

"Umm, I'll keep it for now."

"I don't rent it out for the money, J. I rent it out to help people. If you're not using it, someone else can."

"That's fine."

"I'll keep it for a little longer, but you'll have to keep paying rent. And if you give it up, you've gotta clean out your stuff. I'm not hauling another bedframe to the curb: I'm too old for that shit. Have your boyfriend help you; would be nice to meet him. Let me know if you want to borrow a truck. And I can—"

"I'm done, you can give it up."

"Still . . . you're paid up through the end of the month. And you need to move your stuff. Come back. Does he have a car?"

"I don't know. Sell the stuff . . ."

"Doesn't work that way. Text me a time?"

"The fifteenth?" Two weeks off.

"Got it, penciling you in. Bring the man!"

Hanging up was a relief. Now the circle was closed. She'd never show up on the fifteenth, but there'd be no need for another call. Most of the street kids she knew insisted they were out there by choice, and she understood the sentiment. Better to be responsible for yourself and take the consequences. When she'd been an active fuckup, she'd hated that sense of continual failure, and each final break—with a friend, or with a relative, even with her parents—had come as a relief. *One less person to worry about me.*

• • •

As she walked down Fillmore Street, backpack in hand, looking into the expensive boutiques, she stood up straighter, bracing herself, rubbing her fingertips against the velvety side of her dress for comfort. Her hair was held back with a pink barrette that hopefully camouflaged her receding hairline, just like her glasses hid her prominent brow bone.

Her fire-eater friends were always going off on vacations to Kathmandu or New Zealand or Croatia, but people from all over the world came to visit San Francisco. So why go on a vacation? You're already here, living at a destination.

To Jhanvi, all these strange people on the street were perfect—the pairs of women with their strollers, the young men in tight pants who appeared not to have jobs, the old Chinese ladies pushing groceries in a handcart. All around, the pastel and blue houses climbed up hillsides, trees lined the walks, and flowering vines hung from foyers.

She walked into an ice cream parlor and hung around tasting the weird flavors—the olive oil was surprisingly delightful—and trying to figure out if the ice cream scooper was trans. She was tall, with the sculpted cheekbones that usually came from facial feminization surgery, and a similarly sculpted, artificial voice. The woman's fake eyelashes were thick and long, and her lips were painted a brilliant blue. Jhanvi smiled at her, trying to establish some subtle contact.

"I'm visiting," Jhanvi said. "From Sacramento."

"Nice, I've heard it's a cool place."

"I've heard that too," Jhanvi said. "But it's a hundred times nicer here. You've got *trees*."

"Yeah, but who can afford it?"

Jhanvi smiled hopelessly. She walked out eating her ice cream, into a sunny but quite windy day. She had no ultimate aim—maybe the gay district, the Castro, where she'd never felt quite comfortable as a man. She'd stood in gay bars too, ignored and alone, fat, unloved. But now she was different.

The important thing was to try. By nature, Jhanvi was shy. Her self-consciousness had destroyed her years of high school and college. Even her jokes and routines had required near-blackout levels of intoxication, and natural, normal interaction was impossible no matter her mental state. She'd stood on the outskirts of so many parties, her eyes burning in anger and shame, wondering why she was so gawky and different, so unable to speak—wondering why it was so easy for other people, folks no smarter or more handsome than herself. She'd hated so long and so deeply—hated everyone who'd ever let their eyes slip over her—and she'd vowed a thousand times that she'd take revenge by living well. She'd been an angry young man, and she could've slipped into the alt-right misogynerd rabbit hole, but instead she'd symbolically killed the man inside her.

And that'd made all the difference. Back in Sacramento, she'd slid almost effortlessly into a community. People actually liked her. At the co-op, they were always talking about how friendly she was, how great with the customers, how insightful, hard-working. Within months of starting hormones, she'd begun to yearn for another shot at San Francisco, thinking, *I could do it this time. I could talk to people. I could be a person, I understand now what I didn't before, which is: You need to try . . . you can't rely on people to see you. You need to compete and prove yourself.* And now, years later, here she was. She hadn't entirely failed yet. She had met people, made an impression on them. Life wasn't going too terribly.

The walk to the Castro took the better part of an hour. She strolled into a bar at the top of the street and asked for a hamburger and a soda.

"I'm visiting," she said.

"Oh yeah?"

Henry had said being a bartender in the Castro must be the most enviable job in the city. This guy had thick biceps and a strong jaw covered in a half-inch of stubble. He looked like the love interest in a pop music video.

After her second bite, Jhanvi had a greasy smudge on her dress, and no matter how she wiped or tried to cover it, the mark made her self-conscious. So she headed home. Well, whatever, she'd tried. It was a process. Trying was what counted.

Passing a bar, she saw a group of young women sitting just inside, near the window, their faces animated as they chatted and giggled, all wearing leggings and skinny jeans that accentuated their slender frames. Jhanvi hurried faster, her face already flushed, as she once again mentally lacerated herself for her own worthlessness—her own complete lack of anything to offer the world.

• • •

It was well before six when she got back to the house, but she rang the doorbell repeatedly. It was an electronic touch-screen dealie, and the intercom told her to wait. She saw her own face on the screen and heard a brief ringing, then the door opened.

"Hello?" she said. "Is anyone home?"

She heard a creaking from upstairs, and a door slamming.

Jhanvi shouted, "Hey ... uh ... R ... Roshie ..."

There was no response. Jhanvi went up to the attic room and

knocked several times on Roshie's door. When it opened, the girl was in her pajamas. "What's going on?" she said. "I already buzzed you in."

"Just seeing if you want to hang out," Jhanvi said.

"Why?"

"Because I'm lonely?"

"Sorry. Busy," Roshie said.

"You hardly ever leave this room."

"I'll see you at dinner."

Jhanvi tried again to get an answer, but Roshie shoved the door closed. Jhanvi heard the click of a lock.

Going downstairs, Jhanvi tumbled into the den, but she couldn't concentrate. She needed a friend. She needed something. Someone. And if even this friendless elf ignored her, then how could she have value? Did Jhanvi deserve to be so ignored? Well, yes—she was an interloper here, entirely unwanted, and her plan was to guilt a bunch of better, more successful people into giving her their health insurance. But still! Did she have worth? The idea kept revolving in her head. She thought she did—she was almost positive—and yet at the moment, the evidence was rather thin.

And at exactly that moment, she got a text message from Toni: *It's my break! Want a drink?*

• • •

A Coke was waiting for Jhanvi when she got to the bar, and she put her lips on the straw and found herself sucking it down before she knew better. It was a whiskey and Coke.

The bitter liquid hit her throat and sent warmth through her neck and collarbone. A friendly buzz traveled up into the back of her head, and her mouth fell open in a smile. When it was gone, she thought—*Oh, telling Monica that I still drank, that was a preparation.*

"Nice to see you!" Toni said. "How's shit going?"

Jhanvi found herself talking effortlessly, making jokes about how seriously people took the concept of marriage, even though people knew Jhanvi's marriage wouldn't be consummated or long-lasting. As she spoke, patterns formed in her mind:

"Audrey is happy because it locks her boyfriend down—he'll always be available for her. Katie has a stick up her ass because she thinks I'm not lefty enough or something, like I'm a bad influence. They can smell it on me—the fact I think they're full of shit, just performative—and now she's like, *Oh boohoo, this girl is exploiting Henry.* Or something. But that just shows she's a transphobe and misogynist, because she cares more about his freedom than my well-being. And Henry wants to escape, it's so absurd. I'm like a god, if I lifted up my hand, even slightly, the mouse would wriggle free. But he can't. He can't do it. Or, I dunno . . . And my boss in Sacramento was *so* worried, but the word marriage calmed her down instantly. I love it. What a word, what a scheme. I'm a genius."

Toni's face got serious. "But . . . I thought he was—that you kind of liked him."

"No," Jhanvi said. Her face refracted crazily in the glass bottles behind the bar. All the amber fluids she'd pour into her brain. "Can I get another?"

Toni got her another drink, then she said sorry, they can only comp two.

"I don't get unrequited love," Jhanvi said, even though that was absurd—she couldn't count all her unrequited crushes, even with her shoes off. "If he'd love me, I'd love him. But I don't respect any of them. I'm so much better than them. You are, too."

Toni's break ended, and Jhanvi waited around, hungry for more social contact, but Thursday was trivia night, and the bar filled up with drunken normies. After being jostled by the elbow of another sweaty prick, Jhanvi stormed out.

She stood in front of a convenience store with the liquor

boiling through her brain, and thought, *Nobody would blame me for getting drunk. I could do it. I have nothing and nobody in this world. Surely this is the moment to drink.*

But some voice came to her—it positively growled: *No. Don't give them the fucking satisfaction.* So she went inside the house, and she sat in the den with a big jug of water, and terrible cravings came upon her—She heard voices whistling in the darkness, saying what she needed was to obliterate herself, because her life was over. *Just drink,* they said. *Drink some more.*

She was reminded of Jesus in the wilderness. Or of Jesus in the garden of Gethsemane. Or of Jesus on the cross, asking why God had forsaken him. Okay, wow, Jesus had gotten tempted a whole bunch of times.

Evening turned into night, and she moved around the house, avoiding people as they came in. The knowledge stewed inside her—Henry was avoiding her. All day, he hadn't responded to a fucking text. Last night, she'd been pathetic, opening herself up emotionally, letting him know what she needed. And he'd left her there, wounded, bleeding, and gone off to another girl. If a friend of hers had acted out the way she had, she would've said, *Girl, you're just driving him away.* But this situation only needed to hold for three more days, and she'd be set.

Hey, she texted Henry. *I can find somewhere else to be if you need the room this weekend?*

No worries. I'm staying out tonight, but I'll see you at the house meeting tomorrow? We're discussing ur stuff?

Errr, okay? What stuff? Jhanvi threw the phone onto the bed. It beeped, and she tried to ignore it. When she picked it up, she read:

Just you staying a few more days. Don't worry. Talk soon!

5

The next night, Friday, she finally witnessed the house somewhat close to full. Jhanvi took her plate of bean sprouts and
sat next to Henry, who was hovering over a woman with gray
eyes and bleached hair, her neck encircled with a hundred little
loops of wire.

"Oh hey," Henry said. "This is a friend of mine, Jhanvi, who's
crashing with us."

"And marrying you," Jhanvi said. *Who the fuck is this girl?*
It was coldly amusing to be so jealous. So that's where Henry
had spent last night.

"Wow, marriage? Like in a spiritual sense?" the girl asked. "I
would marry so many people. I just feel such strong connections to all kinds of people. I have to say, I really like your energy
right now. I'm Purpose."

"Porpoise?" Jhanvi said.

"Purpose," she said. "As in, 'My purpose is to help all living
souls self-actualize.'"

"Is that your actual purpose?"

"Yes," she said. "What's yours?"

"Uhhh," Jhanvi said.

"Just tell me the first thing that comes to mind."

"To . . . transition? And become a girl?"

"Oh . . ." she said. "But is that a purpose? Isn't that really a
means?"

"What's the difference?"

"A means can be completed. A purpose is never-ending."

"All living souls self-actualizing is also something that could be completed. It's just very difficult."

"Haha, no, but seriously, what's your purpose?" she said. "I love asking people."

"Err . . . to find friends? And experience an exciting social milieu?"

"Again, that's more of a means . . ."

"Then I don't know if I get the question."

Audrey was sitting in the lap of the guy from the Instagram picture, Achilles, who lazily cradled an arm around her midsection. She was topless, as usual, and her movements were effortlessly sexual, especially with her short hair teased into curls and her eyes heavily painted. Her compact body just seemed made to be picked up and handled.

Did she have value? The idea hadn't ever left Jhanvi. Did she have a purpose? More and more, she felt like an object that yearned to be a human. It didn't have to be this way, but somehow she'd bought into or created a version of herself that couldn't truly exist until people finally accepted her as a real girl. And she knew her definition of "a real girl" was pretty twisted. She wanted to be Audrey, essentially. She wanted to be desired.

Except . . . except . . . she'd said the opposite to Toni, in the bar—she'd said it didn't matter if she never "passed"—and she'd believed it! Back then, she'd felt hopeful, even confident.

"Okay," Katie said, standing next to the whiteboard, balancing a plate in one hand and gesturing with a marker in the other. "Thank you everybody for being here, particularly Jhanvi, who's a temporary member of our community. And our other guests, Purpose and Achilles." She nodded at the guy sitting under Audrey, who waved a little. Jhanvi noticed the strange tension simmering between Audrey and Henry—it was no accident they'd both brought dates. A hard, tight feeling was balled up in Jhanvi, and she picked it apart like a seventh grader dissecting an owl pellet. Wow, she was actually feeling hurt. Obviously, Henry had decided that having only Jhanvi here wouldn't hurt Audrey in the least.

"Uhh," Jhanvi said. "Do I have to stay?"

The words went unnoticed, which tended to happen whenever she spoke around this group.

Roshie sat on a couch at the far end of the room, eating noisily from a bucket of chicken nuggets. Wait a second, she said she never ate out! But there she was, licking her fingers and shoving them into her mouth as Porpoise looked on with distaste.

"This year," Katie said, "will be the year of boundaries."

"Hear, hear," Henry said. "Snaps to Katie for coordinating this."

The agenda had a bunch of technical stuff on it about the separation between their AlternaFest camp Trial By Fire and its offshoot, the Trial By Fire event space where The Guilty Party would be held, which was now being incorporated as its own 501(c)(3), and then more stuff about their house itself, their living space, with Katie drawing a bunch of complicated rules and comparisons about how various activities needed to be confined to their particular spheres. Jhanvi found her eyes rolling, and she simply couldn't stop.

"What are you actually trying to say?" Jhanvi said.

"I think we're discussing that right now," Katie said.

"Are you trying to say you don't want people having group sex at this house? Because I've noticed that's a little over the top."

"No," Katie said. "Excuse me, but it's a really complicated topic, and you're being quite . . ."

"It really seems like you're saying the sex offends you."

"We're a sex-positive space."

"No," Audrey said, giggling, as Achilles's hand probed lower on her shorts, his thumb sliding into the waistband. Jhanvi's eyes were riveted to the scene. "No, no," Audrey said. "I think what Katie is saying is we need boundaries."

Jhanvi's eyes went to Henry, whose hand was nervously stroking Purpose's back.

"Yes," Jhanvi said. "But *what* boundaries?"

"Well, I think Jhanvi is right," Roshie said. "People shouldn't be touching each other in public in gross, unsanitary ways, especially around food."

Her eyes bored into Audrey's body with a look of naked, unvarnished disgust. Jhanvi nodded, then looked around, trying to see what other people were making of this. How deliciously aggressive!

The only thing they'd cooked today that was at all edible was the fried tofu, and Jhanvi forked a cube, ran it through a puddle of sriracha, and lifted the dripping mass to her mouth.

"We discussed the sanitary conditions last meeting," Katie said. "And I thought we addressed those concerns, Roshie."

"It's not really about sanitary stuff though, Katie," Jhanvi said. "Doesn't being a community mean looking deeper? I mean, some real feelings are happening here ..."

But she was talking to herself—Katie went on with the meeting. Each of Roshie's interruptions was managed through a deflection, and the other residents did their best to ignore the negative energy emanating from her. Roshie stewed in her black turtleneck and thick glasses, hunched forward on the couch, not looking away from Audrey.

There was an intermission so people could clean their plates. Most folks decamped to the kitchen, but Roshie and Katie stayed put, so Jhanvi did as well.

Katie knelt by Roshie's couch. "Can you please try to be more constructive?"

"We talked about this!" Roshie said. "We talked about the sex."

"Hey," Jhanvi said. "What's up?"

"This is a private conversation," Katie said.

Jhanvi backed off, but when Katie went back to the board,

Jhanvi leaned closer to Roshie. "You have a good point. Most places, they'd be like, *this kind of behavior is not acceptable in common spaces.* That would just be understood."

"I know!" Roshie looked at Jhanvi as if seeing her for the first time. Then she blinked behind her immense frames.

"So you're an angry, resentful virgin. I love that," Jhanvi said. "Why have we not been friends?"

A moment of quiet followed. Dishes clanked in the kitchen, and Purpose chattered animatedly, running out of breath, her speech almost pressured, like someone having a manic episode, about how the world seemed so sick, and people really need to understand the energy they bring into it.

"No . . . I just have good boundaries," Roshie said.

Jhanvi nodded. "We both do."

Did there exist a place, or some group of people, that didn't spend so much time trying to deny or to evade the obvious? Imagine how much progress people could make if they just admitted the basic facts of what was happening. *Roshie is desperately lonely. You guys doing shit in the hallways makes her feel bad. You make her feel bad.* The solution to the problem wasn't clear to Jhanvi, but at least they could state the problem clearly!

Jhanvi inched over to Katie, who was scrubbing the whiteboard.

"Hey," Jhanvi said. "I think Roshie's just lonely and left out."

"Mmm," Katie said.

"Look at her body language. She's all the way over there. It's corny, but couldn't you just show her some love?"

"Thanks," Katie said.

"Don't just brush me off," Jhanvi said. "People here just brush other people off, as if they don't matter. I have worth. I think . . . err . . . I probably have some worth. Not a lot, but, some."

"We're starting the meeting again."

Wow, Jhanvi mouthed to herself. This place was incredible. She imagined telling Charli about it—her friend would ask, *Why are you hanging out with these people? They seem to have no redeeming value whatsoever.*

But now, looking at them returning from the kitchen, where Henry had thrown water on Purpose, seeing them laughing, skipping sideways, hugging each other—hearing Henry's bluff voice talking about new regulations for AlternaFest-affiliated parties, and how everything was gonna be totally different this year—seeing Audrey slither toward Achilles and put out a long foot, and seeing him catch it and start to rub it as she flexed her body and sighed theatrically . . .

This was the good life. It was something Jhanvi couldn't explain: this was the life people were meant to lead. Except perhaps not so dishonestly.

"Finally," Katie said. "There's some behavior around here that's made me very uncomfortable."

Jhanvi perked up. Maybe Katie had actually listened to her . . .

"I distributed the guest rules and I informed everyone about them at the beginning, and . . ."

Then she went on to make the case, although not in so many words, that Jhanvi was a threat to the house.

Jhanvi was more impressed than surprised. At least Katie was willing to do her own dirty work, unlike the rest of them.

And she was happy with herself for how little she felt, even as Katie studiously indicted her for—wait a second—this wasn't about being a creep or a moocher—it wasn't even about randomly proposing marriage to Henry, it was about—"You've got to be kidding," Jhanvi said. "The police? The police thing?"

"We stand firmly in league against the carceral state," Katie said. "Chris was harassed by the police yet again this morning, and you won't tell me the name of the person who's calling the cops."

"Because I don't want you bothering her."

"What about Chris's right to not be bothered?"

"Chris shouldn't call her a faggot," Jhanvi said.

Audrey's foot dropped and she pulled herself into an upright position.

"Hey, hey," Henry said. They were almost his first words of the meeting, and Jhanvi squinted at him. He'd *known* this was going to happen. "Jhanvi knows the rules, right?"

"Her continued presence makes our community unsafe," Katie said. "And I'd like to know her plan for leaving."

"Uhh," Jhanvi said. "Henry said I had at least three weeks..."

He raised his hands. "Well, I mean, yeah, but..."

"So that would be when?" Katie said. "This Sunday?"

"What?" Jhanvi said. "N—no, I've been here less than a week. It'd be three Sundays from now."

"That doesn't work for me." Katie pursed her lips.

Suddenly things got heated, with everybody weighing in and lots of talking back and forth, negotiating. Audrey slowly slipped down onto the ground, disengaging from the talk. Henry kept bargaining away Jhanvi's time, but Katie wouldn't accept fifteen days or ten days—she held firm at one week. Which, you know—fair enough. It was her house. Her living space. And she deserved to feel safe.

Jhanvi had lived in a co-op during college, and she'd frequently experienced this dynamic. The most intransigent person always got their way. Really, these meetings were a form of highly structured bullying. She sat there, reiterating, quietly, that she needed three weeks, but she could feel herself wavering. She knew they would say, "Oh no, of course we wouldn't just kick you out into the street," but they'd give her a bunch of homework to do to find another apartment or shelter, and when she came up short, they wouldn't call another meeting, Katie would simply speak to her privately and say... well, Jhanvi legitimately wasn't sure. She shrugged to herself. She was curious about what Katie would do if Jhanvi just refused to leave. Katie didn't seem like the type to hold her grievances until they could all practice restorative justice together. Would

Katie call the cops? Ask them to enforce her property rights? That would be entirely too amusing.

And then what? If Jhanvi got on the phone with Monica right this second, she could perhaps keep her old room and her old job. Maybe. Or she had a cousin-uncle, Yadav, who lived in Sacramento. He was intolerably Republican and impossible to be around, but because of that, he was the one cousin she hadn't stolen from or betrayed.

"Can you one hundred percent guarantee you'll be gone in three weeks?" Henry said.

"Sure," Jhanvi said.

"No, that's not acceptable," Katie said. "We talked about . . ."

Roshie was loudly crumpling up her paper bag in the kitchen. Audrey chirped at her to please maybe throw it out outside, since they didn't necessarily want those grease chemicals in their kitchen garbage. Roshie opened the door to the back porch, where they kept their cans, and after a second she slammed it hard, then clopped back into the room with her wet bare feet.

Jhanvi looked at Roshie, watched the emotions mix and congeal in her face. Everyone here was so easy to read. Roshie's face got red around the edges, and the contrast made her acne show a deeper purple.

"This is disgusting. She doesn't have a place to live!"

Roshie had shouted the words. Everyone went silent. She stood up now, her whole body vibrating, and she stuck out a finger. Jhanvi fished in her pocket, wanting to surreptitiously record what was sure to be a crazy moment, but her phone was in her bag in the other room.

The lighting in the room was harsh, with a fluorescent edge that brought out every pit and crag on Roshie's face.

"What is wrong with you people?" Roshie said. The words were choked and high-pitched. "Remember that creepy, dirty guy you all loved, Nasal Xylophone? You were obsessed with him, Audrey! He stayed here for three months! And whenever

I complained, you blew me off. Now you've got a vulnerable person, and you want to kick her onto the street."

There was another moment of silence. Roshie's chin jutted forward, and she stared around the room, daring people to speak first.

"We voted on Nasal," Audrey said. "If you hated him so—"

"I should've blocked him! But if he got to stay, she should too! That isn't fair."

"Nasal was intimate with members of the house," Katie said. "Those rules are different."

"Fine, then I'm sleeping with Jhanvi! Fine, you happy? Are you happy? We're fucking!"

Jhanvi's eyebrows went up. Despite their easy sensuality, there was surprisingly little overt, formal queerness in this social scene. If girls fucked, it was always on ecstasy, or in threesomes, or in secret, as good friends or "roommates." Bisexual men were almost unknown, and Jhanvi wasn't sure if Audrey and Katie even knew about that side of Hen. The fact that Roshie was claiming her as a lover just showed how out of touch she was with the mores of the house.

"You've all had lovers and girlfriends and hookups and street kids here, and I *never* asked for anything," Roshie said.

"Let's take a break," Katie said. "I think we've gotten a bit heated."

"No!" Roshie said. "No! No! You guys, we've been arguing online for a week about how to *help* Jhanvi, and let me tell you, this definitely isn't it. This isn't how a *community* operates. I mean, she's your friend! She's your friend, and she's asking for help! Like, like . . ." Now Roshie licked her lips, and Jhanvi's eyes widened. She knew what Roshie was going to say. "Like Audrey, you didn't have the money to afford the event space. So I paid. And now you're gonna kick a trans woman out onto the street? Do you get that she's literally gonna be homeless?"

Jhanvi emitted a sudden laugh. People looked at her, but Roshie went on fulminating. This was interesting. Not that it hadn't occurred to Jhanvi to play this card, to frame her story this way, as someone who'd potentially be homeless. It made sense, in a certain light. She was homeless right now, potentially. No apartment in Sacramento. No family nearby. Her parents on the other side of the world and not rich enough to help her, anyway.

She tried to make herself feel anxious, but it simply didn't work. This was a matter of social class. Katie and Henry and Jhanvi had all gone to Stanford, they'd moved in the same circles, and they were in a distinctly different social class than Roshie, who always seemed so middle class, despite apparently earning more than anyone else in the house.

Jhanvi couldn't escape the feeling that homelessness was simply not the sort of thing that happened to people like her. Like, during her bad days, she'd spent nights walking around in circles or hanging out in the twenty-four-hour McDonalds, but that was always because she couldn't get home or had lost her phone or was waiting for the bus to start running again. It'd almost gotten to be a routine for her: *Oh yeah, this is happening again.* That wasn't real homelessness, though.

Maybe that was absurd—maybe she was fooling herself. In a college anthro class, they'd read an ethnographic study of homeless magazine sellers in New York. Most had insisted they were out there by choice, but when the French anthropologist investigated their origins, he found that actually poor finances or mental disease or drug addiction made other living situations too unstable. They had framed as a choice something that wasn't a choice at all.

But if Jhanvi found herself on the street, she would simply open her phone and start making calls. Someone would take her in. Or, at worst, she would get a hotel room, spend down the money in her account, maybe apply for some credit cards, spend that, apply to grad school or something, use the student loan money, or take a flight to India to see her parents. She had options.

As the argument raged around her, Roshie was shaking, and Jhanvi had become a bystander as people argued about her life.

"If we're the kind of people who refuse to help our friends, then I don't want to be part of it! I won't . . ."

The other meeting participants, aside from Katie, had started to put distance between them and her. Achilles and Purpose had disappeared. Henry was hunched over on the couch, Audrey's hand on his back. The sight of Audrey sent a cold shiver through Jhanvi—she was like a painting, an object, an expanse of skin that terminated in the waistband of her brown shorts. Everything she said and did oozed with sexuality.

"Henry," Jhanvi said. "I'm your guest. We talked about this."

Katie put up a finger. "You're the house's guest."

"But we know Roshie's right. If I was fucking someone, it'd be copacetic. And Henry and I have sex. Or we do . . . something, anyway. Don't we, Henry?"

"Uhh," Henry's mouth opened.

Jhanvi's teeth ground together slightly. She couldn't read her oldest friend's mind. Whether he was confused because he hadn't told anyone about their cybersex (was that even the word anymore? Did it even count as sex?) or because it was simply so outré for her to claim it meant anything. His golden skin darkened, getting mottled and ruddy—blushing didn't look good on him.

"Jhanvi," he said. "You and I . . . you're a great friend. I want to help. Even if you go back to Sacramento, we can still . . . our plans don't need to change."

"They wouldn't be kicking me out if you weren't on board, Hen," Jhanvi said. "Just be honest. I mean, I'm not worth more than other people, but I'm not worth less either. I'm a human being." She looked at him, and when his eyes dropped, she looked at Audrey, whose gaze went to their tall, blond facilitator. Katie's blue eyes were unblinking, cold, as if examining a medical specimen.

"I'm a human being," Jhanvi said.

"Nobody is disputing that," Katie said. "But we're human beings too."

"Doesn't seem like it."

"Enough," Katie said. "Jhanvi, can you please give the house some room to discuss?"

"Where do I go?" Jhanvi said. "I'm supposed to sit in Henry's room, where I can hear you talk about me, unable to respond?"

"My room," Roshie said. "My room. You won't hear a thing up there."

Once again, Jhanvi was forced to chuckle. But she got up, then drifted into the kitchen, where nobody looked at her. The job board was posted over the breakfast nook—she had a little tile hanging on it. She'd scratched her name into the wood with the edge of a pen. She took the tile down and threw it in the garbage, then walked to the front of the house to collect her stuff.

6

Roshie's room was dim, long, and narrow with sloping ceilings that met in a point. It looked like an attic playroom, an impression created by the peach walls, gray carpet, and rows of white Ikea bookshelves full of graphic novels. The room was full of lamps, and Jhanvi had to turn on three more of them before the space stopped looking like a temple of long shadows.

Jhanvi peered out a skylight window that gave her a view of the fog-cloaked downtown, and slowly cranked it shut. Picking up a blanket, she huddled on a couch next to the clanking radiator, in front of the huge TV.

In a corner, she saw a stack of old paperbacks with very familiar covers: golden Art Deco sculptures, clean lines against a background of stylized green skyscrapers. She thumbed through the paperbacks, amused that Roshie had, like, every single one of Anna Laurent's books. Jhanvi crouched in front of the stack, opening the books, reading through a favorite scene. These were almost like contraband: the author had such a retrograde political philosophy that none of Jhanvi's friends would ever admit to finding the slightest merit in her books.

There was a burst of shouting below, and Jhanvi heard Katie's voice respond calmly, inaudibly, followed by stomping up the stairs. Roshie burst in, slamming the door, turning the lock.

"Fuck you!" Roshie yelled at the door. "And tell Audrey that

I won't pay a dollar more in rent on the event space if Jhanvi can't stay."

There was silence. Roshie sat heavily at her desk, her lip quivering. After a second, she put on her headphones.

"Uhh, hello?" Jhanvi said.

Roshie opened her laptop, her back to Jhanvi on the couch across the room.

"Hello?"

Roshie started to click through browser windows. Jhanvi shouted and waved her arms, and Roshie pulled off her headphones, not seeming the least bit surprised.

"Oh," she said. "Uhh, hey."

"Hey," Jhanvi said.

"Do you need something?" Roshie's eyes closed for a second, then she squinted. "It's bright in here." She shuffled the papers on her desk.

She was about to put on her headphones again, when Jhanvi said, "What happened out there?"

Roshie turned in her wheeled desk chair and scooted across the room with little nudges of her toes across the carpet, stopping a few feet away from Jhanvi. She finally looked directly at Jhanvi's face.

"I'm sorry." Roshie's voice was hoarse. "They can be so clueless. I've been thinking all week about our earlier talk, what you were trying to say, about community and friendship."

"Uhh ... okay?" Jhanvi said. "What've you been thinking?"

"Just what you said? About how a real community is about trusting people implicitly and giving them the resources they say they need, even if you don't necessarily like them."

"Excuse me? I didn't say that. I said real communities *aren't* like that."

"No, no you did. Like, you said Indian and trans people can help you, but Indians are prejudiced and other trans people don't have the resources to assist your transition, so you came here, and you need our help."

"That's . . ." Jhanvi looked up, trying to sort through her thoughts. "I guess that is . . . in a way . . . sort of correct? You are definitely offering a plausible interpretation of the facts of my life."

"Are you making fun of me?"

"No, uhh, I just never took it that seriously, I guess," Jhanvi said. "I knew you guys didn't want to help me. I just accepted that. I never really thought Henry would follow through." Saying it out loud, she wasn't sure if it was true or not. But it felt like her truth now: she'd never expected better from that fuckwit.

Roshie's voice was choked up, almost guttural. "I . . . I don't get it. You *don't* want to marry someone?"

"I do," Jhanvi said. "I mean, I would. But I don't expect anyone to do it. I'm just here because my life was shitty. I'm an adventurer. It's a lark. An adventurer sort of shakes the trees to see what comes out. You break a bunch of unwritten rules, and you cause chaos, and you see if any opportunities emerge from the mess. Everyone here on some level gets what I'm doing, and they resent it."

"But . . . but what about your Sacramento life? I mean . . . you said it would take years for you to finish transitioning. Was that not right?"

"No, it was right."

"So, but . . . but that's okay?"

Roshie's eyebrows were so furrowed that Jhanvi wanted to laugh. But at the same time, her heart was getting heavy. *Oh my god, I am experiencing real, genuine, honest emotions over this. I really need to respect this person. This is really special.*

"N—no, it's not okay," Jhanvi said. "But it's my fate. Some people get their feet blown off by landmines. Others get murdered in their sleep. And I'm doomed to work a menial job in a second-tier town while I save up the money to fly to Spain to get someone to operate on me so I don't look like a monster.

It's a huge deal to *me*, of course, but I don't expect other people to care."

"Except . . . didn't you quit that job? I mean . . . do you have a bus ticket back?"

"No, yeah. I guess that job is pretty much gone."

"So . . ." Roshie shook her head. "What am I not getting here? Don't you want our help?"

"I do," Jhanvi said. "But I don't really deserve it."

"And Chris does? He's a drug addict! You're sober! You're helping yourself. I think it's, I've been thinking about The Guilty Party, and, like, you know how people say AlternaFest is just a bunch of rich people turning SF into their personal playground?"

That was from an article that'd run a few weeks ago in a major alt weekly.

"Yeah . . ."

"Well, I thought that was so stupid. It's so stupid." Roshie's eyes were shining, and the light caught the slight acne scars on her cheeks. "I mean, fuck those people. You want something. You're asking for something. And, you know what? You're clearly smart. You've clearly got your own ideas. You're not just trapped in the default world. So . . . let's invest in you."

Jhanvi knew exactly the words to break this spell. *Okay, so give me money.* Because Roshie wouldn't do that. And if Jhanvi pushed her, this whole edifice would fall apart, and she'd have to accept that Jhanvi, on some essential level, didn't really deserve her help. And yet . . . Jhanvi didn't want to push. In a way, it was absurd. Roshie was rich enough to solve Jhanvi's problems overnight, and yet she didn't. But . . . but that was the essence of friendship. You pretended it was stronger than it was. You pretended your friend would give you the shirt off their back. And maybe they would—but they wouldn't give you the hundred thousand in their bank account.

"You know . . . thanks," Jhanvi said. "What you did is really rare. Like, to actually think about what I'm saying, try to understand me. It's so rare. It's happened, I am not kidding, maybe . . . once in my life, aside from now." Except right then, Jhanvi couldn't think of a second time. What was weird was that she had felt so little desire for Roshie, so little envy for her—had barely attempted to befriend her—and yet the girl had thought deeply about her life.

"No problem," Roshie said. "I'm fucking smart. Anyway, don't worry about the rest of these guys. You know the truth about them? And it's sad, but this is the truth—they're just not as smart as us."

"As us?"

"I mean, I'm probably smarter than you—I can't tell, because my IQ is mostly devoted to my work, and I think you've focused a lot of yours on words and trying to sound good, but yeah—however smart you are, most of these people are dumber. The thing is, wait . . . hold on, you know that friends don't need to be as smart as you are, right?"

"Uhh . . ." Jhanvi nodded. "Yeah. I do know that."

"Good, because a lot of smart people don't. It took me a long time to learn. You choose friends because there's something inside them that's just, you know, totally fucking rad. Something about their essence. Like, Henry, Katie, Audrey, even idiots like Purpose and Achilles, they're just, like, really unique people. But it's like you said, we were all raised in the default world, and the default world is spiritually bankrupt. They don't get it. They don't understand that we've gotta, like, rebuild everything, relearn how to be human beings."

"You're right," Jhanvi said. "I agree. Umm, uhh . . . thanks. For teaching them. Or whatever. So, uhh, what now? Did you talk them around?"

Roshie's mouth twisted. "Don't worry about it. They're being idiots, but I'm used to it. I'll figure it out. Everything is totally in my hands."

"Great," Jhanvi said. "So what do I do then?"

"Uhh," Roshie said. "I dunno."

"I guess I'll get a job or something."

"Yeah I wasn't gonna say it, but why not get a tech job yourself?" Roshie said. "Take a computer class or some shit."

"I probably should."

"Cool! There's a great one for women. They have scholarships and stuff. You need to know a little programming to get in, but I can help . . ."

Roshie reminded Jhanvi so much of her Indian cousins right now: always full of schemes for improving Jhanvi's life. Jhanvi rubbed a hand on the rough fabric of the sofa. This room was like the bedrooms and dens of all her (invariably male) friends growing up. No adornment, lots of books, disorganized, with gaming controllers and wires snaking all over. No sense of intentional design, everything just placed higgledy-piggledy, with a few zones: a TV zone, a bedroom zone, and an office zone with a desk. Roshie dug in a closet and came over with an armful of camping gear and dropped it on the couch next to Jhanvi. She could tell it was expensive, made with space-age materials that were thin and light but trapped heat.

"Here," she said. "The couch folds out, but I don't have sheets for it. And we've got our own bathroom, over there . . ."

Jhanvi gave a sad smile. She liked Roshie. She couldn't help it. Something about the girl was just so adorable. It was in her posture—how she skittered across the floor on tiny feet—how her hands were grasped together in her lap, and how she stared out owlishly from under her straight bangs and thick glasses.

"I'll give you the door code too. Just text me if it changes. Katie threatened to put in a new one, but I said I'd just give it to you. The only problem is if I'm not in cell range—I might need to cancel my camping trip next week."

"Don't," Jhanvi said. "Katie's not gonna do that. It's an empty threat."

"I dunno, she's tough."

"I'll be fine. And it's just for a few weeks. After that—"

"Shush," Roshie said. "Enough with these 'house-sitting gigs.'

Everyone always has a house-sitting gig. But you know what? A lot of the time, they're lying! They go out to sleep in their cars! Or on the street! Or at their parents' place! I think it's so stupid, the way they were like, *Oh, but she has a house-sitting gig.* It was just a way for them to ignore that you need our help."

Jhanvi's mouth formed an O. Her chest leaped, and she didn't know how to fully convey how impressed and touched she was. "That's so insightful," she said.

"It's okay," Roshie said. "I used to get really mad about how dumb people are, but I got resigned to it eventually."

Roshie went into a long, emotional rant about all the ways the people in this house had let her down and been a bunch of fucking idiots. The story of the glory hole returned. Many of the tales dealt with the intricacies of the event space, including zoning, the building code, and dealing with their landlord and the city. She warmed to the topic, getting quite impassioned, and Jhanvi found her attention wandering. She wanted to say, *But you're doing all this work for them, so who's the stupid one, really?* Jhanvi liked and admired Roshie, but the girl lacked charm. She wasn't an easy person to talk to or be around. And Jhanvi got the impression that Roshie maybe didn't even really like her much.

And yet, and yet, when Roshie had gone back to her computer, and Jhanvi was left huddled on the couch, she watched Roshie openly as the other girl got more absorbed in her screen, and the thought came without warning—*I'm home.* It was absurd—a castle in the sky. This girl was socially awkward, at war with her own apartment, couldn't possibly give Jhanvi what she needed.

But right at that moment, the other girl's presence felt like drinking clean water after a very long thirst.

7

Jhanvi tried to escape the wind at the Sixteenth Street BART station by standing between a market stall and a self-cleaning toilet, a large green column whose stainless steel door seemed to be permanently locked. She scanned the entrance of the train station, looking for Roshie, wondering again whether she ought to have dressed in something slinky and see-through like the stuff Katie and Audrey wore.

Jhanvi had actually spent an hour in a thrift store nearby, purchasing a way-too-short dress, but she'd been afraid to wear it on the street—much too presumptuous. And when Roshie showed up, Jhanvi exhaled: the girl was in a hoodie and jeans, without even a backpack.

Jhanvi opened her arms, and Roshie acceded to a hug without returning it.

"Hey," she said. "You ready to see the event space?"

"Err, I guess it's not a dressing-up type thing?"

"What? No," Roshie said. "We're there to work."

"Okay, okay . . ."

Jhanvi had huddled in Roshie's room all morning, afraid to go out, less out of fear of being locked out—Roshie had given her the door code—and more to avoid the pain of potentially confronting the rest of the house.

But then Roshie had texted her a few hours ago, asking if Jhanvi wanted to check out the dungeon, and Jhanvi had said yes without revealing that she'd already asked Katie and Henry a few days before, and they'd basically said no. She hadn't really spoken to Henry since the meeting two nights ago. She'd texted him today to ask if the wedding was still on, and he'd said: *I'll get back to you. Just have some things to research.*

Jhanvi started talking nervously, telling Roshie that she'd gotten stir-crazy and had gone out for lunch, but not before getting a bag together in case Katie locked her out.

"That was dumb," Roshie said. "I turn off my phone while I work."

"Okay, okay," Jhanvi said. "I just wandered around the Lower Haight and the Mission. It's so gorgeous here, with the colors and the murals. I know this is a really basic thing to say, but it's like living in Europe."

"Yeah, it's nice," Roshie said.

They walked together with no conversation, and Jhanvi felt a flicker of resentment. She knew it was just the other girl's social awkwardness, but Jhanvi didn't want to live like this, sharing space with someone so sullen, so difficult.

"You sure they won't mind me showing up?" Jhanvi said. "I asked before, and they said no."

"No, that's dumb," Roshie said. "There's a guest policy. And anyway, I'm the one paying for the place."

"See," Jhanvi said. "This is why white people don't help each other out. What you have is a brown-person mentality. You paid, so you're owed something. And I think that's why you're angry at them."

"No, no," Roshie said. "What you're saying is so self-evidently stupid."

Jhanvi smiled. She almost wanted her friend to repeat the words *self-evidently stupid* so she could hear the bite of emphasis at the beginning of each word.

Roshie said, "Don't get into that whole 'Fire-eaters suck and are selfish and only care about hedonism and sex' mentality.

That's the kind of thing second-raters say: people who can't do or build anything, so they just tear others down."

"You sound like those books you have. The, uhh, the Anna Laurent books."

"Don't talk about that."

"What? I like her work."

"Huh?" Roshie said. "No. Shut up."

"I do. I've always liked them."

"What's your favorite?"

"*The Redness of Mars*," Jhanvi said. "Obviously."

"Yessssssssss," Roshie said. "That's clearly the best. Okay, this is weird. You really like her? It's not a joke?"

"I mean, the political philosophy is dumb—"

"Obviously."

"But I like . . . the integrity of it, I guess," Jhanvi said. "I like . . . you know, when the guy goes to Mars, and he works and works and works, and everyone writes him off. And then when he succeeds, the government comes to take it away. And he gives that speech. The one that's like, *I asked the people of Earth for aid, and you ignored me, and I accepted that as my due—I did not deserve your help, when there were so many more in such greater need. But I see now that your turning away was not due to principle, but to fear and greed and indolence . . .*"

"Wow," Roshie said. "So . . . like . . . you do get it. You actually get it. You really do get what I'm about."

"Sure," Jhanvi said. "I guess."

"Good," Roshie said. "I'm starting to get your sense of humor. But be careful, other people would think you're serious about some of the shit you say."

Roshie opened a gate, and they headed into a dark little alley. At the far end was a spot of sunshine, where Jhanvi saw tables and diners, but Roshie turned to the left, and she bent down, over a cellar door, heaving it up. A little light showed from the bottom of creaky wooden steps, reflecting off the stone foundation of a building.

"Watch your head," Roshie said.

They walked down, Jhanvi behind Roshie, going through another stone corridor, with pipes and bare lightbulbs overhead.

"Where are we?" Jhanvi said.

"Just a basement," Roshie said. "This used to be a furniture factory, and they'd use this for storage. Then I think people lived here for a while."

The hallway didn't have quite the look of a sewer system. It was more like leftover space, the butt-ends of many buildings coming together. The wall on one side was brick, on the other it was wooden siding. They came into a space where the sky opened up, and the sun beamed down on them.

"This trough runs behind this whole block of Mission Street." Roshie bent to grab a cardboard box and propped it against the wall, shaking her head. "Remind me to bring that out when we leave. I don't know what people think when they leave this stuff out—do they think the recycling truck comes back here?"

They passed a wrought-iron gateway going through the brick, which was screened by vines. Roshie hung on to the iron fence, peering through, then she laughed. "Hola, Adriana!" She followed with some schoolgirl Spanish that Jhanvi didn't understand.

Looking through the gate, Jhanvi saw ladders, other branching alleyways, a little handcart, and flowering vines climbing up the side of the wall. A woman wearing gloves was hunched over a planter.

"Wow," Jhanvi said. "Is she the gardener?"

"What?" Roshie said. "No, it's her garden. She's our upstairs neighbor."

"So this is the building's garden?"

"Uhh, it's hers," Roshie said.

Adriana walked toward them, smiling, and she gave a flower to Roshie, gesturing at Jhanvi. "For you to give," she said.

"Oh," Jhanvi said.

Roshie tried to hand back the flower, but Adriana gestured

again, so Jhanvi took it and twisted the stem and put it behind her ear, hoping it didn't look absurd.

"I love your garden," Jhanvi said. "It's incredible."

Adriana looked around, trying to peek around the corner. "Anyone else here?"

"Oh . . ." Roshie looked further down the alley and noticed two guys, both clearly techies, one white and one Asian, who were wrangling a big metal bracket. "Uhh, yeah."

"Later," Adriana said. "I show you later."

As they walked on, Jhanvi said, "She thought we were dating."

"Adriana is great," Roshie said. "Her husband's really, really sick, which under the law makes her un-evictable, but the landlord tried anyway. Adri's been organizing the other tenants to fight back. She thought I wouldn't join in! I've been helping her do repairs."

"Wow," Jhanvi said.

Roshie smiled earnestly, her eyes wide. She bent down to pick up a little wrapper and tucked it in her pocket. "So you get it," Roshie said.

"Get what? That this is awesome? I love this."

"People act like the event space isn't surrounded by anything. But this whole alley is so cool."

Jhanvi's skin was buzzing. She hopped up and down, her heels lightly touching the cobbled alley. Then they caught up to the two guys in leather vests, their bare arms showing—one wore goggles and the other had a pair hanging around his neck. They were holding an odd-shaped metal bracket and had chains looped around their arms and shoulders. As they turned, the bracket banged against the brick wall, and Roshie hissed, touching the crater.

"Hey," said one of the guys.

"What is wrong with you?" Roshie said. "Haven't we done enough damage here?"

"Oh shit," said the Asian guy in vaguely British-inflected

English. "I'm sorry, I'm really sorry." He hefted the bracket again. "Can I fix it?"

That's when Jhanvi saw the whole wall was blackened, and she grimaced. This must've been where the glory hole had been.

"I really have to do something about all this," Roshie said. She rubbed at the blackened brick again. "I think it's just a brick siding—we ought to be able to replace it. But getting it to look right . . ."

The guys looked at each other, and they kept trying to get the bracket through the door.

"Stupid," Roshie said. "Here's how you do it." Then, getting underneath, she lifted from the bottom and executed a maneuver that flipped it around, hooking the edge through an open doorway nearby. She exhaled slowly, ducking underneath the bracket and through the dark door.

"Jeez," said the Asian guy. "You're a wizard."

"Just don't be such an idiot," Roshie said. "If something doesn't fit, don't keep pushing and pushing and pushing. Move it around."

"Hey," Jhanvi said to the Asian guy. He had a short beard, and his arms and shoulders were tanned a golden brown and covered in fine hairs that shone in the sunlight that swept across his upper body.

"Oh hey," he said, awkwardly putting out one hand. "What's up?"

"Roshie is just showing me the event space."

"Aww yeah." The Asian guy's accent was not quite British, maybe from Australia or New Zealand. "I'm Xiao. So you're friends with Roshie?"

Jhanvi held Xiao's hand for a moment. His nail beds were short and broad, and she pulled at his fingers, seeing how they reddened under the pressure.

"Oh, okay," Xiao said, wrenching his hand away. Sweat collected on the back of his neck as he shouldered the bracket. Then with much heaving and grunting, they navigated down a narrow stairwell into darkness. A clear plastic tarp fell around them, and Jhanvi had to bat it away from her ears, even as the sound of electronic music got louder and louder. Then they entered a large space suffused with blue light.

As they all were sorting themselves out, Xiao and the other guy dropped the bracket into a corner and shouted some words that were swallowed up by the music.

The room was a long chamber, running the whole length of the building above them. The floor was polished concrete. In one area, just to the left of the stairs, were a sink and kitchen island. Next to it, between two plywood partitions, a bunch of couches and oriental rugs and a lazy Susan on a low table formed a little hookah bar. But then, you looked farther, and saw an open toilet and a concert stage at the other end. The jumble of disparate settings made the dungeon look like a Hollywood backlot: a nothing-land where fantasies were constructed and taken down.

As her eyes focused, she noted a ten-foot-tall painting, done in an impressionist but still recognizably representational style. It was Audrey, larger than life, with her broad smile and broader shoulders. In the painting, she was completely naked, with a woman and a man kneeling between her legs, their tongues out like snakes, collars around their necks, looking toward the viewer. Jhanvi shivered. The girl had a high blond ponytail, but her eyes were X-ed out. Was it Katie? The guy, who was clean shaven, could've been any white guy.

Next to the painting there was a refrigerator and a set of sinks. On the other side were two toilets just out and about, rising from the concrete floor.

Suddenly, the lights turned bright white. There was a whirl of motion at the far end of the room, and Jhanvi blinked, taking a few steps toward the people who came in. The room was so long that they were still indistinct, but they were all clothed, albeit disheveled. There was a girl with her hair in high pigtails, in a white polo shirt and pleated skirt, like a Japanese school-girl. Jhanvi realized right away, *Oh yeah, that's Audrey.*

"Is this my work crew?" Roshie said. "What's left to get done today? Did we get the wood for the walls?"

The group of assorted guys and girls stared at her blankly. Most of them were dressed sensibly in jeans and boots, with work gloves hanging from a pocket.

"Hey, hey! Rosh, you're here. Were you asking about the wood?" Henry was in a leather vest, his neck encircled by glowing lights. He stood with a circle of other men, all bearded or with long hair or, at the very least, showing chest hair, who were harrumphing and making vaguely man-like noises over a bunch of plywood partitions. The fire-eaters could be oddly gender conforming sometimes.

Roshie walked toward him, and with each step, the other girl lost her withdrawn body language. She straightened, puffed out her chest, and raised her chin, looking like the famous painting of the apes walking through the phases of evolution. When she got to Henry, she asked, "Hey, what've you all done?"

"Hi Rosh," Henry said. "Just spitballing about how to put up these partitions. Achilles here thought we could..." Jhanvi didn't understand what was at stake. She watched Roshie's face as her friend talked. Her jaw set, and her lip thrust out.

"That's the dumbest idea I've ever heard," Roshie said. "Do it like the plan."

Achilles, who Jhanvi had last seen shirtless, groping Audrey, was wearing a blue unitard like a circus strongman, which displayed a rough, bushy-haired chest. But his voice was high and nasal as he said, "I saw on YouTube that if we use these tracks, we can move the partitions on the fly."

"They'll collapse," Roshie said. "Don't be a fucking idiot."

"Roshie," Jhanvi said. "Maybe let them..."

Now Henry reached out and put a hand around Jhanvi's midsection in a weak hug. "Oh hey," he said. "You made it."

The sudden contact was intensely off-putting. She brushed

off his clammy hand. He hadn't touched her very much in public since she got to SF. He hadn't said anything to her until she'd spoken.

"We'll do it Roshie's way, all right?" Henry said. "Come on, Rosh, tell us what to do."

"See, be like Henry," Roshie said. "He's a pretty boy, built for fucking, like all of you. No need to think."

Nobody laughed. Jhanvi was agog. This was *not* how people talked in Trial By Fire, and especially not Roshie.

Roshie's face was twisted into a scowl of contempt. She harangued everyone standing around, got them working. Her bitter voice soured the mood, and conversations ceased when she got close.

"See," Roshie said to Jhanvi. "People here are so incompetent. Don't touch it. No, you can't do anything. You don't *know* anything. Just look pretty, Jhanvi. Someone'll be railing you against this wall in two months, and you don't want it to collapse and kill everyone."

Jhanvi noticed that Henry was sort of a foreman. He trailed in Roshie's wake, asking her questions, fielding questions from other guys. Almost none of the women talked to Roshie, except for Travesty—a short, sporty girl who doubled over laughing at everything Roshie said.

"Is Roshie always like this?" Jhanvi said.

"Oh yeah, she's intense," Henry said.

"Katie must be so pissed."

Henry didn't say anything. But Jhanvi could feel the dagger eyes coming at them from the girls. Everyone was slowly getting to work, but Roshie got more stressed and anxious. She seemed to barrel right into the little groups of people, busting them up, harassing them like flocks of pigeons that inevitably reassembled in their little groups the moment she left. The anxiety was so uncalled for, so outside of normal, that it felt like a solo act, like Roshie was purposefully working herself up.

"Won't anyone tell her to chill?" Jhanvi asked.

"She gets things done," Henry said.

"Come on . . ." Jhanvi said. "This really isn't good."

They threaded through piles of plywood and extension cords, past buckets of paint and big noisy ventilators. Roshie's face got more pinched and her manner more dictatorial. Henry had fallen back as Roshie headed for Audrey's little court—the assortment of colorfully dressed girls sitting on the edge of the stage, laughing, playing with strands of light, dressing the set.

A phone was on a tripod, and Audrey spoke into it, gesturing at various people in the space. Katie had a tablet in front of her, and she was very self-seriously writing something with a digital pen. Roshie muttered under her breath like an insane person. Jhanvi, heart pounding, smoothed down the edge of her dress—she felt lumbering and out of control, like she was flashing someone with each step.

"Hey," Roshie said. "What're you doing here?"

"Designing the trainings for the party," Katie said. "It was the only time we could—"

"Today is for working," Roshie said. "We have to *work*."

Audrey spoke a few words into her headset, then walked to the phone, glanced at the screen. "We were filming a training. You *ruined* the take, Roshie. That is not acceptable."

"There won't be anything to train for, unless you guys do some work," Roshie said.

"You are *not* in charge here."

"I'm paying the bills," Roshie said. "So it's my responsibility."

"That isn't how things work," Katie said, but her voice was more even, and she stayed sitting.

Audrey grimaced, her face turning ugly. It was a funny contrast with her fairy wings and hot pants, her nipples covered in purple pasties. She wore heavy foundation, with glittering purple eye shadow along the edges of her eyes. The wings were a good touch, they broke the outline of her blocky body and created a more sylph-like silhouette. She pressed one small fist into her hip, elbow out, purposefully standing closer to Roshie.

"You cannot act this way," Audrey said.

"Then don't be lazy," Roshie said. "Even your fucktoys put in some work now and then."

"Roshie . . ." Katie said.

"I will end this party," Audrey said. "I'll take it somewhere else."

"Do it," Roshie said. "Saves me the headache of building all this shit."

They were toe to toe, nostrils flaring, and the sheer drama of it was intoxicating: the terrible beauty of the conflict, the physical and stylistic mismatch between the two. Even though their skin tones were similar, Audrey exuded paleness and that strange, feminine kind of brittle strength—as if her power came precisely from the fact that she'd start crying if you put her under pressure. Meanwhile, Roshie was squat, pugnacious, bundled up, and looked like she was made from modeling clay.

"Hey Roshie," Jhanvi said. "You really are being a bit of a dick."

Roshie turned. Her eyes narrowed. "They're fucking idiots. We're two months out, they're doing trainings. All she cares about is being an influencer. It's pathetic."

"I know," Jhanvi said. "I don't disagree. But you're really at an impasse here. Let's get back to work, okay?"

Jhanvi would've savored her victory, except Katie came in like a toreador and jabbed, "We'll have to discuss this later, Medusa."

When Katie and Audrey had left, Jhanvi asked, "Medusa?"

"My fire-eater name. Everyone needs one. You should ask Henry for one. He's great at making them up. I don't understand it, the two of them. You and him are way better. I'm glad you won in the end."

"Won?"

"Glad he fucking dumped Titania. I mean poly is one thing. But she used him."

"You, uhh, really don't like her."

"She's fine," Roshie said. "I don't care. She's fine. I don't let her bother me."

Completely false, Jhanvi thought.

"Get out your phone," Roshie said. "Take down these measurements?"

"Me?"

"Yeah, you," Roshie said. "I changed my mind. Better to have you do some fucking work, so people know you're not useless."

They spent the next hour looking at clamps, marking which ones were corroded. Roshie read off the numbers to Jhanvi, who took them down on her phone. Jhanvi now had lines upon lines of notes, and in her spare moments she'd annotated them so that people besides Roshie and herself could read them.

Maybe this was what it was like to have a desk job: the work was dull and the cause was pointless, but it wasn't so bad if you were around people you loved. Like, by any objective measure, it was disgusting, when there was a housing shortage, to spend tens of thousands of dollars turning a huge basement into a sex dungeon, but the work had an immediacy that Jhanvi imagined was missing from all of the Trial By Fire members' jobs.

Amidst Roshie's shouting and cursing, the dungeon began to take shape around them. Partitions were lifted into place, like in an old-fashioned barn raising, and Achilles would crawl underneath, checking that the tracks were in place. Roshie didn't give a lot of compliments, but they did mean something. Achilles beamed when Roshie said he'd gotten way faster at this lately.

Henry wasn't doing a lot, just drifting around, moving toward Audrey, who was still filming in the back, then over to where some of the chill-out areas of the dungeon were taking shape, like the little hookah lounge and nonalcoholic bar. The latter was freshly painted with a stylized image of a woman burning at the stake, the flames turning into her long hair. This insignia had sprouted everywhere—it was on the sheaf of flyers that lay by the entrance: the burning witch was the logo of The Guilty Party.

"Hey, Perseus, come here," Roshie called.

That was Henry's fire-eater name. He drifted close, giving them both a smile, but his eyes dropped when Jhanvi tried to hold them. As far as she knew, the wedding was still on, but ever since the house meeting the other day, nobody had mentioned it.

"What should Jhanvi's fire-eater name be?"

"You have one, don't you?"

Jhanvi laughed. "Average," she said. "Yeah. It's a joke. I thought, what's the one thing no fire-eater would ever say. And it's the phrase '*I'm average.*'"

"Hmm," Roshie said. "I don't get it."

"I think you do."

"Hmm."

After a few silent seconds, Roshie said, "How're the wedding plans going? I've been thinking we ought to have it here."

Both Jhanvi and Henry were caught out. They shared a glance. Roshie was still bent over some clamps, measuring them.

"Yeah," Jhanvi said. "You still free tomorrow?"

"Totally," Henry said. "But it's a courthouse thing, right?"

"My friend Toni is coming to witness." Jhanvi felt Roshie stirring microscopically down, and she added, "Roshie is coming too. You have anyone coming?"

"No," Henry said. "I'll see if Audrey wants to come."

"So it's happening," Jhanvi said. "It's firm. Tomorrow."

The meeting at the co-op was also supposed to be tomorrow. Monica had sent her a plaintive text: *We can still make it work if you need to . . .*

"Totally," Henry said. "We're good."

The work crews had long since begged off, and now they were in a corner, lounging on pillows and beanbags, cracking open beers. Audrey and Achilles were together again, making out in a corner. Even icy Katie's face was gleaming as she laughed at something that one of the guys said and touched him on the chest. She flirted like a robot, laughing too loud, running through preprogrammed motions, but her just making the effort was enough for most men.

Jhanvi turned back to Roshie and caught a glimpse of her face, distorted by anger and hatred and pain, and some spark leapt between the two of them—for a moment, they became the same person. Jhanvi could remember feeling that exact same thing in the past. Could remember wondering: *Why doesn't he want me? Why does nobody want me?* Back then, when Jhanvi had still possessed hope, she'd been unwilling to accept the simplest solution. *I'm a tranny monster. It's no more exciting or complicated than that.* And while Roshie wasn't ugly, she gave off a relentlessly nonsexual vibe that was a particular turnoff in the midst of a sex dungeon.

Jhanvi followed Roshie, who was kind of stomping in her heavy boots, with her little fists swinging by her sides, and suddenly Jhanvi pounced, wrapping her arms around her friend. "You have so much value," Jhanvi was about to say—it was a bit of graffiti she'd once seen on the sidewalk—but Roshie fought free and whirled around. "What was that?"

"I . . . sorry."

"Don't do that!" Roshie waved a finger.

"Sorry. Sorry."

They stood there, with the long shadows framing them. "I'm really sorry," Jhanvi said. "I was just feeling affectionate."

"Well . . . I don't do that."

"S—sorry," Jhanvi said.

"I don't do that."

Jhanvi looked back. The circle looked pretty convivial and fun. People were lying out on rugs and pillows, someone was drumming. Intense conversations were leavened by casual touching. "Are you gonna hang out?" Jhanvi said.

"For this bullshit?" Roshie said. "No. I'm going home."

"Can I—would you mind if I stayed?"

"I don't give a shit. Do what you want."

8

Jhanvi stood by the stairs for a long time, thinking to herself, *I really should go. I should go. I should follow Roshie. She needs me, and that's the right thing to do. She is in pain, she's basically begging for me to follow her.*

In these situations, you were supposed to pretend you didn't know what the other person wanted, so you had plausible deniability—*I didn't know they needed me, they told me to stay!*

More than anything, Jhanvi hated people who didn't admit they knew what they knew. If she stayed here, she would at least admit to herself that she was doing a wrong to Roshie.

But she had also gone up the stairs so many times—staked so much hope on so many people, imagined so many saviors, so many people who'd made her think: *If this person is willing to just see me as I am, I'd be happy.* And in her experience, the gamble almost never paid off. Like when she'd taken that room from Monica, she'd thought, *Oh, this is a cool, wise trans elder. We'll learn from each other and have a beautiful intergenerational friendship.* But in truth, Monica had a full life and didn't need a new friend, so she never had an incentive to understand Jhanvi for who she was. Or take Henry—she'd come here intending to make him a co-conspirator in her marriage plan, and instead, he'd gotten more and more distant.

And Roshie was a particularly bad bet: prickly and hardheaded and judgmental and not a little selfish. Jhanvi was tired of wanting things from people that they were unable to give. She was tired of giving people the benefit of the doubt or of trying to convince herself that some job or some living situation made sense when she knew, in her heart, that she hated it.

There was something so freeing about not giving a shit. Like, this was fun! She was having fun here right now! So screw the future. She would stay down here and keep having a good time.

Okay, but one second. If I stay here, I can't be the old Jhanvi. I can't be whiny and resentful because people are suspicious of me. I need to win them over. To be my best possible self. To show them that I have value.

She stopped for a second, putting her hand on the wooden doorframe, which was pulsating from the thumping music. In college, she would've needed booze to get past this point. But now she put one foot in front of another, telling herself she would get through the door eventually.

"Hey!"

A man had come out of the dark, holding a plastic cup. He was shirtless, wearing just his boxer shorts. "Henry?" she said.

"Jhanvi!" he said. "You're back! Come on! Come on!"

• • •

She found herself sitting in a little circle with Henry and Achilles and some other guys. They were all shirtless, holding drinks, and someone offered her some, but she said no thanks. She'd shyly changed into a short leather dress and her very high heels, and she tucked in her arms, holding in her stomach, telling herself, *Everyone is welcome here, all bodies allowed*, even though she knew it was absurd. They chattered away, and Henry's shoulder rubbed against hers. He pawed limply at her thigh, maybe to get her attention, and said something inaudible.

"I can't hear you," she said.

Leaning closer, he said, "Hey. I think it's so great you're Roshie's friend."

"Yeah?" Jhanvi said. "She's great."

"Are you gonna go by Average?" Henry said. "I love Average. It's so funny."

"Nobody here laughs when I say it."

"Would you even want them to?"

The two of them had their heads together, and his hand was on hers. Her heart fluttered. He had a red cup by his side. In college, he'd been a notoriously bad party buddy, always abandoning her the moment they got to the party, to the point where she called him out a few times for ditching her. But now it was different. She was his—okay, let's use the corny word—his lover. She knew the things he wanted, knew how he liked to be abused and tormented and topped.

She threw her voice up into her head, trying to make it higher pitched without losing that fullness of tone. She hated trans women who sounded like sexy robots. "Hey . . ." she said. "So you're really going through with it on Monday. That's locked?"

"You're one of my oldest friends," Henry said. "Of course it is. Like . . . I am so proud of you, J. You've changed so much. Sobered up. Found yourself. It's really inspiring."

Her stomach quivered, and she lost that calm. "It . . . it is?" She gulped. He couldn't be flirting with her, here in the open, like she was an ordinary girl. There was a mirror lying on its side against the wall in the corner, reflecting her grotesque forehead, the inarguable mannishness of it, like she was a rock whose maleness constantly bled from its interior. The sounds in the room phased in and out, and she squeezed her legs together, stretched her arm, which was asleep from propping her up. Her entire self-image would explode if Henry was flirting with her right now.

"Yeah," he said. "It's so brave. And this plan—it's smart. I'm sorry people have been weird."

"So . . ." She couldn't help her voice cracking. "You're really doing it?"

"Mmmhmm," he said. "Katie is looking up some things for me, but yeah."

She twisted her lip. "What the fuck is her problem? Why is she messing with this? I genuinely don't get her."

"She's a mother hen. She's protective of her chicks. She'd do it for you too, if you were gonna enter a binding legal contract."

"No," she said. "No . . . that's bullshit. I hate people like her . . . they're so vacuous. They don't . . ."

She couldn't form her thoughts, and anyway she'd said the wrong thing. Henry had flinched away, and now she stretched, following Henry's gaze, and saw Katie whirling around, swinging two balls of flame. Some Arab music played, and a female voice wailed in another language. Katie twisted sinuously, the spinning fire making trails in Jhanvi's eyes. So stupid. Such a fire hazard. They could kill everyone here. And they called Jhanvi selfish? Henry didn't know. Henry had no idea. They wouldn't protect her. Not really. He hadn't even protected her that Friday at the meeting. He'd let them ambush her.

Henry lay back and laughed. There were guys and girls all around them, everyone touching each other, and Jhanvi sat in the middle, propped up on pillows, a little island. People were losing their clothing, but she had yet to see the moment at which someone went from clothed to naked. It all seemed to happen seamlessly, without discussion.

Henry dipped a wetted fingertip into a plastic sleeve of MDMA powder, then licked it off, and offered her the next hit. She dutifully refused, because everyone here knew she was sober. So she watched him space out, babbling vaguely happy nonsense, and then disappear into sensation.

"Hey," Jhanvi said. Henry was rubbing a hand against his own nipple with his eyes closed. "Hey." His eyes flashed open when she touched his leg. "Hey," she said. "How's it going?"

She moved to touch him, and her leg knocked over his wine, sending it across the concrete floor. Cursing, she threw some paper towels on it, wiping up, and when she came back from throwing away the garbage, some random guy—the white guy who'd been holding the bracket along with Xiao—was massaging Henry's feet.

She sat back down and said, "Hey, should I go?"

"No, no," Henry said. "It's okay."

"Hey," she whispered to him a moment later. "Hey, girl. Wanna do something?"

His eyes snapped open. "Just relax, Average. Just relax."

"Let's at least make out!"

The only time they'd hooked up before, at least in real life, she'd been drunk. Ever since, it'd all been mediated by the phone. She looked around at the room. Henry sat up, applauding, as Katie walked past. He reached out a hand, and she fell into his lap, her blond hair spilling over Jhanvi's shoulder. "You were awesome," he said. "Awesome."

The girl was all skin and long limbs, physically pressing into Jhanvi. She wanted to scratch the bitch. All around the room, people were making out. She hated them.

Katie's legs nudged her again. She and Henry were swallowing each other's faces, an ungainly ouroboros, and Jhanvi said, "Hey, watch yourself." She put out a hand, thought of pushing on Katie's bare back, and but decided against touching the girl.

Jhanvi tried to enjoy the hurt. Some people she knew were into being cuckolds—having other guys sleep with their girlfriends. The pain could be pleasurable—confronting intimately the notion you might not be a man, might be worth less than another. Jhanvi had imagined, sometimes, guys brutally abusing her, calling her a tranny, saying she was ugly, that nobody would ever love her. In her darkest fantasies, they took knives to her arms and legs or they tattooed slurs on her face.

If she'd been here, Toni would've said, *Girl, you're gorgeous— you're so tall and glamorous.* But Jhanvi knew it wasn't the case. She was objectively ugly—if she'd been sixty, she would've been one of the sad men you saw on sitcoms—the guy with big jowls and fishnet tights and a red wig. But she was relatively young, so there wasn't yet a place in the public imagination for someone like her.

As usual, her mind turned to hate. *I'll kill them all, light this place on fire.* But why was she mad? They just didn't want to have sex with her. That wasn't a crime. She was, in a way, a little glad for the slight: this was the kind of thing she needed to learn to endure. Not harassment, but its opposite—indifference.

• • •

Oddly enough, Audrey was on her computer, wearing a shirt for once, ensconced in a little nook away from the main party. She chewed on her pencil eraser and typed something. Jhanvi stood looking at her, head cocked. They were in the less-finished part of the dungeon: the floor around was concrete, with piles of boxes and pallets and lengths of wire. Audrey sat on a crate, her computer in her lap.

Audrey stopped typing and glanced up.

"Oh," Audrey said. "Hey."

"Hey. What're you working on?"

"Some emails," she said. "Project launch."

"I keep forgetting you have a real job," Jhanvi said.

"Yeah." Her eyes were tired, hooded and cold. She glanced back down at her computer.

"Uhh, I'll leave you alone." Jhanvi gulped, and she made another circuit around the party, feeling so much like a college kid again. Back when she used to smoke, she'd go outside to smoke a cigarette, nonchalantly, to hide that she had nobody to talk to. Then she'd put out the cigarette, make a circuit of the party, and go back out. Night after night after night, often drinking to black out, she would go to these parties, where everyone was hooking up and having fun, hoping to crack the code: *Why am I not like them?*

All these years later, she had concluded: *I am trans.* It was that simple. She'd wanted to be seen as herself, but she could only be seen as a man. And today she wasn't drunk! That was a leveling up. She'd come back to this city, introduced herself to people, made friends—even a few loyal ones, like Toni and Roshie. That meant something—it must.

But during her third circuit of the party, when she hurried past a grunting girl pinned down in a corner, a hand caught her arm.

"I am so sorry," Audrey said. "I should've told you, but I think Roshie's gone."

"Mmmhmm," Jhanvi said. "I know."

"It's really silly, I'm sorry, but since you're her guest . . . I mean it's only for safety, and . . ."

"Are you . . . are you kicking me out?"

"It's just, there's a training people need, to be safe, and to know consent, so people feel safe, and you haven't done it, and . . ."

"What consent?" Jhanvi said. "There's no consent. I saw Henry pull Katie down as she was walking past, then they started making out. She got all over me. Where's the consent?"

"It's just a rule."

"Like, just be real . . ." Jhanvi's eyes were wet. "Just be real. Just be real. Like, we can cut the crap. I'm a spare cock. Unwanted."

"No!" Audrey said. "We love you!"

"I'm disgusting, I'm a monster. I'm like something from a nightmare. I'm like Buffalo Bill, looking for ladies to skin."

Audrey's eyes were blank. Clearly not up on twentieth-century depictions of transsexual and transvestite serial killers. Jhanvi had watched that movie and had imagined someone making a movie where the skin suit worked—where it actually transformed you into a girl. That would've been edgy as fuck.

"Is something wrong?" Katie had popped up, holding the sides of her shirt closed over her chest without buttoning them.

Jhanvi's mouth twisted. "Oh, fuck this, I'll go home."

But Katie was a shark with an instinct for human blood. Maybe that's what you needed to be to succeed in the world. Jhanvi could feel the other girl dogging her steps as she walked toward the door, and, against her will, she turned as she reached the stairs. She heard a moan from nearby. The ventilators were off, and some blap-blap electronic music was playing, and everyone was horizontal, spread irregularly over circular red carpets, as if they were making out atop a giant pepperoni pizza. At that thought, Jhanvi's stomach grumbled.

"I'm sorry," Katie said. "I wasn't going to say anything, but you really can't be here. People don't feel safe."

"Like who?"

"Umm, me, for instance. You were very close to me earlier."

Henry stopped short, a few steps back. His Adam's apple bobbed as he gulped.

"You were touching *me!*" Jhanvi said. "And it sucked."

"Hey," Audrey said. "Average, is it?" The name, spoken by this girl, didn't feel funny. It felt true. That's how they really thought of her. Some average goon, nobody worth bothering about.

"Henry," Jhanvi said. "This is crazy. I'll leave, but this is crazy. Like, this is gaslighting. I *know* all of you. I was invited here. You're literally kicking me out for being trans and unfuckable. Nothing more. That's so . . . sick."

"I really don't agree with that at all," Katie said. "We have trans members."

"You have Synestra. She's gorgeous. Okay, it doesn't matter. I'll go, okay? I'll go."

And in that moment, seeing the relief on their faces, the little look they exchanged, she thought, *Why am I holding back?* So she straightened up to her full height—she hadn't even noticed herself cringing—and her voice dropped an octave, rumbling in her chest:

"But I just want you guys to know something. Hey . . . can you look here? Can I just say one thing? Maybe I'm a creep or whatever, but can I say something? Audrey, you're great and all, but you're also vapid. Like, nothing you say is meaningful. It's clichéd. *We need more love, more community, more lifelong friendship, nuclear family is a trap*, blah blah blah, we've *heard* it. You don't have community, you have a cult of personality. That doesn't scale. Other people can't do that. And it's built on fucking exploitation, Audrey. Lonely people. I mean, Roshie slaved for you all day. It's actually sick. You're gonna stand around saying I'm such a bad influence, and—"

"Jhanvi," Katie said. "Now isn't the—"

"Let me finish!" Jhanvi shrieked. "Katie, you know better. You're smart. Audrey is an idiot, but you're not. You see it. This is *wrong*. It's fucking oppressive. Henry is in love, so he's holding on even though Audrey treats him like *shit*. Roshie is so lonely she'll fucking pay money so you'll be her friends. That is sick. Don't you see how transactional that is? That is sick. You've normalized it, but it's so monstrous. And, finally, you're in the fucking Mission District. This building is full of brown people. You're smoking hookah here, in this building? You're *spinning fire*?! How many fire exits are there? What the fuck? You're putting people in *danger* so you can fuck. And Katie . . . Katie . . . Katie, me and Roshie are both dark people. Don't you see that? I mean it's absurd, I don't mention it because I went to Stanford so whatever, but I'm literally the most marginalized person here. I mean . . . do I have to point it out? Come on, guys."

Katie's lips were pursed, and her arms crossed, eyes hard. She was armored in her own righteousness.

Jhanvi's eyes were streaming tears. She suddenly giggled. She was literally on a staircase, had literally turned back. And she understood why they called it l'esprit de l'escalier. Because even the fact of turning around put you in a weak position. She gulped, her throat getting hot and stuck. A rabble of voices emanated from the rest of the dungeon. She trudged upward and stood outside, her heart hammering. She realized she was searching on her hip for a pocket that didn't exist, looking for cigarettes she hadn't carried in three years.

And, of course, she had more to say: she'd left out Henry. Fuck him. She had things to say to him too. But when she tried the door, it didn't budge. She was locked out.

9

That's when she realized she hadn't been searching for cigarettes, but for her phone. She banged on the door, hissing at them. It was infuriating to imagine them all confabbing in there, trying to deal with "the Jhanvi situation," while she just wanted to get in and get her phone.

She walked around the building, looking for a way in, and Adriana, the older woman from upstairs, waved to her. She waved back, and asked, "Can you let me in?" Adriana let her into a side staircase: a set of concrete landings. She banged on a metal door, but it didn't open either. Adriana asked her something else, but the woman only spoke broken English, and Jhanvi shrugged helplessly. She thought Adriana was inviting her upstairs, but Jhanvi shook her head, already mentally leaving the building.

She went out into the night and took a breath. Saturday night was in full flower around her: the two San Franciscos coming together on the sidewalks before parting at the doorways to restaurants and clubs. One San Francisco was dark-skinned, often wearing false lashes or long nails, sometimes wearing low-cut dresses, but more often in jeans and blouses. The other was tall, light-skinned, with straight hair, a carefully sculpted "natural" look, wearing leggings or a mini-dress. The dresses were tight and more focused on revealing the legs than showcasing the breasts. Both types of women were surrounded by retinues of a similar hue. Normally, the San Franciscos lived parallel lives: Valencia for the whites and Chinese and Indians; Mission for the Blacks and Filipinos and Vietnamese and Latinx. But on Friday and Saturday nights, white people invaded the nightclub district, jostling in the lines outside El Techo or Baobab—popular nightspots for darker people—queuing up to get into whatever fancy bar or yuppie dive or warehouse party was hot that night.

Jhanvi walked through the crowd in her short leather dress and high heels. A man held up a hand and she slapped it. Another followed her for a block, saying, "Hey, mama." And if she'd repeated these encounters to her friends, she would never have noted their race, but of course both men were dark-skinned. And yet she passed a group of tall white people, and she saw the slightest curl of one girl's lip, and a peal of laughter as she passed, and Jhanvi knew she'd carry the memory of that slight display of disgust longer than she would that of the overt harassment. She held her shivering arms close to her chest—her jacket and backpack and other shoes were inside too. She considered slipping out of her heels for the walk back to Lower Haight.

Looking down an empty alley full of colorful murals, her stomach lurched, but she tottered across the cobblestones, all by herself, feeling oddly safe away from the crowds. If she was to be murdered, at least let her be murdered alone. She took off her tall shoes and let them dangle from two fingers; now she walked barefoot, glancing down once in a while for broken glass.

The light and noise of Valencia smacked her like a sockful of quarters, sending her staggering. A police car idled in the bike lane, sending up spurts of siren noise whenever bikes tried to maneuver around it, leaving the whole street confused. Two cops were huddled around a Black guy sitting on the pavement. She moved on, didn't pretend to pay attention—certainly didn't film it, like you were supposed to these days. She wouldn't have even if she'd had her phone.

Perhaps it was because she'd done it, crossed that Rubicon, tried to play the race card, but she felt so adrift. She understood herself completely. She was, on the inside, no different from Katie or Audrey—she was merely less desirable. Her race and gender identity set her apart. But on the inside, she was lost—fully acculturated into bourgeois hegemonopatriarchocapitalism. Or whatever Katie would call it. She might *look* dark and *look* marginalized, but she had the soul of a skinny white girl who spent an inordinate amount of time worrying about the mild shifts in social dynamics within a small group of similarly skinny, wealthy, and well-educated white people.

The thought brought her a perverse joy. She might have no virtues to speak of, but at least she knew it.

She ducked into several pharmacies and corner stores on the way home. In one, the Indian clerk narrowed his eyes at her. "Are you desi?" he said.

"Hahn-ji, Uncle," she said. "Hum ke Hindustani."

He responded with a torrent of Hindi that she barely understood, and when he started coming out from the booth, she left, waving her arms, and kept walking.

By the time she'd reached the front door of their house, her fingers and thighs were numb, and her torso was sticky with trapped sweat that'd turned cold against her skin.

Then, of course, the fucking code didn't work. The code didn't work! It didn't work! She hissed to herself, trying it again and again, until the lock emitted a loud beep and flashed *ERROR*. After that, even the slightest touch led to another beep. Then a strange voice came out of the intercom: *Who is this? Who are you?* It must be from one of the other apartments.

Her heart beating fast, she stumbled away. People were thick on Haight, all the white techies out for the night. She bumped into one shoulder, and the man shoved her back, so quick she couldn't believe it. Normally tech-yuppies were terrified of physical contact and apologized preemptively for it. She staggered against the stoop, scraping her knee, and the tall guy in his baseball cap leered down at her, "Fuck off, tranny."

The words reverberated so loud in her ear, they could've come from inside her head. She'd literally never been hate-crimed before! And now, here, on the stoop outside her own house! He sneered, then he turned, putting an arm around another guy. Nobody else stopped or even looked. She may very well have imagined the words.

The bar was open, at least, and the bouncer nodded her through—"You're Toni's friend." Suddenly warm, half of Jhanvi's body began to burn, and her vision went white. She staggered to the side, reaching for the back of a chair to steady herself. After she could see again, every pore in her body disgorged its molecules of sweat, and she was suddenly a slick, smelly mess.

"Oh, sorry," she said to the pair of glasses in the chair.

"No worries," it said. "Hold on as long as you'd like." The man wearing the glasses leaned forward, going back to conversing with his date.

She made her way, practically hand over hand, to the far end of the bar. Toni gave her an insouciant wave, and Jhanvi waved back. The other girl had maxed out her femme self-presentation today, wearing foundation and lipstick and a low-cut top that showed the dark roots of her chest hair.

Jhanvi took over a stool, laying her head down on the bar. She raised a finger, and Toni said, "Long night? Where are your friends? I still want to meet them!"

"Ham—burger," Jhanvi said.

"Oooh, good, you're ordering now. The kitchen is just closing. One sec."

She zipped back with a paper sleeve of French fries. "These were left over." Jhanvi dipped them in the aioli Toni had brought and almost gagged, her throat was so dry, but she forced most of them down, and the glass of soda water cleared her airway. Toni blinked at her now. The bar was loud, and Jhanvi could only hear every third word, but Toni leaned far over the counter.

Jhanvi had to stop herself from looking down the girl's top. Gender was so weird. Toni had no breasts, wasn't on hormones, but Jhanvi still wanted to see her cleavage, though she'd have been totally uninterested in looking at a guy in a tank top.

"Everything okay?" Toni said.

"Locked out again."

"Shoot!" Toni said. "It's a busy night, but stay here! What're you drinking?"

Jhanvi took a minute. *I only drank two drinks the other day, and it'll warm me up. I'm half-dead. I need the booze. It's medicinal.*

"Whiskey? A cocktail?" Toni suggested.

"Yeah, to both."

Long minutes passed as Jhanvi assayed the room. Her legs were cold. And her shoes were under the counter somewhere, being kicked around by strangers. Maybe Toni had some socks she could borrow. She ought to venture out, check if Henry or Roshie were back, ring the doorbell, borrow a phone. A thirst for alcohol wasn't usually a physical thirst, but now her mouth was filled with saliva, and her throat and chest burned preemptively.

The first drink was exactly what her body had needed. Her fingers and thighs regained life. Her insides uncoiled. She took it and put up a finger. Toni smiled and said, "One more?"

"My cards are with my phone."

"Don't worry. Want to borrow my phone to get ahold of your friends?"

For the next two hours, Jhanvi drank steadily and fiddled with Toni's unfamiliar Android phone, with its strange menus and browsers and applications. She tried logging into Facebook, but everything was two-factor protected, and she couldn't pierce the barrier of her own identity. She resorted to emailing people randomly at first.lastname at gmail. She seemed to recall Roshie's email was something like that and so was Henry's, though she couldn't remember for sure.

Jhanvi went back to the front door of the house and rang the doorbell several times, then beat on the door. She repeated this cycle at least twice, moving back and forth between the bar and the house. One time, looking back, she realized a different bouncer was at the door, and her heart sank. "I don't have my ID! But I'm not gonna drink."

He said, "Sorry."

"I was just inside."

"We card at the door after eight."

"I know Toni!" Jhanvi said. "She's my friend."

The bouncer took a breath. Then he opened the door, looked inside and exchanged a few words, then waved her in.

Toni checked in a few times, but tonight was busy, and Jhanvi was absorbed in her quest, drinking steadily, not thinking very much or feeling overly sad. It was odd, how alcohol made stress go away. Whatever happened didn't matter. This was good stuff. Good stuff. No regrets.

Then the lights flashed, and the bar emptied out, and people were milling around, and Toni said, "Hey, I've really gotta go if I'm gonna catch the last train. You want to come stay with me? My dad is a lot, but we'll be okay!"

"No," Jhanvi said. "I managed to reach them. They're on their way. Here's your phone."

"Keep it," Toni said. "You'll give it back."

Jhanvi said, "That's the dumbest thing I've ever heard. Just take it."

"Well, at least take some cash," Toni said. "Are you sure you won't come with me? I'll write down my number—just ask anyone for their phone."

Then Jhanvi was clutching a piece of paper and some bills, and Toni hugged her tightly. "Be safe," she said. "Your friends are really on their way?"

"Yes," Jhanvi said. "Literally ten minutes."

"I can stay . . ."

"No," Jhanvi suddenly just wanted *Toni gone.* "No, don't

worry. Anyway, I don't want you outed to my horrible room-mate—she's on the warpath against the person calling the cops on her neighbor, Chris. The homeless guy. It's dumb."

"Well . . . you'll text about tomorrow? Don't you need to get ready for that? Come on, actually, seriously, come home with me . . ."

Jhanvi demurred, and the reason bubbled out of her mind. She wanted to drink more alcohol, and she didn't want to do it around Toni right now.

The moment Toni was gone, she walked into a corner store and bought a bottle of whiskey—it cost her all the bills, or at least when she came out, she didn't have any money anymore.

The first swig made her stomach spasm, and she vomited on the ground, right outside the house. So she scampered off, away from the crime scene. She had her shoes in one hand, and she cradled the bottle in the other as she skipped barefoot through the street. She would crash with another college friend, Simone. Jhanvi didn't have their number, but years ago, she'd gone to a party at their house. She went to their block in the Mission. It was even colder than it had been earlier, and she shivered on the way, not meeting the eyes of the passersby. When she arrived, she walked back and forth, trying to remember which house it was. She pushed a doorbell, but a strange woman came to the door, some early-forties yuppie type who just couldn't figure out why Jhanvi could possibly be at her door.

Nothing about this experience was exciting or interest-ing; Jhanvi had no stake in any of it. She walked back to the Haight—now it was almost midnight—and she banged and pounded and yelled at the apartment door and got no answer. The whiskey bottle tumbled off the stoop during the commo-tion and shattered on the ground.

"Fine," she said. "I quit. I'm done."

She went to a corner store run by another Indian guy—or perhaps the same one as before—and she asked for a phone. But Toni's phone number was gone! Jhanvi stood there, searching all over her body, unable to find any pockets, any place where the number could've conceivably gone.

"Do you need help?" the man asked.

"N—no." The only number she could remember was her parents' US phone, and she gave it a call.

"Hello?" said the voice of her dad.

"Daddy," she said. "Can I get some money? Or a hotel room?"

"What is this? Where are you? Are you in Sacramento?"

"I'm in San Francisco, Daddy." Even as she begged, her voice was high pitched and feminine, she noted to herself. Tacking to one side, still holding the manager's phone, she let a hunched-over man waddle past her to the counter and mumble for something. The manager shouted at her, "Stay close, don't go near the door."

She walked back and forth, and the manager caught her by the arm, pulling her behind the counter. He told her to sit down, then went back to his customer.

"I'm just visiting friends, but I'm locked out."

"Are you drunk?" he said. "How much have you drunk?"

"Just a few," she said.

"No," he said. "No more. You've been told. Stay out all night, if you must. No more for you."

"Wait," she said. "Can we—can we just talk?"

The wheedle came easily into her voice. Maybe this was simply gender practice, the cold part of her brain thought— an attempt to be daddy's girl.

"I cannot talk when you are drunk."

"I'm just locked out!" she said. "It's not my fault! If I had my phone, I'd be fine."

"No more new phones. We've bought you too many now."

"You haven't gotten me a new phone in two years. I bought the last one on my own. Come on, can you put on Mummy?"

"No," he said. "She doesn't wish to speak to you."

"Daddy," she said. "Daddy, Daddy. Give me Meena's phone number."

"Who?"

"Yadav-Uncle's daughter. She lives in San Francisco."

"Nothing doing," he said. "You cannot prey on more friends."

But Jhanvi heard a voice in the background, imagined her mom saying, *Let her do it. The second generation should learn how to support their own too. And anyway, she will need these contacts when we are gone.* Then her dad said, "Fine, take down a number."

Jhanvi scrabbled for a pen, snapping her fingers, and the man put one into her hand. She jotted the numbers down on a pad. When the call was up, she put the phone down, and she was about to hand it back, when his rough fingers touched hers.

"Vo tumhaare paapa the?" he said.

"Mmhmm," she said. Then he spoke faster, and she understood the gist: he was asking what she'd done. And she didn't have the words in Hindi, so she explained in English, then. He clucked his tongue, shaking his head, and she huddled closer on the stool. She gave him piteous eyes and asked for a chocolate bar. He grimaced, then reached up and over the counter, slithering through the glass case, surprisingly sinuous despite his age, and brought back an Almond Joy. Not even a Hershey's bar. The little bits of coconut filled the grout between her teeth and graveled her tongue, making her feel surprisingly full.

Then she made a call to Meena. "Hey, uhh, can I crash on your couch?" Jhanvi said.

"Uhh, what?" Meena said. "Who is this? I'm in Japan right now."

"Jhanvi, I mean Nikhil," she said, trying to lower her voice.

"Oh yeah!" Meena said. "Sorry, I moved up my trip. I should've given you a key before I left. Do you still need somewhere to stay?"

"Yes!" Jhanvi said. "Where's your building, who has a key?"

"Where are you? Are you in a bar? Are you drinking again? Isn't it the middle of the night there?"

"No, no, I have a friend who works at a bar, and they were helping me out."

"What?"

"Do you have a key to your place? Can I get in?"

"Can you wait a minute? I'm going into a meeting."

"I, uhh, how long . . ." Jhanvi said.

"I have meetings all day. Can we text? I'll try to get in touch with my doorman. Can you stay put?"

"Sure."

"What's going on with you anyway?" she said. "What're you doing in SF? Why didn't you get in touch? Your mom is so worried."

"I'm, uhh, I'm just moving here."

"To do what?"

"I don't know. I was—" Jhanvi didn't mention the marriage plan. This girl knew her mom, after all.

"You don't have to worry—your mom swore me to secrecy. I won't even tell my dad about the trans thing. That's fine with me. I grew up in SF, after all. Like, everything's fine with me. But do you have a job?"

"No," Jhanvi said.

"And . . . are you gonna get one?"

"Not sure."

"Come on, you've gotta do something. Didn't you have one of those do-gooder jobs before?"

"Don't you have a meeting?"

"I'm texting my doorman. He's telling me some shit about needing your ID on record. Can you email him your ID?"

"I don't have one," Jhanvi said.

"Shit," she said. "Okay, well, can I book you a room for the night? Nothing fancy, how about like . . . I don't know, the Fairmont in Nob Hill."

"Nothing fancy?"

"I mean, is that a problem?"

"The Fairmont is extremely fancy."

"Sure, sure, whatever. I forgot you're a hippy. Oh yeah, the do-gooder shit. Plenty of jobs like that in SF. You went to a good school—you're trans—they'd love having one of you."

"No, I don't want to do nonprofit stuff anymore. They're just as bad as anywhere. And they don't pay you."

"Good girl! Get a real job!"

The proper gendering shocked Jhanvi so much that she stood up straighter, and she even raised herself on her toes. She smiled, and the thought came to her: *Oh yeah, I forgot that I actually love Meena.*

"Hey," Jhanvi said. "We should hang out sometime."

"Yeah, yeah . . . I'm never around actually, and when I'm there I'm super busy—dates dates dates, gotta find the father of my kids."

"I thought you were engaged."

"Yeah, I thought so too," Meena said. "But no such luck."

"So let's get together and talk about it!"

"Sure sure sure, maybe in a few months, when I've got time."

Jhanvi went cold. It had happened that quickly. She remembered, *Oh yeah, that's the reason we aren't friends. She has no respect for me whatsoever.*

"Just let me know about the hotel room, okay?" Jhanvi said.

"Totally, totally."

"I'm gonna start walking there now. It's not too far."

"That's pretty far!"

"I've done it before," Jhanvi said. "It's nice out. Whatever."

Jhanvi's legs ached from the walking she'd already done, but she made her way east through the city, walking a block or two north of Haight Street so she would be out of the craziness. These were quiet neighborhoods, with few enough cars, and she thought, *Okay, now that I've learned to beg from random Indians, I can survive pretty easily in this city. That's good to know.* She made it up the tall hill, gasping, with a stitch in her side, and her face shiny from sweat—her makeup must be a horror right now. Crossing a major thoroughfare, cars whizzed past, and she looked downhill, into the cold heart of downtown, where cars queued up to enter the shiny artery of the 101. Beyond the highway were the tall, wide boxes of an industrial district, and then the long black sweep of the bay, interrupted only by the lights of container ships.

At the Fairmont, they hadn't heard of her, under either her birth or her new name. She tried calling her parents to get Meena's number again, but this time they didn't pick up, and eventually the hotel kicked her off their phone. It was nearing one a.m., and she thought, *Okay, it doesn't matter, let's go home.*

• • •

Passing the darkened display of a store window, she toyed with her hair, pushing her bangs over to hide a slightly receding hairline. She went back to the house and pounded on the door and rang the bell, but there was no answer. Leaving, she went to a CVS, just to be warm, and spent a half hour walking around, playing hide and seek with a security guard. She'd read that in San Francisco it was possible to steal freely, and neither the guards nor the police would stop you, so long as what you took was worth less than $999, but when she grabbed a candy bar, the guard yelled at her and she dropped it, running into the street.

She walked back to the house and stood in front of it, but then the bright idea came to maybe have some sort of intercourse. In the three years after that one hookup with Henry, she'd had six or seven hookups, all with men, all anonymous and unhappy and mediated by the internet, and she'd never done more than let them suck her dick, but she'd been celibate since transitioning, and she'd never yet had sex as a woman-type person. Maybe it would be different!

Guys cruised for sex out in Dolores Park, by the Muni tracks—or at least that's what a friend had once said.

She walked out there, looking boldly into the eyes of the few passing groups of people—it was really late and not many were out, but she saw groups of Latino people, the real people the neighborhood belonged to, and that gave her an idea. She knew that streetwalkers worked on a street way to the west—Capp, maybe, or South Van Ness.

So she walked past the park, now through empty streets, looking down when cars passed close, thinking *no, not yet.* The walk was long, perhaps an hour, and a man jeered—"Hey baby, hey baby what are you"—and kept walking with an ugly smile. In the past, she'd almost never been harassed, she was too tall and blocky, didn't really read as a woman, but lately with the weight she'd lost and her hair grown out, maybe that was changing.

Now she was in a little dark cluster of houses at one end of an alleyway. Then at a corner, she spotted a girl in a very short skirt, high heels, and a white tube-top, standing looking bored. Jhanvi quickly glanced away, walked past, then circled around to the other side of the block, and saw another woman, almost identical to the first. Both were brown, clearly Latina, one a little taller, the other short and chubby. Jhanvi took another block or two, and then she stood on the corner, smiling into the dark. Her stomach churned with nerves, and now her head ached a bit, and the wind bit into her skin.

Cars flashed their red lights in the distance, then they started again. The girls entered and exited the yellow pools of light. Jhanvi stood for half an hour, and a car came rolling past. It slowed down, but she didn't look, and after a few minutes it went past.

Her stomach growled, and she was wickedly thirsty. The chain pharmacies were closed, but she happened to pass an all-night corner store. The man behind the counter was brown and weathered, not unfriendly, in a sweater with thin glasses that had golden rims.

"Hey," she said.

After a few seconds of browsing the aisles, her hands were full of chips and water. She kept glancing at the front, where both the man himself and a big glass wall stood behind her and all the liquor. A plan occurred to her: bold in its audacity, simple in its execution. The mark of a perfect adventurer. She'd ask him to get down the liquor for her, and then she'd snatch it up and steal it.

So she came to the door, and looking to the side, she said, "I want a bottle of whiskey."

"Illegal," he said. "Come back in the morning."

"No, I, uhh, I can't wait," she said. "I'll pay you more."

"It's illegal. I could get a ticket."

"Not if you just ... give it to me. I can pay you later."

"That's not how liquor licenses work, my honey," he said. "Why don't you go home?"

"I'm locked out," she said. "Come on."

His eyes glinted. Then he stared at the door. He looked there for a long time, and then she found herself crouched in a corner, behind the display of chips, squatting awkwardly on her high heels, her knees almost touching the ground, with one hand bracing her against the shelf, the other spitting and working at his dick.

She barely understood how a blow job worked—most of her tricks preferred for her to top them—but she plunged onward, blindly, licking and slobbering, running her tongue and throat over it as he moaned and grabbed her hair and looked awkwardly at the door.

"I'm coming," he said.

She didn't know what to do, so she kept going until the liquid had shot into her throat, and she swallowed without tasting it. Her whole face and the front of her chin and collar were drenched, not with cum but with spit, and she held out her hand at a distance before slyly rubbing it against the chip shelf.

"Here," he said. "What you want?"

"Umm ..." she said. "Whiskey?"

A bottle was shoved into her hands. Not inexpensive: Jack Daniel's. She was tottering into the alley when the man came out, looked at her, and handed her a paper bag to put it in. Her stomach growled, but the door had already slammed shut. She hadn't felt dirty during the act, but the disrespect after—the way he'd shoved her outside, like trash—that made her want to kick down the door. *Fuck him, I am powerful! I'll get my revenge on the world. I'll burn it all down.* She remembered now other hookups, the greasy, discarded feeling after men had cum. And now that moment from earlier came back to her, when she'd lashed out at the others, but left Henry alone:

You were my friend. You knew I'd never dated anyone, had a relationship. Knew I was a lonely person. You had a sacred duty to be good, to talk me through it, to give some care, and if I fell in love, then so what—you had a sacred duty to talk about what we did, to normalize it, to make me not feel so disgusting, like some phone sex bot. I think with the marriage I was begging you to—to feel or to show—to say—that I had some value. I would never treat someone else like that, like a cheap toy, to be picked up and handled and thrown out. They'd be an expensive toy at least, something I'd value and store on a shelf.

She tottered blindly through the neighborhood, drinking from the bag, then found a darkened porch and climbed onto the steps. She was cold, so she found a newspaper and tore it open, placing it down under her.

She was special and free. Special because of that freedom from doubt. *Oh Daddy, if you could only see the specialness of Alice.* She was like that character in that famous Russian novel who was convinced that if he killed himself, it would free all of mankind and nobody would ever need to feel despair again: *There will be a new man, happy and proud.* She understood Russian novels now! The insane self-regard of those characters, their feelings of destiny.

Obviously, if anyone heard her thoughts, they would laugh. Or think her sad. But she would do great things. Her week of travails had made her lose a few pounds—her clothes were loose. If this went on, she would be gloriously thin. Forget about being a monster, being a mountain, being unloved. She would find a mark, get those surgeries, change her body, become like Audrey, efface her personality.

Fuck them, she thought. *Fuck them. The nice thing about being a con woman, a scoundrel, an adventurer, is that you need not ask for permission. I will die before I ask again for someone to love me as I am. I deserve this. I deserve it for relying on Henry, on anyone. With God as my witness, I will never go hungry again.*

She sat on the porch, lost in dreams—she would turn into something else, something provocative and powerful—she imagined herself on a yacht in a tiny bikini, surrounded by admirers; in a small dress on a black carpet; leather jacket in a smoky bar, grabbing men's glasses and smashing them on the ground, making them hate each other—*I'll be the Estella to my own Miss Havisham—I'll destroy them!*

A man came out and started yelling at her, talking about his newspaper, and she walked halfway down the block, but then she came back. He was on the phone.

"This is San Francisco," she said. "They won't come, bitch! This is our city! This is *our* city! I'll sneak into your house during the day and shit in your closets. You'll *never* be safe."

She turned to walk and heard the footsteps behind her, the man was running. She started to run, but fell, pain in her knees and palms, grit everywhere, the bottle flying—she grabbed for it, unbroken. The man was shouting, she got up, shaking, screamed at him. Windows opened. "Shut the fuck up."

"Techie asshole!" she said.

"I've lived here thirty years!"

"So have I! I was born here!" she said. A lie. She'd been born in Boston, while her dad was in grad school.

She heard the blit of a siren and got spooked, scuttling off. The sirens were closer now, and she kept running, then ducked into the overhang of a driveway, into a narrow pool of shadow, and she stood there, her stinging palms pressed to the painted garage door, and drew a breath.

Moving slowly, she drank more. Her mind spun, time passed, she went back to the daydreams, laughing to herself, then laughing harder. She staggered onward, found herself in a familiar alley, spent time trying to squeeze through wrought-iron bars, and her hands and knees—they *hurt*.

Then she was somehow inside the garden, next to a water fountain, and she sat alone on a bench, drinking and thinking and holding her knees together, trying to cover one with the other, to stanch the flow of her blood.

10

Before banging on the door, she tried to input the code one more time, and it flashed red again. Hissing, she banged on the door with her palm. "Open up! Open up, you rich fucks! Open this fucking door! Techie assholes! Open up!"

"Shut up!" The voice was deep, not one of her housemates'.

Jhanvi hefted the empty bottle of Jack Daniel's and threw it behind her so it shattered on the ground.

"Open this fucking door! Open it! Open it!"

When the door flew open, she saw Henry, bleary eyed, in his sneakers and jeans and hoodie. "Jhanvi!" he said. "You're here! Hold on, let me get Roshie on the phone. She's out looking for you."

She lunged forward, scrambling past him, going on hands and painful knees up the stairs.

Jhanvi heard the distant jangling of voices. Katie stood in front of her, arms crossed. "That is unacceptable," she said. "You haven't ..."

Her voice came in and out, and when Jhanvi tried to step around her, she interposed herself. "Respect for ..."

"Katie," Henry said. "Let her lie down."

"Get out of my fucking way!" Jhanvi said. "Get out! Get out! Get out or I'll ..." Her throat closed up and her body broke out in shivers. She scrambled past Katie, ran up the stairs, and threw herself into Roshie's bed. Voices came through the door: "We should ... sleep ... tonight ... when will ..."

Jhanvi stuffed earplugs into her ears and put on an eye mask. She burrowed her head into the pillow and the room rotated around her.

• • •

"Hey . . . hey . . . what happened to you?"

Jhanvi blinked a few times. Roshie's smudged glasses were inches from her face. Jhanvi bopped forward, kissed her on the forehead, giggled, then grabbed her own head. Something was inside her brain, burrowing its way out.

"Are you . . . have you been drinking?" Roshie said.

Jhanvi blinked a few times. "Not really. A little. A lot. But . . . can I just sleep? I am so so so sorry. Can I just sleep?"

"Yes, I just need to know . . ." Roshie said. "You're . . . the sheets are bloody. Did someone hurt you?"

"Scraped my knees. Fell down." Jhanvi blinked a few times. When she moved, the sheets stuck to her bloody knees. She tugged at them, and they came away, leaving two rust-colored spots.

"I need to go downstairs really, really quick," Roshie said. "But can you tell me what happened? We are so sorry. That'll never happen again. I am being—I'm not good—just can you tell me, please?"

Jhanvi's face flushed, remembering those minutes on her knees. She didn't even remember which corner store! It could be any of them. She'd gone into more than one, she was sure. So many middle-aged Indian men, so much like her dad.

"I, uhh, got locked out. I knocked on the door a bunch, didn't have people's numbers. Decided to stay out all night until morning. Yeah, kind of had a sobriety slip. Where were you?" Jhanvi said. "I came and knocked so many times. Where were you?"

"Inside," Roshie said. "I'm far from the door, and I had my windows closed! I am so so so sorry. I hate myself."

Jhanvi sank down into the bed, but she was disgusted by the sheets now. She drank some water from a glass next to the bed, slopping it on her neck and chest. A half-eaten bag of M&Ms was by the bed, and she squeezed the remaining candy into her mouth, then settled back down in bed, trying to sleep again.

She woke up to Roshie noisily pulling out the couch bed on which Jhanvi normally slept.

"No, no," Jhanvi moaned.

"It's for me tonight!" Roshie said. "Don't worry! And don't worry about cleaning, I can wash your sheets in the morning? Or now, if you're up."

"Morning."

Jhanvi staggered to the bathroom, stood over the toilet, willing herself to vomit, but she wasn't quite there. She got a notification, saying the time for her wedding was coming up, but she ignored it and went back to bed. Over the next few hours, her phone kept beeping, announcing its sadness at her utter uselessness, until it too gave up on her.

The next day, Tuesday, she hung on, gray faced, lying on the sweaty mattress, her head throbbing, if anything, even more than the previous day, until Roshie finally left—though not before writing down the new code on a notecard.

Jhanvi's backpack was there, and she dug in it until she found her phone. Toni checking in on her: *Excited for the wedding! Should I come to your place first? Or right to city hall?*

A few texts from Roshie: *Hey it's 5 in the morning, and you're not home. Are you okay?*

I woke up Hen, and he says you left the party at like 10? Where are you?

Just let me know if you're safe

A message from Henry: *I'm staying home all day if you need me. Just text or call! Hope you're safe.*

Then an unknown number—a message from just a few hours ago. *Hello Jhanvi, I think that I owe you an apology. Don't want to intrude, but let me know when you want to talk -katie*

And, finally, a string of messages from Meena: *did you manage to check in to the room? They charged me so I assume you did.*

They charged me for another day! What's going on over there? Not cool!

I've been calling my doorman trying to get you on the list, but if you're on one of your crazy benders maybe you should stay where you are.

Also, I can get you a job maybe, but you get one shot with me—after that I won't be able to help you find anything—and I refuse to just give you money

Jhanvi rubbed her head vigorously. *Thank you. I actually never managed to check in.*

What??????

They hadn't heard of me.

The bastards charged me!!! How're you doing? You okay? You drunk?

I'm sober. Fine. Thanks for helping. You were, like, the only person who would help me unconditionally like that.

Don't be dramatic. Our families have known each other a long time. Okay, girl, let's schedule a lunch for sometime soon so we can talk about your future.

Sure.

Next week? Tuesday? Noon?

Uhh, sure.

Thank god ur ok. I've been googling dead trans girl san francisco for hours.

Jhanvi got out of bed and pulled off all of Roshie's sheets and threw them into a corner. She didn't feel as entirely terrible as she might've expected. Sort of . . . energized, actually. Empowered.

Raiding Roshie's mini fridge, she started opening candies and sodas, throwing them into her mouth—the taste was exquisite—little explosions of flavor in her mouth. Her entire body felt raw and sticky. She squatted in a corner, between the bed and the wall, eating. All her emails went directly into the trash.

That afternoon, she alternated between binge eating, furious rumination, and masturbation.

Jhanvi's head hurt like a tiny creature was inside, burrowing its way out with stubby little fingers, making it through the flesh using pure abrasion, cutting through her skull a nanometer at a time, slower than a river eroding rock.

But she'd forgotten how pleasurable it was to masturbate while hungover. The dryness of her skin, how it heightened the sensation of every nerve and sliced briefly through the pain, and how with each orgasm, it got harder and harder to cum, but her penis got more tender, making the experience even better.

Years on hormones had completely changed her sexual responses—all her sense memory of hungover masturbation was from before, as a man. Now the feeling was unbearably intense, no longer centered on the dick itself, but almost like her penis was some sort of joystick or touch screen, something that mapped to the rest of her body without precisely being a part of it. The sensation made her legs weak, suffused through her aching head and body. God, she loved this. She was an outcaste, beyond all human law, a personage, an art monster, something defined by rules of its own creation. *You have no clue. You'll never understand. There is a very loud amusement park right in front of my present lodgings.*

She giggled at the interpolation of that quote, then reached up, pulling savagely at her nipple, wondering if it was time to get them pierced—she'd been waiting for breast implants, perhaps—but she'd likely never have the money for that—probably wouldn't live out the year, if she was being brutally honest. *I am spiraling, spiraling, spiraling, and I deserve to be put out of my misery.*

There was no moral defense for her life. She gave no value, served as a leech on better, more productive people—but she didn't care. She simply didn't care. She was outside of society, living in a state of nature, part of the war of all against all. And if they would lock her out, if they would lock her out in the cold, if they with their hundreds of thousands, or millions, of dollars, if they wanted her gone, if they had announced that they were her enemy, well then... She smiled to herself, and she imagined a camera above her, looking down on her body not as it existed, with her hairy skin puddling underneath her on the sheets and her sad, lank hair static charged and standing straight out, framing her boxy face, but as it would someday exist—striking, long haired, with a heart-shaped face, high cheekbones, and big, shining eyes. They could do amazing things now, with needles and saws and fat grafts and implants—turn her into a cyborg, beautiful and deadly, like the assassin killing machines in Japanese cartoon shows.

She didn't understand how it would happen, but she would be beautiful. She would have charisma. She could feel the hesitancy being scoured from her bones. *I am a leech. I am an adventurer. I will avenge myself upon the world for the crime of being born.* The words were so dramatic that they made her giggle: they were the kind of thing you said about a girl born fatally sad and attractive, desperate to be loved, and yet wary of that love. A femme fatale.

She shot bolt upright. Or at least she did in her mind. In reality, any slight movement of her head set it to throbbing. She couldn't believe those words hadn't come to her sooner. She was a femme fatale! That was her calling. That was her purpose.

Jhanvi tossed herself into the shower and then threw open the windows. She was just shimmying into a pair of jeans when her phone buzzed. It was her newest saved contact: Katie.

you ok? Roshie was looking for you.

I'm fine. She was on the verge of texting *I lost my sobriety.* But she pulled back on the words, falling silent instead.

I'm really sorry about the door. It was programmed to change codes on Sunday, and I forgot to warn you. Sorry. Where did you sleep? I can reimburse your expenses.

Jhanvi was about to write *That's bullshit. You didn't forget.* But the femme fatale shouldered aside that instinct. Oh yes, now she remembered her old behavior, the way she'd pissed off her parents and relatives and a lot of her friends. The alcohol had reawakened an atavism. And that part of her brain generated a number:

A thousand should cover it.

That's a little high, Katie said. *Where did you stay?*

The Fairmont, Jhanvi wrote. *They charged me for two nights too for some reason. You can venmo this number thx.*

Can I see a receipt? Katie said. *That's quite a lot of money.*

Are you serious? Jhanvi wrote. *I fucking blew a guy so I'd have somewhere warm to be, and you're haggling? What is wrong with you*

Jhanvi stared at her last words. She was going to let out a stream of insults, but her head ached way too much. The thing was, Jhanvi always did too much work for Katie, always rushed ahead and got angry or confrontational too fast. But Jhanvi needed to dance across this conversation. She needed to tire Katie out, pricking her just enough so that she'd keep rushing around blindly.

I am so sorry you had a hard night! Can I come up?

Let's talk later, Jhanvi wrote.

Please, I think it's really important to clear the air, and I have a tough work schedule for the next week. This is our last free day to really address some of your issues. Audrey and I both want to speak to you about the events of last night

Oh, of course! She'd called them out. They'd need to beg her forgiveness, ease their liberal consciences. Audrey probably didn't care, but the accusations must really be pricking at Katie right now.

All right. What're you thinking? Jhanvi wrote.

They made a date to meet at the Copper Barrel. It was a bar much fancier than where Toni worked, just a few doors past.

With a shaky hand, she dabbed her face. Half her net worth

was tied up in this one brand of Yves Saint Laurent foundation—sixty-eight dollars a bottle—that perfectly matched her skin tone. She normally hated to use blush or highlighter, because if she fucked up, that was the cost of a whole coat of paint wasted, but this time, she rubbed more creams and powders into her face, sculpting it, wiping away smidges of jaw and nose. What she'd realized about makeup was that what you see is what you get. The thing you're seeing in the mirror is exactly what other people are looking at. You don't *want* it to be invisible: you want to create real, visible effects. If you treat it like a painting exercise, as if you're literally redrawing the image in the mirror (within limits, of course), then you can achieve startling results.

When she was finished, her eyes didn't look so dead. She blinked her long lashes then grimaced, looking at where the mascaraed tips had left little black lines on her upper brow. Her phone buzzed. She hadn't even started her lips yet. The lip liner went awry, giving her a Joker smile, and she almost snapped the pen in half. And yet, the desperation was a delicious meal. Thoughts bubbled up—*You're stupid. You're no femme fatale. You're an ugly bitch.*

Jhanvi went down into the den, pulled back the sliding door, and sat at Audrey's vanity. With her head pounding, she started testing concealer colors on her arm and holding them up to the mirror. She found a shade that matched, and she used it to correct the mistake, then pocketed the tube. When she spotted a bottle of gin in the corner, she reached down and took a swig, which cleared her head a bit. Fifteen minutes later, her lips were cranberry red, and no matter how she pouted or frowned, it was impossible to look completely pathetic.

She had somehow avoided stealing more alcohol. She was about to head out when she got a text from Henry. He'd written:
ARE YOU DRINKING AGAIN????

The question made her stomach burn, but then she read what was attached below it. An email Roshie had sent to the entire house.

Dear House,

I am extremely disturbed by how Jhanvi has been treated. On Sunday, someone waited until Jhanvi was out of the house and then changed the door code. She couldn't reach me, and as a result was out all night.

This is totally not okay. It's actually illegal, under the rent control and housing regulations of San Francisco— we are not allowed to kick someone out this way. We have to call the sheriffs if we want someone removed. And there's a reason for that: Jhanvi couldn't find other housing, and she showed up this morning covered in blood.

I don't know if she was assaulted, but I do know she relapsed under the strain and lost two years of sobriety. I couldn't get out of her exactly where she'd been or what she'd done. It's possible she doesn't know herself.

This is not how either this house or this community should function. I keep telling Jhanvi that we are about more than sexual experimentation and wild parties. She doesn't believe me. She says we're spiritually bankrupt, and that all our talk about being best friends is just to make ourselves feel better about the selfishness of our lives. She says we fool ourselves into thinking we'll be there for each other, but really, we know it's a lie, and that's why we never actually try to rely on each other for anything important.

She doesn't expect anything better from you than this, but I do. Jhanvi is a trans woman of color. She was kicked out of her house by family, kept on a long transition timeline by inadequate health benefits, and her only hope, as she saw it, was to basically come here and beg us for help.

You know what she thinks? She thinks you're kicking her out because she's ugly. Because of her in-between body. She said that nobody has ever made her feel more valueless—nobody. Not her family, or the Indian community—nobody. That you reduced her to just a body, and because you found that body to be wanting, you kicked her out.

But she is more than a body. She is a thoughtful, intelligent person, who is full of warmth and insight, and I will not let you treat her this way. If anyone—and I mean anyone—tries to kick her out again, I will call the police on them and charge them with violating the SF housing code.

Please, let's be better. I expect to discuss this further at the next house meeting, but until then, I'd like you to be only open and welcoming toward Jhanvi.

Thanks,
Roshanak

11

Jhanvi tried to sink into the sidewalk and to move her feet along an invisible line, swaying her hips as if she was a real woman, and she was rewarded with a muttered word from the corner.

"What?" Jhanvi said.

"I said you're a faggot." The guy, Chris, narrowed his eyes. "Faggot. Faggot."

Jhanvi walked onward, feeling a little twitch in her side, imagining the man sticking a knife into her kidney.

Her stomach churned as she passed Toni's bar—god, to name one of many places she never wanted to go again. She also had to cross the entrance to the CVS. She made eye contact with the security guard, her face burning, but couldn't remember if he'd been there the other night when she'd tried to shoplift.

The day was brisk and windy, and the sun didn't warm her skin. Her woolen duster flapped around her legs and hips as she walked into the bar. Right away, she spotted two figures sitting in a booth. Audrey, in her work clothes—jeans and a blazer over a T-shirt. Katie was more dressed up: she wore a complete little skirt suit, along with three-inch pumps. Audrey had her hand on Katie's shoulder.

They were sitting in one of the windows, and, shielded from the wind, Jhanvi finally felt the warmth of the sun on her skin, which made her head throb.

"Hello," Jhanvi said.

Both of the girls were wearing sunglasses. The sun was orange and low over the buildings across the street. Jhanvi slid sideways in the booth, trying to get her head into the shadows.

"Oh hey," Audrey said.

"Are you hungry?" Katie said. "Did you want anything?"

"Sangria," Jhanvi said. The two girls looked at each other, and Jhanvi felt a spasm in her stomach.

"I'd prefer if you were sober for this," Katie said.

"Just for the beginning," Audrey said. "So we can clear the air." Her voice was higher than Katie's, and she smiled widely. "It got really tense on Sunday."

Jhanvi felt totally unable to match the tone of whatever conversation she was in. The bandages on her legs suddenly burned, and a chill went all the way up her legs and back. Her head hurt so much, and her throat was harsh and raw, like someone had gone over it with a cheese grater.

"Why do you think we're here?" Katie said.

"Oh my god," Jhanvi said. "Stop. Please. Just get to the point."

Even Katie's slow blink was gorgeous: acres of eyelid sliding up and down, thin as the membrane of a bat's wing, and just as sinuous and alien.

"After you left on Sunday, we spent a lot of time introspecting about your presence, and why it made us feel uncomfortable. It sort of took over the night. I think, ultimately, we came out stronger, but a lot of strong emotions were felt."

"I had strong emotions too," Jhanvi said. "Strongly strong ones."

"Do you know what exactly was so disruptive?"

"I called you out? I don't know," Jhanvi said. "Can we please skip to the end? What is the upshot here?"

"Henry reminded us you've never been in situations like this before. I think that I should apologize, in particular, because I assumed you were more experienced in alternative social circles than I think you are. But Henry says that was, in all likelihood, your first play party?"

"What?" Jhanvi said. "I lost my virginity at a bathhouse in Berkeley. He knows that." After she'd hooked up with Henry in college, she'd mulled for a year over the potential that she might be gay. She'd gotten drunk and high one night and driven up to the bathhouse, hanging around for hours until she got the courage to proposition a gnarled stump of a man sitting in the sauna.

Katie's voice went on, inexorable and flawless, almost monotone, her head shifting slightly, and her eyebrows making little flutters. Audrey took her hand for moral support and introduced murmurs, perhaps to soften the tone. Katie told Jhanvi that many members of the group had a history of trauma, and they'd objected to a stranger's presence without it being discussed.

"But Roshie invited me."

"She left, however," Katie said. "And in any case, usually invitees aren't just friends. They've been intimate with a member of Trial By Fire."

"But . . . you guys have tons of strangers at your summer party. That's, like, the point."

"Different events have different boundaries."

"Okay, so, whatever. I didn't know the rules. Roshie invited me. You kicked me out. I was mad, whatever . . ." Jhanvi's throat was getting raw. She wasn't prepared for this. It was grievously unfair. She hadn't *done* anything. "You . . . you were the one who touched me! I was sitting with Henry, and you started . . . you were basically kicking me."

"No I wasn't," Katie said.

"But . . . you were. I was there. You did. I didn't consent to that."

"If you'd gone to the training, you'd kn—"

"But I wasn't invited to any training! Nobody told me any rules. Shouldn't Roshie be here?"

The bar was loud with the midafternoon crowd, drinking their flights of beer, chirping with each other about their weekend adventures. She looked around at the wooden walls, the little pioneer emblems, the wagon wheels and old maps and flags. On the other side of the bar, a boy was slouched forward, staring at the table as a girl in a cardigan and sundress lectured him. Jhanvi ought to grab him and say, *Let's go. Let's just escape right now.* But she was rooted in place.

"I don't mean to accuse you," Katie said. "I just want you to know that harm was done. Traumas were reactivated. It wasn't racism or transphobia. We'd have done this for anyone."

"Fine—" Jhanvi muttered. "Are we done?"

"Of course!" Audrey said. "I am so sorry, we just thought talking somewhere neutral, not in the house, would be—"

"It's not true," Jhanvi said. "But whatever. It's not true. You wouldn't have done it to a cis woman. Kicking a cis woman out of a sex party. Never. Would never happen."

"That's not true."

"Who then? Who did you do it to?"

"I can't name names, but it's happened."

"Carmen? She was like fifty. And fat. I know your dirty laundry. Henry and I are friends. Fuck you guys."

"I'm sorry."

"You can fuck who you want," Jhanvi said. "That's your right. But don't *lie* to me. I hate you fucking *liars*. Would I fuck me? No. I disgust myself. But don't blame it on *rules*. Don't say I caused trauma. Fuck you."

"Well, you're right," Katie said. "We can choose. And you're acting very entitled right now."

"I'm saying what a thousand people wish they could say. You didn't see Roshie that night," Jhanvi's voice cracked. "You don't think she went home and screamed into a pillow and imagined disemboweling you with a corkscrew?"

"That is—I think we're done here," Katie said.

"You are *liars*," Jhanvi said. "You are liars."

"Let's go."

Katie stood up, gathering her bag in one motion. Audrey scooted out. She started to say something, but Katie was already headed for the door.

"Hey, look," Audrey said. "I hear what you're saying. It's not true, but I hear it. I don't look like Katie, but I . . ." She trailed off. Jhanvi towered over the girl, whose shorts showcased her muscular thighs.

"And?" Jhanvi said. "Should we gram this for your fans? They're all just like me, Audrey. Half of them fucking hate you."

Jhanvi sped out the door. *Those bitches were gonna stick me with the check*, she thought. She intended to walk around the block a few times, but she got a flutter in her stomach and picked up her pace, almost running, until she was at the apartment's front door. She didn't breathe clearly until she'd put in the door code and the light had turned green.

12

Two days later, Roshie woke her at six a.m. "Come on," she said. "Get dressed."

"What?"

"We're headed to the woods," Roshie said. "I'm not leaving you behind."

"Haaaaaaah?"

"Our visioning weekend. To emotionally prepare us for The Guilty Party?"

"Mahhhhh?"

"Come on. Come on. I am *not* letting you out of my sight. I *told* you this was coming."

"How can I keep track? You guys are gone *constantly*."

The members of Trial By Fire had turned weekend getaways into an art form, with a portable generator and a fancy satellite uplink system that gave them many gigabits of internet no matter where they were. Most didn't even bother to take vacation days anymore—they just "worked from home" up in Lake Tahoe or the Lost Coast or wherever the group happened to be that weekend.

"Anyway, I'm sponsoring you for entrance into TBF, and this is our intro-to-new-members event."

Jhanvi sat up, groggy. She went downstairs in her dirty sleeping clothes and stood in the kitchen, drinking coffee. The house was a whirl of activity. Somehow all kinds of equipment had appeared out of the individual rooms overnight, and now Katie was going around with a clipboard, checking labels.

Henry came into the kitchen, but wouldn't meet her eye. She'd texted and called him multiple times over the past few days, pressing to reschedule their courthouse appointments. She'd even banged on Audrey's door and tried to question her. No answer whatsoever. Finally, last night he'd sent one of those long heartfelt emails about how his life was so confused right now and he was so sorry for leading her on and he'd refund her any costs from this trip. She'd been half-drunk and hadn't possessed the energy to tell him to fuck off with his phony offers of financial aid. After all, despite being offered a receipt, Katie still hadn't reimbursed her for the money that Meena had lost.

"Hey, Henry," Jhanvi said.

"Oh hey," he gave a shallow smile. "You're looking good."

She rolled her eyes.

"No, really," he said. "You've really blossomed. I think the city's been good for you. Where'd you get those shorts?"

She was wearing gold lamé shorts she'd found in the house's "free store"—old, stained costume clothes left behind by folks who'd moved out. She snorted.

"Yeah, suck my dick," she said.

"Whoa, hey," he said. "I'm sorry. Guess it's early ... but, I mean, if you want to talk ..."

Achilles came in behind him, clapped Henry heavily on the shoulders, and exclaimed over the coffee. "Oh, thank you god. It's so early." He poured some coffee, then held out the carafe to Jhanvi. "Want any?"

She raised her cup, displaying the contents.

"Hey, Jhanvi!" Achilles said. "I heard you're joining TBF. That's cool. How'd that happen?"

"Roshie is sponsoring me."

"Cool," Achilles said. "Has she ever sponsored anyone, Perseus?"

Jhanvi rolled her eyes. "Isn't Roshie called Medusa? That's so spot-on."

Henry chuckled. "Maybe you should be Pegasus."

"Bellerophon rode Pegasus. You don't even know your own myth?" Jhanvi said. "God, that is such a fire-eater thing. You guys are so . . ." *Vapid*. But she trailed off and never said that last word.

"No . . . it was Perseus," he said. "I looked it up."

"Roshie is already Medusa," Achilles said. "Maybe you *should* be Pegasus. That'd be a little triangle? I love how that happens. I think names have such power, don't you?"

"I'm Average."

"Oh whoa," Achilles said. "No you're not! Why would you say that?"

"She's joking," Henry said. "Average is obviously exceptional."

"Obviously," Jhanvi said.

"Still . . . *Pegasus* is a great name," Achilles said. "You should be called 'Exceptional.' I'd love that for you. I can totally see that. Well, Exceptional, can I call you that? I—"

"No," Jhanvi said. "You cannot."

"Anyways, I—I can't say Average, sorry. Happy to camp with you, though! Medusa is so awesome. She's so handy. It's, like, so awe-inspiring. Any friend of hers has my vote."

"Don't worry," Jhanvi said. "I won't get in."

"Hey, hey . . . see, that's the Average energy. I really don't like that. We've gotta talk more about that. Are you on the visioning board at all? Maybe our chemschedules will sync up, and we can chat."

Roshie kept a fancy spreadsheet where everyone listed what drugs they were going to take and when, along with their particular requirements and preferences, so that jobs could be assigned, and there could be a minimum number of safe and sober people around. Jhanvi hadn't listed herself—she hadn't done anything during her San Francisco bender besides drinking.

"I just meant it won't come to an open vote. Don't you have one of those sorority-style entrance deals where any member can blackball anyone else for any reason they want?"

Achilles looked at Henry. Then he slowly said, "Well, I wouldn't put it like that . . ."

"Katie is definitely going to blackball me. I mean, if it's not her, then it'll be Audrey, but it'll be her. Katie's at least braver than the rest of them."

"What did you say?" Katie popped out of the dining room. Her hair was tied back into a long braid, and she wore a sports bra and yoga pants. "I heard my name."

Everyone looked down. Henry said, "Oh, nothing . . ."

"It's okay," Jhanvi said. "It wasn't an insult. I called you brave."

Katie's smile faded. "Okay," she said. "Well . . ." She shook her head, and then she ran from the room. Achilles pursued her. Henry took a look at Jhanvi, and then he too went into the dining room. Jhanvi heard low voices, and then the murmuring of the two boys.

Katie had been crying a lot lately, ever since their angry meeting at the tavern, and her tantrums required quite a bit of cosseting from the house. Roshie wouldn't tell her the details, but Jhanvi got the sense that her continued presence in the house was creating a lot of argument.

Now that the marriage was off, Jhanvi didn't really have a reason to stay, but she'd made a conscious decision to put as much pressure on these people as possible. Maybe they'd pay her to leave, or something. Or she could sue them: Roshie claimed she had legal rights under the rent-control law.

In a way, it was insulting. Katie had expected that mere social pressure would somehow drive her out into the street or send her home. She didn't seem to get one simple fact: Jhanvi was a fucking transsexual shemale monster who'd once been kicked out of her own parents' house. No trio of skinny yuppies could possibly break her.

Jhanvi got up and stood in the doorway.

"It wasn't an insult," Jhanvi said. "I might be able to bully these others into letting me in, but you at least aren't stupid. You know that kicking me out now will save trouble later."

"Jhanvi," Henry said, briefly unfolding himself from Katie's arms. "Can you not pour fuel on this?"

"But . . ." Jhanvi stopped herself. Shaking her head, she went back into the hall, where Roshie and Achilles were arguing about the sound setup.

Jhanvi shivered as she assembled a bag to take with her. She hated camping. She paused for a second, then she fished out a bottle of whiskey from the back of one of Roshie's bookshelves. Stashing it in her backpack, she went and stood on the landing and waited for everyone to finish packing.

• • •

There were two cars, and Audrey, Katie, and Henry claimed one together. Achilles was about to get in along with them, but Jhanvi waved at him. "Hey . . . come with us. You can convince me to change my name."

"Hmmm," he drawled. "That is something that needs to happen."

When the other car pulled away, Jhanvi hissed, "Yesss . . . can't believe we snagged noble Achilles for Team Average."

"Hey . . ." he said. "Do you know why Katie was so emotional?"

"She hates me, and she's a brittle white girl, and the feelings are shaking her apart?"

"Nah, it's something else. Katie doesn't let that stuff bother her. I wonder what it is . . ."

On the drive north, Jhanvi had a great time, holding forth, making fun of Katie and how the girl couldn't even bear her own internal contradictions. They stopped on a random block for a long minute, and Achilles came back with a stack of pizzas.

"What's that for?" Jhanvi said. "You guys don't cook when you're up there?"

"For the mushrooms. So there's no accidents this time."

"Last year on this trip, Achilles used our tea kettle to make mushroom tea," Roshie said. "Everyone who drank tea from it for the rest of the weekend got a threshold trip."

"That's not my fault! I cleaned it!"

Roshie continued, "Leading to a new rule: no using any of our cooking equipment for drugs of any sort."

"I still think there was ergot in the bread. That was the original shrooms, you know? St. Vitus's dance, you heard of that?"

"Okay, Achilles, you seem . . ." She wasn't sure how to finish the sentence. He was a friend of Henry's from work, and she'd had a nodding acquaintance with him for a few years, without ever really getting to know him. In reality, he seemed extremely dim, even by fire-eater standards. But, oddly, he made her feel safe. Despite knowing Henry for over ten years and hooking up with him and notionally being great friends, she hadn't felt easy with him since the day, four years ago, that she'd told him she was really a trans woman. Even the memory made her burn with rage. He'd assured her there are lots of ways to be queer, and she didn't need to lock herself into an identity. The first of many let's-just-pump-the-brakes conversations she'd had with friends and family over the next few months. But he was one of her closest friends, and he was queer himself! She'd trusted him to understand!

"Achilles," she said. "You seem cool. This whole thing with Roshie holding the stash, you think it's absurd, right?"

"I'm not holding it," Roshie said. "It's my stash."

There was a tackle box in the back of the car with each compartment labeled with drug names, including their exact dosage, price point, and origin. Roshie bought all these drugs from the Dark Web throughout the year, keeping them on hand for the whole camp. She even stocked some generic sildenafil (Viagra) that she vended assiduously to half the men in the camp.

"Why can't people buy their own drugs?" Jhanvi said. "It just feels wrong."

"Shit," Achilles said. He'd taken a bite of pizza. "Is this okay? Should I have, like, asked your consent before dosing in the car?"

"Are you on the chemsched?" Roshie said. "Yeah? Then it's fine."

"That's another thing. You guys keep talking about the chemsched and being safe and being responsible, but what about Rosh? Who's keeping her safe? She's holding felony weights of drugs. And all the evidence is in a spreadsheet!"

Roshie fluttered her fingers in midair, then let them land on Jhanvi's hand. She pressed down, her hand hot on the delicate skin that covered Jhanvi's knuckles. It wasn't totally comfortable, and Jhanvi tugged a bit at her hand, but Roshie didn't let go. They were driving past Alamo Square—the famous Painted Ladies, with their boxy bay window façades, colored red and gold and blue in a nineteenth-century imitation of Renaissance Italy's imitation of Rome's imitation of Greece's imitation of Babylon, which had imitated Eridu in turn, and Eridu, perhaps, had stood alone, the first city of them all—just as, once, three hundred thousand years ago, two apes must've held hands naturally, unselfconsciously unaware that another ape was watching them, jealous of their intimacy, and practicing the gesture for itself, ready to unleash it upon some unsuspecting friend.

Jhanvi liked Roshie—was grateful for and amused by her advocacy. *After all, I'm doing the same thing myself, defending her. So why shouldn't we be friends?* And yet, it didn't feel natural. Their intimacy was too practiced, too sterile. During their hours alone together, they rarely spoke, only to have these fragrant, heavy conversations the moment someone else was around.

"Oh, there's Syn!" Achilles said. "Pull over."

Jhanvi's heart lurched. She'd been dreading this. They stopped near a lanky, brown-skinned girl with bleached-gold hair. The girl was wearing long trousers and a red blouse tucked into her waistband. Between the Hepburn trousers and the Lauren Bacall wave of her hair, she looked like something from a Golden Age Hollywood movie.

The girl waved languidly, then she bent to the window. "Hello, are you Roshanak? Oh, and there's Achilles, hello. I'm Synestra."

"Hey," Jhanvi said. "We've met."

"Oh, yes, remind me of your name."

Jhanvi's cheeks twitched, but she pulled back the grimace. "Jhanvi."

"Pleasure."

The girl went around back to throw her bag into the trunk. Synestra was the other trans girl in their social scene. She was one of those ambiguously creative people. Perhaps a poet, perhaps a musician, perhaps a journalist, but mostly just a professionally sexy person.

She squeezed into the back next to Achilles. "Well," she said. "Can you please make sure the pizza doesn't slide onto me?"

"Want some?" he said.

"It's mushrooms," Roshie said.

"No thank you," she said. "Now if it was MDMA . . ."

"There's some in the trunk," Jhanvi said.

"Ooh," the girl said. "Well, I'll wait. Don't want to be that slut who shows up already loaded—it's so déclassé."

As they drove, crossing north through the city and over the fog-wreathed Golden Gate Bridge, Jhanvi couldn't help twisting around in her seat to look at Synestra, who was on her phone with her headphones in. She saw Jhanvi looking and pulled out the headphones, which were the old-fashioned wired kind.

"And how long have you been in town, Jhanvi?" she asked.

Jhanvi hated how happy she was that Synestra had remembered her name this time. Jhanvi had wanted Roshie to tell Syn there was no room, and that she ought to ride with someone else, but Roshie had insisted it would be rude. Jhanvi had begged, *Please . . . I just don't want to be around her. It makes me so dysphoric,* and Roshie had said, *This isn't a good side of you.* Another tiny insult, another instance of not-quite-rightness. Jhanvi was certain that Katie would've instantly culled Synestra for Audrey.

"Just two weeks," Jhanvi said. "I was gonna hire someone—I mean marry someone—for their health insurance—trans benefits."

"Ahh," she said. "Who?"

"I don't know. Someone."

"Henry," Roshie said. "Isn't it still Henry? They were going to do it last Monday, but there were some delays."

"Mmmhmm," Jhanvi said. "Sure. Delays." She'd been telling herself that Henry would've found a way to back out even if she hadn't gotten locked out and relapsed on Sunday.

"How fun," Synestra said. "It *would* be Henry, wouldn't it? Do you top him?"

"They're not together," Roshie said.

"He's such a submissive little thing," Synestra said. "Always after me. Something of a fetishist? A chaser, I think they're called."

"You know what they're called," Jhanvi said. "Don't be stupid. And I've stopped being able to do that: I always have trouble keeping it up."

"He has little blue pills he carries," Syn said. "Always offering them to me. Be careful around that one."

"Yeah. Sure." That settled it. He wasn't the least bit interested in Jhanvi. Not in person, at least. They'd spent weeks in the same house together, had literally gone to a sex party. It was fucking devastating to be living with a gorgeous guy with a tranny fetish, and he was like, *No, not you, sir, not you—I prefer this handsome golden chit with the Lauren Bacall hair.* Fuck him.

Synestra made more noises about how Jhanvi was absolutely his type, but Jhanvi tried to tune the other girl out. Henry hadn't made so much as a move in her direction in the two weeks she'd been here. He'd made out with Katie while sitting next to her: you don't do that to someone you're interested in. They hadn't had the *We're better off as friends* conversation, but that was only because Jhanvi hadn't made an issue of it. She was such a fraud—a fraud inside a fraud—pretending she'd ever had anything with Henry—had ever been anything besides a college acquaintance. Pathetic.

"Hey," Roshie said. "Katie and Audrey are transphobic as fuck, right?"

"Uhh," Synestra's eyebrows furrowed. "I'm not sure—I've never gotten that impression from them, but it wouldn't surprise me if they were. What have they done?"

Synestra's lips were painted a deep crimson, matte and clearly defined in a way Jhanvi's would never be. Her skin seemed utterly smooth and without pores. She hadn't even transitioned that long ago! Jhanvi had met her once before, when she was a very gay boy. But somehow she'd fallen very easily into womanhood. Nor could you be like, oh, she's one of these rich trannies: she had been rejected by her parents for being gay, had to drop out of college, done sex work. She was the actual thing: the girl who'd aged too quickly, who pretended to an innocence she didn't have. An authentic femme fatale. The only false note was her pretend upper-crust accent. But the falseness was only slight: she hadn't allowed her posh accent to cross the line into overtly mockable Britishness.

"They tried to throw Jhanvi out onto the street," Roshie said. "Even after I told them she's my life partner."

Jhanvi grimaced. "They don't want me around while they have sex. And they have sex everywhere. So, you know, it's no big deal."

"Not here," Roshie said. "I'm not gonna—things won't get out of hand like that. I'm just glad I can finally say it. I've been in this group for three years, and I am so tired of them ruining every one of our events. Audrey is the problem, you know.

Things weren't like this before she bought all those fake follow-ers on Instagram."

"Now, now," Syn said. "I'm told at least half of them are real."

"She turned everything into content," Roshie said. "It's sick. She's got to project to everyone that she's so free and perfect. And she ruins people's lives. Look at Henry. He is such a good guy. It's really sick. She's basically exploiting us, monetizing us. But not this weekend. She promised to respect my and Jhan-vi's boundaries and keep her stuff private."

"So I hear . . ." Syn said.

In college, Jhanvi had spent so many hours pretending she understood sex, knew about it, longed for it, though she didn't actually long that much, and she hated those who were having it. It was all wrapped up in her repressed gender iden-tity, she assumed. Or she was just a loser. So she sympathized with Roshie's disgust and hatred for the other members of TGP, but it was uncomfortable, the way defending Jhanvi had allowed Roshie to turn that hatred outward and cover it in self-righteousness about how the house's overt sexuality was harming and triggering the two of them. Of course, Katie had done the same, turning her disgust for Jhanvi's body into exag-gerated claims of harm.

"Your house always has so many feelings," Synestra said. "Don't you get tired of it?" She addressed Roshie but was look-ing at Achilles, who was staring out the window humming to himself, watching the fog that blew off the Pacific Coast. They were on Highway 1, hugging cliffs near Bolinas. A bicy-cle emerged from the mist, and Roshie stepped on the brakes.

"Whoa, did other people see that thing?" Achilles said.

"Is Achilles okay?" Synestra asked. She pronounced the name "Ah-sheel."

"He's on mushrooms," Jhanvi said.

"I'm gonna take it all away from her," Roshie said, doggedly continuing the previous topic. "That's what we're discussing tomorrow, at the big meeting. We're gonna split everything up. Audrey can choose, either she gets the event space or the house—she's got to give up one. I'll live go and live in the other with Jhanvi and Henry and whoever else wants to come."

"Mmmhmm," Jhanvi said.

"Interesting," Synestra said. "Such drama."

And now it was Synestra's turn to go silent. A while later, Jhanvi looked back again and Synestra had her earphones on and was deeply focused on her phone.

• • •

Roshie and Katie got into a miniature argument at the campground over whether or not Jhanvi should have to help cook. Roshie insisted that as a newcomer and someone not part of the collective, she shouldn't have to work. Katie broke down in tears and started yelling. Audrey came out ready to defend her friend and shook a finger in Roshie's face. Roshie said, "Fuck you, I'll get the locks changed at the event space."

After it was over, Roshie went around stringing up the sound system, outcaste from the rest of the group, while Jhanvi trailed along with her.

"Hey, umm," Jhanvi said. "You know I don't actually think you should cleave the earth in twain."

"What's mine is mine," Roshie said. "I paid for it."

"Well, yeah, but . . . don't be such a prude. At least not on my behalf," Jhanvi shrugged. "I like the sex. The sex is cool. Without the sex, TGP is nothing."

"It's selfish. And exclusive."

"Roshie," Jhanvi said. "These are, like, your friends."

"No," she said. "Like, it's something I've been ignoring for a long time. But they and I are so different. Every time Katie cries, I want to kick her in the teeth. And can you believe Audrey? I'm pretty sure even Henry wants her gone."

"No he doesn't," Jhanvi said. "She's certifiably hot."

"She's not. She's really not. She's just topless all the time so men can't tell the difference," Roshie said.

"All right…" Jhanvi said. "Look, you know…I really…how can I put this? I really like what you're doing for me. And don't think I don't see the Laurent element." She snapped her fingers. "It's just like when, uhh, like … when that financier, Marcus, tries to defend the Prince of Mars by bribing all of Congress."

"You're no Prince of Mars," Roshie said.

"Ouch," Jhanvi said. "I meant … it's heroic in the same way. You've taken on a cause. But … hmm … the thing is, just like the financier was doomed to fail, so are you: You just cannot force a thing to act against its nature. Rich, young, attractive white people are gonna get together and create sexy parties. That's their nature. And they're gonna work to expel anyone who seems like a beggar at the feast. If you want, you know … if you want more than that … if you want someone who'll notice you're lonely and … in pain … these aren't the people who can give you that."

Roshie looked up from her cords and cables. "I know that's how you feel. But I just don't accept that. It's the partying that *makes* them selfish. They don't get that only people with healthy souls can really enjoy a party—for everyone else, it's an empty performance."

That was a line straight out of Laurent, when the Prince's lover goes to a ball and watches the glittering people and says, *But don't they understand that the only true ornament is an untroubled soul?* Jhanvi had loved that passage, underlined it as a kid, and sworn she'd always stay true to her innermost self. But she hadn't, of course, because "an untroubled soul" was meaningless bullshit.

"First of all, I wish you could understand how correct I am," Jhanvi said. "And the second thing is…I like these people. I like the sex, and how free and effortless they try to make it seem. Sex isn't, of course. It's awful, and complicated. But if a group of people can make it seem simple, that's a beautiful thing, even if they have to do all kinds of ugly, exclusive shit to make it work."

The strange thing was, Jhanvi meant it. She *did* like them. Liked Katie the most, oddly enough, perhaps because of her principles—her unwillingness to be buffaloed by charges of racism. Something about the open hostility, it'd freed Jhanvi from the effort of pretending to hate these people. She didn't understand the psychology of it, precisely—or maybe she understood it too well: they'd rejected her, and now she wanted in.

"You're just being cynical," Roshie said. "You don't believe that."

"I have contempt for them, obviously, because the way they talk is so pathetic and false. But . . . look at them . . . they're beautiful." Jhanvi nodded toward the crew of people crowded around a fifteen-foot geodesic dome near the RV. Audrey was hanging from the center in some ropes—she was wearing leggings and a skimpy leather halter top. Katie lay on top of the dome, arching her back, her blond hair, released from its braid, flowing down and fluttering in the wind.

"That's stupid," Roshie said. "I'm the one who built that fuck-ing dome. And it's the same dumb aerial fabrics routine every time, and we have to applaud like we care."

"It's not stupid," Jhanvi said. "It's light, and it's fun. You get together, you make some high-sounding noises, you take drugs, you dream of better things and explore your individuality, and then, when you need real help, you go to someone else. Your family. Your people. That's how life works."

"That's not what you did," Roshie said. "You came to us."

"I was stupid," Jhanvi said. "I had no plan. I just wanted adventure. It could never have worked. I'm basically a week or two from giving up."

"Fine," Roshie said. "Then fuck you."

"Roshie," Jhanvi said. "I really like you."

"No, I mean it, fuck you," Roshie said. "I'm a hundred times smarter than you. You're some dumb, basic bitch. Fuck you."

"Roshie," Jhanvi said. "That's all true. You're really special. I hope you know that. You've got . . . integrity. I just . . . if you want to use that integrity . . . this isn't the place to do it."

"Leave me alone."

"Roshie . . ."

Jhanvi heard her friend growl, then she dropped an armful of cables and stomped off toward the car. Jhanvi stood motionless for a moment, wondering whether to follow her, but then she heard a peal of laughter from the dome and headed back toward it.

13

Without thinking too hard about it, Jhanvi ate a slice of mushroom pizza—Achilles said he would cover her for the cost of the drugs. And a moment later she thought, *Well, I guess I'm not sober anymore*, so she ate another piece. Within an hour, her stomach was tight with psilocybin cramps. She'd done this so many times, in her prehistory, that she automatically associated the discomfort with impending euphoria. She staggered slightly into a field, clutching her cardigan around her shoulders, laughing. Katie was in the open field, swinging balls of flame. Achilles was already naked, his cock and balls shaved completely bald.

"Hey, hey . . ." Henry said. "What's going on? Are you on something?"

The sun was caught between his teeth, and that made Jhanvi laugh. "No."

For once, Jhanvi's brain was sped up, quick enough to make moves—it was like the spectator part, the thinking part, had shoved aside the driver, who moved on instinct, and said, *Here, let me try*, and now with the drug, the spectator was using its foreknowledge and planning to take a neat path through disparate obstacles. She *had* taken mushrooms before—many times, dozens upon dozens, but usually in secret, in college, holed up in dark rooms, screaming into mirrors at the sight of her own ever-shifting face.

"Oh okay, okay . . ."

Jhanvi heard a buzzing around her, the words piercing her, breaking in and out. "Is she—is she—why did we—"

"It's okay." Henry's breath brushed across the hairs on her ear.

Hallucinogens could proceed on many levels, she knew—if you allowed too much silence, you got deep into your own head, transcended social realities, and the earthly world stopped making sense—she didn't want that level. She wanted the level where you looked at pretty lights and laughed at dumb jokes.

Her jaws moved. "Leave me, leave me, save yourself."

"It's okay, come on," he said. "I remember you like to keep it a secret, right?"

He was dragging her to a tall, bearded man who was drumming in front of a fire, a dog barking next to him. The man was shirtless, sitting on a stone, with a few other shirtless guys around. Henry offered her a spot on a log.

"You'll probably want to be touching trees, speaking to the Earth."

"That doesn't speak to me."

She rubbed her own head. She wanted to be touched, and the thought came to her: *I literally always want to be touched, and yet I never just ask for it.*

"Here," Jhanvi said. "I need you to touch me." She pulled on the loop of Henry's belt. He tried to get away, but she pulled again. "I need you." Eyes swiveled to her, but he took a place on the log, the man next to her moving.

She wrapped her arms around him immediately, holding him tightly, her eyes closed, and he whispered, "Don't worry, don't worry, I'm here."

He was probably on mushrooms too, and she was ruining his trip. But maybe he needed this. Their needs would mesh. She slid down onto the ground, her head lying against his side, her arms around one of his hairy legs. But in a moment, she realized her mistake when she heard his voice talking to some other girl who had taken her place on the log.

She wanted to tug Henry back, but instead she got up, tottered to a card table, grabbed a handful of chocolate-covered nuts, took a cup of wine, and stumbled off into the distance as she heard a sound like banshees howling. The trees waved eerily, and children and dogs played across the field, near other tables, in other stories.

• • •

Her walk took endless time, and in typical mushroom fashion, she lived and died in those epochs. She started to freak out, wondering where she was, why she had done this—her mind screamed again and again *This is not a game this is not a game this is not a game*. And then a figure jogged up and stood in front of her, and she saw again those dark eyes, that simple gaze, like a dog's—Henry had arrived.

"Hey, hey, why'd you run off?"

"I want to walk."

"Okay..." Henry squinted. The wind sucked at her ears. "But can I come with you?"

"I don't need you to babysit me."

"Except...I'm happy to. You've done it for me...remember?"

She swayed a little, couldn't remember, had a vague remembrance of branches coming up out of the ground and encircling her, then consciousness broke through. Yes, once. She had sat with him as he raved at the moon.

"Okay."

"You're so, like, independent," he said. "It's no wonder you and Roshie are such good friends. I'm really glad you have each other."

"But we don't."

"Come on," he said. "She likes you. I can tell. You know, it takes her a lot of time to know someone. Hey...hey...where you going, come on." She plopped down abruptly by the base of a tree, and her head grew into its bark, melding spatially with the wood. He threw a coat around her, and she pulled it off.

"Hey." She felt his breath on her cheek and his hand on her neck. "Hey. You okay?"

"Yeah, bro," she said. "I'm just on drugs."

"K."

"Do the Roshie talk some more," she said. "I liked that."

"Oh, uhh, just . . . she's great."

"Know someone."

"What?"

"Continue from before—the monologue. It takes some time to know someone. Come on, man, fill in the gaps, or sorry, my mind is moving too fast."

"No, uhh, well, everyone at work is in awe of her. Have you ever heard of . . ." He said noncomprehensible alien words.

"Huh?"

He said the words again. "It's a technique for speeding up web pages—it's sort of the core of what our company does. She was the one who made it work. Like, this technique spread through Silicon Valley so fast. She invented it. Anyway, people are afraid of her; they think she'll tear your ideas to shreds." He smiled. "But I was like, shit, I'll get her on my project team. And it took a while. She had another guy she liked to work with. But I won her away."

"Cool. I like that."

"She's gotten hurt," Henry said. "Like she's told me some nuts stories. From high school, like, she was out of control. Learned to pick locks . . . break into people's lockers . . . destroy their stuff . . . she's got that angry side, just like you."

"I know."

"But you're both good people . . . like, I think . . . it's just been interesting . . . she needs people to need her. I think she gets on people's nerves. Audrey . . . I don't know . . ."

She tried to reply, but her mind kept slipping away, falling down into the abyss, and whenever she spoke, Henry was far out, spacey, encouraging her to slow down and not speak, so she finally lost touch with the world and slipped into a detached airy-fairy mushroom trip, filled with shimmery patterns and wavering trees and living thoughts that budded and split and then withered, leaving her mind jumping from thought to thought before any could be completed.

"I want you," she finally murmured.

"You're on drugs."

"So?"

They were sitting on the ground, leaning against a tree, laughing, and then she was on him, groping at him wordlessly, rubbing her hands over his chest and throat, murmuring, "Kiss me, kiss me," pushing herself at his lips, and he was laughing, saying, "No, no, no, come on, we're old friends. I don't want to ruin that."

"Sorry," she said. "Sorry. Sorry. Sorry. I'm bad."

"What?" he said.

"I'm bad. I'm a bad person. There's something wrong. I'm a monster, from another world, nobody could ever love."

"Hey . . . that's not true."

"I'm a man."

Henry's eyes were far out too, dilated by the mushrooms or whatever he was on, and she licked her lips, drew close. "I'm a man, I'm a man, so I know the male part of you—evil, terrible, naked. I know you just think I'm disgusting. Don't lie. If it was Synestra here, you'd be begging for her dick. Don't lie."

"Hey . . ." He put two fingers under her chin, looked her in the eyes. "Hey, Jhanvi. You're gorgeous. Don't be like that."

"No, Henry, stop. Don't be nice. Because when you're nice, you promise things, and then your girlfriend complains about your promises to Katie, and then she's mean to me, and you're nice again, and you overpromise, and it's a horrific cycle. But I encourage it, because it's my only way inside. Break it, Henry, break the cycle."

"My girlfriend? Purpose?"

She snorted. "You and Audrey are still together. If you don't know that you're insane."

"Look, it's been complicated. But you really are an old friend—"

"I know," she said. "I get it, and I don't judge."

His words came out slowly. "What is it? What do you know?" And now, for once, he was shaken, not in control.

"That you're not enlightened. That you resent Audrey for fucking other people. That you're not nice or sex positive. That it humiliates you. That you want a dick inside you, and you're worried you're not a real man. It was really me writing those words, Henry. It was really me, your old friend, even if you try not to recognize it. All that time we were texting. It was me. I know what makes you tick."

"Hey . . . we should talk when you're not on mushrooms. I really regret that. I shouldn't have started, you know, talking with you like that. It was wrong. And it . . . it went in a weird direction and . . . and I apologize."

"You can't ever apologize for thinking I'm hideous. I've seen the girls you like: Synestra, Audrey, Katie, Purpose. Unfat, sly, overtly sexual. I'll never be that. But they don't *want* you, Henry. To them, you're the effeminate one: weak, only worth keeping in the back pocket, for fun."

Then his head bumped forward, and his lips were against hers. Instantly, she felt invaded, probed, like an insect was crawling over her. He pulled back, and she took a breath.

"You're gorgeous," he said.

She started to chuckle, but his hands were swarming over her, and somehow he'd pulled her down—they fell like in slow motion—and the insect had gained many legs, and all of them were probing strange parts of her body—her armpits, her knees, her ass crack. She couldn't stop giggling. "This is so weird."

"I know," he said. "I know . . ."

Now he reached down, yanking on her cock, which was

short and dry. He pulled it out from her underwear, and it felt like he put it through a dryer circle—lots of warmth, lots of rotation. "I want you," he said.

She blinked. *I guess this is happening.* Another blink, and his insectoid eyes softened—the insect got big, pouty lips. *That's one fuckable bug!* She giggled. He rubbed his furry chest, tweaked his nipples. She almost couldn't stop laughing. The bug was so cute, so small and so helpless. She felt a weird stirring in her groin. Her penis, after two years on hormones, was a bit of a nub, and now he was tugging on it insistently.

"I want you inside me," he murmured.

"Uhh, huh..."

"I've always wanted that..." he said. His eyes glistened. "I just didn't... I've always..."

Too many thoughts. She couldn't get it up. Couldn't even explain the amount of mental preparation it took her to top a guy. He scuttled around in the leaves, trying to get at her cock, and she waved him off, feeling like the guy on the runway waving the lights. The wrestling was comic, and left them sweaty, slimy, feeling vaguely off.

"I can... I have things to help," he said. He'd produced a pill. "Here... just if you want..."

Now his eyes were big. "I'm really sorry," he said. "I've just... I've never told anyone about... w... wanting that. But we're such old friends, and..."

Now her mind went cold. The insect rubbed a little mandible against her. "Fine," she said. "Give it over." Then the pill was in her mouth, and the first erotic sensation she felt was from his fingers on her lips, and she tried to suck on them, but they withdrew.

She swallowed it dry, and although it couldn't work so fast, she was suddenly erect, all the blood rushing to her head. "I'll do it," she said. "I'll do it for you. For a friend. Because I'm a good friend for you... a good friend..."

His eyes went wide and soft. "Uhh," he said. "Wow."

"Lie back."

She leaned forward, softly rubbing the stubble on his face, and touched her lips to his. She felt for a moment the explosion of a kiss, saw herself as Audrey, topless, wrapped around her man, and then they were together, hands running over each other's bodies. He spat in his hand—she noted the practiced gesture, like in a porn—and then her mind blanked out, when he touched her, and she thought—*Oh this is it, what I ought to have felt*—the holy fire leaping through her chest—the sourceless pleasure, unlike anything else—pleasure without analogy or explanation, overpowering, drifting through her body, and for once, for once in her life, she took in the smell of a man, all salty and gluey, the smell of sweat and semen, and she kissed his neck, sucked his earlobe, drew out his breath. And she was small, like Audrey, in his power.

Slowly, out of nowhere, the fantasies rose up: she was his slave, in a tent, a captive boy—no, a woman—and a weird thing happened, she actually *was* a woman, fully a woman, with not a hint of dysphoria. The sensation was indescribable. She'd experienced hints of it, at times when she was alone, but usually other people's eyes broke it down, and her gender identity became a hopeless contest, like trying to maintain a failing erection, but now she simply was a girl.

Almost all the time, at any moment, she felt like a man pretending to be a girl. But right now, she let herself simply be Jhanvi, a person who was . . . who was . . . who was—her mind blanked. She couldn't go any further . . . had no identity . . . no job, no family, nothing made sense—girl, she was its essence. All the accretion of loathing and cynicism—her deeply personal, gut-level understanding of her own awfulness—even the sense that she needed wanted didn't want deserved didn't deserve love—all of that disappeared. Her gender identity shifted into the background, became the bedrock of herself, so she could, for once, break outwards, take in the other man, shift on his lap, make out, feel his gasps and his awe. The leaves rustled under them, and the trees bobbed with their breath. An ant oozed down the tree's bark, dipping in and out of sight, carrying itself well. Their lips were joined like the stones in an arch, and so were their penises, and they pushed against each other, and her only intrusive thought was *So it's real. So it really exists.* And for a split second, this was her man.

Then he murmured, "Fuck me."

"Hmm?"

"Fuck me, like you said."

The haze took a while to lift, but then she went to it like a technician, tested her cock, its tensile strength. He went down on her, bobbing his mouth on her dick, and she closed her eyes, tried to imagine Henry was servicing her as a woman, but he murmured, "I love your smell."

"Turn around," she said.

He was on his hands and knees, and she pulled down his jeans all the way, exposed his hairy ass, a grotesque, winking hole. Then, slowly, dissociating from herself, she pushed in.

"Oh god," he said. "Oh god, stop."

She paused, pulled back. Her penis felt nothing. It was hard wood, senseless and dead, hewed from the living trunk, fashioned into a dildo, like the ancient Romans did. Splinters. She giggled. A spider fell from her hair, and she wiped it from his bottom. Then she heard a sniff. He'd had a bottle of something in his vest: poppers. Wow, he really was a queer, though he hid it well.

She pushed deeper in, and he groaned. Putting a hand on his upper back, playing with the little marks on his skin, she bore down, went deeper in.

"You're blowing my mind," he said.

"Am I? You're worthless," she said.

"Oh god."

"You're not a man."

She said the words robotically. But he seemed into it, and she kept going. "Your girlfriend cheats on you. Your dick isn't very big." She went further and further, faster and harder, and it seemed to take forever, and then she had a thought:

"Tell me you love me, Hen."

"What?"

"Say you love me. Say it."

"Umm . . ."

She stopped.

"I . . . I love you, Ni—Jhanvi." He'd almost said it. Almost said Nikhil. She drove in, making him groan with each centimeter, until he got so loud she was certain others could hear.

"Yell it," she said.

"I . . . I love you!"

"Say you'll marry me."

"I . . ."

"It's not real, Hen. Just say it. For me. Or else what do I get? What do I enjoy about this?"

He was an animal, back bent, doing an up dog, braying out the words: "I love you so much! Keep going. This is great!" The sight of him sickened her, and she tried to turn him into a woman, into something that might attract her.

She had to guide him, but he got into it, lavishing praise on her, saying he loved her, he wanted to marry her, she was a beautiful goddess. None of it meant anything. Her wooden dick sawed mechanically into and out of him, and she became focused fully on his body, on the rapid breaths or the twitches of discomfort, on the groans when his dick brushed against the leaves, until, finally, slowly, she reached down and brought him to a screaming orgasm. When it was over, he lay on the ground, dirty, covered in leaves, smelling vaguely of feet, while she wiped his semen off her hand onto a nearby leaf.

14

Jhanvi stood next to the fire, a cup of wine in hand, watching the embers flickering and shifting. She was a few steps away from the main crowd, whose unclothed limbs were dancing and twirling, spinning electric lights, beating on drums.

The generator belched, and the air was suffused with the smell of oil. Roshie squatted near it, murmuring, while Jhanvi pretended to listen. Roshie's coarse hair was beautifully shaggy and wild, and Jhanvi's fingers were deep inside it, parting it and moving it aside, picking through it like a baboon looking for nits.

"You're out of control," Roshie said. "What are you *doing* up there?"

"Nice hair, beautiful hair," Jhanvi said.

"I can't believe you got fucked up immediately," Roshie said.

"Why not?" Jhanvi said.

"Because it's falling apart!" Roshie said. "We're totally behind schedule. And it's the new member introduction today. We're not remotely set up, and—"

"Relax, little ant. Winter is months away."

"You are so fucked up," Roshie said.

Jhanvi's sense of identity was returning, but it felt insubstantial, not even a mask—more of a cloak, lightly held around the shoulders. She wasn't sure if the part of herself that had emerged during her time with Henry was her true self, or if it represented something constructed, and she wasn't sure if she ought to lean further into that persona or not. Perhaps, in a world where Synestra existed, Jhanvi could never be a femme fatale. But she could be something. There was something growing and evolving inside her. She wasn't the anxious, silly person she sometimes seemed—she was cold, cruel, and calculating, a creature of rage and desire. *I understand now those bizarre people I've sometimes met in trans groups who think they're fairies or demons or vampires. I'm inhuman, something else is alive in me. Jhanvi is a costume. Nikhil was a costume.*

"Hey."

Katie had spun out of the fire, and now she was a silhouette in the dark, with glowing paint—long notches of purple and green—on her cheeks and thighs and the swells of her breasts. Jhanvi blinked a few times, trying to get a glimpse of her face—that narrow face, her flowing golden hair. The trees loomed around them, and over Katie's shoulder the wooded hills rose up, riven by a single pass.

"Hey," she said. "I wanted to talk. Is now a good time?"

"Sure," Jhanvi said. "I always have time for you."

"Let's talk inside." Katie had a phone in her hand. She gestured in a direction, and Jhanvi walked with her, figures whirling out at them from all sides. She was floating. She ended up inside a long school bus, painted rainbow colors, sitting on a heart-shaped bed at the back. Jhanvi immediately splayed out, hissing, then turned on her side, her head on the pillow, and her own smell rose up, sour sweat and shit and semen and that feeling of saliva coating her body in a sticky layer. She enjoyed the smell of semen, but not that empty saliva smell.

"Hey," Katie said. She was next to Jhanvi, but far away, with her back leaning against a cushion. She reached forward, touched Jhanvi's leg. "I wanted to discuss what happened out there."

"Huh?"

An infinity of time had passed. Jhanvi remembered the feeling, from so many other mushroom trips, of being sad she couldn't retain it, couldn't live forever inside the frozen time. Sad that it drifted away, led her back into the real world.

"Hey," Katie said. "I've spent the last few hours talking to Henry, helping him process what happened?"

"Oh." Jhanvi was about to say, *It was fine. Yeah, I was high on mushrooms, but I consented.* Except she realized, quickly enough for once, that Katie wasn't going to be on her side. Instead, she thought, *What is the most absurd possible interpretation of what happened?*

"Is he okay?" Jhanvi said.

"Why?" Katie said. "What do you think happened?"

"Hmm," Jhanvi said. "I guess I'm assuming he had a really intense sexual experience that put him in a submissive posture—perhaps it was even his first time with receptive anal intercourse—and he has lots of strong, conflicting feelings. Perhaps about his masculinity, perhaps about what this means for his sexuality and his relationship with the women in his life, perhaps about the social stigma, perhaps about HIV—endless possibilities, really. Thank you for helping him."

"So . . . you don't think this is something you should've thought about?" Katie said. "He seems really . . . stunned. Not to mention sore."

"Yes, Katie, you're right," Jhanvi said. "I should've practiced the fine art of aftercare."

What she didn't say was, *What about aftercare for me? What about the homeless girl, alone in the woods and high on mushrooms with her best friend and crush, someone she is transactionally tied to in a complicated plot involving her transition and housing? What about her being manipulated into doing something sexual, topping a guy, that she absolutely never wanted to do?* Jhanvi didn't say those things, not just because Katie wouldn't give a shit, but because they weren't *true.* She hadn't been sober; she'd been newly relapsed, in fact, and according to Katie's value system, she'd been incapable of consent. What Henry had done might've easily been characterized as an assault—or at least uncool—but it hadn't been. She had consented.

"I can't tell if you're joking," Katie said. Her eyes flickered, took on a shifting, multi-hued aura.

"Are you sober?" Jhanvi said.

"Yes, why?"

"When do you cut loose?" Jhanvi said. "You're always so tightly wound."

"Okay, just . . . the thing I don't understand is . . . if you knew all this, why did you just leave Henry out there?"

"It was my first time," Jhanvi said. "I don't know much about dominating people . . . I haven't taken the trainings . . . I was confused too . . ." She parroted Trial By Fire phrases she had heard, saying exactly what she needed to say.

Katie sucked in her breath. "Okay, this is fine. Everything is fine. It could've turned out *really* badly, but in the end, Henry is happy. He had a great time."

"I'm glad," Jhanvi said. "Me too."

"But you have responsibilities to someone like him," Katie said. "Someone's first time doing something, that's sacred. If you mishandle it, you could really hurt them . . ."

"Oh, I know," Jhanvi said. "I have a lot of anger toward people who treated me like an object."

"That's the worst," Katie said. "Okay, I think . . . I think when we get back, you and I should talk more. Do you think . . . can you come to some trainings? I really love Henry. He's one of the few queer guys in Trial By Fire, and I just think, like, if he'd felt differently—a scandal where our only bi guy got sexually exploited? That would be awful. As it is, he's super worried about the stigma. We've always known he had that side, but he never really explored it around us. A lot of fire-eater spaces have terrible biphobia, you know. At least toward men."

"I'm aware."

"But . . . I'm glad." She gave a thin, light smile. "I'm really happy for both of you. He doesn't want people to know yet, is that okay?"

"Mmmhmmm," Jhanvi said. "Thank you for being so . . . tactful." Her voice was monotone, and she couldn't help smiling. Katie could've really hurt her here, right now, today, but Jhanvi had deflected her.

Katie's head was cocked. There were light wrinkles around her eyes. Jhanvi kept her gaze from falling to the bandeau that kept the girl's small breasts contained.

"I'm sorry," Jhanvi said. "For . . . for calling you out. You're not racist or transphobic. That was wrong."

"No, no," Katie said. "You were frustrated. I get it. You've seen now how complex this stuff can be. It's not simple. We need to be so aware and so respectful to keep this group running. I totally heard your accusation of transphobia, and there's probably work I can do to be more accepting to gender-diverse people."

"No, you don't have to apologize." And with her fingers lightly brushing the vellus hairs on the back of the girl's wrist, Jhanvi smiled with her dead eyes, and she said, "It's okay to say I was full of bullshit."

Then, pausing for a second, she found the most devilish brick to fit into the gap in her rhetorical appeal. A person like Katie always needed a political reason to feel how she felt.

"Women are trained to suppress their instincts," Jhanvi said. "I see this as kind of a war, what you're fighting—the men rely on you to keep their environment free and safe and to minimize conflicts before they occur. Normally, you keep out people like me—you know, people who are potential scammers, dangers, drifters, whatever—without asking—but that causes resentment. People think you're bossy, think you're a bitch."

"I don't use that word," she said.

Jhanvi saw now the value of controlling and channeling Katie's responses, of building in outlets for her to make objections. That way, Jhanvi could manage the flow of the conversation and stop Katie from taking control.

"Totally," Jhanvi said. "The point is, you know I'm, like, not one of the real trans women. I mean, no offense—it's not politically correct—but I'm not underprivileged, like Roshie says."

"How do you mean?"

"It's just a class thing," Jhanvi said. "I spent a night outdoors, that's true—and that was your fault."

"I am so sorry for that!"

"Totally," Jhanvi said. "But that doesn't mean you should have to live with me. I get that. You're right. You're a hundred percent right. That's not transmisogyny. I feel bad. Like, you're a good person, and—"

"So are you!"

Jhanvi frowned. She hadn't quite expected that. It gave her a lower opinion of Katie than she would've thought she could possess.

"I just see everything you do for the house," Jhanvi said. "It's really thankless. You make enemies on other people's behalf. They're really irresponsible, actually—they play with dangerous stuff. Like nobody else, no one, would've thought to check up on what happened with Henry and me. It wouldn't even have occurred to them. I bet you've seen a lot of things."

"You have no idea," Katie said, shaking her head. "I'm sorry. I should've talked to him. I should. And . . . you know . . ." She took a deep breath. "I don't know. It's not impossible that . . . I mean . . . like, let's be real . . . we're all white. It's not an accident that I singled you out . . . I mean . . . I had concerns . . . but . . . Do you see what I'm saying?"

"No," Jhanvi said, thinking, *This can't be right. I can't possibly be allowed to be so insincere.* But now that she'd embarked on this course, she wanted to see how far it could go. "I actually disagree. I think you'd have subjected a white guy to the exact same scrutiny. I mean, I came in with no exit plan, no close friends in the house, basically saying I wanted to exploit people for money."

"Huh? How?"

"Well, for a place to stay, for one. And then for the health insurance."

"Oh," Katie said. "Yeah. I didn't—that wasn't—"

"It's dumb. It would bind people to me in a way that would let me trap them later on. If I wanted to. Roshie said as much."

"Well, yeah," Katie said. "She's kind of ... she's an odd one. Has she ... has she given you money?"

Jhanvi shook her head. "I wouldn't take it. I have limits. I don't know ..."

"Oh! You should! I mean ... look ..."

And now Katie seemed to transform. Her voice took on a husky tone, and her shoulders dropped. For the first time, she smiled, and gained some of the shy, vulnerable look that Jhanvi had previously only seen from a distance.

"Look, let's be honest," Katie said. "I can only afford to do public interest work because my parents paid for college—I don't have a dime of student loans—and I can always fall back on them. It sounds like you and your parents aren't as close."

"Well, I've given them reason to distrust me."

"Life is complicated," she said. "I get it. But still, I know from my clients, nobody is perfect. People take drugs, drink, whatever, even tell lies or whatever, some of them ask me for money. I don't blame them. I have good boundaries when it comes to my space, my body, and that's something I pride myself on. Roshie is really lonely. I think you've been good for her. I just ... I don't know, maybe I can trust you to be there for her. I don't know."

Jhanvi smiled. They'd locked her out a week ago, but a wet dick was a skeleton key. She'd fucked a man inside their circle, and now she was inside as well. Roshie hadn't, so she wasn't. No amount of money could bind people together the way an exchange of seminal fluid could.

"Look," Katie said. "I've got to get back out there. Are you all right? I realize I should've checked in with you too. Do you need to talk to anyone?"

"Yeah," Jhanvi said. The word hung there in silence.

Katie blinked a few times, and now she gripped Jhanvi's shoulder. "Hey. I do care about you as well."

"Are . . ." Jhanvi felt a lump in her throat. She did want to talk about her and Henry, about that moment. She had taken control. Had fucked a friend for the first time. Had a guy tell her he loved her—and more than that, she had been, in some sense, desired. Not in the usual way, the way she wanted to be, but she had aroused something in him. Her body had provided him with some value.

But no. To talk about that would be to surrender. Jhanvi shook her head. "Fine. Totally fine."

"Okay," Katie said. "Well, just checking. Hey, stay here as long as you want."

When Katie was gone, Jhanvi lay back on the bed and took a dozen slow breaths. She saw the bottle of gin on the counter, and she grabbed it, hunted for some tonic, and marveled at its glow under the black light. She poured herself a cup and drank and watched the party through the window. The anger inside threatened to flare up, consuming her—the old Jhanvi would've screamed, smashed bottles. But instead, she banked the fire, left the embers smoldering—her day would come.

The next morning, Jhanvi woke to rapid knocking on the window of the school bus. When Jhanvi slid it down, Roshie said, "Hey, I've been looking everywhere for you. I'm going home. You want to come?"

"Err, what?"

"Come on," Roshie said. "I know you're hungover, but it's ten o'clock, I've waited long enough. Katie and Audrey have been gaslighting me for hours. Let's get the fuck out of here."

"Uhh . . ." Jhanvi blinked. She was wearing a pleated leather skirt and nothing else. She vaguely remembered digging this thing out of a costume bin last night. She yawned. "Roshie," she said. "Can I get coffee?"

"Fine," Roshie said. "But ten minutes and I'm leaving, with or without you."

The sun and the clouds were interpenetrating, but the wind was still cold, and everyone was huddled in jackets, except Audrey, who was topless and wearing spandex shorts, of course. She rushed up, hugged Jhanvi. "Hey!" she said. "You're awake!"

As Achilles poured her coffee from a saucepan, she asked, "What's wrong with Roshie?"

"She's annoyed we didn't have the new member greeting last night," Audrey said. "But we all talked, and we like you, you're in the club, so what's to get mad about? Did anyone tell her?"

"I did," Katie said. Her hood was drawn tight over her head, showing just a narrow aperture of face. Audrey shivered and Jhanvi thought, *Put on a shirt*. Jhanvi could feel herself losing sensation in her arms. Just then, Roshie came back, dropping Jhanvi's bag on the ground.

"If you're coming, get dressed!"

"Eggs are almost ready," Achilles said.

Henry was on the other side of the fire, and he flicked a wave at Jhanvi but didn't come closer.

"Come on, come on, come on," Roshie said. "Jesus, I'm literally setting a timer."

Jhanvi rustled around in her bag, found a shirt and a pair of jeans, and got dressed in front of everyone. Her makeup must be a horror, caked onto her face, clumping around her beard hairs. She took a wipe and rubbed it over her cheeks and lips—it came away stained red and black and pink. Someone blew a note on a conch shell. "Brunch is ready!"

"Fuck this rabbit food," Roshie said. "I'm going to Denny's."

"I'm in," Jhanvi said.

"Really?"

Her stomach rumbled, but more importantly, she didn't want to be bare faced around these people. *Besides, time to bank my gains.* She grabbed her bag, and then she was forced into a series of goodbyes, including with Synestra, who murmured, "I hear you had an interesting night."

Then she was in Roshie's car, and they took off just as the alcohol and mushrooms met the coffee and let loose a horrendous pounding behind each of Jhanvi's eyebrows.

• • •

On the road home, Roshie's phone started blowing up. Jhanvi reached for it, and Roshie said, "No, leave it."

"But it's Henry."

"Fuck him," Roshie said. "He wants his fucking drugs."

"Wha . . ." Jhanvi said. "You didn't leave the drugs?"

"Fuck them," Roshie said. "Fuck them so hard right in their dirty little asses. No offense."

A bolt of sensation shot through Jhanvi's heart. She'd reflected that morning on the events of last night, on the craziness of it—the instantaneous switch—the nakedness of the in-group/out-group dynamics. *All it took was prostituting myself.* Her phone buzzed. Henry had texted:

Hey heard Katie and you had a good talk last night. Welcome to TGP! Can you put Roshie on?

No, Jhanvi wrote. *She's absconding. I had a good time too*

It's sort of serious, he wrote. *Can we meet you anywhere? I'm in a car, which Denny's are you going to?*

Jhanvi grimaced, and, oddly, her eyes got wet. It didn't take a PhD in psychology to figure this out: she was upset that he'd gotten aftercare and she hadn't. But fuck her, an adventurer doesn't have *feelings.* An adventurer collects gold, instead of metaphysical rewards. And she'd fucked her way inside: *Thank you, Mr. Dick.*

She wrote back, *I'm running out of battery,* and then she turned off her phone.

Roshie said, "I don't let people push me around. I just don't do it."

"So what's wrong?" Jhanvi said. "You're mad they didn't discuss me last night?"

"Yeah," Roshie said. "They completely fucked our schedule. Fuck them. I am so tired of them. I spent all fucking night working the lights, the sound system. Fuck them."

Her voice was strained, loaded with tears. She clenched the wheel. They were in the hills now, on a two-lane road, headed away from the campground. It hadn't rained in a while, and the hills were bleak and golden, dotted with occasional cows. Roshie drove fast, tailgating cars and pulling around them on straightaways.

Obviously, Roshie was mad that everyone had started fucking, and Jhanvi was about to call her out for it, but then she thought, *I spent so much effort managing Katie's emotions. Don't I owe Roshie the same thing?* So Jhanvi stretched, letting out a long moan. Then she pulled one bare foot up into her lap.

"I admire you for getting mad," Jhanvi said, slowly, feeling out each word. "A lot. You know . . . it's weird, I was just thinking, my whole life, I've felt, like, this envy for people who are beautiful, smart, carefree—"

"They're pathetic."

"Well, yeah, okay. But I envied them, and I felt like they had no reason for having me around. That I needed to offer them . . . I don't know. That I needed to be unobtrusive. Or be helpful. Be a listening ear. Do services."

"Well, you sure as shit don't do any services now."

Except I do. I did a service for Henry at least. And for Katie, too.

"That's true," Jhanvi said. "That's on purpose. Because, if you do things for people, they don't respect you. Not unless you force them to. And I can't do anything for people anyway. It's weird—the more people are put out for you, the worse you make them feel, the more you impose—the more they like you. A certain kind of person, anyway. They think, why would I be doing this if I didn't like and respect this person? Like . . . ever since we started hard-core calling out Katie, she's really softened toward me."

"That's weak," Roshie said. "People like that don't deserve to live."

"Well, how do you think Audrey gets away with so much?"

There was a long silence. The rejoinder was obvious: *because of her sexuality.* But Roshie wouldn't allow herself to think of that difference between the two of them. And Jhanvi spun out this conversational thread, expanding on how these people took up space, and that's why they had power.

". . . so now you're taking up more space," Jhanvi said. "And I'm proud of you."

"I always took up space. I demanded that my room's bathroom be for just me, when I moved in."

"That's good," Jhanvi said. "I think the thing about you is ... you're willing to do things if you understand why. Like if someone needed the bathroom for some reason, you'll do it. But not for an abstract reason. Not just because someone else tells you it's the right thing."

"I don't know ..." Roshie said.

Jhanvi said, "Is it okay if I touch your shoulder?"

"If you want."

Jhanvi reached up and put her hand on the other girl's shoulder. Roshie was in a T-shirt, with her hair pulled back underneath a newsboy cap. Jhanvi rubbed her shoulder with the fingers and thumb of one hand, keeping her eyes fixed on the other girl's unflinching stare. Then her hand went down, and she gripped the other girl's hand, held it tight, stroked her fingers.

"Stop," Roshie said.

"Sorry," Jhanvi said. "I didn't have any real friends for a long time. Maybe I still don't. I used to think ... nobody will ever touch me. There's a book with a line in it, where a lonely old woman talks about just being untouched—about the shock of heat to your groin from a busman's chance touch on the shoulder ..."

The silence hung between them. Jhanvi sighed and let go of Roshie's hand.

"I'm not a lesbian," Roshie said. "Or bisexual. I've tried to be. It didn't feel right."

"That's funny," Jhanvi said. "That's really funny."

When Roshie didn't say anything, Jhanvi replied to herself: "It's funny because to you I guess I'm a girl. No, you know, I always admired, when I was a guy, the sort of—the sensuousness of being a girl—of how you could touch people ... be touched ... how friends touch each other. The aesthetic of it. Maybe that's stupid. It's not part of being a girl for everyone.

But . . . Roshie, I mean . . . we really should turn back. These are your friends. You choose to hang out with them."

"I'm taking the event space away from her. I told her it'd happen, if she broke her promises. And she did. Maybe she can't be trusted to keep her word, but I can. If I tell the landlords I'm worried about the party, they'll break the lease, even give back half my money—they're so scared of liability."

More silence. Jhanvi had started to wonder what would happen if she didn't cut into Roshie's silence. She wasn't stupid, she understood that she would have to choose between Roshie and the rest—and she knew the right choice to make. She knew that Roshie was a better person. That Roshie liked her more and would treat her better.

And yet . . . life with Roshie would be lonely, and it would be sterile. Compared to last night's moment of connection, this one was . . . well . . . it wasn't even good conversation. Choosing Roshie would mean choosing a kind of cloistered loneliness as well.

Roshie fulminated nonstop. Jhanvi only broke in to say *You're right* and *I totally understand it* and *Don't go to this Denny's, it's the closest one, and they'll be waiting for us.* It was so easy just to agree with Roshie—to feed her anger and say things that were true and necessary. Roshie *had* been exploited. They *didn't* have any respect for her or her boundaries. And she was permanently, unbearably, on the outside of this group, and she probably *should* stop being friends with them. But Roshie also needed to hear something else: *This is all about sex. You resent them because you're not fucking. If you were fucking, you wouldn't resent them. So, regardless of what you do, begin the fuck-fest soon.* The very idea was appalling—Roshie belonged in some cozy twosome with a guy who'd worship and adore her— she shouldn't need to hawk herself at some sex party. And how had the fucking worked out for Jhanvi? When she thought of herself and Henry, she was surprised by the lack of joy, the lack of self-love. Instead, she felt the sudden urge to smash her

boot against his face, forever and ever, until the world understood how much she'd been wronged. Her hatred of him felt,
if anything, increased by her amatory success, as if in taking
him, she'd finally allowed herself to feel the full depth of her
anger for the promises he'd broken and the care he hadn't given.

As they got onto the 101, Roshie recovered some of her equa-
nimity, and she went into a long rant about all the stupid things
they were probably doing up there, all the stupid faux-Native
rituals and the stupid games and the stupid partner-swapping
and the stupid dancing. And her ire focused more and more
sharply on Audrey, and how she was such a dumb, empty-
headed, *stupid* person who didn't really care about anything.
And Jhanvi wanted to ask, *What do you care about?* But she
didn't, because she knew that she was already on thin ice.

16

Over the next week, Jhanvi tried to embrace her role as Roshie's sidekick. She accepted every invitation her friend made, from "happy hour after work" to "help me pick up these lengths of rebar from a friend in Oakland." It was nice, in a way, to be so needed. Roshie asked, but she took it for granted that Jhanvi would want to accompany her on the most mundane tasks.

"Hey," Jhanvi said, as they came out of the wash-and-fold spot where Roshie took her laundry. "I hope you don't think I come with you to these things just because I'm crashing with you."

"What?" Roshie said. "No, why would I think that?"

"I dunno, just that . . . I didn't want you to think that I thought that you were buying my friendship. Because I actually really like this."

"Why wouldn't you want to come with me?" Roshie said. "You're not doing anything else. You don't really know this city. And I like having you around."

"You do? Why?"

"Uhh . . . you're smart. Who else is gonna talk with me about how dumb everything and everybody is."

"Oh," Jhanvi nodded. They were on their way to a coffee shop where they almost always stopped. Jhanvi got them a table while Roshie ordered two cappuccinos and two chocolate croissants. When Roshie rejoined her after ten minutes, holding the drinks, Jhanvi continued the conversation.

"It just surprises me," Jhanvi said. "That you have that insight. That you know how much you like to complain."

"Of course I like to complain. That's like the number one thing people say about me. *You complain a lot.* Or even, *You complain too much.* Whatever. I like that you've never said that."

"This is just so much," Jhanvi said. "It's really changing how I feel about you. It's so much . . . insight."

Roshie rolled her eyes, pulled apart her chocolate croissant. She immediately started talking about something dumb somebody had done at work. Roshie's job, unlike the job of almost every tech person Jhanvi knew, was actually not uninteresting. She worked for a startup, developing tools to make the internet load faster. She worked by herself, and could actually explain what she was doing—the specific technical problems involved. Jhanvi repeated to her that Henry had said the whole company was in awe of her.

"So you actually like your job," Jhanvi said.

"Of course," Roshie said. "This is real coding work, deep problems, stuff the smartest minds in the world are working on, and I get paid a boatload of money to sit around all day and do that shit. Why wouldn't I love it?"

"Most people don't."

"Yeah, most people don't do shit. Like, Henry doesn't do anything, but at least he knows it, and he just stays out of my way."

"That's just really cool," Jhanvi said. "I really respect you. That's such a strange feeling." She shook her head.

"Hey," Roshie said. "You don't think it's weird I haven't offered you a job at my company or whatever?"

"What? No no no no no no no no," Jhanvi said. "That would be a really bad idea."

"Good."

"Terrible idea. I never want to be subjected to your standards for performance."

"What does that mean?"

"Oh come on."

Roshie pretended to be confused, but to Jhanvi it was obvious. Her standards for Jhanvi were much lower than for almost anyone else in her life. If she really evaluated Jhanvi as she was, Jhanvi couldn't help but being classified "a fucking idiot."

Roshie did a lot of monologuing: whether it was the details of her job, or TBF, her building projects, or the lives of her various friends and acquaintances. And she didn't really ask Jhanvi very much about herself. She rarely even said, *How are you doing?*

Jhanvi knew Roshie simply wasn't that kind of person. Life with her, as her sidekick, would be safe, but unexciting. And sometimes she wondered if Roshie actually respected her very much at all, or if Jhanvi was nothing more than a person in need. If Jhanvi hadn't shown up at her doorstep and provided a convenient way for her to get out her frustrations with Audrey, Jhanvi wasn't sure they even would've become friends in the first place.

Of course I would choose Roshie if it was right. If we really were a match, if our life together was effortless—if I felt like she just got me in some way nobody else does—then I would say fuck the rest of these people, and I would choose her. But she doesn't. The truth is she's a pretty simple, honest, direct person, and she could never understand my true nature.

• • •

The marriage plot had been more or less on hold since the woods. Henry hardly looked at her in the hall, and when she brought it up, he said, "Oh god, I am so sorry. We need to talk about that."

She said, "Look, are you trying to get out of this?"

"No, no, we just need to talk."

It was pathetic that he couldn't even openly say no. But, whatever, maybe she'd let him off the hook. Jhanvi had recently pondered the idea of asking Roshie flat out for the money to do her procedures. To Jhanvi, the most important one was her face. She absolutely hated her face: with its broad jaw and protruding brow bone, she could never really be mistaken for a cis woman. On the phone, she almost always got "ma'am," but in real life, people usually called her "sir" even if she was wearing a dress and high heels. It was instinct more than insult: they saw her face and, before seeing any of the rest, they thought, "that is a man."

To do her face surgeries would be at least $15,000 even in Spain or Thailand or Mexico. Then she would ideally also do a hair transplant: another $3,000. And top surgery—she wasn't sure about that, but maybe $10,000. And some body contouring—liposuction and fat grafts to give her less of a blocky, sagging, paunchy shape. That would be, let's say, another $5,000. And then full-on intense lasering and electrolysis for the facial hair, let's call that $3,000. And throw in the bottom too, assuming the rest went well, so call it $60,000 in total. Roshie had paid more than that so Audrey could keep her event space, and she didn't even *like* Audrey.

But it would take years to get all the procedures done, and during that time, Jhanvi would owe Roshie. Just like she'd owed her old landlord. Monica had texted her a few times to ask how things were with the boyfriend, and Jhanvi had responded, *Really busy. Interviewing for jobs.*

List me as a reference, Monica had said. *I won't mention all the stuff you left behind, that I had to pack up. When're you coming to get all that?*

Jhanvi didn't answer. After a few exchanges, she texted Monica, *I kind of need space.*

Fine, Monica had written back. *You think I do this for my own good? You're being unbelievably selfish.*

Either you're trying to help me, or you're not. If you're trying to help me, then refusing your help is selfless, not selfish. If you're not, then you're the selfish one.

Monica sent back a long message that Jhanvi deleted unread, and afterward, she blocked the other woman's number.

Would that be Jhanvi and Roshie someday? The idea exhausted her. And Roshie might say no. People surprised you sometimes with their cruelty.

But already the question had been on the tip of her tongue a few times.

What stopped her was—she wasn't sure. She liked Roshie, but somehow, she just felt angry. The idea that Katie hadn't even considered that Jhanvi might need just as much support as Henry did? Fuck that guy.

More than anything, Jhanvi wanted to *win*. It wasn't something she could explain to anyone. Not because she didn't have the words, but because the implications were so horrifying.

And ever since talking to Katie during the camping trip, she'd been groping toward a solution. She'd realized these thoughtless rich people had *needs*, and Jhanvi could meet those needs. All this time, she'd thought, *When I call them out, they feel nothing*, but talking to Katie, she'd seen—oh, it's not that Katie ignores my callouts, it's that she finds them so existentially terrifying that she's forced to ignore them. But that provides an opportunity. It's not the calling out that gets me in with them—it's the absolution I offer afterward.

To put it more plainly, these people needed a flatterer—someone from a lower social station to reassure them that their lifestyle was good and morally unimpeachable. And that was something Jhanvi knew well how to offer them. Katie was the weakest one—the others were too self-indulgent to care much, but Katie, with her effortless efficiency, couldn't help seeing clearly at times. She was in desperate need of someone to blindfold her, and Jhanvi could be that someone.

One morning, after Roshie had left for work, Jhanvi was star-
tled by a knock on the door. "Hey, Jhanvi, it's Katie. Can I come
in?"

"N—I'm not dressed." She wasn't made up, was only wearing her pajama pants and shirt. She looked like a boy with a
slightly rounded chest.

"It's okay!" Katie said. "I just need a second! I wanted to
discuss Henry. I had another thought."

"Umm, later?"

"I just wanted to say, maybe you can write him, saying you've
reconsidered the marriage idea. I think he's embarrassed about
that. But now that you guys are, umm, it's just a lot. And there's
plenty of other people around with good benefits. You can find
someone else."

Jhanvi caught her response before it exited her mouth: *Are
you fucking serious? What's wrong with this picture?* She was
homeless, poor—her only prospect was an interview at Toni's
bar, where she'd bus tables and get paid fifteen dollars an hour,
with no guaranteed shifts and no health insurance. And she
was supposed to give up on Henry?

"I don't know . . ." Jhanvi said through the door. "Have him
tell me himself."

"Come on," Katie said. "You're his friend. Just table it for a
few months."

The conversation went on for a few more exchanges before
Jhanvi managed to brush her off, saying she'd think about it.

She was angry, and she ought to have been discouraged.
*Katie can't be manipulated. I am wrong. I am bad. I need to
disappear.* But instead, a heaviness grew inside her, and she
thought, *I must defeat them, even at the cost of my own life.*

That night, she sent Henry the email: *Hey, let's rain check
the marriage thing. I think we're better just as friends with*

occasional benefits. I'm totally down to hook up again, if you'd
like, but you're in the driver's seat, all right? Take whatever time
you need.

• • •

Afterward, Henry was beaming, and he started being affectionate around her. He even hugged her and kissed her head. He
texted her a few times, saying, *Should we get together?* At some
point she needed to say yes.

Katie was radiant, holding Jhanvi by the shoulder, her blue
eyes full of life, and saying, "That was so perfect, so wonderful
and brave. I am *sure* you'll find someone else soon. Thank you
so much!"

Everything was good, everything was fine, everyone was
happy. But here was the ticket—she needed disequilibrium,
or she wouldn't gain anything. Somehow the mushrooms had
rewired her brain, and now she sat in her room, moving the
pieces around in the air above her head, plotting to secure her
future.

For the next few nights, after coming home, Roshie dominated her time, but Roshie also worked a lot, and finally her
company had a release. Jhanvi got word that Roshie would be
pulling an all-nighter.

That night, she opened the bottle of whiskey she'd taken all
the way to the woods and back, and she poured herself a stiff
drink. The first gulp kicked up immediately, and she spewed it
into Roshie's toilet.

The next one she mixed with some Coke out of Roshie's
fridge, and she sipped it slowly, letting the warmth fill her head
and heart, letting that voice arise from deep inside. The one that
told her she was strong and bold and powerful—a monster in
her own right—and that everything would crumble before her.

All her life, she'd had these delusions of grandeur: the
vain sputtering of a kid who wasn't quite smart enough, and

definitely not attractive or friendly enough, to make an impression on the world, but who nonetheless believed so deeply in his own specialness.

Ever since transitioning, those delusions had decreased, but they had also become more concrete. She'd admitted to herself that she wasn't a genius, she wouldn't set the world on fire. But she did have power. Look at her now. This house had tried to kick her out, to unhouse her, and she was still here. She had come to this city almost friendless, and now look. Roshie needed her, Toni idolized her, she had Meena offering to help her, and perhaps that was enough—perhaps—but she also wondered, *How far can I go?* Part of her wondered if she could somehow enlarge her power, bend the world to her will. *I want to be part of it. The sex, the drugs, the money, everything. And Roshie can never give me that. I want to force people to love this terrible body of mine. I want to make them lie, make them say, because they have no choice, that I'm an object of desire.*

She would never admit it to a soul, but there was something sexual in her attraction to Katie. And not just sexual, but aggressive too—she wanted Katie, and she envied and hated Katie—wanted badly to harm her. *And why shouldn't I? She's a transphobe. She tried to harm me!* And Jhanvi knew this was true, knew Katie was, in some sense, a bigot, and that if she told the story to another trans person, Jhanvi could make her own actions sound very fair and well merited: they were rich, I had nothing; they were selfish and turned the world into their playground, and I took some well-merited reparations; I caused them a brief discomfort, and in return they changed my life and allowed me to live for the first time.

But I can't help thinking that if I do these things—if I wrap her around my finger, make myself at home in her life, the way I want to, then I will be the bad tranny, the male-socialized one, entitled to a woman's time and attention and body, forcing herself on women who don't need or want her.

And yet, if Jhanvi forewent this power—if she moved away

with Roshie, if she diminished, and went into the west, and remained Galadriel—then nobody would ever know. They would look at her for now and for always without ever under-standing the Dark Queen she could've been.

These thoughts blossomed in Jhanvi's drunken mind with-out coming clearly into focus. She would not have said that she intended to do violence to Katie. In fact, if forced to fully enunciate her plans, what they might've come closest to is "I want to be her friend." But the form they took, and the imag-ery in her mind, and the feelings behind that imagery, were so violent that the feelings themselves felt wrong.

After finishing the second cup of whiskey, she got up and looked at herself in the mirror. Her lipstick was ugly, spread down over her lip, and her mustache was showing in dark spots on her upper lip. She smiled to herself, and she licked two fingers of her right hand, and she drew them lengthwise across her face, smearing her foundation and lipstick in a way that was subtle but unmistakable. She looked *wrong*—no real trans woman would ever allow herself to be seen this way.

Jhanvi took off one of her dangling earrings, laid it on the counter, and went downstairs in search of Katie.

• • •

Katie's room was the smallest in the house. It didn't even have a window to the outside, just to an air vent that looked across to the kitchen. She slept on a bamboo mat, and aside from her standing desk and one beanbag chair, she had no visible posses-sions—everything must fit neatly inside her closet.

"Hey," Jhanvi said, sitting cross-legged on the beanbag chair. "How's it going?"

"Okay," Katie said. She was leaning into the desk, her knees resting on little pads set into the column, the blue light of the computer reflected on her rimless glasses. "Lots of emails. Lots to make up from the weekend."

Jhanvi didn't hesitate. She had gamed out the beginning of this interaction in her head.

"Hey," Jhanvi said. "If Roshie goes to your bosses, let me know. I'll speak up for you."

Katie turned and frowned. "What?"

"I mean, she threatened to. I said not to. But she's a loose cannon."

"Why would she talk to my bosses?"

"About . . ." Jhanvi paused. "Locking me out?"

"Oh," Katie said.

There was a moment of silence. She turned back to her computer. The pointer slid aimlessly across the screen. Her long arms were milk pale, her body white, deliciously white, like the women who'd followed their husbands to Bombay two centuries ago—the memsahibs who'd sat on Victorian furniture, chatting with each other, waving their fingers at coolies to bring them more gin and tonic.

"That's really troubling," Katie said. "That's not how this house normally operates."

Jhanvi had told herself to expect trouble. Katie wouldn't fold immediately. She was armored in purposeful ignorance. Watching Katie murmur to herself and get herself worked up into self-righteousness, Jhanvi had a thought: *I'm letting myself be sidelined. Turning myself into a eunuch or handmaiden. How do these girls do it? How do they get me to kowtow to their version of reality?*

Jhanvi had intermittently, in the past, gotten into reading pick-up-artist books. These were books by nerdy guys who tried to crack the code of picking up women. At first, Jhanvi had read them as one of those guys, but even after transitioning, she had wanted to understand how to have charisma, how to make people want her. The pick-up-artist guys talked about the power of holding frame: the power of imposing your reality on someone and holding on, until they acceded to it. Beautiful, confident, well-off girls like Katie—the guys would say—have a powerful frame by nature. You need, through training and willpower, to match what their upbringing gave them.

"Well, yeah," Jhanvi said. "She was upset. I was almost raped out there. Well, I mean, I did actually blow a guy."

"Wow," Katie said. "I . . ." She turned, nudging the side of her glasses. "I didn't know. Do . . . do you . . . I mean I'm probably not the person you want to talk to about . . ."

Jhanvi stayed silent, looked at the girl. She was in uniform: yoga pants, sports bra, loose T-shirt with large armholes, cut a bit short to show her belly.

"That is . . . I mean . . . if you . . . I mean . . ." Katie took a long sigh. "It's very generous of you. To warn me."

"I blew a corner store owner," Jhanvi said. "So I could have somewhere to be. My phone was out of battery. When I was drunk, and he was sober. I, like, couldn't really consent."

"Wow," Katie said. "Do you . . . do you . . . is he somebody you want to . . . I mean . . . he's a local . . . someone here who . . . the police probably wouldn't do anything, but we could protest to the neighborhood . . ." The girl kept stuttering, rambling. Jhanvi let her eyes bore into Katie, dragging out the moment, thinking, *I will remember this for the rest of my life*. There was a knock on the door, and Audrey said, "Hello . . ."

"I actually don't want her in here right now," Jhanvi said.

"Oh . . . uh . . ." Katie looked at the door. "Can you give me a second?"

"Are you okay?" Audrey said.

"Did you text her?" Jhanvi asked. She knew from the cadence of her voice, which was getting low, that she sounded like a serial killer. Seen from the outside, with her hulking body lying on the chair—her eyes purposefully empty—this couldn't help but seem dangerous, like the monstrous fantasy of every trans-hating radical feminist, worried about women's spaces being invaded by *men*.

"The thing is," Jhanvi said. "I'm not mad at that guy. He

helped me. I felt valuable, like someone wanted me. You're the one who hurt me, Katie. I'm a human being."

"And I'm sorry," she said.

To Jhanvi's surprise, the other girl was crying. Jhanvi had to struggle to keep her face straight. She thought, *How pathetic.* She didn't complete the thought, but if she'd had the time or the presence of mind, it would've been, *How pathetic, to be unable to bear the consequences of your choices.* Jhanvi waited for a second, and the crying got deeper and more prolonged. Katie didn't sit down. She lay against the side of the desk, so Jhanvi expected the computer would go tumbling, or something would fall over, and Jhanvi would have to rush to catch it—and wasn't that part of it, these women, who acted out this fragility—Jhanvi knew that everything depended on not showing an ounce of pity.

"I'm sorry," Katie said. "I'm sorry. I'm sorry. I don't know what happened." She crumpled inward, rubbing at her eyes.

"You think I'm disgusting," Jhanvi had intended to make her voice low, manly, but somehow it escaped from the front of her mouth, surprisingly high and pure in its tone.

Katie's phone chimed a few times, and Jhanvi yearned to tell her to get it, except if she did, then Jhanvi would lose. Holding her frame—*I have been wronged*—was intensely difficult. Everything in her background and personality had acculturated her to cosset the skinny white girl.

"I could've died," Jhanvi said. "And I get why you did it—you think I'm dangerous and disgusting. Everybody here is naked all the time. Has sex. My body horrifies you."

"No!" Katie said. "No, no, you can't think that. I wasn't thinking. That's what happened. I just . . . I didn't realize your safety net was . . ."

And a bell rang in Jhanvi's head. Her plan had simply been to come here and put pressure on Katie and see what would happen. But now her brain spun: What did she want? A permanent spot to stay? Or an even bigger prize?

Katie was still crying. It was terrible how prolonged the sobs were, how red her face had gotten. "I just never thought."

"Get off it," Jhanvi said. "Every single interaction we have, all you do is try to protect other people from me."

"No! I'm sorry if it seemed that way! You were inexperienced with Henry, there's so much to learn. You're going to take trainings and . . ."

She sounded so sincere. It was in the catch of surprise in her throat. Like her tears, it didn't quite accord with Jhanvi's image of her. *I'm obviously more sociopath than she is.*

Jhanvi took a breath.

"Just come off it," Jhanvi said. "Aren't you ashamed? Just admit you think I'm a danger."

"I mean, I didn't know you, but—"

"You just texted Audrey! Because you felt threatened, by me! Why are you lying?"

"I did text her, but I thought maybe she could help intercede to—"

"Katie," Jhanvi said. "You don't think I'm a woman."

She was quiet for a second. "I—no—no—nothing like that. That's not. I don't. I definitely think you're a woman."

She held Jhanvi's gaze while saying it. Jhanvi shook her head. "You are such a liar. Do you admit it even to yourself? We're alone here. Look at me. I'm bigger than you. I'm hairy. I have a penis." Jhanvi stood up. She raised her arms, then she clutched at the sides of her dress, pulling them out, making herself large. "Katie," she said. "I walked into your room, stopped your friend from coming in. I crashed at your house, made myself at home. I came to parties where you take drugs, get naked, are vulnerable. If you thought I was a predator, what you did at least makes sense. It's the only way it makes sense."

Jhanvi maintained eye contact with the girl, who looked away. "I just want you to know I'm not dangerous," Jhanvi murmured. "I've never hurt anybody."

Even saying the words to herself, they sounded false. Jhanvi took a deep breath.

"Have you ever thought about what it's like to walk around like this? To be so instantly not wanted, not needed?"

"You *are* wanted."

"Marrying Henry would've saved my life. With those procedures, I could've gotten a new face, gotten my hairline changed, maybe I could've passed, maybe not, but at least I could've felt *safe.* I go out on those streets, and I'm scared, Katie. People like me get murdered out there." She'd thought this was just a line, but unexpectedly, tears came to her eyes, and a stream of thoughts came down: *Maybe I am actually scared. Maybe I'm just that good a liar . . . either way, this is perfect.* "I am fucking wasting my life, Katie. You know how you've got a life, and you do things, and you have boyfriends, and you go on adventures, and have a career? I have a life, just the same as you. But mine is *empty.*"

"It's *not* empty," Katie said. "Don't say that. You've done so much good here. You've changed Roshie, changed Henry, helped so many people."

"It's not enough," Jhanvi said. The silence crept between them, and Jhanvi waited. Her plan was for Katie to somehow reintroduce the idea of marrying, but she said nothing. So Jhanvi said, "You talk about community, but nobody here thinks it's their job to help me."

"That's not true," Katie said. "We're really looking."

"I can't do it alone," Jhanvi said. "Someone needs to step up. I will die out there."

"Don't worry," Katie said. "Don't worry. You have so many friends . . ."

"I just . . . like, I don't even know who to ask. Henry had good trans benefits? Who else does . . . ? Like . . . like . . ." She paused, the moment had come. "Like . . . what about you, Katie? Does your nonprofit . . . do they have anything like that?"

"I—" Katie said. "I—I—I'm not sure."

"That was only an example!" Jhanvi said. "I just . . . I need help."

"No, no," Katie said. "You're right. Let me think. Let me talk to Audrey. Let me . . ."

Now Jhanvi gulped. She could leave at this moment, but something hung unsaid between them. And the mention of Audrey brought Jhanvi's last chess piece into the match. "And . . . I could talk to Roshie," Jhanvi said. "About . . . about the event space. About the party. I could talk to her. About keeping things, err . . . keeping it copacetic."

"Oh!" Katie's lips were the bud of a pale, pink rose. "I—"

"Let me talk to her."

"You don't have to!"

"I will," Jhanvi said. "It's what friends do."

Jhanvi went to the door, and she put her long fingers on the knob, caressing the silver handle. She stood with her arm extended, and she looked at Katie, who was still pale and withdrawn, still leaning against the desk. Jhanvi smiled at her, and she smiled back, wanly. Then Jhanvi left.

17

Over the next few days, Jhanvi got two check-in emails from Katie. One was terse, saying she was researching her org's trans benefits. The other was vague and long-winded, sent late at night, delving deep into Katie's history of activism, and apologizing again for being so emotional, for centering herself, for robbing Jhanvi of her voice. Jhanvi had heard about emails like these—emails that had that Maoist self-criticism quality of people being beaten down psychologically until they were forced to confess to thought crimes—the sort of email that arose when a leftist whose whole identity was rooted in always being politically correct suddenly found themselves forced into the wrong—but Jhanvi had thought this kind of breakdown was, at least in the modern world, a lurid fantasy concocted by conservative writers. Maybe it had been, initially, and the leftists had believed the conservatives and thought, *Well, this is what I have to do now.*

In any case, Jhanvi was both attracted and repelled. The lack of moral integrity—that word, *integrity*, was one she found herself using a lot these days—the lack of moral integrity was appalling, but Jhanvi liked the rawness and honesty. Jhanvi couldn't figure out what to write back, and while she dithered, she got a text from Henry: *Hey I never see you anymore. Are you guys ever gonna come down for dinner?*

Roshie, no. Me, yes. Just lazy about my makeup and stuff
You don't need that tho
Lol
I mean ur still a girl even if ur not all glammed up
Lol
*Hey are we not friends anymore? Bc just tell me and I'll leave
you alone*
We're friends
*Then come down. Spend the night down here sometimes. I've
got a room! Roshie'll like the break*

Jhanvi's ears burned. She scratched the outside of one
eyelid. After a few seconds, she wrote back: *you free tonight?*
Totally
I'll be down soon

She got up, stepped over Roshie, who was dialed into a
book about theoretical physics—the girl was a surprisingly big
reader, of real books, not just comic books and Anna Laurent
polemics—and went to the bathroom. Her cosmetics were
pushed into one small corner, along with a terse Roshie missive
penned on a Post-it: *Can you keep tidy?*

Getting ready took some time, and she fumbled a little bit,
needed the concealer to clean up an errant line, and she made
the classic mistake of putting on her face before getting dressed,
then had to maneuver carefully to avoid smearing foundation
on her collar. But in an hour, she knocked on Henry's door, wearing a short denim skirt and a mesh top over her bra.

He grinned out the corner of his mouth: "Hey." He looked
down the hall.

"Nobody saw. Not even Roshie," Jhanvi said. "She's in her
own world."

The words only made his smile larger. When she walked in,
the door clicked shut. She sat on his bed, feeling sweat spring-
ing from every pore. Her body had that clean but damp feeling
she remembered from her high school prom—the sense that a

layer of filth was accumulating between clean skin and clean clothes.

"Hey," he said. "I just wanted to debrief with you. How're you feeling?"

"Good," she said. "Oh . . . Katie talked to you. What a fucking pimp."

"Yeah, she's awesome."

"No, I mean she's a literal pimp—she's like your procurer. I love it. You guys are so strange here. It's just weird she hasn't found someone for Roshie."

His laugh was high and warm. He sat on the arm of his loveseat, and they stared across the distance between them. "You, uhh, want something to loosen you up?"

"What're you offering?"

"I've got some, uhh, MDMA, I think?"

"That would be awesome."

He went through his drawers and his closets. He thought it was in an old pair of pants. She stayed on his bed, sweating desperately. The sound of women's laughter flowed in from the bars outside. Women's voices were higher, carried farther, like the flutes in an orchestra.

He pulled out a small clear bag with white powder. "I think this is MDMA. Or 2ci or 2cb or 2ce or something like that."

"But not cocaine."

"No, I don't touch stimulants anymore," he said. He slapped it against his palm, and they stood there for a second.

"So, umm, you were debriefing."

"Oh!" he said. "Yeah, just . . . that was one of the most awesome sexual experiences of my life. I, like, you know . . . I'm sorry, I thought it was just a phone thing . . . but that was amazing. I've never thought of myself as really *queer* queer, but . . ."

Her face froze, but he didn't notice, going on about really loving her dick and loving the feeling of being full. They heard voices outside, and he lowered his voice. She remembered now, he'd slept with Katie and Audrey, both of them—she snorted, impressed with her steadiness and utter contempt for this person.

"Come here, bitch," she said. "Give me that . . ."

• • •

She enjoyed parts of it, mostly when he sucked her dick with her skirt pulled up over his face. But topping him was excruciating, of course, and her cruelty this time wasn't purely playacting: it had a tinge of reality. "You are pathetic. You're not a real man," she said to him.

Later, when he was asleep, she crept back upstairs and showered, and as the steam boiled away the remnants of her makeup, she spoke to herself the words she would've wanted, looking back and forth and doing different voices, like a crazy person:

So, that was really intense, how did you feel about what we did?

Not great. It makes me dysphoric to fuck a guy. I don't totally enjoy it. I mean, it was consensual. I got off on making you happy, but it's not sex sex for me.

Hey, I feel the same a lot of the time! I feel so much pressure to perform. It's hard for a dude here. I know that seems like a weird thing to complain about.

No, I totally get it. And I figured me topping you kind of released you from that pressure, and it's great. By the way, I don't think it makes you queer at all—like, it's psychosexual, you want a woman to dominate you, mistreat you, everyone knows that. This is a safe way to do it, because I know you. And, hey, I am sorry I didn't do all that aftercare stuff. I'll do better next time.

Cool. What can I do for you? I mean, assuming you want to hook up at all?

Just, treat me like you'd treat a real girl. I know I'm not one, but pretend.

You are, though!

This was the part that devolved into wild fantasy:

I'm not. You wouldn't do this with me if I was, you wouldn't expose yourself.

Hey, when you were a guy, we only hooked up that once, but I didn't want to go further—because to be honest, I wasn't really into you. The girl part of you is what I love. And you're so beautiful.

I just feel fake sometimes. Like I'm a lonely dude with shaved legs and little tits, who's eunuched himself to worm his way into women's company. I, like, am so hung up on your roommates. I love and hate them, it's so confusing.

Same with me. Same with them together! You wouldn't believe the crazy fights Audrey and Katie have with each other. Life is complicated. Every girl I meet is obsessed with those two—they have their own gravitational pull! Believe me, you're not sick. There is nothing male about you. If you believe anything, you should believe that.

Jhanvi laughed to herself. In her mind, it all sounded so safe, so sane, so consensual. But in real life, such conversations never happened, she was pretty sure.

• • •

Jhanvi had expected the manager at Toni's bar to berate her, to call her a terrible dishwasher, to constantly correct her, like the old-timers at Green Magic had. But instead, he was ridiculously pleasant, and so grateful, saying, "I am so happy you can come in" at the beginning of each shift.

"I literally live next door," she said.

"That's incredible," he said. "Most of the staff are in, like, Vallejo." His voice was high and distant. He was always tossing his wavy hair around, and he seemed really young. But he was the nephew of the owner or something. "I'm so glad you can fill in, we're so short-staffed."

Most of the back-of-house staff was Mexican—as in, literally from Mexico—and the front-of-house staff, like Toni, were mostly white and Asian—a racial distinction that didn't seem to interest anyone, not even Katie, who shrugged whenever Jhanvi brought it up. Jhanvi got the impression that her having such a working-class job made the other members of Trial By Fire a little uncomfortable. She liked when people at house gatherings asked what she did and she could say: *I wash dishes.* She still felt like she was slumming, even though the money was genuinely helpful—she'd spent down half her savings over the last month on booze and food and drugs. She still didn't pay any rent—she'd offered to Katie, but the girl had said, "Let's figure out the marriage first."

Although they didn't see each other much during work because Toni was front of house and Jhanvi was back, they still found time to talk. She told Toni about the hooking up.

"With your roommate?" Toni said. "The marriage guy! The gorgeous one? I thought you were already together!"

"No marriage anymore." Jhanvi's face reddened. "I might've oversold it when we first talked, but now I'm his whore."

"He pays you?!" Toni said. Her eyebrows were plucked now, and they displayed surprise excellently. The smell of disinfectant and beer rose from the counter, and Jhanvi leaned back so it wouldn't get on her.

"No, just a metaphor," Jhanvi said. "I've been feeling a little . . ." She took a breath. "Off-kilter. I dunno, my roommates. They're so gorgeous. It makes me insecure. I feel, I don't know. They make me feel . . ."

"I've seen them," Toni said. "They're basic. You're the gorgeous one. I said it the first day we met."

Toni's voice was higher, and Jhanvi's heart melted, looking at her, this girl, roleplaying the best friend. Toni had an appointment booked to get on hormones and was out at work now, but still hadn't told her dad.

Toni said all the things a trans friend ought to say, about how Jhanvi was beautiful and didn't need work done, but it made sense if it would help with dysphoria. She was more tapped into the rhetoric than Jhanvi was. Sometimes Jhanvi felt bad for not being closer to more trans-femmes.

Synestra unexpectedly texted her as well, and they got coffee together. Synestra spent a lot of their conversation boasting and talking about her tricks, but the intimacy of the chat was nice. She allowed Jhanvi in, talked to her one-to-one, as a trans friend.

"Of course you don't pass," Synestra said. "But your friend isn't wrong. You've got striking eyes and long legs, and I bet Hen goes wild for your cock."

Jhanvi giggled at the foreign lilt Synestra gave the word: *cawk*. And even Synestra said, "You're more girl than any cis bitch can imagine. It's a secret power, don't you think? Actually choosing to be a woman. Something we know—like, to use that terrible cliché, the red pill. We know our own power."

"I don't feel that way," Jhanvi said. "I feel awful."

"From my perspective, you've done well."

But in some ways, the pep talks made her feel more alone. This sense of being a monster, being set apart, even from other trans girls, didn't abate, even though she knew it was such a trans cliché—how they all thought, *Every other trans girl is normal, but I'm the unique monster who's really a sick one.* Internalized transphobia and transmisogyny, she knew. She needed therapy, which she couldn't afford.

Because the final piece of the puzzle, the thing she didn't reveal to anyone, was the promise she'd made Katie. It was clear, although without an explicit quid pro quo, that the marriage plan hung in the balance. The other girl had already asked, *Hey sorry for the delay. Still researching our trans benefits. In the meantime, do you mind talking to Roshie about the event space? She's threatening to pull out, and we can't find anywhere else for the party.*

Everything came to a head at a house meeting—more of an

ambush—where Katie and Audrey showed up at Roshie's door. They pushed in and sat on her couch, amidst the neat piles of books and the trailing video game controller cords. Audrey was in jeans and a tank top; Katie had just come from work, and wore a tan suit and a blouse with an open collar.

"Roshie, we've asked you to suggest mitigations," Katie said. "For your concerns about noise, sound, and fire. But you've been completely unreasonable."

"You guys have no assets," Roshie said, tucking her chin down, staring at the floor. "I'm the one who's liable."

Jhanvi was on the loveseat with Roshie, the two of them sitting with their knees barely not touching. Jhanvi picked up a pillow and handed it to Rosh, who held it close to her chest, as a barrier.

"I still don't understand what happened," Audrey said. "Why did you leave the camping trip?"

"Because you lied to me. You said the first day would stay inclusive even to those of us who aren't nonmonogamous, and you broke that—you all got together immediately! And I just don't trust that you'll keep good order in the event space. I can't take the risk. And I owe it to all the marginalized people living in that building."

This was the new strain in Roshie's language: social justice rhetoric about the rest of the building, particularly Adriana, whose husband was ill and who was worried about noise from the party.

"I promised her she'd stay safe," Roshie said. "And maybe that doesn't matter to you, but it matters to me."

Katie and Audrey double-teamed Roshie, arguing incessantly, words spinning on top of words, but everyone was too well trained. Even Roshie knew how to say the right ones to make the party look unconscionable, which admittedly wasn't too hard to do, because Trial By Fire members were spending hundreds of thousands of dollars to have a sex party, with lots of noise and a pyrotechnic display, in a working-class Latino neighborhood.

After an hour of this, Audrey's fists clenched, and she let out a shriek. "This is bullshit!" she said. "You don't care about any of this, Roshie. I'm sorry your feelings are hurt. I'm sorry you felt uncomfortable. I can't stop people from having sex. That is crazy! You sound like a crazy person!"

"Audrey," Katie said.

"No . . . no. No. No!" Audrey said. "This is so problematic. This is exactly what TBF is *not* about. She's trying to dictate how people express themselves sexually."

"I'm not dictating anything," Roshie said. "Find your own fucking place for your fucking exclusive transphobic racist fatphobic yuppie sex parties. You're done. You're both done."

But neither of them left. And when Jhanvi tried to suggest they leave and regroup, nobody responded, not even Roshie. The other brown girl's lip was twisted up, and Jhanvi got the sense she was enjoying dominating these two, making them listen to her. Jhanvi didn't think Roshie's concerns about the building or about Adriana were totally fake, but she also didn't think they were sufficient for this behavior. She was acting out her hurt feelings, and everyone knew it.

Jhanvi had stayed silent throughout this scene, making calming gestures and sometimes holding Roshie's hand. But now she spoke. "Roshie," she said. "The event space is paid up for a year. Let them have the party. It looks petty otherwise. Then give them the chance to fundraise to take over the lease, so you won't be financially at risk anymore? Does that sound good?"

"It won't make the whole thing safe or right," Roshie said. "I mean, last year we had fifteen hundred people come. Can you imagine the stampede if a fire broke out? Everyone would die."

"You don't have to come," Audrey said.

"But who'll work the fucking lights?" Roshie said.

"They'll work it out," Jhanvi said.

"No," Roshie said. "There's nothing in it for me or for anyone else. It's just her fucking ego. So fuck you."

"There is for me," Jhanvi said.

Roshie blinked. Jhanvi had said the words quietly, but they got everyone's attention.

"TBF has been really special for me. It's really opened me up," Jhanvi said. "This is . . . it's a chance for me to feel seen. And, uhh, there's somebody I'm planning to go with."

"All right," Katie said. "Let's . . . let's take a break."

Roshie went to the bathroom and locked the door, turned on the shower, and didn't come out for a long time.

18

Roshie didn't talk to Jhanvi after her betrayal. When Jhanvi tried to speak, she turned her back. But Jhanvi caught her crying once in the corner. She knelt by her, said, "I am sorry, Rosh," but the other girl was too overwhelmed to respond.

Jhanvi spent that night in Henry's bed while he fucked Audrey next door. And the same thing happened the next night—another lonely stint in his boy-bedroom, with its futon and standing desk and lack of decor. On the third night, she was going to go upstairs, but Henry dropped in and said since Audrey was out, maybe he and Jhanvi should spend a whole night together.

Then Jhanvi got an email from Katie with notes about the wedding, which they'd conduct at The Guilty Party to make everything look real. Meanwhile, Jhanvi was feted by everyone as the savior of the party, and Henry in particular came and said, "That was really brave. I know this wasn't totally your social scene at first, but I appreciate your sticking up for everyone. It's not something a white guy is really qualified to say, but I knew what Roshie was saying was unfair, but everyone was afraid to say anything. Sometimes I think people are so dishonest with their social justice rhetoric. They say things that are just not true. Like, we are so not racist here, not transphobes . . . but everyone was too polite to push back on her . . ."

After that, Jhanvi added a new twist to their games: she

called Henry a bigot that night, and he came so hard that the squeezing of his sphincter actually aroused a hint of sensation in her normally nerveless dick.

• • •

Over breakfast with Jhanvi, Katie was all jittery in her freshly pressed work clothes. "Okay, I'm part of a small org, and they'll really be unhappy if they think the marriage is fake, so we need to document this. I'll announce the engagement on Facebook. You should do that too. Audrey will get a wedding license, and she can marry us at The Guilty Party."

Jhanvi nodded. "Sounds good." She slathered butter on toast. Henry came in, shirtless, wearing pajama pants. He poured milk into a jar of granola, then took it into the dining room. She drifted in after him and sat down at the dining room table. He dipped his spoon into the jar. After a moment, he lifted the whole jar and drank some of the milk straight out of it.

Then he looked up with a big smile that somehow got even larger as it settled on his face. He leaned back in his chair, and everything about him—his hands and his feet, and even the hairs on his arms that stood out in the light of the sun—seemed oversized and expansive.

"You really settled down okay," he said. "Like, it all really happened for you. I'm happy."

Her back prickled. She hated when people discussed the wedding. "Thanks."

Audrey popped in: "Oh, hey, you're all here! This is such a poly moment."

Jhanvi forced herself not to grimace. Audrey had taken the revelation way too well, and it almost seemed to have strengthened her relationship with Henry. If she'd been asked, Jhanvi would've said learning about her and Henry's hooking up would've ruined him for the other girl, but Audrey was a bit more open-minded than that, she guessed.

Audrey gave them both a big smile and let her hand drift across Jhanvi's back. The touch was sudden—Jhanvi didn't have time to jump—and then it was over, and Audrey was next to Katie, taking a coffee cup. The dining table was long, meant for guests, and the four of them were clustered all at one end of the dim room, watching the tip of Sutro Tower catch the light in the distance.

"Hey, Jhanvi," Audrey said. "How're you feeling? Are you worried at all?"

"About what?"

"Don't put that on her," Katie said. "My problems aren't hers."

"I'm just asking!"

"Err, no, I'm not worried," Jhanvi said. "I'm excited. Katie got me some papers from her provider—" Katie's employer contracted with a separate nonprofit that sold trans healthcare policies. "It's insane, they have everyone, they pay for everything. I've been calling doctors and stuff, which I guess you're allowed to do, even if you're not authorized yet. I'm getting appointments. They even cover electro." Jhanvi touched the bottom of her nose, the stray hairs that couldn't be shaved. "I got laser done, but I have some stubborn hairs that need to be shocked. It's like, life-changingly good."

"I'm glad," Katie said. She got up, still looking twitchy and jittery and pale, and grabbed her briefcase. "See you guys for dinner?"

"Hen and I are out," Audrey said. "He's my date for a play party in Pacifica."

Jhanvi frowned. People have group sex in Pacifica? It's so dark and cold. Seems absurd. But Audrey said, "Oh you're upset! Did you want him? I can reschedule."

"What? No," Jhanvi said. "He's not our kid."

"Don't kink-shame," Henry said. "What if I was into that?"

"No, uhh, I was just wondering why anyone would have a sex party in Pacifica."

"It's so hip over there now!" Audrey said. "I love the ocean!"

Katie gave them a tight smile, then she said goodbye and walked out. Audrey yawned, filling up her lungs with a breath, then she threw out her arms. "I'm so happy for you. Jhanvi, when's your natal day? I'll add it to the calendar."

"Your birthday," Henry clarified. "She keeps track for all my lovers."

The whole thing was just too grotesque. Jhanvi couldn't tell if this was territory marking or not. If so, it was misplaced. Jhanvi didn't at all value the sex she had with Henry—it was purely transactional—part of the complex psychodynamics that kept her tied to this lifestyle. Looking at him, she couldn't believe they'd once been friends. Maybe this was what it was like for a young girl to have sex with some old fuck—they appreciated it so much, and yet mistreated you to put you in your place.

"Hey, now that she's gone, we've gotta be careful with Katie, okay? She's not telling anyone at work that this isn't a real marriage. She's afraid they'll be pissed if they knew she was exploiting their benefits," Audrey said. "She 'came out' to her bosses. Played it totally straight. Told her parents too. She's gonna be public with it, so everything online tracks."

"She told her parents she's a lesbian?" Jhanvi said. "That's absurd."

"Yeah, she told them something. Her bosses would be really pissed if they knew she was taking advantage of them. So this needs to stay on the down-low. People have to think you're at least lovers. Have you told your parents the truth?"

Jhanvi shrugged. "They've been blocked online forever. So they won't see the announcement. They're in India, anyway."

"So do you, like, talk to them at all?" Henry asked.

Jhanvi rolled her eyes. "Yeah, of course."

"Cool. Cool," Henry said. "Welp. What're you gonna wear?"

"Oh . . ." Jhanvi pursed her lips. "I, uhh, I have no idea."

"Katie has a wedding dress already," Audrey said.

"What? No, she's not gonna use that for this. She'll use that for her real wedding," Henry said.

"Hold up," Jhanvi raised a hand. "Are you joking? She has a dress already?"

"Yeah, like two years ago a coworker broke up with her fiancée, and Katie bought it off her, cheap," Audrey said.

"That's . . . weird," Jhanvi said.

"I dunno, she likes a deal," Henry said.

Jhanvi wanted to pursue the topic further. Nobody thought it was insane that uber-minimalist Katie kept a wedding dress in her tiny little closet? But the conversation moved on, Henry and Audrey discussing what Jhanvi ought to wear and asking questions about the wedding party. There was a ripple of slamming doors, and Jhanvi shouted, "Hey Rosh!"

But the footsteps didn't stop. "Rosh!" Jhanvi yelled. "We're in here!"

The front door opened and slammed again.

"She never eats breakfast anymore," Audrey said.

"Yeah," Henry said. "What does she eat?"

"Cereal," Jhanvi said. "She keeps, like, Frosted Flakes and milk in a mini fridge upstairs."

"Thank you so much for supporting me, by the way," Audrey said. "It was *so* healing to hear you speak up."

The conversation continued, circling around various topics, the three of them lightly bantering. Audrey touched Jhanvi on the back again, and it made Jhanvi wonder, *She can't possibly be into me, can she?* The idea left Jhanvi oddly cold. Strange to think of Audrey embodied, as a person, with desires—fucking her would make Jhanvi utterly anxious.

As the conversation went on, it became more and more about that unlikeliest of persons, Roshie. Henry and Audrey wanted to know so much about her: what hours she kept, what she did all day, how much money she had, what she ate, where she went on weekends, how she'd learned all the little contractor's tricks she knew.

"From YouTube, I think," Jhanvi said.

"Oh," Henry said. "I remember once, the toilet at the event space was clogged, and the plumber canceled on us, and she was like, whatever, and just snaked the drain herself. Who even owns a snake?"

"She rented it from Home Depot," Jhanvi said.

"I just wish that I knew what was bothering her so much," Audrey said. "We're not perfect, but we're a force for good! She's acting like we're these horrible rich people who don't care about anyone else."

"Maybe that's her experience of you."

"But she's richer than any of us!" Audrey said.

"Yeah, and she kinda—" Jhanvi was going to say *bought your friendship*. But she paused and thought, *No, I cannot be agent provocateur anymore. I cannot sabotage myself—I'm no longer that kind of drunk.* "I agree," Jhanvi said. "You guys have been good about taking me in, right?"

"Except when you were homeless for a night," Henry said.

"That was an accident. Like, can you imagine most of our college friends?" Jhanvi said. "I've been here for *weeks*. They'd have called the sheriffs. You didn't. That means something. I don't think you're hypocrites."

Unexpectedly, Audrey's eyes got wet. "Thanks," she said. "That really . . . that means so much." Audrey's eyelids nictitated, whisked away the moisture, but her sad smile remained.

• • •

"Okay," Meena said. "I'm gonna do the annoying older cousin thing right now and hand you a phone with your parents on the other side. Sorry."

Jhanvi grimaced, taking the phone. They were having dinner in the financial district, at a fancy Thai restaurant near Meena's office. Meena was in tight slacks and a pin-striped blazer cinched low around her waist. In some ways it resembled

Katie's professional outfits, but Meena's entire manner and coloration were different. She had a waterfall of raven hair, not really parted in any particular direction, which she constantly teased and tossed to either side as she spoke. She wore light lipstick and kitten heels, and she spoke with a loud, brash voice, shoving her strong jaw forward into conversations and gesticulating to punctuate her words.

Jhanvi had walked for an hour to get to the restaurant, just to have something to do. She'd gone through a pretty bad part of town—the part where drugs were essentially legal, where there were tent camps and safe injection sites—and she'd wondered if the unhoused people might hassle her. But no, they'd let her pass without a word. The thought had occurred to her lately that she was only a few steps from becoming one of them. That nothing was stopping her from simply sitting down in one of the long lines of people outside the soup kitchen and just staying there, becoming part of this life. But of course that was a fantasy—that would never happen. She might play the role of marginalized person, but there were infinite gradations of marginalization, and for some reason, she felt compelled to retain rigorous honesty with herself about where she belonged. Except, she'd also wondered, maybe that was only an illusion: maybe she was a pathetic declassed person hanging on to vestiges of lost status.

Her mom's tinny voice came from the phone. "Hello, hello..."

"Oh, go ahead," Meena said. "Answer it. I told them you're alive and okay, but they didn't believe me."

Jhanvi put the phone to her ear. "Hello?"

"Ni—Jhanvi," her mom said. "Can you hear me?"

"Mmmhmmm."

"Are you there?"

"Yep, I'm good."

"What is happening? Why are you still in San Francisco? What happened to your job and your house in Sacramento?"

"I moved here. Staying with friends. I told you this..."

"We know you're drinking, but what other drugs are you taking?"

"You don't know I'm drinking," Jhanvi said. They'd tried the *We know you're drinking* sneak attack on her a few times while she was staying with them. It'd only worked once, but they were very proud of it. "But I am drinking. I'm actually not an alcoholic. Turns out that was just gender dysphoria."

Jhanvi had said this so many times she wasn't sure whether or not it was true. It certainly *sounded* true.

"How much cocaine are you doing?"

"I'm not rich enough for cocaine," Jhanvi said. "I did, uh, I did mushrooms once with friends. That's literally it. But you don't have to believe me, Mom. I'm free. I'm a launched little birdie. I'm sorry I worried you, but I have a place to live."

"What's this about marriage?"

"Ohhhhhhhh," Jhanvi pursed her lips.

"Sorry," Meena said. "Had to tell them about that. Should I give you privacy?"

Jhanvi shrugged. Meena took the phone back.

"Hi, Auntie," she said. "I'm going to go to the bathroom and give you some privacy. And Jhanvi, the waiters know what I like here—I definitely tip them enough—just tell them you're with Meena and she wants the usual."

"Yeah," Jhanvi said, taking the phone back. "Umm . . . about the marriage, it's just to get the trans benefits my friend has."

"Isn't that illegal?" her mom asked.

"No, I don't think so."

"It sounds very illegal. I am almost certain it is illegal insurance fraud."

"Yeah," Jhanvi said. "I guess so. Probably."

"Do you think this is such a good idea?"

"No," Jhanvi said. "Not really. It's not the best idea."

"Then why are you doing it? Jhanvi, dear, haven't your schemes landed you in enough trouble? If I or your father had wanted, we could've reported you to the police when you opened those credit cards, and you'd be in jail."

Her mother went on like this for a little while, with interruptions from her dad and her sister and her sister's husband as well, all of them asking her to think of them, and not be so selfish. The worst moment was when her dad started shouting about how his dad had been an alcoholic and a gambler, and how, at twenty years old, Jhanvi's dad had needed to go out and search the streets for his dad when he didn't come home, and he would find his dad in a ditch, and he'd have to carry the man home.

"But that's not me," Jhanvi said.

"How do you know, son?" he asked. "How do you know? Everyone thinks it is not them, but look at it from our perspective."

"No, from your perspective the way you're acting makes total sense," Jhanvi said. "But believe me, I'm doing the right thing for myself. I just, you know, I have to find my place in the world. Sacramento wasn't . . . I wasn't at home there. I didn't have a good life."

"Your friends won't be there for you," her dad said. "They won't be there for you when you're in the ditch. My dad's friends abandoned him there. Simply left him! Always, it was me and my mom picking him up. Your family is all you have, but your mom and I are reaching our breaking point. And someday— someday we will not—it is simply too painful, son."

"I know," Jhanvi said. "I'm with you, one hundred percent. More than you can possibly know. Friends are bullshit. I know they won't be there for me."

"Then why are you doing this?"

"Because you just called me 'son,'" Jhanvi said.

"What is this nonsense? We have been more than supportive!" her dad said. "We tried to keep you on our insurance, did we not? We wrote letters to keep you on! We offered even to pay for your pills! We pushed back our retirement plans, cut into our income, so you could get sober at our house. We have—"

"Dad," she said. "Dad, sorry. I should've been clearer. I just need to be myself. I'm sorry. It's okay. You're totally right to be worried. I would be worried too if I were you. But I've got this."

"How many times can you say this? Your judgment is simply not good. You simply cannot be trusted. And I am warning you, Nikhil, if you do this, you are dead to us. Absolutely dead. We cannot be the parents of a criminal. If you are willing to work and to help yourself, we still have some contacts—Meena's father needs someone to run several stores—but if you are not, then you are absolutely dead to us. We will have no son."

"Daughter," Jhanvi's mom said.

"What did I say?"

"You said 'son,'" her mom said.

"Arai, what does it matter compared to what he's done?"

"It matters because he's saying that he cannot transition with us!"

Jhanvi snickered. She had no doubt that her father was serious. But he hadn't given her any money in years now. She regretted stealing from them, she supposed, but the events seemed so abstract: she'd been crazed, taking the first steps into her transition, and had needed cocaine just to put on a wig and go out at night and feel like a real woman. That wasn't true anymore! Here she was, drinking again, but *not* a thief—or not much of one, aside from a few sips of stolen liquor here or there, and that one time stealing candy from the store.

19

When the food came, Jhanvi said, "Goodbye," and hung up the phone. It rang again, but Jhanvi turned it off. Meena took a long time to return, so Jhanvi started eating without her.

"Sorry," Meena said. "Call on the work phone."

"No problem," Jhanvi handed the phone across.

"How was it?"

"Usual."

"So you're gonna do this marriage thing?" Meena said. "It's a real marriage, right? You were just telling them it was fake so they wouldn't be angry."

"You think a real marriage would make them more angry?"

"Shit," Meena said. "If I got married to someone my dad had never met." She shook her head. "That would be . . . wow."

Meena started to talk about her own life—she usually couldn't be diverted from the topic for too long. Mostly her life consisted of work, and she talked about office politics, about the deals she'd made and about being overlooked by the partners at the most recent compensation meeting. She tossed around numbers in the millions when she talked about her earnings, and Jhanvi shrugged. Then she talked about her struggles trying to find a normal guy to date and how everyone was so bland and colorless.

"All right," Meena said, looking at her watch. "I've got a meeting. Let's cut to the chase."

"What's the chase?" Jhanvi said.

"You wanted to stay at my place, remember? While I was in Japan?"

"Oh yeah," Jhanvi said. "I don't need that anymore."

"You can do it, but you've got to look for work. There are these short software dev courses you can take. I took one when I switched into product, so I could show I had the technical chops. And my company is always looking for new developers."

"Sure," Jhanvi said.

"That's it? You're in?"

"It's a good life," Jhanvi said. "Why not?"

Her answer surprised even herself. Maybe it was all the doctors' appointments she had coming up. The intake forms asked about her social support—was she housed, where would she stay, who'd take her home from the hospital. She'd need a place. And besides . . . she had a vision of herself passing, looking truly like a girl, going unclocked—she'd need a place of her own, somewhere to bring people back to. In fact, maybe she'd change her name, cut off Trial By Fire entirely, say "Katie, thank you, but farewell," and move to the Marina, where the fire-eaters never went, and just sink endlessly into cisgender life, complain about those trannies in the bathroom. Fuck this world. Fuck being trans. Fuck being special. She'd get expensive manicures and browse restaurant reviews and go on dates with self-obsessed man-boys and sneer at fire-eaters over lunch with the girls from work.

"I'm completely down," Jhanvi said. "I don't think I'll need rent. I can keep living where I am. But I want my own life in San Francisco someday, like you have."

"Well . . . that might be a bit much," Meena said. "But I could loan you, like, the down payment for a studio—no, that's a terrible investment—maybe a small house? In Pacifica or the Sunset? If you ever got to the point where a bank would give you a loan!"

Now she was talking like Monica, the last woman who'd tried

to help her out—full of all sorts of plans. In no universe would Jhanvi, a single girl, live in Pacifica, which was a fog-shrouded surf town full of ruddy-faced old men. But still, Meena had a good heart.

"I'll look into coding school."

"Totally, you should go to the one where I went. I'll give you my books."

"Thanks," Jhanvi said. "That would be great."

"No problem, Cuz," Meena said. "We're, like, blood sisters. Our dads helped each other out when they first got to this country, and our kids will too. And . . . hey. Look, I know the older gen can be bigots. Heck, our office can be too. But . . . you know . . . I think . . . I've kept your secret from the other uncles and aunties, because your mom asked, but . . . but I don't think you should be . . . is 'in the closet' the right phrase? You're not in the closet except to Indian people. And I don't think you need to be."

Jhanvi shrugged. "Thanks," she said. "You know, you're the one I always liked the best. You're . . . straightforward."

"Learned it from my dad!" Meena said. "And, hey, I like you too—I mean, all the rest of the kids of our dads' friends are total straight arrows, hardly anyone's not in finance or tech. But you changed fucking genders! I mean shit, out of all the rest of us, there isn't even a regular gay person. You're just . . . different. I'm glad when we get together in two decades, my someday-kids will know about you, and they won't have to, like, go through what you went through." Meena put out a hand. "That's, like, really brave. You could've . . . well, I don't know . . . I don't know if you could've stayed being a man or whatever . . . but you could've not . . . you know . . . not been yourself . . ."

"Yeah, thanks," Jhanvi said. "Thanks."

They ended the dinner with an embrace, and Jhanvi took a slow route home, feeling somewhat better about herself. She probably owed her parents more. They were okay. She should take their calls. Everyone described their parents as, like, terrible people or bigots or narcissists. Her parents weren't any of that. They were just confused. They'd hardly asked her about her transition, except to wonder if hormones would somehow be dangerous or make her depressed. Honestly, it was just the same old disgust. The same disgust she aroused in other people. Her parents were fine. Their sense of responsibility for her was laudable. It was just the emotional connection that was missing. They were like Tolstoy's unhappy family, whose members had no more in common than a group of people chance-met at an inn.

Her dad's story was haunting, though. And she agreed with him. If only she could sit down with him, tell him her friends had thrown her into the street, tell him that Meena, who hardly knew her, and whose politics were totally different (she was a Republican) had shown more concern for her than all the liberal activist types, and how her activist "friends" had only come to her aid after she'd manipulated them. Tell him she agreed totally with his view of social relations and the value of family . . . but if she did, she would get too quickly to things she couldn't explain, like what she was doing out here in San Francisco, instead of back home.

· · ·

Over the next few weeks, all talk was about the upcoming party. Roshie tried to stay out of it at first, but people came to her with so many questions that she eventually reentered the fray, stomping around, more foul tempered than usual, calling everyone fuckers and fuck toys and assholes. She became so intolerable that nobody even spoke when she was around, and all the talk in her absence was about how to kick her out. Jhanvi, for her part, rarely spoke up to state the obvious: they *needed* her—not just her money, but her logistical support, and Roshie was only still involved in this party because Jhanvi had convinced her.

For Jhanvi, the next weeks were purely, unambiguously *good*. She had absolutely no money, but it didn't matter. She did all the things. She went to the parties, stayed up late sitting in the kitchen, learning about how her roommates and the other members of The Guilty Party spent their nights, about their problems and dramas, and learning to joke with them, too, the way they joked with Audrey and Katie about their codependence or with Henry about his continual waffling over his various lovers—whole schemas and universes of jokes that she hadn't known existed. And whenever she stopped to think *Why am I here? What do I offer? Do I deserve this?* she remembered, *It's because I manipulated them.* The fact of her impending marriage to Katie had created such a stark reality that they couldn't help but accept her. And she didn't need to offer them value, or to be anything other than another warm body, because she no longer wanted anything nonmaterial from them, not even the affirmation that she was a person worth knowing.

And yet, it was her very standoffishness that slowly started to draw forth exactly the attention she'd always craved. The first to break was Henry, who said, "Hey, uhh, do you ever, uhh, get mad that, uhh, I'm not public about us?"

"Hmm," Jhanvi said. "I didn't expect anything different."

"Because I could be. At, err, The Guilty Party. It'll be, like, your first party like this, won't it? I don't want you to be, uhh, keeping secrets."

"Are you asking to be my boyfriend?" Jhanvi said.

"Like, not exclusive. But . . . I really love what we do. And Audrey and Katie've been helping me work through it, and I think I'm ready to be public."

"If you're ready then I'm ready," Jhanvi said, still smiling slyly, while thinking: *I revile you.*

Audrey was the next to reach out: she commandeered Jhanvi one weekend to go dress shopping at a boutique that fire-eaters liked. Jhanvi told her it was too expensive, that nothing here would fit her, and Audrey said, "Oh come on, just give it a try, for me. Stormcloud"—Katie—"is my best friend, and this is a big moment for her!"

Audrey dragged her into one of those impossibly chic high-end vintage stores that only had like two hundred items, culled from estate sales across the country. The owner and Audrey came together, kissing cheeks, and then the owner said to Jhanvi, "Are you ready for the event? I can't wait."

"This one is going to be so special," Audrey said. "Did I tell you Storm's getting married? To Average here."

"Oh no, no," the owner said. "Don't say that. Don't say you're average. You're so big! You're like a model!" Her voice was high and wispy, and she cocked her head. Jhanvi couldn't tell her age: midthirties, maybe. She had blunt-cut bangs and big, empty eyes, her arms full of tattoos, and she floated through the store in a long white skirt.

Jhanvi gritted her teeth and said, "I totally get if nothing here works."

"You're lucky, minidresses are so in right now," the woman said. She brought out a black gown with an Empire waist that was probably made for a short, chubby woman. Jhanvi wrestled the dress on in a dressing room but had to ask the woman for help zipping it. The Empire waist hid Jhanvi's belly. She still thought she looked pregnant, but at least it was a feminine bulge and not a manly paunch. On Jhanvi, the dress was scandalously short. "A pair of tights will fix that, no problem," the woman said. "You'll be a vision. And let me have my assistant run out to get some fabric for a veil."

People came in and out—the shop did a surprising amount of business—but the assistant took care of them. Audrey held out her phone, held Jhanvi close, their faces together, addressing her followers: "Just dressing my *gorgeous* friend for her wedding to Stormcloud! It's going to be so beautiful. It'll be during the party, if you stay to the end."

"I can tag you if you want," Audrey said. "But the attention can be a lot."

"Please don't," Jhanvi said.

Jhanvi was veiled in the video, so all the attention in the comments was focused on Audrey—a lot of slut-shaming, of course, and people talking about how she was a whore, and then other people arguing with them.

"That *is* a lot," Jhanvi said.

"Yeah . . . I've been thinking about writing a book. So many journalists talk to me, you know, and they get things wrong? And I just want to tell my own story? I've been thinking about how beautiful this wedding is, how it brings together so many needs. How much *you* have brought us, Average . . ." Audrey pulled her close, and Jhanvi felt the workings of her sinewy shoulder. "You've changed Henry and my relationship so much. Like, for the first time, there's really a future between the two of us."

Once again, the idea occurred to Jhanvi, *Maybe Audrey's marking her territory. Or maybe she's just being nice!*

Audrey put the black gown on her credit card, and she wouldn't let Jhanvi see the bill. Jhanvi thought of clarifying, *I would never ever even offer to pay this bill, I'm just curious.* But she let it go.

"How're you feeling?" Audrey asked as they ate salads at the tiny place next door.

"Great," Jhanvi said. "What about you? Oh . . . how's prep for TGP? I guess it's been hard, with Roshie so mad."

"She's being *so* unreasonable. Now she's worried the ventilation system is too loud. I was like . . . but that was *your* job . . . and she keeps threatening to shut things down. It really might all fall apart."

"Don't worry," Jhanvi said. "You've got this. Rally the troops. She's just a smart person who watched YouTube videos. You're the group's heart."

"Oh my god, no. Definitely not. But thank you for saying that! The only nice thing is it's made me realize how important we are. And we really need to advocate for ourselves, really make the case to the public, that this isn't just a lifestyle, it's a revolution in consciousness . . . it's about making people freer and happier and more fulfilled."

"Totally," Jhanvi said. "Totally . . ." This line of talk signified nothing to her, though it was weird how much people like Audrey believed they were communicating something really *deep* and *vital*.

On the drive home, Audrey was silent for a long time. And as she pulled into a parking spot in the Haight, she sighed heavily.

"You okay?"

Audrey was in a sundress—the day was unusually warm and sunny for San Francisco—and her powerful shoulders flexed under the loose cotton. "I just . . . do you think Katie is okay?"

Jhanvi was about to say, *Of course not, she's doing this marriage thing that she doesn't really want to do.* But that was dangerous territory. If Audrey got up steam, then Katie would slip free from the marriage, and then, almost like a mathematical equation, they would need to turn on Jhanvi, to demonize her and force her out. And yet . . . perhaps because she was in fact a demon, Jhanvi heard herself saying:

"Have you been trying to talk her out of the wedding?"

Audrey turned, her eyes going wide. "Oh no," she said. "I mean, yes. Was it obvious? I'm so . . ."

"Don't be sorry," Jhanvi said. "You're being a good friend."

"It's just so . . . what if she meets someone? Or . . . but then . . . you really need the help. What would you do, if she didn't marry you?"

"Probably drink myself to death."

"Oh Jhanvi, no! No."

"It's not a choice I'd make. Just weird how I haven't really gone overboard with the drinking lately. And I've been studying these coding books. Because I have *hope*. So, yeah, if that went away, I'd put on a good face and say, *Oh yeah, I'm hanging in there*, because you can tell yourself things are about to look up, day after day, even as you struggle, and make bad decisions, like stealing money, pissing people off, that eventually leave you no other choice but to end yourself."

"Jhanvi, that is so dark! I am so so sorry! I never should've . . . if Katie . . . she'll be *fine*."

"No, that's silly. This marriage is an objectively bad idea. You'd be a terrible friend if you didn't tell Katie not to do it."

"But . . . but you need us."

"So? So what? I mean, Audrey, can I be honest with you?"

The other girl was clutching the steering wheel, and when she turned to face Jhanvi, her smile was wan.

"Do you guys ever—how do I put this—" Jhanvi said. "Why can't you guys just accept that you're sybarites? Like . . . why do you need to be good people too? I mean . . . you spend lots and lots and lots of money on . . . you know . . . on your own pleasure."

"I don't . . . what are you saying?" Audrey said. "We don't spend money. Our rent is $3,000 a month. We purposefully keep things minimal."

"Well, yeah," Jhanvi said. "It's a rent-controlled apartment. That makes it worse, not better. You're hoarding that for yourself too. I mean, you earn like, $200,000 a year. And the event space—that cost more than $100,000."

"But not when we first leased it. After the rent increase, I was gonna give it up, but Roshie paid."

"I'm just saying," Jhanvi said. "You're a small group of rich kids who want to fuck and be beautiful and have fun. Why does it need to be more than that?"

"It's—I'm sorry," Audrey frowned. "We should talk. We should talk when Katie is around. I just think . . . there is so much . . . I mean . . . our event space is for everyone. It's for the whole community."

"Not for queer people, not for dark people. Or poor people. Or . . ."

"We're trying to be more diverse."

"But why?" Jhanvi said. "Why not just be white and straight? Why carry this guilt?"

"I . . . I understand how it looks, from your perspective. But we really try to be a positive force for the community. I just feel like that's our duty. We owe that to the world. We've been given so much, and I know we're so far from being what we ought to be, but we're gonna get there! But that's why I am *so* glad you're a part of this. And I want to say, if you know other queer people who want to attend—I heard what you said to us about our exclusivity, we trust you—just talk to us. I really, really want you to be more involved in the years to come."

"Okay." Jhanvi thought of Toni, and she smiled. "All right. I do know at least one more person."

Later that afternoon, she texted Toni, who said, *Oh my god, I thought you were keeping me apart from your other friends on purpose.*

No, of course not. Just wanna warn you, this might be more anthropological than fun. It'll be eventful, but I dunno how friendly it'll be.

Aren't you getting married there????? Of course I'll be there to support you!

• • •

The weeks passed, and the event space took shape, and Jhanvi became increasingly preoccupied with the idea of what her misshapen body would do at what was, essentially, a sex party. There was a limit, after all, to what you could get by guilting people. When everyone was naked, no amount of guilt or pity would shield Jhanvi from the disgust in people's eyes.

And every time Jhanvi tried to speak to Roshie, the other girl would spew something bitter like, "They only care about themselves," or "Now I know how the Morlocks felt about the Eloi."

But one night, when they were cleaning up after dinner, Jhanvi said, "Hey . . . are you actually gonna go to the party?"

"I have to," Roshie said. "I promised the other tenants I'd stop the fun instantly if anything dangerous happens. Responsibility might not mean anything to *Audrey*, but it matters to me."

"What're you gonna wear?"

"I don't know," Roshie said. "I'm there to work, not to screw."

"You know I can, like, spell you if you need? Give you a break?"

"Why?" Roshie said. "So I can be lonely and alone and pathetic?"

"Hey . . ." Jhanvi said. "I'll be right there with you."

"You've got Henry." Roshie's face twisted up hatefully. They hadn't discussed that either—the fact that she and Henry were fucking. What was Jhanvi supposed to say: *I'd give him to you if I could?* Nothing would make it better.

"I understand you, Roshie," Jhanvi said. "I'm the only one who does. Seriously . . ."

Jhanvi put a hand on Roshie's shoulder, but the other girl shook her off and went back to rinsing the dishes.

20

Jhanvi offered to help Katie lead the safety trainings for potential partygoers. "It'll create the illusion of inclusivity," Jhanvi said.

"This is a mess," Katie said. "We have so many cancellations and reschedulings. We're going to have to do trainings on the day of the event."

"Makes sense," Jhanvi said. "I'll be flexible."

The event space was completely different now—it had wooden partitions sectioning it off into a series of rooms that ascended in terms of the outrageousness of the activity planned for it. The ventilation system overhead was loud and the room was viciously cold, but Katie had assured her it'd warm up.

Jhanvi was the demonstration subject. Katie was in a leather halter top and matching shorts and a leather cat's eye mask, holding her whip. Jhanvi wore a backless minidress.

They went through the motions together, with Katie rehearsing her lines, speaking intensely, putting Jhanvi through the paces.

"You're such a natural domme," Jhanvi said.

Katie didn't respond. Jhanvi mimed The Guilty Party's various ways of indicating she needed help, including some that were private and should be visible only to the spotter.

"We should emphasize that it's totally safe and normal to want to slow down or end things."

"Sure," Jhanvi said. "Okay . . ."

"What? Does that not make sense?" Katie said.

This new thing had begun happening, where the members of the house had started listening to her, including to the undertones of what she said. She was so used to being ignored that it was a shock, and it had forced her to revise her opinion of their intelligence. All those weeks when she'd been haunting their house and making sardonic comments, they hadn't been dumb or unperceptive: they'd simply been choosing to ignore her.

"Umm, nothing," Jhanvi said. "Just . . . like . . . I imagine the scene will stop if the crowd thinks it ought to stop, and the woman will take her cue from the crowd; if they don't seem disturbed, she'll ignore what she's feeling, and she'll go on. It's really our job to stop things. And that's fine, it's normal."

"No, see, that's the attitude we don't want. And why do you say woman? Plenty of men use their safety signals."

"Sure. Totally," Jhanvi said. "And plenty of women don't. You just lie back and wait for it to be over. And that's okay."

"No," Katie said. "That isn't okay. Jhanvi, this is really worrisome. We've gone over this training a half dozen times. Is this how you treat Henry?"

Jhanvi untied her wrists from the flogging post and sat down quickly—she didn't get real spontaneous erections anymore, or not very often, but she was feeling substantial heat under her skirt and didn't want to risk anything. Holding her legs tightly together, her eyes fell onto Katie's bare arms and traveled to her gloved fingers.

"I'm sorry," Jhanvi said. "I'm always making trouble. I'll reassure them that they really can stop things."

"Jhanvi, I am so anxious," Katie said.

Katie unbuckled her gloves and stripped them off, then reached behind her head and pulled off the mask, which left behind a smear of sweat just under her eyes and on her fore-head. "I am so anxious," she said.

"About the marriage?"

"That," Katie said. "And this event. It's going to be so big this year. Way too big. Hey . . . you'll be sober at this, right? Every-one is supposed to be, but . . ."

"Yeah . . ." Jhanvi said. "You're right to be anxious. This place is a tragedy waiting to happen."

"Jhanvi!" Katie said. "You're supposed to reassure me."

Jhanvi actually felt like they were bantering, for once—she made a macabre joke about a fire starting down here that would burn them all up, and about the headline and the general glee that would follow.

"Can I tell you something horrible?" Jhanvi said.

"Yes, yes," Katie said. "I'm used to it, from you. That fire joke is going to haunt my dreams."

"I don't miss being friends with Roshie."

Katie went silent. Then she nodded for a second. "That doesn't make you a bad person."

"Doesn't it? I think not missing and not sticking by a person who put me up rent-free, stuck her neck out for me, shamed you guys into liking me, that's pretty terrible."

"She's just—I don't know. It's hard to explain. She has a nega-tive energy."

"Desperation," Jhanvi said. "Loneliness."

"No, not that . . . I think . . . a lack of . . . it's a surprise she got so mad at us for being transphobic and racist, because she didn't really seem to care about that kind of stuff at all before . . . most of the time, she seemed so apathetic."

"She wasn't apathetic, she was unsophisticated."

"Yes, that, but more . . . her ideas were regressive."

Jhanvi tried to get Katie to say what they both knew: the problem wasn't that Roshie was too bourgeois, but that Trial By Fire was too aristocratic. Roshie might have more money than them, but she had middle-class values. She valued fairness, community, hard work, competence. And her unwillingness to jettison all that cultural baggage marked her as someone who didn't belong: someone not worth respecting, not worth listening to, not worth fucking. A person to be used, rather than included.

Maybe because Jhanvi had gone to a more elite college—Stanford instead of UC Santa Cruz—or maybe because she was just more observant, spoke the language better, and leveraged her marginalization more effectively than Roshie had leveraged her wealth—Jhanvi had finally found a way to belong.

That's why it'd always struck her as absurd to claim discrimination. Yes, she was discriminated against, but so were so many people: the pie was so small, and the number of free pieces was even smaller. Moreover, only maybe twenty percent of the pie was up for grabs, was being allocated to newcomers who could make the best case for their own need and merit.

Oh well, this was stupid. Roshie had money. She would always be fine.

"What's funny is all our training is about what to do if too much attention, too much desire, comes your way," Jhanvi said. "But how often is the problem actually *not enough* attention?"

Katie blinked. "I don't understand. You know we try to keep things fifty-fifty, but there *always* end up being more men, somehow."

"Sure, but at the same time . . . I mean, you couldn't know this, because you're gorgeous, but for most of us, there's just not enough. I can't explain the math of it. I've been on both sides. Guys are like, *Girls are too picky.* Girls are like, *There aren't enough good guys.* I've been the good guy who was overlooked, so I know . . . and if you're a guy and you come to a party like this and no girl pays attention to you, what happens is you get angry, you go home and write on Reddit about how they're such bitches, but what if you're a girl? Maybe that never happens to cis women. I don't know. I've accepted I know nothing about cis women, by the way. Like, I'm done pretending. Don't let this go beyond the two of us, but I know nothing about being a cis woman. I mean, you all complain about street harassment, and on the *very* infrequent occasions I get it, I'm like, *Wow! Someone thinks I'm a woman!* You complain about the creeps out there. But I don't know—I don't know—I've known lots of women—like Roshie—she never complains about the creeps, and women when they get old, hit forty—they're like, *Suddenly I'm invisible*, and—"

"But that doesn't mean they liked that style of attention before."

"No, of course not," Jhanvi said. "I just wonder why cis women come here. Is it good? Do they enjoy it?"

"It's really good," Katie said.

"You said that so quickly," Jhanvi said. "So it's good. You can have genuinely satisfying sex here."

"It takes practice, but . . ."

Her lips went narrow, and Jhanvi couldn't help imagining Katie losing control, really becoming herself for once.

"Well, I don't know," Jhanvi said. "Part of me is like, cis women have this thing—their femininity—they can run away from it, suppress it, or embrace it—but they always have to deal with it. But I was a man. I was a man. And I went to parties in college, and I looked at the girls, and I thought, *People love them, they're desired, they have value—if I was like them—*" Jhanvi shrugged. "I don't know. Maybe my gender presentation is just me indulging a fetish. I don't care."

She didn't really think being trans was a fetish. It was clearly a natural, biological condition. But being trans messed you up. Having to hide it, grapple with it, figure it out. Having to wonder for all those years what was wrong with you. And then after you transitioned, you were expected to just be normal, and it simply wasn't possible. The damage was done. You were broken.

Katie nodded. Something in her eyes had gotten a little cold, and she was slightly distant, looking at the door.

"Hello?" Jhanvi said.

"No, that's really interesting," Katie said. "I think it's the same for cis women. We want a safe place to embrace femininity. To dress up, to express the most outrageous elements of female sexuality, where we won't be judged for being promiscuous..." She shrugged. "I don't think it's very different. I don't think you need to feel bad."

"But I do," Jhanvi said. "I do feel bad. I don't know why. I come to this place, and I'm like, *This is not safe. This is a temple to human misery.* I think of all the people getting dressed up, putting on their makeup, stepping into high heels, their hearts pounding, googling anxiously in the cab, *What do I do at an orgy?*—And I know this isn't exactly an orgy, but that's what they google—and then all the guys, queueing up, got their best shirts on, maybe took a few shots before coming—you know they're doing it, you know they're drinking or on drugs even though they're not supposed to be, Katie, don't frown!—and they come here, hang around the edges, see girls who're so in command of themselves, girls like you—"

"And you—"

"Sure, and me, if you say so—girls like us, who are so in command, so desired. And then these girls stand around in their sparkly dresses, their long stockings and garter belts, their cat ears and face paint, they're all standing, staring, nervous, maybe dancing a little, hoping for something to happen, for something to be different, for tonight not to be awful. Their eyes, their envy, their desire, are the fuel we need to make this work, but it's just this horrible human sacrifice, this terrible engine for misery, and—"

"This is not how I see this at all," Katie said. "Not at all. I don't know what scenes you've been part of, but here, it's friendly, welcoming, accepting. That's the ideal."

"It's not, though. I mean come on, I've gone to AA meetings—the whole purpose of the place is to provide fellowship to losers who walk in off the street—and even those are lonely and cliquey. People are shy. They don't reach out. At a place like this, the girls are concerned with their own friends, they don't want to be tied down—the guys are mostly really shy, uncertain—the ones who aren't, the people like Henry—there are too few to go around."

"So to you, Henry is an ideal? More men should be like him?" Katie said.

"I mean . . . yeah," Jhanvi said. "He's not great, but he's a good-enough guy. Better than he needs to be . . . he has feelings, sometimes . . . I mean the standards aren't too high, are they?"

Katie shrugged. "We'll have to talk more about him sometime."

"Oh, he's sleazy," Jhanvi said. "In subtle ways. Like, you know, back in college, he's the first guy I ever hooked up with? Before him, I was a virgin. And he *knew* that, but he acted like I was an old pro, and he didn't have any responsibilities to me *as a friend*."

"Do you even want to be at this party?" Katie's eyes locked onto Jhanvi's. "It sounds like you have a lot of doubts."

"Don't I have to be?" Jhanvi said. "I mean . . . we have the marriage license."

They had gotten it a few days earlier, at the courthouse, giving all their information and IDs, and then handing over the license to Audrey, who'd insisted on being the one to marry them.

"It would make better pictures if we had a lot of friends there, but we can do it somewhere else."

"Thanks for asking," Jhanvi said. "No, I do want to be there. I desperately want to be there. This place is at the core of my life and my identity. I just wonder, I just wonder, if we could tell people—don't tell them the sex is incredible, tell them instead it's some obscene ritual—it's supposed to be a torment. I think that's how they feel anyway, it's a story to tell people later. Ninety percent of people don't really experience it for itself, but it's a ritual—it means . . . I don't know what it means. It's a crucible . . . you learn something about yourself. I don't know—either that, or we need to step up, you and me and Henry and Audrey and the rest—we need to step up and make things less miserable."

"Well, I think that's what this training is about," Katie said. "Keeping people safe."

Jhanvi was about to say, *No, it's about the opposite, it's about telling them: People will try to rape you, and if they don't, you're undesirable, but if they do, and they succeed, then you're weak, so there's no way to win. What if we could say: I understand, I get it . . . I know you feel small right now . . . I know you feel unsafe, and I know you're going to be hurt tonight, in one way or another.*

But these people would never understand that. Not because they'd never felt small, but because . . . Jhanvi didn't know why, didn't understand why they were so empty . . . why they lied to themselves so deeply and so frequently. Jhanvi wasn't sure what made her so different and so special, so unwilling to turn away from the truth.

She liked them and even sort of respected them, but she couldn't help thinking sometimes: *I came to you shy and lonely, and if you'd accepted me then, I would've loved you forever. But I'm glad you didn't. I'm glad you forced me to grow. And yet, I'm still angry, and perhaps that's how I'll always be.*

21

On the day of the party, Henry pulled Jhanvi into his room, which was crowded with Achilles and several other fire-eaters Jhanvi had only met in passing.

"Normally Roshie does this," Henry said. "But I'm self-nominating this year. I've got the blue pills, of course. But do you want anything else? TGP is a sober space, so you won't be able to get anything there."

"Uhh, I dunno. Amphetamines, I guess. It'll be a long night."

"Good choice!"

Her wedding gown was stashed at the event space: Audrey had said it might get dirty, so she should save it until the moment of the ceremony.

When it came to her outfit for the party itself, Jhanvi had been debating all day whether to wear the chastity cage she'd bought a year or two ago during a particularly self-hating period when she had imagined people mocking her and denying her sex. If she did, she might go completely naked otherwise, except for a pair of high heels, because that would minimize the gender-bending element of her appearance, and minimize, in turn, the loathing she was likely to see in people's eyes. But she suspected that the more male she appeared at the party, the more she would hate herself, so she still wasn't sure. Even after several years on hormones, she still felt like her femininity, to the extent it existed at all, was an illusion created by clothes and makeup, and that if she was forced to appear in an outfit that was closer to her skin, she would be indistinguishable from a man. Instead, she'd dressed to fit in with the other girls, wearing furry knee-high boots, spandex booty shorts, a velvet vest, and cat ears, with strands of light-up ornaments surrounding her body.

"You know all about drugs, so you probably don't need a spotter or anything, do you?" Henry said.

"No," Jhanvi said. "Of course not. Just get me hopped up and let me loose with a bunch of strange guys."

"I mean, I'll spot you if you want," Henry said. "I'll stick to you like glue."

"Yes," Jhanvi said. "I would like that, actually. Every single fucking moment."

Jhanvi and Henry hadn't ever talked again about the subject of them being official, but somehow people knew they were hooking up.

"Oh, shoot, okay," Henry said. "Well, we have a list of available spotters. Let me hook you up with—"

"Are you joking?" Jhanvi said.

She looked at Achilles and at the other women and men crowded into the room with their cute outfits, enjoying their little in-group preparty. And now she raised her voice. "You *offered* to look after me, Perseus. You offered."

"Totally," he said. "And I'll keep an eye on you, but if you need a real spotter, I can—"

"What did you think offering meant?"

"I just—I'm sorry—you're getting mad at me, but I don't really know why. Can we . . . can we maybe talk right after this is done?"

"No," Jhanvi said. "You know what, I don't need you anymore, Henry. And, no, I don't need a spotter. I've done all these drugs a thousand times."

"That's what I thought!" he said. "Come on, let's talk soon."

She spun on her heel and walked out, then retreated upstairs, back to Roshie's room, where she waited, alone. Nobody came to find her, not even Henry.

• • •

The attendees crowded into the alley. A Latina woman tapped Jhanvi on the shoulder, saying something in Spanish, and Jhanvi put out her hands.

"You are Roshie's friend?" the woman said. "I haven't reached her."

"Oh, sorry," Jhanvi said. "She's around. Sorry about the noise."

"It is okay," the woman said. "We trust you."

"Sorry," Jhanvi said. "Thank you, thank you so much. Adriana, right? We should be done by one or two a.m."

Henry was at the door checking tickets, and the queue of people streamed down, flooding into the anteroom, where Trial By Fire volunteers waited, one with a tablet and another with garbage bags to hold people's clothing. In moments, outerwear was flying everywhere, and already Jhanvi could see a discordant note: the guests had followed one of four different dress codes, depending on what they were familiar with—raver (like Jhanvi); leather and bondage (like Katie); boudoir style, with hints of their expensive underwear peeking out from trench coats; or clubwear—the tiniest, briefest possible dresses. That was the women.

The boys stripped down to boxer shorts. A few wore vests. Some of the gay guys were in chaps or jockstraps or leather. Towels were handed out by TGP volunteers and gratefully wrapped around midsections. The party guests stood shivering in the cold, waiting for direction.

• • •

The party had crossed the initial hump where the attendees percolated through the room, clustering around drink tables that held only soda. The more experienced members of Trial By Fire took the lead, with couples and other pairings coming together on couches, hugging and touching, chatting easily, though aware they were being watched. The eyes spurred them to kisses, led them to various rooms to negotiate scenes, to start things off.

Jhanvi's heart was thumping in time to the music, and she danced in her sweaty, uncomfortable shoes—she'd stashed a pair of sneakers in the space but wanted to stay in her high-heeled boots as long as possible. She towered over the other women but didn't care—sometimes she raised up her massive hands, those meat-hooks, and flailed at the sky, pretending to be a god, lording over them all.

A hand stroked her back, and Jhanvi turned. Toni was in her femboy best, wearing a long blond wig, heavy makeup, a short black skirt, and thigh-high boots. She mouthed a few words, and Jhanvi leaned down. "You're a goddess," Toni yelled.

"You look great too," Jhanvi said. "How's it been?"

"Weird," she said. "My ass has been groped so many times. This is insane."

Jhanvi's smile froze. Not a single person had made a move on her. Now her lips twitched, and she tried to hide the coldness in her eyes.

"Well, you went to the training, right? You know the safe signals."

"Totally," Toni said. "But is it okay if I hang out by you?"

"Absolutely," Jhanvi said. "Stay all night if you need."

"No, no, it's your wedding."

"What is it about weddings?" Jhanvi said.

Toni mouthed, *Huh?* The music had changed, gotten louder. Jhanvi gestured, pulling Toni with a finger toward the narrow cool-down room for people of the femme persuasion. The room was packed with girls who huddled together on the couches and giggled on the carpets. Toni stopped at the door, but Jhanvi pulled her in, whispered, "Don't let them think you might not belong."

A pair of girls got up, and Toni and Jhanvi settled on a corner of the couch. The background chatter was like a babbling brook, loud enough that Jhanvi didn't worry she could be overheard. She looked at the network of pipes and wires above. The place reminded her of IKEA: everything was staged, just an illusion.

"I said, *What is it about weddings?*" Jhanvi said. "People know it's fake, but they act like it's not."

"Well, it's legal, right?" Toni said. "It's a big deal. It's so incredible that you made this happen. I tell everyone about it. Like, I saw it happen, you just rolled up here, hopped off the bus, a girl from Sacramento with nothing but a suitcase and a dream."

"Stop," Jhanvi said. "It's not that impressive."

"It is! And aren't you already getting appointments and stuff?"

"Mmmhmm," Jhanvi said.

"Your life will be so different," Toni said. "And you did it all yourself."

"Well, if I ever get a job with good benefits, I'll marry you," Jhanvi said. "We'll make a chain, pulling each other up."

"Really?"

"Totally. Why not?"

Purpose drifted out of the crowd. She was utterly alone, not moving in a pack, and was wearing a very spare golden leotard, like something from an eighties exercise video. She cocked her head at them. "Oh, hello there, Average," she said. "It's so nice to see you."

Jhanvi introduced Toni to her as a coworker, and they accumulated a few more people. If it wasn't for the girls making out around them and the yells from outside, it would've been a pleasant afternoon hangout.

Then the mood shifted. The girls straightened, craned their necks, then preened a bit, like a harem when the king walks into the courtyard. Audrey was in a white halter dress with a high skirt and white stockings. She looked like a fifties pin-up. She swirled on her high-heels, the skirt spinning out, and then she leaned forward and embraced another girl. Within seconds, she was so deluged with hellos that it took her a few minutes to get to Jhanvi. She leaned down to speak to her. "Hey, has Katie talked to you?"

"No," Jhanvi said.

"Okay. Henry said you were in a weird mood. I thought she might've said something."

"Audrey, this is my coworker, Toni."

"Hey." Audrey's face was small and heart-shaped, like it belonged to a much smaller, much less well-built woman. "I, uhh, Katie is having some second thoughts, as you know, and we thought about delaying this for a few days. Is that all right?"

"No," Jhanvi said.

"I, uhh ..."

"I said no," Jhanvi said. "If she doesn't want it to be public, that's fine. Let's just get together and get the certificate signed. But if she wants to back out, let her be honest about it."

"She doesn't want to! It's just The Guilty Party is so important to her, and she's got a sort of act she does, and there's a conflict, and ..."

"I don't care," Jhanvi said.

"Okay ..." Audrey said. "Look, let's talk when you've cooled down a bit ..."

When she was gone, Jhanvi sat in silence, not looking at Purpose or Toni. The latter said, "That was intense."

"Is everything all right?" Purpose said.

"No."

"Shitty of her to try and back out," Toni said.

"She doesn't want to do it, Toni," Jhanvi said. "What can I say? She doesn't want to do it. She doesn't want to do it. People don't want things sometimes, and I'm that thing."

"Let me get Henry for you," Purpose said. "He's always so comforting ..."

She was off before Jhanvi could stop her.

"Can . . . can I get you something?" Toni said.

"No," Jhanvi said.

She'd watched *Citizen Kane* recently, and the idea came to her like she'd seen it in a snow globe: Roshie. That was the person she needed most right now.

• • •

Roshie was dressed in jeans and a big flannel shirt, with her smudged glasses high up on her nose and her forehead obscured by the usual spray of bangs.

"Roshie!" Jhanvi said. "Roshie! Over here! I've been looking for you."

The other girl turned, and her jaw locked.

"Roshie," Jhanvi said, tapping her on the shoulder, but the other girl kept pushing her way through the crowd. Jhanvi followed.

They were just past the foyer where everyone had changed, which was filled now with bags and clothing. Then they were in the chill-out space, which was covered in carpets and pillows and sofas. People in various stages of undress were lounging all over, and as always, Jhanvi's eyes were drawn to the long, tawny bodies of the girls—mostly white girls, some East Asian, hardly any brown skin in sight. And, of course, the men were clothed, and most of the women were awkward, but the sheer languorous beauty of the few who *were* comfortable was enough to create an atmosphere of glamor and luxury.

A loud metallic clanking sound filled the room. Roshie had opened the door to a side room, which expelled a gust of hot air and dust. The guests turned to the side, drawing away.

"Hey," Jhanvi said. "Hey. Hey. What're you doing?"

Suddenly the clanking shut off, and there was relative silence in the room before the voices rose up to fill it. Roshie had a phone to her head. "Is that okay? How is that?"

"Roshie," Jhanvi said. "What are you doing?"

"I, uhh." Roshie looked at Jhanvi. Then she shielded the phone with one hand. "Remember Adriana, our upstairs neighbor? I introduced you once. Her husband is recovering from surgery, and he can't sleep. I guess the ventilators are really, really loud."

"Oh, uhh, okay," Jhanvi said. "Well . . . is it okay for them to be off?"

"Not really," Roshie said. "We have a thousand people down here. Let's see what happens. H—" She looked Jhanvi over, and it was like she forgot to be mad. "You're looking good. Just like one of them."

"That's the idea," Jhanvi said.

"You told me once to wear the uniform, do you remember that? To wear the uniform if I want to fit in."

"I don't remember that, but it is how I feel. You'd be so much more comfortable with your ass hanging out right now."

"You don't know," Roshie said. "What it gets like here. It's disgusting. I am pathetic. God . . ." They were in a little nook, a pool of light in a red-lit room, and bodies were moving around them, moaning and twisting, people trying to put on a show.

"No, I get it," Jhanvi said. "Katie is backing out."

"What?"

"She's trying to back out of the plan," Jhanvi said.

"I won't let her," Roshie said. "Fuck her, I won't."

"St—no," Jhanvi said. "You don't have leverage anymore. The party, it's happening. That's all they care about."

"So I'll shut it down."

"Stop," Jhanvi said. "Why are you doing this? Are we even that good friends?"

Roshie's lip pushed out, and she set her jaw. Her finger traced through the dust behind the panel. They heard Achilles's voice cut through the noise, amplified, telling people about something happening on the main stage. The music was muffled, but the bass shook the walls, and the smell was grotesquely organic, like a thousand people's BO, even though everyone had scrubbed before coming here, Jhanvi assumed.

"You might not be," Roshie said. "But I am."

"Roshie," Jhanvi said. "I just want you to know, you're not weird or wrong or bad. I've been thinking about us a lot, and we became friends during that moment when I said, *Oh, we're both angry sexless nerds*. That's when you opened up. And I said that, you know, because I wished someone had said it to me. That there's power in knowing who you are, and in not being ashamed, and you've taken that power on."

Roshie's pout had deepened. She looked down. Jhanvi put a finger under her chin and lifted it up, the gesture feeling unbearably intimate. "We're unwanted."

Roshie blinked. "What? Nothing else? No pep talk?"

"We're unwanted," Jhanvi said. "That's it. I hate fucking Henry. I feel nothing when I do it. It's not nonconsensual, but, you know, I hate him. He could've treated me well. But he didn't. I hate him. I hate everyone here. I hate everyone. Well, that's not true. I don't hate you, but I hate enough people—too many of them. And I hate myself. But I just wanted you to take a shortcut around all my years of, you know, being confused, not knowing who I was. And you did! So . . . thank you. I'm sorry I wasn't a better friend."

"Yeah, you sucked," Roshie said.

"It's true."

They took a breath. Roshie's phone was ringing again. She stared at it for a moment, then took the call. "She says it's loud but a little better."

Another figure entered their orbit.

"What's going on?" Katie wasn't in her dominatrix outfit. Instead, she stood in front of them wearing a short skirt, knee socks, and a crop top. The clothes were slightly off, striking a bit of a discordant note, especially given her straight stance and aura of command. But she didn't give Jhanvi so much as a glance.

"You're killing someone," Roshie said. "Adri's husband: he's sick. None of you have asked me about him."

More people drifted into the conversation. Roshie had to repeat herself several times, and she held out the phone first to Katie and then to Henry, but both refused to take the call.

The party seemed to grow louder each moment, and every time Jhanvi looked around, there were more people, acting with more abandon. She saw the surreptitious gulps of alcohol, saw the glazed expressions, saw the men with hungry eyes looking at lone women.

"I have a scene," Katie said. "Can you guys handle this?"

"Sure, sure," Henry said.

"Not really!" Jhanvi said.

Audrey arrived, and Jhanvi's eyebrows went up. Her shoes were extremely high, her hair was pinned up elaborately out of her face, and she had a white riding crop that she swished absentmindedly against her leg.

"Hey, do you guys feel like it's getting a little stuffy?" she said. "And kind of hot?"

"The ventilators are off," Katie said. "The neighbors are complaining."

"It's nine o'clock," Audrey said. "And this used to be a factory."

"I mean, they probably don't run factories at night."

"Adriana is super cool," Roshie said. "And normally she'd never complain. But I think her husband is really sick." Her phone lit up. "This is her."

Roshie ducked out to the side to take the call, and the little clique of people—Katie, Audrey, Henry, and a few bystanders—drifted into a corner behind the bar.

"What's going on?" Audrey said.

"Roshie says the ventilators are really loud upstairs," Katie said.

"Well, she installed the ventilators! Or . . . she made them work . . . she did something with them. That's her problem, isn't it?" Audrey said.

"I don't know . . . someone is sick? They just had surgery?"

"Can't they hold out until one a.m.?" Audrey said. "I mean it's a Saturday! Am I crazy, or . . . ?"

"Just let us handle this . . ." Henry said. "There must be a half-power setting on the ventilators. Or we'll run them half the time. Go do your scene."

"Yeah, we'll just do the usual thing," Jhanvi said. "Turn down the music for a bit, then slowly turn it up until they complain again. Repeat until the party is over."

She had expected Katie to disagree, to be insulted, in fact, and she was surprised when Katie turned her blue eyes to Jhanvi. "That's a plan. Can I detail you to do that?"

"Umm, sure," Jhanvi said.

Now Katie pulled her into a hug, and her mouth touched Jhanvi's ear. "Thank you so much, I really owe you."

"No problem." Jhanvi shrugged, and in a moment, she was glad that she held back.

"Sorry I got emotional," Katie said. "But I'm looking forward to the wedding . . ."

Katie and Audrey went bustling through the door into the farther recesses of the party—places where Jhanvi still had not been.

When they were alone, Henry gave her a shy wave. "Hey, uhh, are you okay?"

"Fine."

"Just, because . . . you were mad earlier."

It was almost Pavlovian. The slightest kindness and tears came to her eyes. "Uhh . . . just emotional. Sorry I got mad."

"No, no, you've inherited Roshie's job—calling us on our bullshit."

Now she looked into his eyes, which were visibly dilated— tight bands of brown around fat black pupils—and he gave her a lazy smile. "Watch this," he said. Then he gripped the sides of his shorts, and pulled on them, tearing them away. "Cut-away shorts!" His cock leapt straight out, immediately hard. He'd shaved his balls and his bush. He wasn't the only fully naked person in the room, but he was the only one not passing from one place to another. Now his hand went down, and one finger traced along the top of his penis. Circumcised people were so gross—and circumcised white boys were the worst—with their pale worm penises and that little band of scar tissue.

"That was Adriana," Roshie said, returning. "It's really serious. I guess her husband got a kidney transplant a few days ago? From her daughter? And they're both resting at home? And her husband's super constipated, and he hasn't been able to sleep, and this really woke him up, and she's just kinda worried."

"Hey," Henry said. "You're doing a good job."

Roshie looked at him now, and she blinked a few times. "Why are you naked?"

"Why are you not naked?"

"Okay . . ." Jhanvi said. "Katie put me in charge. Is there a half-power setting on the ventilator?"

"No, not exactly, but—"

"Lower the power," Jhanvi said. "And see how it goes."

"Adriana called me and said even with the ventilators totally off, her walls and floor were still shaking. I think Achilles is using a lot of bass? She's really worried."

"Can we put her in a hotel?"

"I offered! She was like, no. I guess her husband is immuno-suppressed? From the transplant? So he really shouldn't go to new environments and stuff . . ."

"Let's do the hotel," Henry said. "Get them a suite at the Four Seasons."

Jhanvi and Roshie both looked at him, standing in the corner with his erection and his lazy smile.

"Adriana's calling again," Roshie said.

"Okay," Jhanvi said. "Let's forget the ventilators now and go find the sound system. Can you ask her about the hotel?"

Grabbing Roshie by the sleeve, Jhanvi stumbled over her own feet, and she gasped. She bent down, stripping off her high-heeled boots, with their stupid furry ruffs, and kicking them into a corner. Then, walking barefoot across the concrete, she followed Roshie into the next room.

• • •

This room was dark, filled with strobing lights and pounding music. The edges were obscured by black curtains and there was a cutout in the corner wall, like a glory hole, with men queueing up nearby, rubbing their junk, though nobody seemed to be on the other side to service them. The men in this room were mostly naked, or in their towels, and a lot of people were grinding heavily on each other, groping, pinching. A lot of glazed, closed eyes, people dancing in a frenzy by themselves.

Achilles stood in a corner, shirtless, sweat streaming down his face, showing off his hairy chest and impossible musculature—he was severely buff, in a way that was almost uncool. He was dancing in front of his laptop, intoning nonsense words that came out over the music.

"Hey," Jhanvi said, bending close to him. "We have to turn this off."

"What?"

"Turn it off."

Jhanvi reached for the red switch, and he batted her hand away. Jhanvi went and got Roshie, and she pointed at the board, and there was a lot of shouting and squabbling. Finally, Jhanvi pulled a plug out of the wall, and there was a squealing noise from the speakers.

"What the fuck!" Achilles said. "You can't do that shit!"

"Then stop when we tell you to, asshole."

"This is twenty thousand dollars' worth of equipment!"

"Fuck you," Jhanvi said.

With the music and the lights cut off, they had only the red emergency lights above to guide them. The two doors opened, letting more light in, and revealing dazed people standing on the dance floor, some of them still trying to dance. Everyone was sweating; the women looked worse, makeup glistening, gone liquid and oily.

Random comments drifted out of the crowd.

"Why is it so hot?"

"Just a lot of bodies."

Shaking her head to clear the ringing that'd broken into her brain and wasn't going to leave of its own accord, Jhanvi looked at Roshie. "How is this?"

"She's gonna try..." Roshie said. "But it's still really loud. This sucks. Shit. I got mad, I never finished soundproofing."

"Yo," Achilles said. "You didn't put up the soundproofing? What the hell? These are..." He let out some audiophile gobble-dygook, talking about how this much noise in this small a space needed to be managed, and they had *talked* about this, he'd given her *plans*, and Roshie said, "I thought it'd be enough. And you didn't check! You didn't do shit about—"

"Hey, this is the heart of the party," Achilles said. "If we can't have sound, we might as well pack up. I hate to be a bitch, but aren't the neighbors being a little uptight? Like, it's the Mission: shit is loud."

"God," Jhanvi said. "Shut up. Now come on, Roshie, bring the, uhh, bring the spark plugs or whatever you disconnected, I don't want him putting this back together."

"Dude!"

• • •

They took all of his surge protectors, carrying them by their cords, and Achilles followed them, still complaining, until they disappeared through the fire-safety door. "It's locked," Roshie said to him. "If you come out, you can't get back in."

The stairwell was concrete, dimly lit with fluorescent lights, and it hummed with a forbidding, alien energy.

Roshie leaned against a railing: "Adriana called, said her husband is acting kind of delirious. Kind of confused. She's really afraid. I'm gonna do it. I'm gonna shut everything down."

"How?" Jhanvi said.

"Just switch on the lights and tell everyone to leave."

"Roshie, you're basically their landlord right now, and you know what happens when someone's landlord tells them to stop partying? The tenants say, *Oh totally, we'll turn the music down*, and then they keep going."

"But they *promised*."

"And you've told them. You've told everyone."

"You're always defending them. It's pathetic," Roshie said. "You're like I used to be . . ."

"Tell Adriana we're moving people around down here," Jhanvi said. "Look . . ." She looked at her watch. "We've killed an hour this way, just waffling around. It's almost ten. Just three more to go."

Jhanvi looked at Roshie, expecting to see something fierce, some condemnation. But the other girl was blank faced.

"Hey," Jhanvi said, putting a hand on her shoulder. "Are you okay?"

"I just . . . don't know what to do," she said.

Jhanvi sighed to herself. It wasn't *really* a big deal. The dude upstairs wouldn't die. It was a guilt trip. A party couldn't kill a person.

And yet it was also morally indefensible: if there was even a one percent chance of hurting someone, you couldn't throw a sex party. But wasn't this like her parents worrying that Jhanvi's grandparents would die if they found out she was trans? Like . . . it wasn't unreasonable to have a party. They were fine. But the optics were terrible, obviously.

The noise was outrageous, even with the music off, and Jhanvi could hardly think. Roshie was hitting her phone, trying to talk to someone. "What's wrong?"

"She's here," Roshie said.

"What?"

"She's here. At the stairwell."

• • •

The fire door behind them vibrated from the sound, and then, after a few seconds, they heard the thump of the music start again.

"Guess they found more surge protectors."

"Fuck!" Roshie said.

Then a bunch of Spanish words floated down the stairwell. Adriana was standing at the top of the stairs, not looking accusatory at all, just worried. Roshie went up a few stairs, and Adriana came down, and the two of them talked at each other across one flight of stairs. Every sound refracted and shattered, growing and shrinking, and Jhanvi felt the noise clattering inside her brain. Roshie stood with one foot on a higher stair, looking up, like Romeo to the balcony, gesturing with one hand and the other hooked into her belt. Jhanvi could hardly hear what they were saying, but Adriana kept repeating the same sounds over and over.

"No, I'll stop it, I'll stop it," Roshie replied.

"Don't say that . . ." Jhanvi whispered.

"I'm gonna stop it."

"Hi," Jhanvi waved.

Adriana stood there, her face helpless, wringing her hands. And then her voice was raised, and she started to scream. "Stop this! Stop this noise! Stop it!"

"I will."

"Just stop it!"

The lament continued for a few moments, and then Adriana went away, and the two of them were left in the almost-quiet stairwell.

Roshie looked empty eyed, staring up the stairs. Jhanvi came to her, put a hand lightly on her back. Roshie shook like a cat, but Jhanvi kept running her palm across her friend's shoulder blades.

"Stop it," Roshie said. "Stop it. I don't like that."

"Sorry. I'm sorry."

Roshie's face was haggard. "This is my fault. I should've worked harder. Should've done more soundproofing."

"No."

"It is," Roshie said. "Fuck!" She beat her hand against the concrete wall. "FUCK!"

"You're gonna hurt yourself."

"I *knew* her husband was sick. I should've checked with Adriana, checked about the date of his operation. I could've told Adriana—they could've changed the date. I could've said, it's gonna be so loud."

"You told them about the party," Jhanvi said. "They knew it was tonight."

"But I also told them it wouldn't be loud."

"That was dumb, but they should've known better. It's okay, it's not totally your fault."

"Jhanvi!" Roshie said. Her voice rose momentarily above the hum of the fluorescent lights. "He could die."

"Roshie!" Jhanvi said. "He is not going to die. I get that she's worried. I get that he's uncomfortable. But he'll probably be fine."

"You don't get it."

"No, I get it completely. He is sick. He is fragile. He needs sleep. His body could reject the kidney. Anything that disturbs him is dangerous. His wife is worried. But he'll probably be fine. Anyway, you've done what you can—they're not gonna end the party."

"I just don't get it," Roshie said. "Did I not explain it right?"

"You explained it perfectly. I mean, Roshie, come on—literally nobody in the world would end their party over this. The house has been planning it for like four months."

"But he could *die*."

"Sure, if you phrase it like that, obviously it's immoral to keep this party going. Like, no party should involve even a one percent chance of someone dying. But they're just ignoring you. It's what they do. You know that. So come on. Let's, uhh, let's go home or something. It's gonna be a bad night. There is no way to feel good about this. But we'll all survive."

Roshie's eyes were blank. She stared aimlessly ahead, and then looked into Jhanvi's face, uncertainty and confusion on hers, and Jhanvi wanted, for a minute, to lean forward, to kiss her on what she had just noted were plump lips, to take the bottom lip between her teeth and run those teeth over the soft hairs beneath the lip. Jhanvi wanted to hold on to Roshie, to crush their bodies together, to both smother and protect the other girl's vulnerability and to turn the two of them into one person.

"You don't get it," Roshie said. "That's fine. I knew that, but you just don't get it. I don't give a shit. I'll pull the fire alarm."

Jhanvi shrugged. "Sure, cause a stampede. That'll help."

Roshie had drifted to the door, and now she turned back, her face red. "What I hate about you is that you almost get it," she said. "You understand everything, but you still won't do the right thing. You're like the . . . you're like the Commissioner."

That was the villain of *The Redness of Mars*—a government agent who knows that his role in life is to steal other people's hard work and is unapologetic about it. "Ouch!" Jhanvi put a hand to her heart. She smiled. "That's not so bad, I suppose. There's something operatic about that."

"You're a bad person."

"Maybe," Jhanvi said. "But what's a bad thing I've done?"

"You're letting someone die."

"Know what's funny? Nobody else in there gets what you're saying. They're like, *it's a party, what's the big deal?* And I have *so much* more reason to delude myself. Because, let's face it, if this party ends, there's a ninety-five percent chance my marriage thing won't go through—"

"Is that why you're—?"

"But I agree with you. I see the truth. You're right. This party is wrong. And yeah, if you weren't so lonely and angry, you wouldn't want to stop it, but so what? Maybe angry and lonely people are good for something. But I am not going to do it, Roshie. I'm just not going to."

"You're, like, pure evil."

"Maybe," Jhanvi said. "You have no idea the things I think. The hatred, the violence, disgust—I think terrible things . . . I want to physically consume other women sometimes, just drink them up and take their essence, as if I am everything some crazed right winger thinks about trans women. But I am just so tired of being worthless. Being pitied. And yeah, I could dress it up and say that for a trans woman, transitioning is everything, and it'd even be true. But there's the interior truth and the exterior one. And the interior truth is, I want to look different. I don't want to transition, I want to cut the transness out of me, so I'm just like any other girl. I hate this body, and I hate the life it gives me."

"But . . . but," Roshie sputtered, "if you looked different, and . . . I could afford plastic surgery, too, but I tell myself if I looked different and someone loved me just for that . . . then . . . ?"

"You're probably right," Jhanvi said. "Henry loves my dick, and I hate him for that, because it's not really a part of me. So, what if I felt like my new face or my new tits weren't a part of me? But . . . I don't know. I'll risk it. Or if not, I'll be even more beautiful and terrible than I was before."

"Can you keep quiet?" Roshie said. "She's up there. Adriana. She's right there."

Jhanvi could've gone on speaking, but Roshie wouldn't have understood. Sometimes she hated this girl who *almost* got it. Nobody else had drawn more truth from her, had seen further inside her, but Roshie was damaged, mute, maybe incapable of talking about her own feelings.

Roshie was on the step now, and she was quiet for a minute,

with her head in her hands. Jhanvi went on: "You know, we act like they're especially bad people in there, but they aren't. They're just rich. I don't get it, why they pretend to be better than they are. But it's what they do. But don't punish me for not pretending. I am so tired of the bullshit."

Roshie didn't say anything, and Jhanvi was about to go on, and then she noticed a small catch in Roshie's voice. The girl looked up, and her face was covered in tears.

"Hey ... hey," Jhanvi sat next to her, put an arm around her. "What's wrong? What's going on?"

"I can't do it!" Then suddenly her face was buried in Jhanvi's neck. "I can't do it. I can't stop it on my own. I'm pathetic. I'm a fucking second-rater. I just can't do it. I don't know what's wrong. I can't do it. I can't stop it."

"Shh," Jhanvi said. "Shh ... stop. It's okay. It's okay."

Roshie's eyes were a brilliant black, set off by lustrous eyelashes. More tears spilled from those eyes.

"It's okay."

"I can't do it. I can't do it."

"Shh," Jhanvi said. "You can."

"N—no, you're right. I can't pull the fire alarm. I can't call the cops. I—I know I can't do it. And they won't listen to me. It's just ..."

"You're not the Chaplain."

"I am."

This was another character from *The Redness of Mars*: a chaplain on Mars who's given stewardship of the colony while the Prince is gone. He cracks under the pressure from the Commissioner and betrays everything the Prince stands for. The Prince says the Chaplain is the worst amongst all men, because he knew the truth and yet couldn't stand firm.

"No, it's human," Jhanvi said. "You can't base your life on that shit. There aren't heroes in real life. It's all ... it's all ... I don't know. It's all social dynamics. Economics. Human nature ..."

Roshie drew away from her, and she shrugged Jhanvi off

when she tried to console her. They leaned against the railing there for a few minutes, and Jhanvi watched her, trying to feel some sort of emotion. She started to prepare another speech about how nobody could stop this party, about how it was foreordained to go on, and then she stopped. What a crock of horseshit.

"You know what?" Jhanvi said. "Let's do it. Let's just kick everyone out of this stupid party."

"W—what?"

"I mean, yeah, what the fuck are we doing? Of course we have to stop this party. It's just a fucking party. It's not a force of nature. We just need to end it. And that's that."

"Right?" Roshie said. "Is that—but you said it couldn't be—"

"I say stupid things constantly," Jhanvi said.

"You—you do. That's true."

"Totally, I say them all the time. Sometimes I even believe them. But this takes the cake. Yeah, let's just end this dumb party. Why are we even wasting time talking about it?"

"Are . . . should we wait until after your wedding?"

"No, they're too smart. They put the wedding at the end."

"Jhanvi . . ." Roshie said. "I, uhh, I'm not as rich as . . . I don't know if I can pay for you to . . ."

But the words didn't register with Jhanvi. The future didn't matter. She was too caught up in the moment, in making Roshie happy, in . . . just being a good person for once. Purely, unambiguously good—sacrificing herself. Even in her stupid male body, she'd always have this. *I was good. I did a good thing. I was the Prince of Mars and not a pathetic Earthling like the rest.*

"Let's just do it," Jhavi said.

"Because . . . so . . . should I call the cops?"

"What? No, these people are sheep. They'll obey any firm voice. Let's just tell Audrey and Katie to cut the bullshit." Jhanvi rolled her eyes. She wanted Roshie to argue, to say, oh no, they're not gonna want to do this, they're not going to want to end things. Jhanvi was completely certain she could convince them to end the party. People were so simple. They would obey her, if she wanted them to.

• • •

They passed awkwardly through a classic orgy. Men and women, many in masks, most of them naked, going at it violently in some places, and in others just writhing on top of each other in piles. Everywhere, the problem was the oversupply of men. They'd talked about this in the run-up to the party. Giving women a safe place to retreat removed them from the floor, creating a tipping point where, at the moment of contact, each woman was outnumbered by the men. In this environment, even Jhanvi felt men looking at her hungrily, speculatively. As they queued for a second at the door to the final room, the heavy one, where all the rough shit went down, Jhanvi made eye contact with man after man—most looked away, but one of them, a big guy with a beard, came up to her, smiling. His eyes didn't waver as he drew closer. She waved hello and he reached out, like some slow-motion nightmare, for her span-dex shorts. Shoving his hand between her legs, he groped and grasped at her penis, mixing her balls around, making her yelp. She turned around, and he reached for her butt. She felt something wet, and saw he was bending down, literally licking her shorts with his tongue. The whole experience was like being attacked by a dog.

I knew it. I knew the communication wouldn't be good. I knew all of this consent stuff was just talk.

She moved forward a few steps, and the man drifted away, but she felt hands all over her. A guy turned back, smiled, and he pulled her close, kissed her on the head, kneaded her butt, and she felt the beginnings of arousal. Okay . . . this might work.

The crush was too loud, but she tried to say something, and he nodded at her. Then their lips were crushed together. She succumbed to the kiss, but felt a persistent tugging on her shoulder. Roshie was pushing forward, and there was a grumbling. A man was saying, "Line up! Line up! There are too many!"

Jhanvi started elbowing, pushing her way through. A hand grabbed her shoulder, but she just moved and moved, her heart and head throbbing. She fished in her wrist satchel for another dose of Adderall—someone's ADHD meds, misdirected by fire-eater wealth—put it in her mouth, crushed it under her teeth—made a face at the foul taste. And then she walked suddenly into an empty space, and she stopped. Katie was on the ground, on her knees, her top pulled down around her waist, her stockings torn, a set of fake eyelashes—she hadn't even been wearing fake eyelashes before!—pasted to her cheek by sweat, and her head was bobbing up and down on a strange man's penis. Audrey was standing over her, holding a whip of some kind, her tiny face transformed, shouting the foulest of language.

"How do we get to them?" Roshie said.

The temperature in the basement had gotten steadily hotter. The room was divided between those who were naked and those who'd hung stubbornly on to their clothes. Aside from Jhanvi and Roshie and Katie and Audrey, almost everyone was a man. There were some exceptions, a few women hanging around the edges, and one tall white girl was at the front of the crowd, cackling enthusiastically—Audrey had to keep slapping away her hands as she tried to touch Katie's neck. Audrey looked at Henry, who went and talked to the woman and stood in front of her.

Most of the men stood more or less silently, or talking to each other, sniggering. One had his phone up, and one of the TBF members, Stanley, reached up and grabbed it out of his hand, and there was a brief altercation.

Jhanvi was transfixed. There was a wildness in Audrey's eyes. "You little whore," Audrey said. "You think anyone cares about your rules? All they want is to fuck you. Look at these guys..."

That sort of dirty talk went on and on, Audrey berating Katie, reducing her to an object, stripping away, in very personal terms, all of her sense of herself, attacking in particular her dignity and her reserve.

"You think you're so much better than other people? Well, you're just an animal."

Audrey's eyes were gleaming, ferocious. She pulled Katie off that guy's dick and dragged her by the collar around her neck to another one. Jhanvi vaguely recognized both guys from the Trial By Fire scene, so clearly this was mostly a staged thing. Katie and Audrey exchanged a brief glance, and Audrey jammed her onto the guy's dick.

Oh, so this actually does sometimes work how it's supposed to.

"Can we stop them?" Roshie asked.

"This is the most incredible thing I've ever seen in my life," Jhanvi breathed.

Katie's body was drenched in sweat, and the lighting, overly bright and stagey, didn't show her paleness to its best effect. She looked like an overexposed nightclub selfie. Her legs really were incredibly thin in those stockings, and as she skittered around the mat, she was a fantasy come to life. Actually, they were reenacting a popular genre of porn: the public humiliation video.

Audrey played to the crowd, which was still shy. She picked out a guy wearing just a pair of boxer shorts—a small, nebbishy guy with short, bushy hair—she pulled him out of the crowd and she told him to call Katie a whore.

"She's not a human anymore, is she?"

"Uhh, no."

"She's a filthy slut."

"Y—yeah, in this context."

Another guy was maneuvering around to get between them, and Audrey dropped character. "Hey!" she said. "Boundaries! Back. Shoo. Shoo."

At this, the crowd stepped back again, but then Audrey worked it up, purposefully drawing out the kind of energy that, Jhanvi assumed, people elicited in gang rapes.

Jhanvi dawdled, stepping forward a little, then forward a little more. Audrey and Katie were sharing an intimate scene.

Then Audrey suddenly slapped Katie, loud and hard, and the whole room exhaled.

"Umm, hey," Jhanvi said.

Audrey looked around, standing up.

"So, uhh . . ." Jhanvi leaned so close, she could smell the spit and semen on Katie's body. "Umm, I think we have to end the party."

"What?" Audrey said.

"The noise stuff, it's too loud."

Katie stood up, shaking her head. She wiped her face, looked at her hand, grimaced, then wiped it with her other hand. Some slightly older guy from the fire-eater scene leaned toward her, trying to grab her waist, and she batted him away absentmindedly. He reached around, kissing her neck, and she started to push him away with one hand.

"What's going on?"

"Yeah . . ." Henry said. "Are we done?"

"No, wait . . . we're . . ." Audrey looked at her watch. "We have fifteen more minutes. What's going on?"

The crowd milled around—a few of the guys were still stroking their erections hopefully, and now Katie was getting crowded by the men.

"Stop!" Audrey said. "Stop it! Stop!"

After much shouting and pushing, the guys extricated themselves from Katie. Audrey went to her, gave her a look, then turned on the guys. "Not cool!"

"Hey . . . hey . . . relax . . . we . . ."

"Go to the front room," she said. "Cool down. Come on. Go. Can you go?"

The tension started to dissipate. Henry pushed forward into the circle, and so did other members of The Guilty Party. Jhanvi realized that there were at least ten or fifteen people in the crowd who'd been working it, trying to control it.

"Are you okay?" Audrey said. "Come on . . ." she said. "Let's take you backstage . . ."

"I'm . . ." Katie blinked a few times. "What's . . ." She was still half-naked, slick with various fluids—her hair disheveled, she was pulling at it with her fingers. Audrey passed her a hair tie, and she gathered it into a ponytail.

"Here." Henry handed over her glasses, but they were fogged and smudged, and she looked around, blindly.

"Come on," Audrey said. "Come on."

She put a hand around Katie's waist, and they limped off to a corner that was hidden behind a curtain. Katie immediately went for the blue bucket of water in the corner. She stripped off all her clothes, throwing them into a corner, and started vigorously attacking herself with a sponge.

"Take your time," Audrey said. "Can I . . . ?"

Katie's teeth were gritted. Henry looked in and then looked away.

"I, umm . . ." Jhanvi said.

"Sorry," Audrey said. "I can't leave her right now. Can you talk to anyone else?"

"Well, yeah," Jhanvi said. "Henry, we're shutting down the party."

"What?" Audrey said. "What's happening?"

"It's just not right," Jhanvi said. "The guy upstairs is really sick. He can't get moved. He needs to sleep."

The little antechamber got crowded with people, and Audrey looked back between the naked Katie and the rest of them, hanging at the door. One of Katie's boyfriends swooped in, touching her on the shoulder, and she clutched tight to him, pressing her face into his shoulder. Jhanvi was absolutely riveted. He spun her around, covering her with his body, as she clung, wet, to his T-shirt.

Audrey looked at him, and then she stepped out into the room, which other crew members were already mopping and cleaning.

"Why is it so hot?" she asked.

"Oh hey," Achilles said. "We've gotta talk. I need the rest of my surge protectors."

"We're shutting down the party," Jhanvi said.

"It's 11:00," Audrey said. "They can't wait two hours? Two hours? They live on Mission Street. I mean, come on!" She looked back at the closed curtain, and she shivered a little bit.

"We can play the music quieter," Achilles said.

"Can you just deal with this?" Audrey said.

"No," Jhanvi said. "We can't. I mean, come on, Audrey, you know we need to shut this down. There's just no way to defend this."

Katie stepped out from behind the curtain wearing a bathrobe. Audrey rushed to her, and Katie gave her a tight smile, even as Audrey picked one set of fake eyelashes from her cheek.

"You okay?" Audrey said. "I am so, so—"

"Totally fine," Katie said. "Don't worry. You were perfect." She smiled for the rest, although with her lips pursed tightly, the effect was eerie and forlorn.

"Yeah, so . . . Roshie is gonna turn on the lights now," Jhanvi said. "Roshie . . ."

Roshie tapped her phone, and the lights came up. They were suddenly under merciless, unforgiving floodlights, and all the naked bodies came into view in their full grotesqueness. Katie was wan and drained. Audrey was red faced, with little blemishes on her neck and shoulders, in the spots where her outfit gaped open. The men had hairy thighs and wrinkled elbows. The women had sagging buttocks and cellulite. *This ought to be a picture in an art book*, Jhanvi thought. *What an orgy looks like under unfavorable light.*

"What's happening?" Katie said. "Can't you just take care of this?"

"Hey, sure," Henry said. "I'll talk to them. Let's just get you—"

"No," Jhanvi said. She could hardly bear to look at Katie. What she'd just witnessed her and Audrey doing had been too intimate. Now, looking at the girl's body, at her hollow eyes and pale skin and wet hair, it was impossible to see her in a sexual way, or even to envy her. Jhanvi's stomach lurched.

"I'm kind of tired," Katie said.

"Come on," Audrey said, drawing the curtain to the side.

"Hey." Jhanvi grabbed the curtain. "Hey. Katie. Look, look at me. You know that you're the leader, right? And if you say the party ends, it'll end. Nobody else can do it."

Katie's eyes looked up, and they gained focus. She breathed in, and her commanding aura came back.

"Talk to me," she said.

Jhanvi looked at Roshie, who was hanging at the edge of the group, not really speaking.

"Well," Jhanvi said. "The woman upstairs can't be moved. I mean her husband. He's a transplant patient. Immunocompromised. It's just time. Like, she's calling begging us and stuff. And Roshie knows her. Maybe it's bullshit and they could last two hours, but we can't party when somebody could die. We just can't do it. And you know that, even if nobody else here does."

All eyes went to Katie. She thought for a second. "Yeah, I guess you're right."

"So we're doing this?" Henry said.

Now the weakest pylon was Audrey, and all eyes went to her. She shrugged. "I guess we have to."

"Yeah," Jhanvi said. "Sorry. No way to wriggle out of it."

"Okay . . ." Audrey said. "Let's get people out from the front rooms first. If we do it from here, people will just clog up."

"Yeah, and we need to make sure they don't hang out in the alleyway, either. We need them to move," Henry said.

"Good point," Audrey said. She shivered again, then she looked at Katie, who was in the arms of her boyfriend. "All right."

23

The logistics of ending the party had seemed insuperable to Jhanvi, but apparently the members of Trial By Fire were used to sudden changes of plan. The word simply had to be spread, and people started sharing their ideas. Achilles said they should just take down the plywood partitions, turning the area into one big room, but that seemed too hard and time consuming. They got frustrated trying to set up the amplifiers again, so they used the human microphone, with the members of TBF repeating whatever Audrey said until the combined din overpowered the room and brought it to silence.

"One of our upstairs neighbors is very sick," Audrey said.

"One of . . ."

"He might not survive the night."

"He might not . . ."

"He needs quiet."

"He needs . . ."

"So please collect your belongings and exit calmly up the stairs . . . do not hang around . . . move up to the alley, and then out to Eighteenth or Sycamore Street."

TBF members went through the corners, rousting people in amorous clinches, and one girl, who was completely passed out, had to be handed around until they found a member of Trial By Fire who knew her and could take her home.

Through this, Katie sat on the raised stage in her bathrobe with her knees together, her head propped on her hands, staring blankly at the floor.

"Is she okay?" Jhanvi said.

"Just decompressing," Achilles said.

Roshie was deeply involved in the closing down of the party, with Henry and Achilles and the others coming to her constantly with questions about the space. But at one point, she came to Audrey and held out the phone. "Adriana is so grateful. She wants to talk to you . . ."

"Uhhh," Audrey smiled. "Sure."

At some point, Audrey had changed out of her pin-up outfit and now she was in a pair of yoga pants and a loose T-shirt. For once, Jhanvi didn't even look at her breasts: she'd seen enough of them—ninety percent of the breast-viewing time in her real life to date had consisted of seeing Audrey's nipples jiggling while she scrubbed a pot in the kitchen or something. Even breasts sometimes got old.

"Totally," Audrey said. "Yeah. Yeah. No, we're sorry. We're so sorry. Give him our best. We're really sorry. No, no, it's really our problem."

When their conversation was over, she gave the phone back to Roshie. Then she walked through the edges of the crowd, checking first on Katie, and then on the various operations. Finally, she approached Jhanvi. "Henry said you had some amphetamines?" she said. "Do you have any left? Otherwise, he'll run home to get some for me. It's gonna be a long night here."

"Sure."

"And can you give the neighbors my number?" she said.

Jhanvi was left alone, her brain buzzing from the sudden cessation of anxiety. When she came across Henry and some of his friends in a corner, pouring little paper cups of some concoction out of a plastic juice bottle, she took one, and took a sip, then went to the sink and poured it out. She wasn't sober again, not exactly, but she still felt a headache coming on, and she was trying to opt out.

The level of self-congratulation in the room had become overwhelming. She could feel their self-image reconfiguring itself—they weren't decadent rebels, now they were principled activists who absolutely wouldn't let their partying harm their neighborhood. Henry was talking loudly about something called sustainable partying, which he claimed he'd just invented. Jhanvi wasn't sure if he was on mushrooms or something, but he cornered her and said, "Okay, get this, we've just been trying to party in a way that does no harm, but what if we did the opposite? Partying that does good! So the more you party, the better it is! The neighborhood actually *welcomes* a party, because it's so good."

"What would that look like?" Jhanvi said.

"Okay, take this building, right? It looked terrible before. Now we've got new paint, toilets, plumbing, ventilation, lots of cool stuff. Maybe we take run-down places, and we descend on them, utilize that partying energy to fix them up, then bam, when the party is done, someone's got a place to live."

Jhanvi raised an eyebrow. "That's . . . not insane."

"Right!" Henry said. "Right?!" He shouted, "Yo, even Jhanvi thinks it's a good idea."

"You're encouraging this?" said Audrey. "Okay, well if even Jhanvi thinks it's worthwhile . . ."

"I mean it's conceptually exciting . . ."

Jhanvi tried to move away from the conversation, but Henry followed her, drifting behind her, offering her another drink, then asking if she needed anything. When they'd gotten a little away from his friends, Henry said, "Totally right call. You're, like, our moral center."

"Sure," Jhanvi said. Oddly enough, she didn't feel a sense of loss. She'd never truly believed the wedding would happen, or that her life could ever change for the better. But she felt no triumph, either. Even though she'd done the right thing and had known how right it was, these people had vacuumed up all the excitement and gotten high off it instead.

Her main feeling, to be honest, was relief: *if I don't get married, at least my family won't disown me.*

"You're, like, my moral center too," Henry said. "Hey . . . you're, uhh, hey, like . . . Syn, Roshie, and Katie have all had talks with me tonight. Called me an asshole for how I've treated you. It's a lot to think about. I, uhh, should've been better to you. Like, your emotional needs. You're a really good friend. And, uhh, you just hit my buttons so hard that, uhh, I got a little . . ."

"Same here," Jhanvi said. "I mean not the buttons—I don't really enjoy what we do—but I should've checked in with you. Like . . . you've got . . ." She gestured at Audrey, who was sitting on the stage, her arms around Katie, pressing her face against her hair. "You've got a lot to deal with . . ."

"Totally," he said. "But, uhh . . . maybe we cool it for a bit?"

Her inclination was to say, *No, I can keep fucking you! If it does so much for you, that's fine. It's a favor to a friend.* But that was exactly how guys like Henry got you.

"Maybe," she said.

"All right, c—cool," he said.

This group was good at cleaning, and they worked with an efficiency that mostly didn't require words. Roshie reported that Adriana's husband was asleep, and there was a cheer that Audrey immediately shushed.

"Decibel meter," Henry said. "Automatically connected to the music. We put one in their apartment and boom . . ."

Jhanvi usually half-assed group tasks like this, but today she went around seriously, collecting half-drunk cups of whatever and pouring them down the sink. She worked for a long time, not thinking anything in particular, just tired and emotionally weary. But finally, she felt tugging at her arm.

"Hey," Audrey said. "Come on . . ."

When Jhanvi approached the group, there was a light smattering of applause, and Katie stood up, wearing her plain white wedding dress, her face drawn in a wry grin. "The girl of the hour," she said.

I should have predicted this. It makes total sense. Jhanvi was too tired to explain how or why, but of course the wedding now needed to go through.

Jhanvi looked around. "Where's Roshie?"

"I think on the phone," Audrey said. Now Jhanvi felt something forced into her hand: a black gown in a plastic garment bag. She looked at it. Henry was wearing a little priest's collar, and he lowered a screen that had the silhouette of a mountaintop scene printed onto it. Someone started humming the wedding march.

"You can change over there, if you're shy," Audrey said.

Then Jhanvi was left holding the dress. Everywhere she saw smiles. Katie came up to her, put a hand on her arm, murmuring some words, but Jhanvi didn't understand what she was saying.

"Are you sure?" Jhanvi said.

"Y—yes," Katie said.

This could've gone further: *You don't sound sure / You sound like you have doubts / I don't want to do it if you're not sure.* But that wouldn't have been true. Jhanvi wanted to do this even if it, in some way, ruined Katie's life. She would happily trade Katie's future for her own. A dark thought, the logic of human sacrifice. And yet . . . not the actuality of it. Jhanvi kept having to remind herself, *This actually involves very little concrete harm for Katie, and almost limitless good for me.*

These people fetishized consent and mutual enjoyment, but so little of life worked within those frameworks. They had ruined the night of the residents of this building, and possibly endangered the health of one, and done it for their own pleasure. They'd chosen themselves. And now Jhanvi did the same. Her trans friends would say, *Well, yeah, but for a marginalized woman to choose herself is a revolutionary act.* That was certainly *a* truth, but Jhanvi wasn't certain it was hers.

Jhanvi's eye caught a movement by the stairs. Roshie was

putting on a coat. Jhanvi looked down at the dress, and she tried to hang it on the corner of a plywood barrier. It fell down, but she didn't notice, just drifted closer to Roshie.

"Hey," Jhanvi said, licking her lips. "Why're you leaving?"

"I, uhh . . ." Roshie looked at the circle. "I . . . hey, we'll still be friends, but is it okay if I . . . don't . . . if I'm not here for the wedding?"

"Sure," Jhanvi said. "But . . . just stay for a little bit."

"No, it'll be a whole big party, and, I dunno."

"How many of these parties have you actually stayed for?" Jhanvi said.

"Enough!" she said. "You think I don't know what'll happen?"

"Okay . . . okay," Jhanvi said. "You know. You'll be lonely forever, probably. But . . . could you still stay?"

Audrey was in Henry's arms, and he kissed her neck. Her liquid peals of laughter rang out through the room. Katie relaxed on the stage, her long legs kicking rhythmically. She reached out, kicked Audrey lightly, and there was more laughter. Jhanvi tried to recollect Katie on her knees, Audrey yelling at her. *They could teach me so much. They're everything I've wanted, loved, envied.*

Then she looked down at her body—really looked—and saw her belly, saw her knobby knees. She rubbed a hand over her cheek, felt stubble. And she looked back at the crowd of people, cuddling and enjoying each other. Nobody all night had made a move on her. Wait, except for that gross guy who squeezed her balls like they were a stress management tool.

"Hey, actually . . . I need you to stay so you can bully Katie if she tries to back out," Jhanvi said. "I'm serious. I need the moral support."

"Oh . . ." Roshie frowned. "Okay. Sure."

Things don't normally work out well. Usually when there is a buildup to something, that thing is a letdown, and when there is an expectation, those expectations turn to disappointment. But in this case, when Jhanvi guided Roshie back, there was a sustained ovation and a long round of hugs. Roshie sat on a velvet couch next to Jhanvi, who felt free to hug her and wrap her arms around her.

For once, the sexual games were slow to begin. They drank a little wine and relived the night. Henry kept talking up his sustainable party idea, turning it bigger and bigger, and Toni looked up at him, absolutely riveted, drinking in the idea, saying, "That's so brilliant. That's so smart," in her increasingly nasal voice.

Roshie got heated, saying it was fucking stupid, but Jhanvi whispered to her, "Let them have it."

"But it's stupid."

"Well, maybe not."

"Except it is."

"Still . . ."

Roshie shrugged like a horse angry at being bridled, but she stayed quiet.

Then, Katie, refreshed and dressed in white, took charge of the group, and Jhanvi found herself in a corner with Roshie and Toni and Audrey and Katie, getting dressed.

"Hey, you don't have to do this, Kate," Jhanvi said.

"Yes she does," Roshie said. "She absolutely does!"

"It's fine," Katie said.

Jhanvi shrugged. She had offered the girl enough chances to escape.

Roshie had a bullish look, her head lowered, her eyes fixed on Kate and Audrey. She was still in the past, still living in the world of an hour ago, ready to defend Jhanvi's rights as her new pet cause.

Jhanvi looked at herself in the black dress, suddenly noticing its broad shoulders—did it have padded shoulders? She absolutely hated that. She couldn't even remember picking this thing—whether she'd had any say in it, or if Audrey had just snapped her fingers and said, "That's the one!" Maybe she'd *wanted* Jhanvi to look bad. The transsexual woman stared at the length of mirror propped against the cinderblock wall and evaluated herself. The idea came to her again: *I am a man. A man in a dress.* She sucked in her gut. So many things created the effect: her hairline, receding in that unique way; the power of her chin; the little smudge of hair on her upper lip. She was the transvestite in a sitcom, looming over the bride in her white dress. Jhanvi held her large hands in front of her, fingers splayed, and the effect magnified.

"Are you all right?" Audrey said.

"I'm hideous."

"No!" Toni said. "Hey . . . come here. What do you need? You look fantastic!"

Jhanvi swallowed. "You're right," she said. "I'm gorgeous. I'm a goddess. An Amazon."

"There you go!" Toni said.

"Isn't that right, Rosh?" Jhanvi said.

The girl's face colored and went red, and she kept looking down at her phone.

"Rosh, come on," Audrey said. "Tell her she looks good!"

"What?" Roshie said. "What? I was checking something for work. I need to fix the Wi-Fi down here, it sucks."

"Tell her she looks good," Audrey said.

"Uhh."

"Roshie!" Audrey said.

"What?" Roshie said. "I mean, like, good in what way?"

"Gorgeous," Jhanvi said. "Tell me I'm tall, like a model. That's something people say."

"Well, sure," Roshie said. "I guess that's true. Come on . . . uhh . . . shit."

There was more consternation, more fuss, and Jhanvi found herself rolling her eyes. Then she shouted, "It's okay, it's okay, let's start. Just leave me with Roshie, okay?"

She was in a trance as the members of Trial By Fire all arranged themselves. Audrey walked onto the makeshift stage in front of the mountain scene, and Katie went with her. They stood upright, together, as the wedding music played. And Jhanvi looked at them, thought of the darkness they'd displayed. They'd laugh it off as *safe, sane, consensual* kink play, but Jhanvi knew the truth. The play was play, but the feelings underneath were real self-hatred, real anger, and real agony. *I can't believe I wasted so much time feeling bad when these two had that kind of evil in them that they needed to expunge.* It made Jhanvi think, like, perhaps even her manipulations had a role. Maybe Katie needed this wedding in some way. For weeks, Jhanvi had thought: *Oh, I'm so evil, I'm scamming this girl.* But maybe, in some dark way, the scam satisfied the part of Katie that wanted martyrdom. Perhaps this ecosystem needed Jhanvi's evilness, just as the bay needed the scuttling crabs to consume the dead fish. Without her, there would be no cleansing scorn to clear away the bullshit and allow these people to really live.

Roshie was by her side, staring at an empty spot on the floor.

"Hey, I feel, like, so much dread for some reason," Jhanvi said.

Now Roshie looked up, her brows beetling. "What? What's wrong?"

"I think . . . my family? It's dumb, but I don't want them to disown me." She explained the call she'd had with them, and how, yeah, they were transphobes, but she'd stolen money from them, and they thought she was a criminal, and she wanted to look like she'd made good.

"Oh, that's fucking stupid," Roshie said.

"No, I know, but—you don't think I should cancel this?"

"Err, you know how I feel about this plan," Roshie said. "But, just, if you're not comfortable then wait for a bit . . ."

"Katie will back out."

"So what? Then Henry will do it. Or I will. Somebody else."

"Roshie," Jhanvi said. "That's not—"

"Trust me," she said. "I never would've believed we could've stopped the party, all of us, but look what we did. Trust me. We'll do it differently, on the down-low, or get you a job. We'll take care of you."

And the pitch was so seductive, Jhanvi didn't know what to do. All her neurons screamed that this was a fantasy, and that they'd leave her in a ditch, just like her dad said.

"Everyone here loves you," Roshie said. "You don't have to do anything you're not comfortable with."

"Yeah?" Jhanvi said. "You promise?"

"Uh huh. I do."

Jhanvi stroked the top of Roshie's hand, and she looked into the other girl's tired eyes. *I love you* felt like a lie, but Jhanvi had no other words. Roshie looked a bit like a fish, with her round cheeks and pursed lips, her bleary eyes, blinking from tiredness under those big glasses. She was smudged and sweaty, had taken off her flannel to show a white undershirt, unshaven pits and arms—the Persian girl's curse, she was hairy as fuck. Not beautiful, never beautiful, never that. But alive, in a sac of skin and flesh.

They touched now, skin on skin, their clamminess intermingling. And the other girl gave her a tired smile. "What're you looking at?"

"I don't know. Some boring, banal shit."

"Hey!" Roshie said. "That's my face!"

"I dunno. I love you, I guess . . . I think I do."

"S—" Roshie's eyes flickered, and then she said the words also, the same way, without emotion, because the moment called for them. "Me too."

The words weren't right. And perhaps that was the point. Maybe life was just filled with relationships that were strange and necessary, sensual and vaguely transgressive, and because people had no idea how to label, or even describe, what they meant to each other, they just said, *Oh, I love her, she's such a good friend.*

ACKNOWLEDGMENTS

This book had the longest and most difficult gestation of all my novels, and that means it had many midwives. I'd like to thank everyone who read drafts of the book and gave comments: Courtney Sender, Amber Burke, Peng Shepherd, Chris Holt, Kelly Loy Gilbert, James Sie, and Michelle Kuo. This book went through many rewrites, and without your comments it never would've been published.

My agent, Christopher Schelling, is a prince. Everyone gushes about their agent, but most people are lying. The agent-author relationship is the most contentious one in publishing. Christopher is a delight; I am proud to count him as a friend.

Thank you to my editor at the Feminist Press, Margot Atwell, for her undying enthusiasm for the book. She is, quite literally, the reason you're reading this. I'd also like to thank Mia Manns, my copyeditor, and Lauren Rosemary Hook, FP's editorial director, and Tanya Farrell and Jennifer Medina at Wunderkind PR. And of course John Elizabeth Stintzi, for their beautiful cover, which really captures the soul of the book.

I can't talk about my wife, Rachel, except in sappy clichés. She was with me through the whole process, every up and down, every rejection, every rewrite, every missed opportunity. She's read three separate drafts of the book, and she knows Jhanvi practically as well as I do. Thank you for everything you've given me.

And my daughter, Leni, who is four years old, and who contributed nothing to the writing of this book, but who I will thank anyway, because that's what you do.

NAOMI KANAKIA is the author of three YA novels and a nonfiction book, *What's So Great about Great Books* (Princeton University Press). Her stories, poetry, and essays have been published in *American Short Fiction*, *Asimov's*, *Gulf Coast*, and others. She has an MFA from Johns Hopkins and was an Emerging LGBTQ Voices fellow at Lambda Literary's 2015 Writers Retreat. She lives in San Francisco with her wife and daughter.

Amethyst Editions
at the Feminist Press

Amethyst Editions is a modern, queer
imprint founded by Michelle Tea

**Against Memoir: Complaints,
Confessions & Criticisms**
by Michelle Tea

Black Wave by Michelle Tea

Fiebre Tropical by Julián Delgado Lopera

Margaret and the Mystery of the Missing Body
by Megan Milks

The Not Wives by Carley Moore

**Original Plumbing: The Best of Ten Years
of Trans Male Culture**
edited by Amos Mac and Rocco Kayiatos

Panpocalypse by Carley Moore

Pretend It's My Body: Stories by Luke Dani Blue

Since I Laid My Burden Down by Brontez Purnell

Skye Papers by Jamika Ajalon

The Summer of Dead Birds by Ali Liebegott

We Were Witches by Ariel Gore

amethyst editions